MAGGIE'S
STRENGTH

a novel

PEGG THOMAS

Spinner of Yarns Publishing
Ossineke, Michigan

ISBN: 979-8-9850278-2-2

More Books

BY PEGG THOMAS

SARAH'S CHOICE

Forts of Refuge – Book One

IN SHEEP'S CLOTHING

a novella

EMBATTLED HEARTS

a novella

LUMBERJACKS & LADIES

an anthology

THE BLACKSMITH BRIDES

an anthology

THE GREAT LAKES LIGHTHOUSE BRIDES

an anthology

THE BACKCOUNTRY BRIDES

an anthology

A BOUQUET OF BRIDES

an anthology

THE PONY EXPRESS ROMANCE COLLECTION

an anthology

This book is dedicated to those men and women who forged head, those who adapted to change, and all who built a country such as had never existed before. All races, all religions, men and women. It takes extraordinary people enduring challenging times to produce exceptional results.

Praise

FOR *MAGGIE'S STRENGTH*

Pegg Thomas gives us a pitch-perfect story in *Maggie's Strength*. She provides just the right amount of historical detail without overwhelming a love story of two wounded people we can cheer for. It doesn't get any better than that.

—JANE KIRKPATRICK
NY Times-bestselling author of *The Healing of Natalie Curtis*

Deeply redemptive and realistic, *Maggie's Strength* takes an unflinching look at frontier America, immersing you in the wilderness so fully you'll feel you're an eyewitness. Pegg Thomas has crafted a remarkable heroine that embodies the grit of countless women who overcame tremendous obstacles and endings yet lived to embrace new and better beginnings. *Forts of Refuge* is a series you won't want to miss.

—LAURA FRANTZ
Christy Award-winning author of *A Heart Adrift*

A redemptive tale of loss and survival, vengeance and forgiveness, and love and longing, *Maggie's Strength* contains all my favorite elements of authentic historical fiction. Both Baptiste and Maggie are fully fleshed in their hopes and struggles, and

Thomas paints their place within an uncertain social and political landscape with sympathy and warmth.

—SHANNON MCNEAR
2014 RITA® nominee, 2021 SELAH winner
Author of *The Blue Cloak* and *Daughters of the Lost Colony: Elinor*

With meticulous historical detail and compelling emotional connections, Pegg Thomas's newest release, *Maggie's Strength*, will sweep into your heart and not let go until the final page. Set during a turbulent time after the French and Indian War, emotions run high as danger lurks around every corner while the promise of home stirs the fires to keep fighting. Poignant and suspenseful, readers will find this tale one worth savoring.

—J'NELL CIESIELSKI
Bestselling author of *The Socialite*

Acknowledgments

I'm pretty sure I thanked everyone except my 10th grade English teacher in *Sarah's Choice*, so for this book, I'd like to thank Diana Wakeford for telling me I could write all those years ago. I should have listened to her back then.

To all those English teachers out there today, looking over the desks of rebellious teenagers and hoping in some small way that you are breaking through, you may be. But you may not see the fruits of your labors for another 40 years.

Be patient. Some of us take time.

Author's Forenote

For the reader's ease of reading and remembering the Native American names, fictional characters in this book will have the English version such as Walking Fire Stick and Stone Foot. The real-life Native Americans in this story will be known by their historical names. These include Pontiac, Teata, Takay, and others.

Much of the dialogue in this story is in French. French words, therefore, are not in italics, but are used to clue the reader that the entire conversation is in French.

MAGGIE'S
STRENGTH

Prologue

Fort McCord, Pennsylvania, April 1, 1756

Screams ripped through the afternoon air, knocking the strength from Maggie Kerr's eleven-year-old knees. It was happening. What the adults most feared. What she'd heard Mama and Da whispering about for the past fortnight when she was supposed to have been asleep. Those same whisperings that had kept her sleep at bay.

She snatched her brother from the floor, hugging him to her hip as he clung to her.

"Mama!" she yelled at the closed door.

"What is it?" Catherine, Maggie's younger sister, clutched the arm not holding little Donald.

Gunshots blasted from outside, answered by shots from below. Shouts in English mixed with the screams. One word carried above the rest.

"Indians!"

The word dried Maggie's mouth. Her skin itched as if from a hundred mosquito bites.

Catherine buried her face against Maggie's shoulder.

Donald wailed.

1

"Mama!" Maggie shouted. The adults were gathered on the ground floor of the blockhouse in Fort McCord, except for a small group of men who had gone for supplies, including Da and her older brother, Reggie. It wasn't a proper fort, Mama had said, but it was all the protection they had. Would it be enough? And if not, would Da, Reggie, and the others return in time to rescue them?

Maggie had opened her mouth to yell again when a crash came from below that shook the floor beneath her. She searched the room, a stark square with nowhere to hide.

A woman screamed.

Children cried from the three other rooms in the blockhouse's upper story.

"Slide under the bed." Maggie pushed Catherine to the floor. "All the way against the wall. Take Donald and hold him close." She grabbed her sister's arm and looked her square in the eye. "Keep him quiet. Hold your hand over his mouth if you must. Neither of you can make a sound."

The wrenching of wood and metal hinges came as Maggie whirled toward the door. She flared her petticoats as much as possible to hide her siblings, hoping that Catherine had gotten them both out of sight.

The Indian who burst into the room wore nothing but a strip of leather held by a belt. Raised in his fist was a hatchet.

A hatchet stained red.

Maggie couldn't stop the whimper that rose in her throat.

In three strides he was across the room and had her by the arm, dragging her to him. Another Indian entered and, with a guttural cry, tore the ticking and blankets from the bed and threw them to the floor.

Catherine screamed as the man dragged her out by the foot, Donald howling in her arms.

"Catherine! Donald!" Maggie pulled against her captor.

He wrenched her arm and garbled some words at her.

She slapped him with her free hand. "Let me go!"

He grinned then, like the opossum the McCord brothers had cornered the week before, a terrible expression showing stained teeth.

The second Indian, carrying Catherine under one arm and Donald under the other, passed them and went below. The cries of her siblings mingled with more cries as the other children were pulled from the upper rooms.

The Indian holding Maggie stayed until the rest were gone, looking her over as if she were a lamb at market. He grunted, then pulled her down the stairs, keeping her behind him. An Indian at the bottom jabbered to him and pointed out the doorway, the door missing from its hinges. The Indian holding her arm shook his head and hauled Maggie outside.

Mama huddled with a small knot of women and children surrounded by more of the mostly naked Indian men. The one carrying Catherine and Donald shoved them into the group.

"Mama!" Maggie cried.

"Maggie!" Mama stepped forward but was pushed back by one of the Indians standing guard. She would have fallen if the other women hadn't steadied her. Catherine threw her arms around Mama's waist. Donald thumped to the dirt on his backside.

"Mama!" The word tore Maggie's throat.

The Indian wrenched her arm again and garbled more words at her, his face pulled into terrible lines. He towed her behind him, striding away from Mama and the others and toward the forest.

Maggie had to move her feet or be dragged. With her face still turned toward Mama, Maggie tripped and nearly fell, but her captor's fingers dug into her arm, and he jerked her over a body.

A body.

Lifeless eyes stared at her from a face she knew. His hair had been cut away from the top of his head. Blood trickled from the corner of his mouth. Mr. Lowry. One of the men left behind to guard the fort.

Maggie's stomach cramped. Before she could give in to being sick, the Indian dragged her away. There were other bodies littering the ground, mostly men but some smaller. Some wearing dresses.

A series of shrill yips filled the air as Indians set the block-house on fire. Within minutes, a plume of inky smoke rose to the clouds. Catherine and Donald wouldn't have been safe even if her attempt to hide them had worked.

Her captor stopped at the edge of the forest and watched, his expression unchanging.

Another Indian approached, speaking more of the nonsense words. Her captor slashed his hand through the air, then pointed to the trees. Their voices rose. Her captor's grip on her arm never lessened.

Maggie's heart beat so hard that the Indian must have heard it. So hard it hurt. Almost as much as the fingers biting into her arm. Almost as much as seeing Mama out of her reach.

Several Indians with spears herded the women and children like a flock of geese in the opposite direction. Away from her. Leaving her behind.

"No!" She yelled. "Mama!"

The Indian holding her cuffed the side of her head. Maggie's vision swam, but she managed to focus on Mama. Donald in her arms, Mama hung to the back of the group until she was prodded by a spear.

"Be strong, Maggie," she yelled. "Someone will come for you. Be strong!"

Chapter 1

She'd come too far to be eaten by wolves. Their gray-and-brown bodies swarmed over a freshly killed doe and its fawn that had come to the water to drink. Growling and snapping, they sorted out their hierarchy of who fed where and on what. Maggie Kerr was not inclined to be the next morsel they squabbled over.

Backing away, her moccasins silent in the damp forest, she left the edge of the lake. She'd yet to come to the big river that would turn north to Fort Detroit, but it must be close. For three days she'd skirted the water and watched her back trail. Nobody had come after her. Yet. But he would.

Tree Sleeper.

Maggie squelched the urge to gnash her teeth like the wolves she'd left behind. Squinting at the setting sun through a canopy of pine branches, she angled to the northwest. Word should have reached him two days past, but she'd traveled fast and slept little. Speed was her only chance against the man who could track a beetle across a dry rock. She'd done her best to cover all sign of her passing in the beginning, and maybe that had bought her more time, but if he found her tracks a day's walk out, he'd know where she was heading.

5

Fort Detroit was the only British outpost she could reach without crossing the big lake they called Erie. She had no canoe, nor the strength it would take to paddle across that vast expanse by herself even if she had one.

She settled into a ground-eating lope along a deer trail, keeping her pace until darkness gathered beneath the trees. Her stomach growled in a good imitation of the wolf pack from the lake. There was precious little pemmican left in her pouch. If only she'd had more time to secure provisions before she'd fled. More time to make a plan.

New vegetation sprouted along the sides of the trail. Nothing of use to her rumbling middle. Winter had loosened its hold on the land, but it offered little in the way of fresh edibles this early in the season.

In a gathering of cedars, she found a large windfall that was dry enough to make a good resting place. She gathered handfuls of old needles and lined the depression with them. With the small metal hatchet she'd been able to steal, she cut a few cedar boughs and laid them within reach. Now that leaving signs behind her no longer mattered, she could sleep more comfortably, even though she couldn't allow herself to sleep much. Dropping her leather pouch onto the makeshift bedding, Maggie sat beside it with a sigh. She dug out the almost flat sack of pemmican and chewed on the greasy mixture.

The fort would have bread. Real bread. The type Mama had made.

She stopped mid-chew. When was the last time she'd thought of Mama? A week? Marking time in the Indian village had been difficult. Many weeks? Perhaps longer for Da. Their names came to mind without sadness anymore. Without expectation. She closed her eyes and tried to picture them, but the images were fuzzy and dark in her mind, like looking through murky water at the stones below.

Swallowing the mouthful of pemmican, she put the rest back in her pouch and curled into a ball in the shelter of the windfall. She pulled the boughs over her. Frost was not uncommon during the nights, but she'd been unwilling to add a blanket to the weight she carried. It would have slowed her down. Her doe-hide dress was thick and warm, as were her leggings and knee-high moccasins. She wriggled into a more comfortable position and grasped her hatchet, holding it close.

Maggie had dreamed of her escape for years, though she hadn't always believed it would happen. At times she'd been sure it wouldn't. She'd stayed strong and adapted to the tribe she'd been sold to. She'd learned to survive. When the British had chased the French out of the country two summers past, she'd thought maybe it was her chance, but the Huron village where she lived had seen nothing of the British. Very little had changed until the Ottawa chief, the one called Pontiac, had come to ask Chief Teata to join with him in a great fight against the British in a place called Fort Detroit.

There had been much talk around the fire that night, enough for Maggie to learn she could follow the lake and then a big river to find Fort Detroit—and that it was filled with British soldiers.

The British. Her people.

The Huron chief had listened with a stoic face, seemingly unmoved by the younger Pontiac's passion for a fight to annihilate the British and restore the French to power. But the more Maggie heard as she'd brought food and drink to those listening to the Ottawa chief, the faster her heart had beat. It had beat for freedom. It had beat for a future among her own people. And it had beat with a hope she'd thought long gone, left at a burning blockhouse on the frontier of Pennsylvania.

Ears tuned to the noises of the forest at night, Maggie let her mind wander to the possibilities ahead. A strong fort filled with soldiers who would keep the Indians out. A return to the world into which she'd been born. A chance to find her brothers and sister again.

If they lived.

Of course she hoped they did. Wanted them to be alive and well and not captives of another tribe somewhere. Wanted them to be together as she remembered them. Which was foolish. They would be older now, as she was. Although she'd no clear idea of her age. Indians marked time differently than her parents had, and they didn't mark it at all for a white captive.

What if she never found her family again?

Her arms ached for the warm press of Redwing's sturdy little body. The chill of the hatchet was no substitute for the boy she had left behind. She couldn't have brought him with her. Couldn't have escaped with his weight to carry, his mouth to feed, his body to keep warm. And Redwing was Huron. The son of her only friend among the Hurons, Wind Over Waters, who had died bringing the boy into the world. Maggie had promised to care for the child, and she had.

Until three days before.

With a wispy sigh, she burrowed deeper into the pine needles. She must find the fort. She must find it before the one who followed found her. And she must be on the move again before the sun broke the horizon.

Clenching the hatchet to her chest, she slept.

———

THE SUN SANK BEHIND THE TREES ON THE OPPOSITE bank of the river. Baptiste Geroux stretched and yawned, thankful to put a long day behind him. Tomorrow, he would plow the field for planting peas. Those seeds liked the cool ground of early spring and would shoot forth in its dampness.

Then he would plow more and plant his wheat, and after that, the corn and squash.

The rhythm of the land was in his blood. Grand-père had toiled in fields across the vast ocean, a body of water Baptiste had never seen. The third son of a large family, Père had left France and brought his young wife to this land.

Here Baptiste had been born, the oldest of five children. Here he had worked from his earliest days, following behind Père and the oxen, dropping seeds into the freshly broken soil. Here he had run ahead of the oxen, an impulsive child who'd tripped and fallen, his leg trampled and twisted. Here he'd survived and learned to live with his limitations. And here he had stayed.

But his eyes were drawn again to the western sky.

Where was Henri? Would he return this summer? It'd been more than two years since his brother had paddled away in his loaded canoe, heading to places west in search of furs to trade, leaving the land he'd been born on to the British.

Leaving Baptiste behind.

He rubbed the thigh of his lame leg. The bunched muscles under his breeches helped him compensate for the twisted calf below. But not enough to sail with Henri.

They'd stood on the riverbank and argued, something they rarely did, the morning Henri'd left. He'd done his best to persuade Baptiste to go west. He'd pleaded, argued, and even bullied, but Baptiste knew the truth. With his lame leg and inability to run, he would have placed Henri in more danger.

The tribes to the west owed no allegiance to the French. They could be hostile to anyone. Probably were. Was that why his brother had not returned? Had he fallen without Baptiste at his side?

He refused to believe it. Nobody was as silver-tongued as Henri or better able to talk himself out of trouble. French,

English, or the Indian trade language, Henri was fluent in all three.

So where was he?

One of the oxen snorted and snapped Baptiste out of his melancholy thoughts. He left the riverbank and picked up his willow switch.

"Beau. Pierre. Come up, boys."

He swished the willow branch through the air, and the oxen leaned into their yoke. It didn't take much encouragement for them to head to the low-roofed barn for the night. Once in the shelter, Baptiste removed their yoke and tossed a handful of grain into each trough. It should be more for all the work they'd done, but he was almost out until the summer's crop was ripe. With the grass greening more every day, the oxen had been finding plenty to eat without it.

With a brush in one hand and an old strip of cloth in the other, Baptiste worked over each beast, brushing and wiping the winter hair from their hides. Père had instilled in him the importance of a well-kept team of oxen. Without them, a farmer was at a loss to provide what he needed for his family, much less the gifts the Indians expected as a form of rent for use of the land.

Not that Baptiste had a family anymore. His parents rested under the spreading branches of a tall oak behind the cabin Père had built with his own hands. His sisters were buried beside them in three smaller graves. And Henri was...

What if Henri did not return? What would Baptiste do then? What did he want to do?

He tossed the brush and rag into the box where he kept his few barn tools, then dusted off his hands. That was the question he needed to figure out. And soon. Tensions were rising between the Indian tribes and the British in the fort.

Baptiste's little farm sat smack in the middle of it all.

The two farmers nearest him had pulled up stakes and moved out last fall. Both had urged him to do the same, and he might have if not for Henri.

But he couldn't spend his life waiting for his brother. He loved the land, the river, his sturdy cabin, even the mismatched colored oxen in the barn. It was home. His home. It was all he knew.

So why weren't the everyday chores and rhythm of the farm enough for him anymore? Was it the unrest of those surrounding him? Or was it something else?

The aloneness pushed in on him as it often did toward the end of the day. He scraped the bottoms of his moccasins on the board positioned for that task. A half-smile tugged at his mouth and in his mind's ear, he could hear Maman telling him to do a good job. She'd been so proud of her wooden floor, put in years after the cabin had been built.

He stepped into the cabin on that floor, littered with clumps of dirt, dried grass, and leaves tracked in since he'd swept last, which had been sometime last fall before the snows came. He took a deep breath and grimaced. The barn smelled better. He scanned the single room for his broom. It must be around somewhere.

The gurgle in his middle distracted him in the direction of his meager larder. He wished—not for the first time—that a hot meal bubbled over the hearth, and with a warm smile on her face, Maman stood nearby.

Or someone else.

He rubbed the back of his neck. The pull of nature was for a man to have a mate, but what woman would want a lame husband?

Something jerked Maggie from sleep. Heart racing, muscles tightened to the point of pain, she slowed her breathing and remained motionless, keeping her eyes closed. The sounds of the forest surrounded her. The brush of a bat's wings against the air, the clicking of insects on the move in the dark, the sway of branches sighing in the breeze.

A grunt, the scuff of a foot against last fall's leaves, a whuffling snort.

She relaxed and opened her eyes but kept a firm grip on the hatchet.

Old wood popped beneath powerful claws, followed by the slurp and smack of a tongue lapping bugs from their hiding places.

Hungry from its long sleep, the bear would be feasting on everything it could find, but not on Maggie. It hadn't smelled her yet, or she wouldn't have heard it. Bears were solitary creatures, not given to provoking trouble with people. Unless, of course... she strained her ears, but no sound of cubs reached her. A single male then, or perhaps a female too old to breed.

Maggie remained motionless until the bear had moved past her range of hearing. She couldn't see much of the sky through the branches covering her but judged she'd slept half the night. It was enough. She pushed the boughs off and rose from the windfall, brushing debris from her clothing and hair.

Eyes accustomed to the darkness, and with the aid of a half moon, she picked her way along the deer path she'd been on the evening before. Her sense of direction was generally good, and when the trees parted, she could see enough of the stars to get her bearings. Da had taught her of the North Star. She only needed to find it and keep it on her right.

Where was Tree Sleeper? Did he rest yet? Or was he also on his feet, slipping beneath the trees, perhaps not far behind her?

She quickened her steps and ignored the chill that had little to do with the damp night air.

She'd lost count of the years since Fort McCord. Sold after two winters by the Indian who'd captured her, she'd been bought by an old Huron medicine man and his elderly sister. Stone Foot had treated her fairly well—he hadn't beaten her, at least. Long Pouch, his sister, had done that. Until the old woman had died, she'd worked Maggie like the slave she was.

Had been.

She was free.

Gaining her freedom had come unexpectedly and far too easily. Easy except that she'd had to leave Redwing behind. Keeping her freedom? That would be the challenge. She'd seen an escaped captive who'd been returned to the village. What had happened to him had both solidified her desire to escape and instilled a terror that had prevented her from forming a true plan of action.

Then Pontiac had arrived, and everything had fallen into place.

As the inky sky behind her showed the first blush of a new day, her feet were almost flying along the path to find Pontiac's river. All her hope rested on finding and following it to Fort Detroit.

Once there... her steps faltered for a couple of strides.

Would the British in the fort believe her? Would they let her stay? Would they protect her from Tree Sleeper?

Or would they turn her away?

She was Maggie Kerr, a British citizen. She'd stayed strong and survived. They must listen to her. They must protect her.

Her stride faltered again, and she slowed to a walk.

Why would they, though?

Nobody else had protected her. Nobody had come for her. She'd been abandoned. Someone should have come for her.

Someone should have cared about her.

She pressed her fingers against the stinging in her eyes. Crying was not permitted. Crying earned Long Pouch's hard slap. And crying—even in the depth of night when no one in the longhouse was awake to hear—solved nothing.

If Maggie was going to survive, she'd have to do it on her own.

Again.

Chapter 2

Baptiste Geroux swatted the gnats buzzing around his hat. He leaned against the curved handles of his plow, resting himself as well as Beau and Pierre. He eased his weight off his lame leg and sighed, taking in the land around him. Once his fields were planted with corn, squash, peas, and wheat, he would work to remove the stumps from the trees he'd cut during the winter, enlarging the field by nearly two rods along the eastern edge.

The flat ground along the river that he'd cleared with Père ten years past would produce a nice crop if the weather held. If the Indians stayed out of it. And if the British in the fort left him alone to tend it. Yet despite all possible—probable—pitfalls, he held on to the land, the last strip of cultivated farmland to the north of the fort on the east side of the river.

The oxen dozed with their noses almost to the ground, enjoying the warm spring sun on their backs. But dozing wouldn't get the crops in the ground. Baptiste lifted his willow switch and brushed it across their rumps.

"Come up, boys. Come up."

With reluctant snorts, the two muscular animals leaned into their yoke and ambled down the field while Baptiste applied his weight to forcing the plow downward into the soil. They'd gone less than half the length of the field when a chain snapped and one side of the plow broke loose from the oxen, driving the point upright into the dirt.

"Whoa!"

The team stopped, heads dropping low. Baptiste wrestled with the plow, its point stuck fast. He couldn't budge it. He slammed his palm against the handle.

"Back. Back, boys." Neither beast moved, so he walked to the front and shook the willow switch in their faces. "Back, I say." The oxen shuffled two steps to the rear.

Baptiste returned to the plow and worked it backward, releasing it from a large rock. It'd hit the rock and dug in along its edge rather than going over the top of it. He twisted the plow and examined it. The sturdy hickory wood had survived intact, saving him hours of labor to fashion another.

He picked up the broken chain and ran his fingers down the links. One had snapped clean. He might be able to rig a rope or leather strap as a temporary mend, but two other links showed signs of stress, one of them with a clear fracture. He didn't have enough strong rope or leather to repair the whole thing.

There was nothing else to do but take it to the blacksmith at the fort. He cast a glance at the sky. The sun hung east of the zenith still. With luck and the British blacksmith's cooperation, he might be back in the field by early evening.

He unhooked the plow and laid the chains across the oxen's backs, then retrieved the switch.

"Haw, boys. Haw."

The oxen shuffled to their left, quickening their steps when the plow didn't drag against them, and headed for the barn. They weren't dumb animals. They knew their work was done.

Baptiste's was only beginning.

By the time he'd put the beasts in their pen and filled their water trough, the sun was directly overhead. Baptiste ate a round of coarse bread, a mixture of ground wheat and corn he'd baked on a griddle, then looped the heavy chains around his shoulder. He grabbed a paddle and his coat before heading to the canoe he kept concealed near the riverbank.

His weather sense told him it might rain in the night. The ache in his leg agreed. If he could get back into the field by early evening, maybe he'd finish enough ground to plant the peas the following morning.

Maybe the British blacksmith would cooperate. Maybe the Indians would leave Beau and Pierre alone while he was gone. Baptiste stopped his uneven march to the river and turned to look over his field again, paddle leaned against his side. Maybe he should pack up and move east to Montreal or Quebec. Maybe it wasn't worth hanging on to this plot of land.

So many maybes.

The weakened chains *chinked* in his tightened fist.

He pulled off his hat and swiped the sweat from his brow before pushing the battered felt back on his head, decision made. He'd stay one more summer.

For Henri.

THE RIVER GLISTENED IN THE EARLY MORNING LIGHT. It flowed past Maggie as wide and powerful as Pontiac had described it. Too wide and powerful to swim across, at least here. There must be a ford somewhere along its length. Pontiac had said the fort was on the western bank. She'd have to cross somewhere.

She squatted at the edge and drank handfuls of cold water. It mixed with the meager remnants of the pemmican to fill her belly. If she didn't find the fort today, she'd need to find food. She filled her waterskin before standing.

A narrow path cut through the dense brush around the river. Hoof and paw prints pressed into the exposed soil, but no moccasin prints. She followed it for half the morning, her eyelids drooping in the warmth of the day. The warmth, lack of adequate sleep or food, and muscles pushed to their limit in her flight to freedom had taken their toll.

Someone coughed.

Maggie froze, the hairs on her arms tingling.

Something rustled near the water.

She dropped to a crouch and waited, afraid to move lest she make a sound. A whiff of smoke reached her, followed by the high squeal of a child. Whoever was near the water coughed again. The splat and slap of someone washing clothes and words uttered in the Huron tongue put her in motion.

Heart pounding in her ears, she eased off the path. Using both hands and feet, she kept low and moved as soundlessly as she could while squelching the urge to run. How could she have been so careless? Hunger and fatigue were not acceptable excuses.

Not if she wished to live.

She'd almost walked into a Huron village. Chief Takay's village probably. His was nearest the fort, according to what she'd overheard. What she should have remembered. He'd have lookouts, of course. How they'd not spotted her already, she couldn't guess. If only her luck would hold.

It took her most of an hour, scuttling like a crayfish, until she deemed herself far enough away from the village to avoid lookouts. Poor lookouts, as it were, but even poor ones could spot a careless person.

And she'd been very careless.

That wouldn't happen again. Discovery by any Indians would

raise questions and suspicions. Her auburn hair and pale skin peppered with freckles made it impossible for her to blend in, even if her clothing and language matched theirs. But there were people in Takay's village who knew her.

They would know she was an escaped captive.

Even more than food, she needed rest, but she didn't have that luxury. She poured water over her face. It had warmed in her waterskin but was still enough to refresh her. Eyes darting, ears straining, she continued along the river but not too close. She stayed concealed in the trees, skirting what looked like farms. She hadn't seen one since her childhood, but they fit her memories.

Perhaps someone on a farm would take her across the river, but more than likely, they would be French, not British. And the French were friends of Pontiac. She kept the brushy growth between herself and the clearings and buildings.

Around mid-morning, the clink of metal caught her ear. Not close enough to have been from one of the farms she'd passed. Folded into a crouch again, she picked her way along the bank of the river. Across its width rose a wall of logs standing upright and pressed together. It must be the fort, but it looked nothing like the blockhouse her family had taken shelter in all those years ago.

Not that it had kept them safe.

The fort was huge, spanning a long swath of the shoreline with something like the blockhouse she remembered thrust up at each of the corners, towering over the wall of logs. There must be many people inside something so large. The ring of metal and other sounds escaped. Even though the land sloped down to the river, the walls were tall enough that only the rooftops of buildings were in view.

Surely she'd be safe there.

Maggie rested and watched for a few moments. There was no

easy ford in sight. The water rushed and swirled, its powerful currants visible from the land. Perhaps she could locate a ford further up the river. She didn't have the luxury of wasting time, but going back toward Takay's village was out of the question. If she couldn't find a ford, she'd have to risk swimming it. She continued upstream.

It was close to midday, and although the river was much narrower than where she'd first encountered it, it also appeared more turbulent. She still hadn't found a place to ford. She considered climbing a tree for a longer view when she almost stumbled on a concealed canoe. Maggie peered inside the vessel. No paddle. The canoe appeared solid, the birch bark tight and well-sealed. It hadn't been abandoned, not as cleverly hidden as it was. Yet a canoe without a paddle would do her no good unless she could fashion one from—

A rustling in the grass came from her right.

She drew her hatchet and backed away from the canoe.

A man limped toward her swinging a paddle in one hand. He was tall and lean and...

White.

Maggie swallowed. She hadn't seen another white person in many months. There'd been several captives when she'd been sold to Stone Foot of the Hurons, but none were left. Two had gone to another village. What had happened to the others she'd done her best to forget.

His white woven shirt under a waistcoat and the knee-length breeches brought back a long-forgotten memory of Da walking toward their cabin. But this man's skin was almost Indian-dark, not Da's ruddy hue. His black hair was not plucked or braided in the Indian way. It was tied at the back, nothing like Da's unruly reddish curls. And he didn't have Da's bushy beard, although a blue-black shadow covered the bottom half of his face.

He reached the canoe and set his paddle and a coat inside

while he unwound a chain from his shoulder. The chain clanked as it hit the bottom of the canoe. Checking the river first, apparently no more wanting to be seen than Maggie was, he eased the canoe from its hiding place and dragged it toward the water.

Her chance to cross the river was leaving without her.

"Monsieur?" The word slipped out before she'd formed a coherent thought. He spun around, hand gripping the knife handle at his belt.

"Who is there?" He answered in French. Not the guttural French the Indians spoke, but the nasal tones of one born speaking the language. Like the Jesuit, Père Potier, who lived among the Huron.

Fear skittered around inside her, but she'd already exposed herself. And she must cross the river. She must reach the fort before the one who followed found her. The man before her might be a friend of the Indians, but he was infirm. If need be, she could outrun him. She took a tighter grip on her hatchet and straightened.

"I am looking for a way across the river."

"Who are you?"

"I am..." She almost said Dappled Leaves, the name Stone Foot had given her, noting her freckles looked like sunshine on autumn leaves. "Maggie Kerr."

THE WOMAN WHO STOOD BEFORE BAPTISTE LOOKED nothing like an Indian aside from her clothing, which was from the Huron tribe by the distinctive flap on her pouch. She pronounced the French words like many of the Indians did, but with a slight accent. When she'd said her name, it had the ring of English in it. Even more alarming, she clutched a hatchet in her hand as if she knew how to use it.

"Let go of that hatchet, and we will talk."

She hesitated, her eyes going to his own hand on the handle of his knife.

He pried his fingers loose but kept his focus on the hatchet until she dropped it into its loop at her side.

"I must cross the river."

He nodded but didn't move. There was a story here, one he was fairly certain he didn't wish to be involved in. "How come you to be here?"

Her eyes flicked to the river and back at him. "I followed the river."

"From where?"

The mulish slash of her mouth and the hardness that entered her blue-gray eyes said she wasn't likely to answer that question. Perhaps it was best he didn't know.

"Can you handle a paddle?" he asked.

Her chin dipped and rose again.

He grunted and pointed toward his cabin, hidden by a screen of willows. "Come. We will fetch another and return to cross."

"I will wait here."

"So you can steal my canoe? I think not."

She looked at the ground, her shoulders pulling in. So… that had been her intent. He'd be smart to leave her standing here and paddle off on his own. He was wasting precious daylight with a woman who reeked of trouble in every way imaginable.

But when she raised her eyes again, he saw something that changed his mind. Something… vulnerable. He could paddle them both across by himself, but in the high spring current with her added weight, a second paddle would make it easier. It would also keep her hands away from the hatchet. Her chin dipped again, and she moved in the direction he'd pointed, her back turned to him.

He could do little else but follow.

Maggie wanted to argue with the man, to tell him to get into the canoe and she'd paddle with her hands. She'd wasted enough time skirting Takay's village and looking for a ford. Even as swiftly as she'd traveled, Tree Sleeper would be close behind.

He knew where Fort Detroit was.

While she'd had to search and work her way on the scanty information she'd gleaned from listening to Pontiac, Tree Sleeper had been to Fort Detroit before.

So she turned her back on the man and walked, seething at the delay. He came alongside her in a few steps despite his odd gait. They rounded a thick patch of willows, the type that grew close to water, and a cabin came into view.

Maggie paused.

He stopped beside her, his forehead puckered into a question.

How could she explain why the sight of a simple square cabin made of logs, chinked with moss and roofed with cedar bark, made her eyes misty? She took a deep breath and marched on, ignoring the tidy log barn with one black ox and one red ox grazing in the fenced corral beside it. She stepped onto the shady porch, covered with a deep overhang that must have kept the snow from building up against the cabin's door in the winter. She half expected a black-and-white dog to come racing around the corner, tongue lolling from its mouth. Dutch had been Da's loyal companion on the farm.

"Wait here." The man brushed past her and entered the cabin, leaving the door open.

The inside looked nothing like Mama's tidy home. Instead, it looked like a bear had pawed through it. Smelled a bit like that too. He took a paddle from a hook on the wall and returned, pointing the way back to the river.

A man of few words.

She half-trotted to keep up with him despite his limp. At least he wasn't wasting any time, whoever he was.

"What is your name?" she asked.

He shot a glance at her but didn't lessen his pace. "Baptiste Geroux."

"Thank you, Monsieur Geroux, for taking me across the river."

His mouth quirked, something less than a smile. "My pleasure, Mademoiselle Kerr." He stopped and faced her, spiky black brows drawn close. "Or is it Madame?"

Heat defying the cool spring breeze warmed her face. "Mademoiselle."

That seemed to satisfy him, and he continued toward the river. Had he thought her a runaway wife? But then, he was closer to the truth than he could know. If she hadn't gotten away—

He thrust the paddle at her, and she grabbed it, still hurrying at his side. Without stopping, he seized the front of the canoe and finished dragging it to the riverbank. He pointed to the vessel. "Get in."

She scrambled aboard, her slight weight barely rocking the sturdy vessel as she sank to her knees at its peaked front.

With a mighty shove, he launched it from the shore, leaping in with an awkward jump that kept his feet dry. On his knees, his paddle met the water, and they slipped into the current. Maggie dipped her paddle and matched his rhythm, sending the canoe in a straight line for the opposite bank.

When they reached near mid-river, he dragged his paddle and angled them downstream.

"Where are we going?"

"I go to the fort," he said.

"That is where I wish to go as well." Her heart lightened as it hadn't done in years when the log wall and its corner block-houses came into sight.

"Then perhaps we are well met, mademoiselle."

Indeed. Perhaps they were.

The rippling current doing most of the work, Maggie had little to do but keep the canoe steady as it whisked her toward her freedom. Freedom from the fear of being sold again.

For any reason.

Chapter 3

The fort's gates were closed. Baptiste stopped, and the woman bumped into his back.

"What is wrong?" Her voice was shallow. Was she afraid? Or out of breath from keeping up with him? She was a tiny thing, even though she filled out the Indian leather dress in all the right places.

"The gates, they are shut."

She took hold of his arm and leaned to the side, peering around him.

The touch and her nearness disturbed him enough that he took his attention from the fort and the surrounding area.

"Are they not normally shut?"

"Non." He snapped his eyes back to the imposing structure. "They are not." But they were, and it had the skin on the back of his neck prickling. He continued along the narrow path from the river.

"Who goes there?" came a shout in English. The face of a British soldier appeared at the top of the palisade.

"Baptiste Geroux."

"State your business with the fort."

Baptiste patted the chain slung around his shoulders. His

English wasn't the best, although he could understand more than he could find the words for. "The blacksmith."

The face disappeared and moments later one of the gate doors swung open wide enough for them to pass. They entered, and it banged shut behind them. The *chunk* of a heavy beam securing it in place.

To keep them in? Or others out?

"Is this your woman?" the soldier in front of him asked.

Before he could find the right words in English to explain, she stepped in front of Baptiste, chin high, and said in clear English, "I must see the commander of the fort."

"Must you, indeed?" The soldier's tone and the feral gleam in his eye as it roamed over Mademoiselle Kerr combined to set Baptiste's teeth on edge.

The woman clenched the paddle she carried as if she might take a swing at the soldier. That could land them both in trouble, and trouble with the British was something Baptiste didn't need. He moved to her side. "She must."

The soldier rubbed his ear and squinted at Baptiste. The woman watched him too. Both appeared to weigh his words carefully.

The soldier moved first, calling to a lanky lad in uniform. "Show this woman to the major. Take the Frenchie too. And keep an eye on them."

The lad nodded. "Follow me." He pivoted to his left and marched down the street.

Baptiste had no choice but to follow, even though the blacksmith's shop was two streets over and in the other direction. So much for plowing more of his field before dark. Still, he wouldn't see the woman bullied by that British guard. And he had to admit, he was curious why she'd insisted on seeing the major.

He was curious about her, a white woman dressed as an

Indian, able to speak both French and English and doubtless Huron too. She was brave enough to have faced him alone by the river, and she'd stood up to the guard. Like a little spitfire. He controlled the twitch of his lips. He may have sworn allegiance to England to be able to stay on his land, but he tread warily around British soldiers. They had no more love of a Frenchman than he had for them.

No longer hiding behind Baptiste, Mademoiselle Kerr marched behind the young soldier. Marched was an apt description. From behind, with the sway of her hips distracting him, he sensed her drive and purpose. Whatever her reason for coming to the fort, she gripped the paddle in a white-knuckled fist.

She wasn't completely at ease.

Good. Neither was he.

They entered a building, and the soldier told them to wait while he disappeared behind a door. Murmuring reached them. They spoke English, of course, and too low for him to puzzle out the words. The mademoiselle tilted her head like a chicken watching a spider, eyes fixed upon the door. The voices stopped, and she relaxed as the young soldier returned.

"Major Gladwin will see you now."

They followed him into a sparsely furnished room with maps on the wall and an imposing figure in a white wig behind the desk. The young officer stopped and faced them. "State your business to the major."

Mademoiselle Kerr took a step closer to the desk. Shoulders back and chin high, her voice rang clear in the room. "Indians plan to attack your fort."

MAJOR GLADWIN PRESSED HIS FINGERTIPS TOGETHER in front of his nose and peered at Maggie above them. "Tell me something I do not already know."

He knew.

She gritted her teeth to keep her mouth from falling open. Never had she considered that possibility as she'd fled from Stone Foot's longhouse. Fled from Tree Sleeper. Grabbed her one shot at freedom.

Now what leverage did she have? What could Maggie promise the major in return for her safekeeping? What use could she be to him? Would he turn her out of the fort? A shiver worked its way up under her ribs.

"Which Indians?" Monsieur Geroux's stilted English rumbled beside her.

The major's attention swiveled to him. "Who are you?"

"Baptiste Geroux." He performed a short bow. "At your service."

The action tickled a memory long buried. Had Da done the same when meeting someone important?

"Where have you come from?" the major asked him.

"I farm across the river to the north. As my père before me."

"Have you sworn allegiance to the Crown?"

"I have."

He didn't sound very pleased about it, and from the major's narrowed eyes, he'd caught that too. But Maggie didn't have time to worry about Monsieur Geroux and his feelings for the British.

The major grunted and lowered his hands to the desk. "How do you know this woman?"

"I do not. She ask to cross the river, and I come here." He shrugged. "She come with me."

Maggie tried not to squirm as the major's flinty eyes focused back on her. "Who are you? 'Tis God's own truth you are no more an Indian than I."

"Maggie Kerr." Her English name came easier this time. "I was taken captive at Fort McCord."

"Fort McCord?" The major's bellow bounced off the walls. "'Tis seven years past. How can this be?"

Seven years. That meant Maggie was eighteen years old.

"Where have you been all this time?" Was that doubt in the major's voice, in the squint of his eyes?

"I was taken from the fort by a Lenni Lenape warrior. He took me away from the other captives including my mama, sister, and younger brother. I was given to his sister, or maybe half-sister, I am not sure. I was barely eleven years old. After a while, I was sold to a Huron man and taken to his village." Would he want more details? In truth, she didn't know much more, having been too young and hampered by language to understand a lot of those early months. "I have been there ever since."

"So, Takay has been harboring captives after all." The major leaned back in his chair. "I always thought that one lied to me."

"No, sir, I was in Chief Teata's village."

"Teata?" The major sat upright. "Are you saying that Teata is getting involved in this plot of Pontiac's?"

Hope surged within her. "He is. Not because he wants to, but because Pontiac has forced him."

"Forced him how?"

"Teata's village is small, the warriors few. Pontiac gave them little choice. He told Teata to fight beside him or be killed by his Ottawas."

"That pompous, conniving—"

"What is this plot of which you speak?" Monsieur Geroux asked.

The major quirked a brow at the other man. "You know nothing of it?" Distrust vibrated through his voice.

"Non. I do not."

Maggie believed the tall Frenchman. Not only did he sound sincere, but she'd seen no sign of preparation at his farm. His oxen had been in plain sight, tools leaned against the wall outside his barn, his cabin door unbarred.

"Do you know Pontiac?" the major asked him.

Monsieur Geroux hesitated a heartbeat. "Him, I have seen, but I do not know him—how you say—close."

There was a wealth of meaning in the Frenchman's simple phrase. The major must have caught it too, for he leaned back in his chair and took the other man's measure more fully.

"Will you stand with the fort if it comes to a fight?"

Monsieur Geroux shifted his feet. "I keep to my farm, away from the fight, as much as I am able."

The major grunted, then stood. "I would appreciate you selling your produce here at the fort and not to the Indians." His brow quirked again. "Providing those heathens do not steal you blind first."

The Frenchman's mouth pulled into a flat line. "I will bring to you what I can, you have my word."

The two men faced each other, and powerful undercurrents swirled between them. Maggie knew the French and British were no longer at war, but they were obviously not on the best of terms either. However, they could wage their battle of silence after she learned what was to become of her. She cleared her throat, and the major's attention turned her way.

He swiped his hand from Monsieur Geroux to the door. "Very well. You are dismissed." His eyes never left Maggie. "And now... what are we to do with you?"

Monsieur Geroux did another short bow to the major and,

much to her surprise, another toward her before he left, his uneven steps thudding across the wooden floor.

Maggie swallowed and met the major stare for stare. "I do not wish to go back to Teata's village." Her voice was firm despite the uncertainty that battered beneath her ribs.

"Return? Of course you will not return." The major sank into his chair. "No British citizen—colonial or otherwise—shall remain captive of these heathens if we can find and release them." He cocked his head at her. "Or if they find us."

The tension melted from her neck and shoulders. "Then I can stay at the fort?"

"Precisely." The major's attention turned to the stack of papers on his desk. "Ensign Willabay will show you to the fort surgeon. I trust he will know what to do with you from there." He lifted a sheet of paper from the stack, not looking at Maggie again. "I will have more questions for you after the surgeon has had his say."

The soldier still standing by the door cleared his throat. "If you will follow me, miss."

She did, with a lightness to her step and Monsieur Geroux's paddle clenched in her fist.

———————

DISGRUNTLED AT SUCH AN ABRUPT DISMISSAL AND further disgruntled that he felt that way when he needed to be about his business in the first place, Baptiste stomped down the dusty streets to the blacksmith shop.

He'd been in the fort many times over the years, especially when it'd been held by his fellow Frenchmen. In the past two and a half years, he'd only come of necessity or to sell his produce. The British may not trade as extravagantly with the Indians as the French had done, but they paid good coin for his corn and wheat. Money that covered the needs he could not produce on his farm. Like mending the chain.

The blacksmith was banging away on a bar of iron when Baptiste entered the smithy, orange sparks kicking up with each strike. No one else was in the shop. Baptiste waited until the bear of a man tossed the metal into a bucket of black water where it hissed. Acrid steam billowed in the low-roofed building.

"What can I do for you, Frenchie?"

Baptiste was used to the name. More soldiers than not called him the same. "My plow chain, she is broke." He plunked the damaged metal onto the room's central table.

"Indeed, it is." Massive hands, blackened by years at the forge, he lifted and examined the links. "I can fix this, but not today."

"I must have it to—"

The blacksmith slammed the chain onto the table. "The major's musts come before yours. Take it back with you or leave it with me and I will fix it tomorrow."

Another trip to the fort. More time wasted. Seeds not planted. And Indians openly talking war. What else could go wrong?

Maybe a pair of blue-gray eyes, under hair more red than brown, looking at him as he turned to leave the major's office. Eyes that lacked the confidence she'd held in the woods. How would a young woman taken as a child and raised by Hurons adapt to life as a white woman again?

Not that it was any business of his.

"I will return early."

"I cannot promise it done before supper."

Baptiste pushed his hat back and scrubbed the front of his head. "As you say. But I will return early."

The blacksmith palmed a pair of tongs and grabbed the iron

bar from the bucket, thrusting it back into the glowing coals as he pumped the creaking bellows. "Suit yourself."

Baptiste left, heading for the same gate by which he'd entered, swinging his paddle in one hand. Paddle. Mademoiselle had his other paddle. Not that he needed it to cross the river on his own, but it was his paddle, and he didn't fancy having to carve a new one. He paused, but had no idea where to find her. He would look for her when he returned the next day.

More urgent were his farm and his oxen. He strode on toward the gate. If the Indians stole his oxen, he'd have no way to farm his land. No way to support himself. Which he must. He must remain on the farm.

Where else would Henri look for him if—when—he returned?

Chapter 4

Maggie tugged at the uncomfortable and unaccustomed clothing. Some of it she remembered wearing before, but some she did not. Mrs. Roberts had demonstrated the wearing of it all when she'd handed the clothing over last evening.

Whyever did white women wear stays? They pinched and pushed and all but spilled her from the top of the dress she'd been given to wear. The gauzy white square of fabric, tucked around her shoulders and into the front of the dress, was all that kept her decent.

Something of Mama must have stayed with Maggie. After years of seeing Indian women with their breasts bared, Maggie could still think in terms of proper English decency. Mama would be proud. Maybe. If she still lived.

If she ever thought of Maggie anymore.

There was no belt from which to hang her hatchet. She glanced at it on the small round table beside the bed. Perhaps she wouldn't need it. Perhaps she'd be safe here. Wasn't that the whole point of coming to the fort?

A tap sounded on the door of the room she'd been given as

Maggie finished braiding her hair into one long plait, taming the thick waves.

"Maggie?"

"Yes?"

Ruth Roberts eased the door open. "Are you hungry?"

Maggie nodded.

"I have corn cakes and ham keeping warm. My husband has already eaten and left. We will see little of him in the days ahead, I fear." Worry lined the corners of her eyes.

Not used to making conversation, Maggie simply followed when Mrs. Roberts led the way down the stairs to the main room of the house. The scents coming from the hearth started her mouth watering. She shut her eyes for a moment and breathed deeply.

"Does it smell good?"

Not only that, it brought back an early memory of Donald and Catherine seated at the table while Mama filled their plates. Maggie'd been proud to be old enough to fill her own and had helped herself after Reggie.

"Please, have a seat." Mrs. Roberts gestured to the bench at the table.

"Thank you." Her response brought a smile to the older woman. Not that the Robertses were old, exactly, not like Stone Foot and Long Pouch, but older than Mama and Da had been the last time Maggie had seen them.

She fidgeted on the bench while Mrs. Roberts brought a plate from the tin warming oven in front of the hearth. All the thoughts of her parents were... disquieting. Letting go of Mama and Da had been necessary for Maggie to adapt to living in the Indian village. To remain strong. Here, surrounded by the things of white people, it was as if she'd stepped back in time.

And yet, it was different.

Maggie picked up the fork and knife beside the pewter plate, juggling them awkwardly for a moment. Mrs. Roberts busied herself at the hearth, keeping her back turned. Maggie appreciated the moment of privacy to figure things out. It'd been the same last evening when Ensign Willabay had brought Maggie to the Robertses' house. She'd been greeted with calmness, allowed to retain her dignity. Phineas Roberts, being the fort's surgeon, had told the ensign that he and Mrs. Roberts would take charge of Maggie and to let the major know. Then, he had examined her and pronounced her both healthy and free of vermin.

Mrs. Roberts had asked the most uncomfortable questions, those of a sexual nature. Maggie knew what happened between men and women. Life in the Indian village was more open than she remembered life with her parents. But she'd been a child when sold to Stone Foot, and in his care, he had sheltered her from any type of abuse other than the occasional beatings by Long Pouch. He'd never touched her in that way, perhaps due to his advanced age. Or perhaps because he knew he'd get a larger bride price when he sold her to one of the young men... like Tree Sleeper.

Maggie finally managed to work the fork and knife together, and got the first bite of ham into her mouth. Her teeth sank into the tender meat, and she resisted the urge to groan.

Mrs. Roberts glanced over her shoulder. "Do you like it?"

Maggie nodded, swallowed, and worked to free another bite from the slab on her plate while the older woman sat on the opposite bench.

"You are not very talkative, for a young woman."

Maggie put the knife and fork down, then met the other woman's eyes. "It has been a long time since anyone talked to me other than to tell me what to do." Months since Wind Over Waters had died.

The clear blue eyes softened. "I cannot imagine what you

have been through. If you wish to speak about any of it, I would listen and keep your words in close confidence."

There was meaning under the words. Maybe not the words, but the way she said them. Maggie nodded, then set about mastering the fork and knife again, puzzling about that meaning. While she chewed, Mrs. Roberts rose and tidied the room.

The kind woman's subtle warning must have been about speaking too freely with others in the fort. A warning Maggie intended to heed, even while she pondered the necessity of it. She was back among her people. She was no longer a captive, bound to do the bidding of her master.

She was free.

Her stomach full and stays tighter, she took her plate and utensils to the wash basin. She remembered clearing the table for Mama in such a way, but she wasn't sure what to do next.

"Just leave them," Mrs. Roberts said. "We can wash them later. Is there anything you need to do?"

"The man who brought me to the fort, Monsieur Geroux. I must return his canoe paddle."

"Oh, my dear." The woman pressed her hand to the base of her neck. "You cannot leave the fort. 'Tis not safe."

"He was taking something to the blacksmith. I could ask if he will return for it. Perhaps leave the paddle there." Although she wouldn't mind seeing the Frenchman again. He'd been kind to her, all things considered. He could have refused to bring her to the fort. He could have... acted very differently. Although with his infirmity, she may have been able to escape him despite their considerable size difference. He was much taller than the Indians she was used to, and broader as well.

"An excellent idea," said Mrs. Roberts. "I can give you a tour of the fort when we are done there."

Maggie had seen enough of Fort Detroit the previous day to know it was many times larger than Teata's village. It was larger inside than she'd imagined from the river. Larger than the town they'd lived in before Da had moved them to the frontier, if she remembered correctly. Perhaps more like a city, although she'd never been to one.

Mrs. Roberts seemed to be waiting for a response. "Thank you." Maggie'd have to get used to responding to people. Long Pouch had never desired to hear her voice, especially in the early years, when it drew the old woman's ire and a swift cuff to Maggie's ear.

She fetched the paddle from the room she'd used the night before.

Mrs. Roberts handed her a three-pointed strip of cloth, then wrapped a second one around her own shoulders. "'Tis a shawl for you to wear. This close to the river, 'tis still a bit chilly and damp most mornings."

Maggie mimicked the other woman. She had no memory of wearing a shawl before, but it wasn't much different than wrapping a blanket around herself. It was softer, however, and less bulky, a beautiful blue that matched a summer's sky. It fit across her shoulders and didn't require a hand to hold it in place. Her being so small, the Indian trade blankets had practically swallowed her. She tied two of the ends in a knot as Mrs. Roberts had done.

They stepped outside into a bustling street. A pair of young boys raced toward them, scattering a small flock of chickens that pecked in the dirt. A brown-and-white dog barked from a space between two houses. From the other direction, a wagon piled with hay approached, the sleepy-looking driver smothering a yawn. A woman tossed a rug onto the porch railing of a house across the way and smacked it with a stick. She stopped when she noticed them approaching, shielding her eyes from the slanting sunlight.

"Who be that with you, Ruth?"

Mrs. Roberts pressed her hand between Maggie's shoulders. "This is Maggie Kerr. She will be staying with us for the next while."

"*Och*, what a poor time to come, what with the Indians making trouble. Arrived with the ship last evening, did she?"

Another wagon rumbled toward them, its bed filled with barrels and crates. "Speaking of the ship," Mrs. Roberts said, "it looks like it brought more supplies. 'Tis a welcome sight." Mrs. Roberts took Maggie's elbow and resumed their walk, speaking once more over her shoulder. "Good day to you, Mary."

Maggie scurried to keep up. Why had Mrs. Roberts side-stepped the other woman's question? She knew the dangers of the forest, and the dangers in the Huron village, but it hadn't occurred to her that there would be different dangers within the wooden walls of Fort Detroit.

———

HE'D AWAKENED WITH THE NAGGING FEELING THAT someone was watching him. Impossible, of course, with the shutters closed and barred over the cabin's two windows. The door barred as well, and all six gun slits sealed from the inside. Baptiste had been born and raised in Indian territory, where taking precautions was as second-nature as breathing.

That watched-over feeling followed him as he dragged his canoe and headed for the river. With any luck, whoever watched hadn't seen where he'd stashed Beau and Pierre. The oxen needed to graze, but it was too risky to leave them in plain sight. Indians weren't well-known for taking the long view. They'd eat the oxen without giving thought to his need of the animals to work the land and produce the wheat those Indians had grown fond of.

Baptiste hadn't lied to the major. He fully intended to bring as much of his grain to the fort to sell as he could. But when the Indians showed up and demanded what they viewed as their share, he would hand it over. That was the cost of staying on his land unmolested.

With a shove and leap, he landed in the canoe. Out of the corner of his eye, he caught movement from the tree line of the bank he'd just left. The hairs on the back of his neck prickled.

With firm strokes, he guided his canoe to the middle of the river, past arrow range but still vulnerable to muskets. Not that it mattered. If they'd wanted him dead, he'd be dead. A man alone in Indian territory lived there only because the Indians tolerated him. Viewed him as useful. For Baptiste, it was his wheat they coveted. Others also saw him as a friend.

They trusted him because he was French, and they assumed all French were enemies of the British. He supposed it was true back in the old country, but while the animosity remained, it didn't seem as important on the banks of the Detroit River.

Baptiste may not completely trust the British, but they were not his enemies. Neither were the Indians. If a fight broke out between the two, where would that leave him? Would he be able to stay and resist being drawn into the fighting? He hoped so, but only time would tell.

He landed the canoe on the opposite bank near the fort and strode along the path. The fort's gates were closed again.

"Who goes there?" came the call from the top of the palisade.

"Baptiste Geroux."

"State your business with the fort."

"The blacksmith."

The gate opened and he stepped through. The same soldier as the previous day eyed him up and down, then jerked his head in the direction of the smithy.

"Go on with you then."

41

He'd turned the corner onto the blacksmith's street when a pair of women hurried past on the other side. One was tall and straight with wisps of blond hair escaping a white cap. The other was small and slender, her uncovered reddish hair swinging in a braid that reached almost to her hips. If not for that and the canoe paddle she carried, he wouldn't have recognized Maggie Kerr. She was encircled by the folds of a proper dress and wrapped in a shawl. The transformation was... startling.

Following them down the street, his attention kept returning to the gentle sway of her skirts. She barely reached to the other woman's shoulder, but she was perfection in miniature, her womanly form accented as it hadn't been in the shapeless Indian garment. Although she'd filled that out admirably enough. Dressed as a proper white woman she was... stunning.

Heads turned as the pair moved along the street ahead of him. One man all but fell from his wagon seat for gawking. Baptiste hastened his steps until the pair turned into the smithy. He followed them into the building.

"I seek the Frenchman who brought you a chain to mend yesterday." Mademoiselle's voice was clear and strong, much like when she'd addressed him by the river. A woman to take notice of. Her years in captivity had not cowed her.

"I am here," he said.

She spun, canoe paddle in her fist. There was no welcoming smile, but then again, why would there be? It wasn't as if he knew the woman or she knew him. However, getting to know her was a tantalizing idea.

"You must be Mr. Geroux." The tall woman had also turned. "Thank you for assisting Miss Kerr to the fort. We owe you a debt."

"No debt. But perhaps the return of my paddle, oui?"

Mademoiselle Kerr handed it over. "I am in your debt,

monsieur, whether you think so or not." She'd switched to French. "If I had been recaptured, it would not have gone well for me."

Captives who bungled their escape attempts rarely survived, and the means of their deaths were brutal. Knowledge of that kept most of them in place. Not this little spitfire. She'd risked it all for her freedom.

"What will you do here at the fort?" he asked.

Her brow crinkled as she shot a glance at the older woman, then back to him. "I do not know."

"We will take care of her and endeavor to locate her family." The other woman touched the mademoiselle's shoulder and spoke in accented French. "If any survive."

The mademoiselle's brow remained crinkled, as if that reassurance didn't amount to much. "Merci, Monsieur Geroux."

He offered a short bow. "I am at your service, mademoiselle."

When he straightened, her blue-gray eyes bored into him as if to decide how literally he meant that traditional response. A little surprised himself, he meant the words very literally.

Mrs. Roberts continued with the tour of the fort, speaking with people they passed and introducing Maggie as if she were a long-lost friend. It was both reassuring and odd.

Many of the women greeted her much as Mrs. Roberts had. The rest of them were less friendly, less open, and some downright rude. More than one had scowled at her. More than one had turned away before Mrs. Roberts could introduce her, and several had hidden whispers behind raised hands as they'd passed.

As a captive, she'd been told many times to not bother trying to escape, that her people wouldn't want her back, that they'd see her as tainted from her captivity. She'd not believed it, had assumed it was a threat to keep her in place.

Maybe not. It might explain Mrs. Roberts's lack of candor on several occasions when direct questions were asked. Not that she told an untruth, but she avoided telling the whole truth. And the underlying warning in her tone at the table that morning. Perhaps what the Indians had said was true to a point. But obviously Mrs. Roberts didn't hold that view, nor her husband.

Nor Monsieur Geroux.

Since Maggie was inside the fort, it was too late to change her mind. They waited in line to fill a bucket at the well, and she turned her back to a trio of whispering women. After all, she was used to not fitting in.

It was odd to be surrounded by walls, fenced off from the river and the forest, unable to see farther than the end of a street. Towered over by tall houses. Watched over by the men stationed in the blockhouses. She shuddered inside at the memories those resurrected. The upper room. Catherine and Donald huddling under the bed. The Lenni Lenape warrior who'd grabbed her by the arm. The Indian whose name she refused to remember.

"Are you cold?" Mrs. Roberts asked.

"Not cold, remembering."

The soft sympathy in the woman's eyes was a comfort, as was the patient air of understanding. Once their bucket was filled, she touched Maggie's arm and guided her back toward the house, walking in silence.

One question—trivial at best—kept poking through all the other things she'd seen and heard that morning. Why did a French farmer who lived by himself at the edge of the woods have need of a second canoe paddle?

Chapter 5

B aptiste dribbled peas from the pouch strapped to his chest and pressed dirt over them with the toe of his well-worn moccasin. The newly broken ground was damp and sun-warmed, eager to accept the seeds. He rolled a few between his fingers before letting them fall. So small, and yet so much depended on them. His harvest and the feeding of himself and his oxen. Extra to trade at the fort for necessities to see him through the winter. More to gift to the Indians, which allowed him to live in peace along the river.

Movement caught his eye, and he stopped, staring over the backs of Beau and Pierre as they grazed along the edge of the field.

"You finally see me, my friend." A square-chested figure slipped from behind a tangle of blackberry canes, his long topknot decorated with a single feather. He wore a breechclout and nothing else save moccasins in the same style as Baptiste's. He flashed a wide smile.

"I suppose you have been watching me for hours, non?" Baptiste returned the grin.

Walking Fire Stick came to meet him, and they grasped forearms.

"Many hours."

Baptiste chuckled. "Many hours without raiding my bread cupboard? This I cannot believe."

"You will happily give me your bread today, my friend." Walking Fire Stick reached behind him and tugged something from the belt that secured his breechclout. A new pair of moccasins. "My sister does not forget you."

Baptiste took the fine leather footwear and admired the craftsmanship. "You must thank her for me and take her a sack of flour." Although he had little to spare, the moccasins were worth it.

The other man frowned and shook his head. "You must come and thank her yourself. Let her see you."

"You know that is not possible. This is the time to prepare the land and plant my seeds."

Crossing his arms over his tattooed chest, the Indian grunted. "Yesterday, you traveled to the British fort."

So, he had been watched. Not that he was surprised, but hearing it confirmed made the hairs at the nape of his neck itch. "To have my chains repaired. A man cannot work the ground to grow food without the proper tools, non?"

"A man needs a woman to do such work."

They always came back to this argument. Walking Fire Stick saw farming as women's work. For a man to scratch in the dirt and grow food was a foreign idea to him. Men hunted and fished and smoked pipes around the fire. Women did the heavy labor in the villages.

"I do well on my own."

"And the woman in your canoe two days past? You took her to the fort with you. Two trips in two days."

Someone had been watching then too. Baptiste mentally kicked himself for missing it at the time. Probably not Walking Fire Stick, as he would have made himself known. That others

had seen and reported his activity was more than a little discon-
certing.

"She wished to go to the fort. I was going myself, so I let her
into my canoe."

"A white woman with a spotted face who was dressed as a
Huron."

They missed nothing, his Indian neighbors. Baptiste
shrugged, which seemed the safest response.

Another grunt. "You come and see my sister." Walking Fire
Stick gestured to the field. "She would return with you to tend
your crops and warm your bed."

Baptiste had resisted this tactic for two years, but he
schooled his face to show no hint of his reluctance. He was not
like Henri. He couldn't slip between the white world and the
Indian world, even though the man in front of him was his best
friend. Especially not with thoughts of Mademoiselle Kerr
dogging his steps and interrupting his work. "I am too busy to
bring a woman here."

"You are a fool."

Baptiste forced a grin and pounded the Indian on the shoulder. "You may be right, my friend. Come. I have bread in the
cabin." He slipped off the seed pouch and dropped it where he'd
sown the last pea.

Heading toward the cabin, Walking Fire Stick asked, "Have
you word of Henri?"

"I have not."

The other man gazed to the west. "Perhaps Dances Away has
lived up to his name. Perhaps we will see our brothers no
more."

That thought left an empty spot in Baptiste's middle that no
amount of bread would fill.

Her third day at the fort brought warmer temperatures and disquieting news. Rumors of Indians on the move fairly echoed off the palisade walls. Maggie listened as she waited her turn to draw water from the central well. Most spoke in English, and it pleased her that she'd fallen back into her birth tongue so readily. Stone Foot had wished to learn English from her, and they had spoken it often enough for her to remember. Other women at the fort spoke in French, the more fluid dialect of Monsieur Geroux. She had to concentrate to capture all the words and meaning.

Maggie also understood the trade language of the Indians, and the Huron language as well as the Lenni Lenape from her first captor. Her ability to learn languages had been the reason Stone Foot had purchased her from the Lenni Lenape. Her first captor had bragged on how quickly she'd learned to speak. Stone Foot, being the Huron village's medicine man, had thought to use her to gain more stature. She'd been thirteen at the time, a slave for two winters and half-starved. Since a medicine man rarely lacked food, he used it to tempt Maggie to learn more and faster.

She had. She'd stayed strong and survived.

"My husband said there were hundreds, maybe thousands of them," said a woman in rapid French as she hauled her bucket from the well. "He would take us from the fort if we had anyplace else to go."

"Better some protection than none, non?" asked her friend. "Even if it is with the British."

The first woman looked around, noticed Maggie, and sniffed, her nose tilting toward the sky. "I am sure 'tis nothing." She switched to thickly accented English. "Indians move every spring." She turned and marched away, a water bucket dribbling at her side.

Maggie stepped up and secured her bucket before lowering

it. At its soft plop into the water, she steadied the rope and waited while the bucket sank and filled.

"Have we met?" asked a woman of about Maggie's age, her face framed with blond hair that curled beneath her cap.

"No," Maggie replied in English. "I am newly come to the fort." She cranked up the filled bucket.

"I hope you do not regret being here with all the talk of Indians." The woman flexed her knees, an action of casual greeting that Maggie remembered. "I am Esther Boggs."

Maggie heaved the bucket onto the rim of the well. "Maggie Kerr." She steadied the bucket with one hand and copied the other's bobbed greeting.

"'Tis nice to meet you. There are not many women our age here. But then, there are not many women on the frontier at all. White women, I mean."

"'Tis a hard place." Maggie shielded her eyes from the sun. She needed a straw hat like the British women pinned over their linen caps. For that matter, she needed a cap if she were to fit in. None of the other women around the well were bareheaded.

"Indeed, but one must follow one's husband." Esther sighed. "And make the best of it."

"Indeed." Had that been Mama's life? Following Da wherever the wanderlust took him? Toting four children, losing two others to the fever. Losing Maggie at Fort McCord. Perhaps losing her life.

The other woman smiled. "Perhaps we can—

The staccato thump of drums reached them, and the hairs on Maggie's arms tingled.

"I beg your pardon. I must go." She barely waited for Esther's nod before lugging the heavy bucket to the Robertses' as fast as she could, spilling a good portion of the water along the way.

Mrs. Roberts stood on the porch, watching those milling

around in the street. Nearly every house had someone waiting outside of it. Listening. Watching. Tension flowed along the street like the river between its banks.

"Slow down, Maggie." Mrs. Roberts rushed to meet her, taking hold of the bucket's rope and sharing the burden of carrying it the last few steps. "What has upset you?"

"The drums."

The other woman's eyes wrinkled at the corners. "Do you know what they mean?"

Maggie glanced at the people gathered in doorways up and down the street. "Maybe inside?"

Mrs. Roberts nodded, and Maggie followed her into the house and shut the door.

"War drums." Maggie's heart thumped against the stays that held her chest. "They are preparing to attack the fort."

WITH A HEAVE, BAPTISTE HAULED IN THE FISH TRAP made of cedar branches and thick hemp twine. It was heavy from flipping silvery-green bodies with their eerie gray eyes as he settled it into the bottom of the canoe. There were at least two dozen as long as his forearm. He plucked out the smaller fish and tossed them back in the river. The large ones he left in the trap.

Walking Fire Stick had been right about the fish and where to find them. Baptiste had baited and dropped the trap the evening before, after his friend left and the peas were in the ground. He would have the fish cleaned and in the smokehouse before midday, then start preparations to plant his wheat in the afternoon. Always there was work to do. Always the struggle to stay alive.

And for most of the past two and a half years, always the loneliness.

The sun shone on the sparkling water and reflected off the fort on the opposite bank. It was good that Mademoiselle Kerr had gone into the fort. The British would protect her. Maybe they would send her back east to whatever remained of her family. He hoped they would, and yet...

She was British.

He was French.

It wasn't likely they'd meet again. It wasn't as if she'd look his way if they did, him with his lame leg. A farmer scratching out a living on the edge of civilization. She'd want to be returned to her family, far from this place. Far from its unpleasant memories. Who wouldn't want that after being held captive for so many years? If not for the hope of Henri's return, Baptiste would...

Would what?

He grabbed the paddle and turned the canoe around, heading toward his farm. On the water, his lame leg didn't hold him back. With arms muscled from years of use, he sent the craft skimming over the water against the current.

In a town, he might find work in a store. He knew his sums and could write a decent hand. In French, anyway. Montreal would have towns large enough for a lame man to find work he could do. Blacksmithing took strong arms, not legs. He could learn. But any of that would mean leaving the farm, leaving the place Henri would return to.

If he returned at all.

The pounding of drums broke across the gurgling river. Many drums.

His blood chilled, slowing in his veins despite the speeding of his heart.

War drums.

Sound carried a long way across the water. It was hard to say how far, but it came from the south and across the river. The Potawatomi village of Chief Ninivois lay in that direction. If they'd joined with Pontiac's Ottawas and Takay's and Teata's Hurons, then three tribes were banding together to move against the British. Neither Ninivois nor Takay were considered strong chiefs, by reputation, and neither was Teata according to the mademoiselle, so it made sense that they'd follow Pontiac's lead. Or in at least Teata's case, be coerced to follow.

He rubbed the hairs at the base of his neck. Maybe the fort wasn't as secure as he'd thought. He hadn't seen that many soldiers when he'd been inside, but then, it was a large fort and they weren't all in one place. The French inside who had businesses, they would fight with the soldiers or risk losing everything. But how many men did that make? Not as many as the combination of warriors from three tribes.

Less than half as many.

That many braves making war on the British posed another problem. When they fought, they did not hunt or fish. The Indian women would grow their corn, beans, and squash, but the people needed meat too.

Baptiste dug his paddle into the water and once more sent the canoe against the current. His meager options tossed and turned in his mind. How was he going to keep Beau and Pierre from filling the kettles of hungry Indians on the warpath?

He had a few true friends among the Indians, like Walking Fire Stick, but mostly he survived on his farm with an uneasy understanding. His oxen were not a secure part of that agreement. Without them, he could not produce the wheat or other crops. Without those, his position was much less secure.

So much depended on keeping those animals safe.

He beached the canoe and dragged it into the willow thicket, then grabbed the fish trap. He trotted along the path to the cabin, inwardly seething over his slow gait. The lopsided trot was the best he could do, and the bulky fish trap banging against his good leg didn't help.

Tossing the trap and fish onto the cabin's porch, he kept going into the woods behind the barn and didn't stop until the oxen came into view. One red and one black lump rose from the small opening in the forest where he'd left them tethered. Lower jaws swung in rhythm as they chewed their cuds.

He stopped, hands on his knees, and pulled in a few long breaths.

Beau and Pierre watched him with calm eyes. They had no idea what might await them if a full-blown war erupted across the river.

Baptiste did.

THE DRUMS STILL BEAT THEIR WARNING, A CONSTANT thumping that wouldn't allow Maggie to settle. She paced between the walls in her upstairs room. The evening meal over and the dishes washed, she had nothing else to do. The Robertses were sitting in the front room, Mrs. Roberts mending a shirt and Mr. Roberts napping in his chair. Maggie couldn't understand how either of them remained so calm.

But then, they hadn't been at Fort McCord.

They hadn't heard the screams of the warriors or the cries of the women and children. They hadn't been dragged away from everything they'd ever known. They hadn't lived as captives, treated as slaves. They'd never been abandoned to their fate.

Maggie had.

All the way to Fort Detroit, fleeing who knew how many hours ahead of Tree Sleeper, she'd thought that once she reached the fort, she'd be safe. For all its high log walls and pretty-coated soldiers, it wasn't the sanctuary she'd imagined. It wasn't stuffed to the gills with men ready to take on the horde of warriors gathered around those drums. She didn't know the exact number of soldiers, but it was nowhere near as many as the warriors of the combined tribes. Instead of a bastion of safety on the frontier...

Maggie was trapped.

If the Indians breached the gate, their vast numbers would overwhelm the soldiers in minutes. A shiver worked its way across her shoulders, and she rubbed her palms up and down her arms.

Tree Sleeper would be with them.

There'd be nowhere she could hide that he wouldn't find her. They'd burn the buildings as they had the blockhouse at Fort McCord. She'd be dragged away by Tree Sleeper, taken back to the village, and then...

It would be better for Maggie if she burned in one of the houses.

She must find a different sanctuary.

Chapter 6

The drums grew louder as Baptiste's canoe sliced through the rush of the river in the waning evening light. He was a fool to come and poke his nose in where it might get cut off. Along with his hair. He harbored no illusions about his safety. Two sacks of flour rested on the bottom of his canoe. Flour he couldn't spare, but to come empty-handed would only cause increased suspicion. He couldn't afford that.

He beached the canoe and left it exposed on the bank, a sign that he intended to return to it quickly. Lookouts would be watching him, and his skin fairly crawled with the pressure of their eyes. With the flour sacks slung over his shoulder, he followed a well-worn path toward the sound of the drums.

Nobody stopped him.

Nobody greeted him either.

Sweat poured from his hairline and flowed between his shoulders. The evening was mild, the walk short, but the outcome less than certain. He kept his steps measured, a steady rhythm to his limping gait, and his eyes straight forward. He wasn't looking for trouble.

But he needed answers.

If war broke out, he'd be sitting between a pair of powder kegs while playing with a piece of flint.

Walking Fire Stick stepped into the path in front of him, arms crossed and feet braced. "This is no place for you, my friend."

Baptiste eased the sacks from his shoulder to the ground between them. "I come bearing presents."

"This is not the time or the place for presents."

"Since when do you turn away my wheat flour?" And why? To the Indians, wheat was a treat like molasses candy to a child in the fort.

The drums stopped.

Walking Fire Stick didn't move.

"What happens here will impact me as well as the fort." Baptiste kept his eyes on his friend's face. Something flickered behind the dark eyes, but before he could decipher it, Walking Fire Stick stepped aside and jerked his head toward the camp. Baptiste hefted his sacks again and walked on.

"You take a risk, my friend. Say nothing unless one of the elders speaks to you." Walking Fire Stick pointed to an open spot in the loose circle of braves around the drummers. "And then say little."

There were no women in sight. That alone marked it as a serious meeting. The crawling sensation was back, and it took all Baptiste had not to scratch. There were a few other Frenchmen and a Jesuit in his dark robes. He recognized several warriors in the crowd. Two were Hurons from Takay's village. The others were Pontiac's Ottawa. A couple of them dipped their chins in acknowledgment. One frowned and turned away.

Baptiste didn't know any of the Potawatomi. Several studied him as if measuring his scalp for their lances. Then all attention turned to the man who stepped into the center of the drummers and raised his hands.

Pontiac.

Indians seated themselves on the ground around him by age and rank, as was their custom. Walking Fire Stick grabbed Baptiste's shoulder and pushed. With his bad leg, sitting as the Indians did was difficult, he grunted and worked to position himself. It wouldn't hurt to let those who didn't know him see his infirmity. A lame man posed little threat.

Pontiac launched into a condemnation of the British in a mixture of the Indian trade language and a bit of French with expansive gestures to match. He went on at length about how the French had treated them as brothers, while the British were stingy, greedy, and not willing to meet the needs of the tribes. His voice rose and fell in a sort of cadence that was almost mesmerizing. His fiery eyes, eloquent movements, and commanding presence dominated the space.

Then he said that the leader of the French—the Great Father —had told him to raise a force and strike against the British.

That couldn't be true.

The French army was gone and not returning. They'd made it plain that Baptiste and all the French farmers needed to flee with the army or pledge loyalty to Britain. They would not return. France had turned its back on this land.

Pontiac was lying.

One swift glance around the circle of faces was all he needed to know that the Indians believed the charismatic leader.

Then Pontiac stared directly at Baptiste and spoke in French. "If there are any French who side with the British, let us strike them down as well." He repeated it in the Indian trade language.

A roar of assent came from hundreds of throats.

Baptiste swallowed the lump in his.

Pontiac launched into a plan to invade the fort disguised as a friendly visit. The other council members asked questions and added thoughts until, several hours later, with the council fire

57

casting dancing shadows over those gathered, they had a plan firmly in mind. A plan to take the fort. And there was nothing Baptiste could do to stop it or even warn the garrison.

Or remove Mademoiselle Kerr.

Walking Fire Stick rose, jerked his head toward Pontiac, and strode toward him.

Baptiste gathered his sacks and followed. Pontiac wasn't physically imposing, but he was strong and solid, somewhere in his middle years. His personality more than made up for the inches he stood below Baptiste.

"Why is he here?" the leader asked Walking Fire Stick.

"He is a friend to the Ottawa, the one who grows wheat upriver."

Pontiac's eyes lingered a moment on Baptiste's lame leg, hidden by his buckskin leggings. The Ottawa chief remembered him, at least.

"It is not good that he is here."

"He will not side with the British. He is French and remains loyal to his Ottawa brothers. His brother is the one who traveled west with Dances Away."

The Ottawa chief grunted, eying Baptiste as a hawk eyes a mouse.

Baptiste held out the bags of flour. "My present to you. My pledge that I only wish to work the land and grow food for myself and my friends the Ottawa."

So much for not speaking until spoken to.

Pontiac's brows drew together, as did Walking Fire Stick's.

But the chief took the sacks, and relief washed over Baptiste. "You bring more to the village."

"But of course. This I will do in the fall after the harvest." Baptiste kept his face passive while his mind whirled about how he'd keep his word to both Major Gladwin and Pontiac, because now more than ever, he was a man caught in the middle.

MAGGIE CURLED INTO THE SOFTNESS OF THE BED'S mattress. The crinkle of its dried grass stuffing and the faint fragrance of a summer meadow should have comforted her. It didn't. The memories of Fort McCord washed over her. She'd spent years pushing them away, fighting to stay strong, to stay alive.

Since the drums had ceased, she'd allowed herself to remember.

Catherine with her brave face as she'd clutched Donald and pulled him under the bed. How old would her sister be now? Seven years had passed, Major Gladwin had said. Fifteen then. Her little sister was almost a grown woman. And Donald? He'd be nine or close to it. No longer the toddler who had plopped to the dirt at Mama's feet. What of Reggie? Had he made it back with Da? Reggie would be twenty, or maybe twenty-one. She couldn't remember when his birthday was.

Mama and Da, were they still alive?

The Indians would have taken the children and kept them, as they had her. She pressed her hand against the ache in her chest. But what of the adults? None had come looking for her.

A quiet tap sounded on her door, then it eased open a crack. "Are you well?" whispered Mrs. Roberts.

Maggie sat up, legs crossed in the middle of the bed, nightgown and blanket bunched around her hips. "I am, ma'am."

"You came up so early, I was concerned perhaps you felt unwell."

"There were memories I needed to rethink."

"Important ones, I should think."

Were they? Was her family important to her anymore? She'd been strong for so long by turning her back on all of them. By refusing to think about them. Refusing to remember. To her dismay, a tear trembled from her lashes and spilled down her cheek.

"My dear." Mrs. Roberts pulled the room's only chair beside the bed and sat, taking Maggie's hand. "Is it anything you can talk about? Sometimes that helps."

Maggie worked furiously to contain the emotions bubbling within her. What was wrong with her? She'd retained a firm control of her emotions for years.

"I cannot imagine what you have been through, but if you wish to speak of it, I will listen and keep your confidences as if they were my own." Mrs. Roberts's tone was warm, her eyes kind, and the way she leaned forward as if what Maggie might say was of vital importance to her... the combination battered down the last of Maggie's defenses.

"I was eleven years old when Fort McCord was attacked by Indians. I was pulled from my family and made a captive." She drew in a shuddering breath. "No one ever came for me."

"I'm sure they would have"—Mrs. Roberts squeezed her hand—"if they could have."

It was probably true. Da had likely died in the fighting, Reggie too, if the men had arrived in time. If Da'd followed after her, he may have died in another fight at another place and time. Over the years, it had become easier to think him dead.

"The man who owned me most of that time, Stone Foot of the Hurons, had recently decided to marry me to one of the Huron warriors."

Mrs. Roberts's breath hissed between her teeth.

"I was given no choice. Before I was exchanged for the bride price, Pontiac, the Ottawa chief from this region, came to our village. He spoke long and earnestly of striking against the British here at Fort Detroit." Maggie wiped her cheek with the back of her hand. "Teata, our chief, was reluctant to get involved, and Père Potier did his best to convince him not to, but Pontiac threatened to turn his warriors against ours if Teata didn't agree."

"He threatened?" Mrs. Roberts sat straighter.

"Teata's village is small, his warriors few, and so he agreed. But before setting out, he sent several of the young warriors on a scouting trip to see if what Pontiac had said was true. Tree Sleeper, the man Stone Foot had chosen for me, went with them. I knew it was my one chance to escape—my last chance— and so I ran. I had listened to enough of Pontiac's talk to know how to find the fort."

"That took great courage."

Maggie met the woman's eyes. "If I had been caught, it would have been very bad for me." She couldn't bring herself to describe how bad.

"This warrior, do you think he will follow you here?

"He will. He is likely outside the fort with the others beating the drums."

"Then we must keep you safely inside the fort at all costs."

But was she safe behind the walls? Or trapped?

BAPTISTE EYED THE LOOMING WALLS OF THE FORT from across the river as he paddled against the current by the light of a half moon. He owed nothing to the British, no matter what words he'd dutifully repeated after Robert Rogers all those months ago. Those words had been to secure his position on the land, not as allegiance to some foreign king.

But what the Indians were planning didn't set well with him. It was one thing to declare war and attack your enemy. Armies had been doing that since the beginning of time. The plan the Indians had devised was something else. It was trickery. It was... evil.

61

Of course, evil had been around since the beginning of time as well.

Mademoiselle Kerr had warned the major that something was afoot, and her warning hadn't been news to the man, so the army wouldn't be caught completely unaware. They could hear the drums. But would they be on the lookout for such a form of treachery?

The fort's soldiers were vastly outnumbered by the combined forces of three Indian tribes. Did the major realize that? He must. He wasn't some wet-behind-the-ears recruit on his first assignment. Baptiste's meeting with him had been brief, but it'd been long enough to recognize the competence and confidence in the man. A natural-born leader.

As was Pontiac.

Baptiste thrust his paddle into the dark water and moved his canoe past the fort. There was nothing he could do. To warn the major would be suicide. There were eyes on him even now. His was one of a handful of canoes in sight as the Indians returned to their own longhouses. They would make sure he passed the fort and landed on his own side of the river.

He'd already been watched. That surveillance would double after his appearance at the council fire tonight.

The spot between his shoulder blades itched furiously.

He'd been a fool to go, but at least he knew what was going to happen and how to stay out of everyone's way.

What of Mademoiselle Kerr? Had she left one precarious situation only to find herself in another?

He refused to glance over his shoulder at the fort. Besides not wanting to draw any attention from other canoes, it wasn't any of his business what the woman did or didn't do. She was British and under the army's protection. If a whole garrison of red-coated soldiers couldn't protect her, what chance did he, Baptiste Geroux, have?

None.

She was as safe as anyone on the frontier could make her.

So why did he have to fight the urge to throw caution to the wind, turn the canoe around, and go find her? For the same reason her reddish-brown hair, smoky blue eyes, and petite womanly form had badgered him since she'd approached at the riverbank. She stirred in him something he'd worked for years to subdue.

The elemental pull of a woman on a man.

But what could he offer her? A small cabin on the edge of Indian land, constant danger of being discovered by those who'd held her captive, and continued separation from her family.

He slashed the oar deeper into the dark water and spurred the craft toward the riverbank. Best he forget all about Mademoiselle Kerr. Best he concentrate on keeping himself and his oxen alive.

NOT SINCE THE LENNI LENAPE WARRIOR HAD PULLED her from the upper room at Fort McCord had Maggie felt so helpless. Outside the fort, a large force of Indian warriors gathered. Inside the fort, a meager handful of brightly coated soldiers waited.

Freedom wasn't turning out to be what Maggie'd thought it would be.

Memories of running through Da's fields, the newly turned earth warm between her toes and the sun on her face promising another outbreak of freckles, came back to her. Catherine's high-pitched giggles, Reggie's shouts of encouragement, even Donald's merry chuckles, these were the things she'd left behind all those years ago. It was foolishness to think she could find them again, but some part of her—perhaps the part she'd worked so hard to seal away for years—longed for them.

Instead, she was surrounded by walls awaiting another Indian attack.

She had to leave. It wasn't safe for her. The ships in front of the fort must sail somewhere. Perhaps the major would put her on one of them and send her east to... whom?

The helplessness of her situation pressed against her chest and beat painfully between her temples. She couldn't stay, but where could she go?

The messy cabin with its small barn nestled back from the riverbank came to mind. No one would look for her there. Would Monsieur Geroux take her in? Maggie had no illusions about what that would entail. A man would shelter a woman, but there would be a price to pay. Was she willing to give herself to a man she didn't know? A cripple who would be scarce protection in a fight? But he'd been kind to her. He hadn't scorned her for being a captive. He'd stood up for her with the guard at the gate. He didn't frighten her.

He wasn't Tree Sleeper.

Chapter 7

A quick rap on her door woke Maggie, followed by the surgeon's voice through the thick wood.

"Miss Kerr? I must speak with you. Please dress and come downstairs."

His footsteps faded as she sprang from the bed and wiggled into her clothing. What could the surgeon need with her? She pulled the curtain away from the window. And in the dead of night?

Maggie smoothed her braided hair as best she could and hurried down the stairs. Mrs. Roberts stood next to her husband in the dimly lit room, its single candle throwing ominous shadows against the wall.

"Would you accompany me to a meeting with Major Gladwin, Captain Campbell, and an Indian who has requested to speak with them?"

Mrs. Roberts gripped his arm. "Phineas, should you not summon Mr. La Butte to interpret?"

"The Indian says he will only speak to Major Gladwin. He claims his French is good enough for Captain Campbell to understand. I thought if Miss Kerr were to act as a servant, offering drinks and waiting in the back of the room, she might understand something the men could miss."

Maggie stepped forward, her knees not entirely steady. "Who is the Indian?"

The surgeon shrugged. "An Ottawa from Pontiac's village. 'Tis all I have been told."

She let out a deep breath. Not Tree Sleeper or anyone from the Huron village who might recognize her. "I can do what you wish."

Mrs. Roberts asked, "Is there any danger?"

"No, my love. None. She will be in the room with one Indian and two of His Majesty's finest soldiers." He winked at Maggie. "Plus myself."

"Take a shawl, Maggie dear, 'tis still hours till dawn." Mrs. Roberts handed her the blue one from its peg behind the door.

The surgeon kissed his wife's forehead and then opened the door for Maggie. She hesitated only a moment before walking through. Strange to walk in front of a man as if she were a person of importance, but she would adapt to it. Never again would she be another person's property. She settled the shawl a bit more snugly across her shoulders and walked with her head high into the night.

"'Tis important that the Indian does not know you speak several languages," Surgeon Roberts said. "You should only speak if needed and only in English. Do not react to anything you hear."

"I understand."

"The captain said to instruct you not to make eye contact with the Indian or in any other way draw his attention to yourself." He glanced at her and then motioned for her to turn down the street to their right. "However, I suspect you will know best how to comport yourself."

She nodded. If there was one thing she'd perfected over the

past seven years, it was how to remain invisible to the Indians around her.

They arrived at the same office building she'd first been taken to. The surgeon held out a hand to stop her and then entered ahead of her. Maggie gritted her teeth against once again being treated as a slave, then reminded herself that this was her choice. She hadn't been ordered to do it.

She stepped into the room, and when she didn't recognize the Indian, let out a shallow breath of relief.

He stood with his back against the wall, eyes roving the room, arms folded. He didn't fool Maggie. He was nervous. His lips were drawn down, but one side jerked, and the last finger on his right hand tapped against his left arm. Only the slightest of movements, but telling.

She moved to the side table with its oil lamp, pitcher of water, a rum jug, and a few pewter mugs. Surgeon Roberts remained next to the door. Major Gladwin sat at the desk with another man in uniform standing at his side. That one spoke first. "Girl, pour water for our guest."

"Rum," the Indian said before Maggie could move.

The man in uniform shook his head. "Water first."

The Indian grunted.

Maggie poured the water and kept her eyes on the floorboards as she walked it to the Indian. He took it, emptied it in three gulps, and thrust the mug back at her. She retreated to her spot beside the table.

"What is your name?" The uniformed man asked the Indian, while the major observed.

The Indian's lips tightened, and it was plain that he didn't want to respond. The silence stretched tight as a bow string. "Mahiganne of the Ottawa."

The man interpreted the rough French words for the major. Then he asked, "What have you come to say?"

67

"The tribes gathered yesterday and today." The Indian's guttural French was easy for Maggie to follow. "Pontiac will come after the sun rises carrying a wampum belt and demanding to speak to Major Gladwin." He lifted his chin in the major's direction. "He will bring a following of warriors with him. After they enter, more Ottawa will come into the fort. They plan to attack at Pontiac's war-whoop."

The uniformed man interpreted again, then leaned forward and asked in French, "Why do you tell us this?"

The Indian bared his teeth. "Pontiac asks our people to do something they should not. He threatens other tribes. It is not good. Too many young men will die."

Maggie believed him. That he was here at all was astounding. Should Pontiac learn of it, the man's death would be a gruesome event witnessed by the entire tribe. Perhaps by all the tribes.

The major spoke too softly for Maggie to hear, but the other man said, "Let us give you gifts—"

"No gifts." The Indian raised his hand, palm out. "Your word. You must tell no one that I came here. If it is found out, I am a dead man."

"Rum, then." The man in uniform nodded at Maggie, and she splashed a liberal amount from the jug into the pewter mug and took it to Mahiganne.

He drank that even faster than he had the water and thrust the mug back at her. "Tell no one." With that, the Indian left, muttering in the Indian trade language on the way out the door.

The door shut, and Major Gladwin turned to Maggie. "What was he saying as he left?"

"I did not understand all of it." Maggie pulled her shawl closer and wrapped her arms around her middle. "But he said, 'The man is evil.'"

68

The men in the room exchanged glances. "Which one of us?" the major asked.

She suppressed a shiver. "Pontiac."

When Pontiac had spoken to Teata and the other Hurons, he had been compelling. The younger men had hung on his words. The older men had nodded and frowned at intervals. Only Teata had appeared unconvinced. And of course, Père Potier, the Jesuit missionary who lived with the tribe. And Stone Foot. The old medicine man had called the Ottawa leader crazy. Crazy or evil, he was a leader many men listened to, but he didn't fool everyone.

Mahiganne was brave for coming to the fort and reporting to Major Gladwin. Or maybe foolish. But he had given warning, and for that she was grateful.

It deepened the urge in her to flee the fort.

Smoked fish and a chunk of bread made for a quick meal before working in the field. He yawned, scratched, and stuffed his mouth with bread. The sun's first morning rays broke through the trees and shone through the cabin's open door. Baptiste hoped to finish planting the wheat before the sun set. He'd broken more ground with Beau and Pierre the day before.

"A woman would make you a hot meal to start your day."

Baptiste almost choked as Walking Fire Stick stepped into the open doorway.

"I catch you by surprise again, my friend."

"You did." Baptiste motioned to the bench on the other side of his small table. "Sit. Eat with me the food that my own hands have provided and prepared."

The Indian grinned and sat.

Baptiste uncovered the bowl holding the rest of his bread, then he broke the fish in half and pushed part of it toward his friend.

They ate in silence, then Walking Fire Stick belched and leaned against the table. "Stay away from the fort."

Something cold puddled in Baptiste's belly.

His friend pointed a finger at him. "You were very lucky the other night at the council fire. Pontiac was in a fine mood. If he had not been, you would be dead."

That something cold curled tighter. Mademoiselle Kerr was in the fort. The fiery little woman refused to leave Baptiste's thoughts. If the fort were overrun, if the Indians found her, if any of the Hurons recognized her...

"You will stay here." Walking Fire Stick shoved away from the table and walked out the door, his voice drifting back to Baptiste. "You will tell no one." His friend's warning was loud and clear.

The mademoiselle had warned that the Indians would attack the fort. Had the Redcoats listened? Would the fort withstand an all-out assault? And if it didn't, what could he do?

Nothing.

If he'd been whole, he'd have gone with Henri to the west. They'd have discovered new places to trap beaver together after Père died. The beaver in this area were gone. That was why Père had switched to farming when the French had parceled out the land on the east side of the river, in agreement with the Indian tribes. And now farming was easier for his lame son. Baptiste thumped his fist against his bad leg.

Two years. More than that, closer to two and a half years since the British had driven the French from the fort. Since Père had died. Since Henri had walked away rather than swear allegiance to the Redcoats. And since Baptiste had been left behind.

He would stay on his farm, mind his own business, and wait for Henri's return.

But if the fort fell, he would go in search of the little spitfire who wouldn't leave his thoughts. He had nothing to offer her, but even he was better than what awaited her if she were recaptured by the Hurons.

But how could Baptiste protect her, and what he would do with her?

He had no idea.

THE WINDOW IN MAGGIE'S ROOM WAS AT THE FRONT of the Robertses' house. Taller than most of the houses around it, its vantage point allowed her to see much of what was happening in the fort. It was a bit like watching a beehive. People scurried along on whatever missions they had, men in buckskins and homespun, a few women, and a pair of boys playing with a dog. Soldiers in bright uniforms passed by in straight lines with measured steps.

The house wasn't tall enough for her to see over the palisade, however. The feeling of being trapped still pressed on her. Trapped and waiting for Pontiac to strike. For Tree Sleeper to come through the gate.

Major Gladwin had asked that she repeat none of what she had heard in the wee hours of the morning. Everything must appear normal when Pontiac arrived with his warriors. The soldiers knew, however. She could see it in the way they moved, the way they watched, even the way they handled their weapons. She wasn't the only one. A woman down the street called the two boys and dog into the house, looking around before closing the door behind her.

Tension thickened the air inside the fort, even if the people didn't know the reason.

Maggie couldn't see the main gate from the window. Part of her had wanted to go and watch, to see Pontiac enter, but Surgeon Roberts had requested that she and Mrs. Roberts stay in the house. The house she'd thought so large when she'd arrived five days ago was now much too small. Too confining.

"Maggie," Mrs. Roberts called up the stairs.

Maggie rose from the floor by the window and joined the other woman in the front room.

"I need something to keep my hands busy, and I suppose you must too," the older woman said. "Have you ever carded wool or used a spinning wheel?"

A flash of memory skipped before her mind's eye. Mama at the spinning wheel, her foot making it turn round with a rhythmic rattle. Catherine separating locks of wool. Donald sleeping in a basket nearby. Maggie with wooden paddles in her hands, brushing the locks of wool Catherine handed her.

"I remember something of it. Mama used the spinning wheel while I brushed the wool."

Mrs. Roberts smiled. "It will come back to you in no time. This far north, one cannot have too much wool spun and ready to make stockings, mittens, shawls, and mufflers." She pulled a sack from behind the spinning wheel. "I have a lovely fleece I dyed brown with old tea leaves last fall. You could have your own shawl for the winter."

After a quick lesson on sorting and carding wool, Maggie was busy with the fibers in her hands. In that way, life wasn't too different from the Indian village. The women were always busy, always preparing something, either food or clothing or shelter. Getting ready for what they would need in the next season.

Maggie's flight to freedom had been something else entirely. No planning, no preparation, nothing to help her move into the next season of her life. Should she try to travel east to find her family? Would the major allow her on one of the ships? Was there anyone left for her to find?

Or should she find a way to cross the river again and go to Monsieur Geroux?

She slapped the wooden paddles together, catching the wool fibers and giving them a yank. The time for such questions had passed. If Mahiganne spoke true—and she had no reason to doubt him—the fort was already surrounded by Pontiac's forces.

Having something to do with her hands helped ease the tension. It gave her another memory, another link to her past. It helped her feel a little more British again. But it didn't change anything.

Pontiac's attack could begin at any time.

BAPTISTE MOPPED HIS BROW WITH THE BACK OF HIS sleeve. The last of the wheat seed was in the ground, and he'd just buried most of his powder and shot in the corner of his field. If a full-blown war broke out, the Indians would not have enough of either. They'd ask for his—demand it—and if he didn't hand it over, they'd ransack his cabin. They'd never find it buried in the corner of his field.

The morning was barely half over, but the sunshine had already warmed the newly planted dirt to give off its earthy scent. He was pulling in a long breath and stretching his back when the soft *shlup* of paddles through water reached him. Fingers tightening on the handle of the knife at his belt, he made for the river.

Indians, a lot of them, were passing his farm. Baptiste stayed behind the screen of brush. They were Ottawa warriors, painted for battle and not trying to remain unseen. They paddled in the middle of the river, letting the deep current propel them along.

Pontiac's second wave.

Baptiste fought the urge to follow along the banks. For what purpose? He owed no loyalty to the British or to the Indians either, even those he would count as friends. He, Baptiste Geroux, was a man alone in the wilderness with only a pair of oxen.

Until Mademoiselle Kerr had appeared beside his canoe.

Why could he not stop thinking of her? He'd spoken the truth to Walking Fire Stick. He had no time for a woman. At least, that was how he'd felt until five days ago.

With a muffled oath, he lumbered toward the riverbank in his limping trot, keeping behind the brush and willows. What he would do—what he could do—when he arrived across from the fort, he had no idea.

But he must be there. He must know what happened.

And he must be out of his mind.

Chapter 8

Maggie's fingers froze on the wooden handles of the wool cards, a tuft of brown fibers dangling between their metal teeth.

"What is it?" Mrs. Roberts asked.

"Indians." Three of them trotted down the street in front of the house. Painted Indians with feathers in their hair. Warriors.

The spinning wheel's rhythmic clatter stopped, leaving a palpable silence in the room.

"There are many Indians who come to the fort." The hesitancy in Mrs. Roberts's voice said she knew. Her husband must have told her what had been said in the meeting in the middle of the night. Of course he had. He'd have given his wife some reason for ordering her to stay in the house.

Maggie went to the window. Groups of three to five Indians loitered at the corners of the street that she could see. She didn't recognize any of them. By their paint and clothing, they were Ottawas.

They would be waiting for Pontiac's signal.

"Are there more?" Mrs. Roberts's fingers toyed with the satin ribbon tied at her neck.

"Many." Maggie glanced at the bar secured in its brackets

across the door. They'd barred it and the door at the back of the house after the surgeon had left, following his orders.

"Perhaps we should close the shutters." The older woman came to the window.

Maggie swallowed, her mouth drying at the thought of being trapped in the house. Trapped behind the fort's walls. Trapped with warriors surrounding them. Warriors who would break through the door and race up the stairs.

Just like at Fort McCord.

Her fears of the past few days were coming to life, but she helped close the shutters and bar them. As they closed the last one, a woman in the house facing the Robertses' was doing the same, her pale face visible for a moment before the wood covered it.

Maggie slid the last bar in place. "I will watch from the bedroom window."

Mrs. Roberts took down the long gun from its rack near the front door. "We both will." The gun wobbled in her shaking hands, but she followed Maggie up the steps.

Maggie stepped to the window, but Mrs. Roberts pulled her back. "Not too close, or they will be able to see you. Stay back."

The concept of glass windows had taken Maggie a few days to get used to. Sometimes it slipped her mind that not only could she see out, but others could see in. Hurons had no windows in their longhouses, glass or otherwise. The block-house at Fort McCord had openings without glass, but they had been kept shuttered while she'd been there. She couldn't remember if glass windows had been part of their cabin. Her memories before Fort McCord were sparse unless prompted, as she'd shuttered that part of her life away.

Mrs. Roberts sat in the chair next to the bed, the gun across her knees. Maggie paced in front of the window, keeping her distance, angling to look both ways down the street.

The Indians stayed in their groups, several clutching the handles of knives and tomahawks hanging from their belts. None were dressed or painted as Hurons, so Tree Sleeper wasn't among them.

Not on this street.

Why had the soldiers let them in? Major Gladwin knew what they were planning. Why hadn't he kept the gates barred?

Panic beat against her ribs, held in only by the tightness of her stays. Perhaps that was why white women wore the uncomfortable garment.

Red and white flashed down the street as a group of soldiers, four rows across and marching in step, guns to their shoulders, deadly bayonets gleaming in the sun, turned a corner. They ignored the Indians, passing by without glancing to either side.

The show of force had an effect. The Indians huddled together. Maggie couldn't hear them, but from their gestures, she could guess what they spoke of. Pontiac had not issued the war-whoop. Soldiers were marching in the street, armed and ready.

Major Gladwin had taken precautions after all.

A second group of soldiers marched around the corner, and the Indians began to slink away. Not all at once, but a few at a time. When the third group of soldiers appeared—or was it the first group returned?—the last of the Indians walked down the street, heading toward the front gate.

Maggie had started to turn from the window, when one of the Indians caught her eye. He wore a tribal tattoo on his chest, had plucked the hair from one side of his head, and wore the old-style kilt some Hurons favored. He wasn't a large man, more lean and wiry, but the look of pure evil on his face threatened the strength in Maggie's legs. He turned the corner with the others, and she backed away from the window, hand clenched at her throat.

"Maggie?"

She startled at Mrs. Roberts's voice.

The woman rose from her chair and set the gun on the bed. "Maggie, dear. What is it?"

"'Tis him." She could barely get those two words past her tight throat.

"Pontiac?"

Maggie shook her head, then pulled in a deep breath. "Tree Sleeper."

"Here? In the fort?" She whirled and took up the gun again.

Maggie sank to the floor and leaned against the wall, drawing her knees up and wrapping her arms around them. "He is gone now. They are all gone."

"Is it over?" asked Mrs. Roberts. "Did Pontiac retreat?"

"For now."

"You fear he will return?" Mrs. Roberts's face was lined with worry.

Maggie glanced out the window but could see only rooftops from where she sat. "Men like Pontiac do not give up. I imagine he saw the soldiers and decided that his plan had been discovered. He was counting on the advantage of surprise."

"And Tree Sleeper?"

"He will return."

Maggie couldn't be there when he did.

BAPTISTE SWATTED AT THE GNATS BUZZING AROUND his ears. The pungent scent of decaying leaves and damp riverbank surrounded him. A cow lowing in the distance reached him. It came from one of the farms across from the fort, his being the last upriver before the wilderness. Before Pontiac's village.

Across from him, the fort shone in the mid-morning light. Canoes lined the riverbank, too many to count. A handful of warriors stood watch, guarding them. The rest had made their way to the other side of the fort, likely to the main gate.

Something bit his ear. He squashed the bug between his fingers. Blood smeared across his thumb. How much blood would be shed this day? And when? By his reckoning, the attack should have started some time ago.

Yips rose from the warriors guarding the canoes. Trotting toward them were more of Pontiac's men. There was no celebration among those returning. They were a silent, grim-faced lot.

Something had gone wrong. Or right, depending on how one viewed the outcome. But something had stopped the attack. If someone had tipped off the fort...

Baptiste crossed himself and dredged up the names of the saints he could remember from his mother's teaching. Then he wiggled back from the riverbank, past the screen of willows, and broke into his fastest pace. If the Indians arrived at his cabin, and he wasn't there—

Never before had he wished for two sound legs as he did at that moment.

MAGGIE DIDN'T MOVE AS MRS. ROBERTS STOOD BACK from the window, watching the street below. The sounds of normal activity reached them. A cart's wheels on the packed dirt, the steady plod of horse hooves, a door slammed shut. Someone called to a child or maybe a dog. Chickens squawked. Normal sounds for the fort in the six days since Maggie had arrived.

By now Tree Sleeper was outside the pointed log walls.

Stone Foot had treated Maggie fairly well. Once Long Pouch

had died, her life in the Huron village had been tolerable, even satisfying in many ways while Wind Over Waters had lived. Maggie hadn't been exactly fond of Stone Foot, but she'd grown to respect him. Then the old man had told her that she was to be sold to Tree Sleeper for a bride price, and she'd nearly hated him.

Hated the fact that she could be bought and sold for a few blankets, furs, and beads.

But underscoring that hatred was true fear. Maggie had done what Mama had told her as the Lenni Lenape warrior dragged her away. She'd stayed strong. She'd adapted, even accepted the ways of first the Lenni Lenape and then the Huron. After a time, her thoughts were often more Indian than British, even though she'd clung to her native language, whispering it to herself when she was alone.

She might even have been content with a Huron man for a husband.

Not Tree Sleeper, though. Never him. His cruelty was well-known among the tribe. He not only participated in some of the worst behavior that Maggie had witnessed—against another captive who'd dared to escape and had been recaptured—he'd enjoyed it. Reveled in it.

He was as close to pure evil as Maggie could imagine.

"I cannot stay here." Maggie rubbed her arms to rid them of the prickly feeling.

"My dear, you must." Mrs. Roberts eased herself to the floor beside Maggie. "'Tis not safe outside these walls."

"'Tis not safe inside."

The older woman sucked in a breath, her hand going to her throat.

Maggie shouldn't have said that. Shouldn't have brought more worry on the woman who was helping her—or trying to. But Mrs. Roberts hadn't lived through what Maggie had. Hadn't seen what the Indians could and would do. Didn't know Tree Sleeper. She couldn't understand.

Maybe it was better that she didn't.

"The fort is large and well situated. The soldiers will protect us. They are trained for times such as this." Doubt crept into Mrs. Roberts's voice, whether she realized it or not. "We must do as they say, and all will be well."

Maggie understood the doubt.

"Come." Mrs. Roberts rose, using the stock of the gun still in her hand for support. "We will busy ourselves downstairs. Busy hands keep the mind from lingering on what-ifs and might-haves."

Maggie followed her down the stairs and helped unshutter the windows, but even as she sat and picked up the wool and carders again, her mind whirled, seeking a way out of the fort. An escape from the walls that penned her in like a fish in a trap.

If the fish were smart, they'd find the one opening to swim through, but instead they knocked their heads against the sides of the trap and remained inside until the fisherman pulled them from the water.

Maggie Kerr was no fish.

SOMETHING CAUGHT BAPTISTE'S FOOT. FORCED TO catch his balance with his bad leg, he went down in a heap on the forest floor. Pain left him lying there, gasping for breath. When he could move, he pulled a snare from his foot.

One had gone missing during the winter, as snares some-times did if a coyote or owl found Baptiste's dinner before he did. But now, it had snared far more than a rabbit. Even so, he slipped it over his shoulder. One didn't waste materials on the frontier, not even a simple rabbit snare.

He tried to raise his bad leg, pain stabbing at him until he dropped back onto the old leaves and new growth of the forest. He waited until his heartbeat returned to normal, then pushed himself into a sitting position. Gingerly, he ran his hands down the length of his leg. It didn't feel broken, but it wasn't good. He scooted to a tree with some low branches and managed to get himself upright and steady on his good leg. Walking was questionable.

Running was out of the question.

A quick glance around told him he wasn't more than a quarter of a mile from the cabin, but he might as well have been ten miles away. The Indians would be there soon, if they weren't already.

Beau and Pierre.

He grimaced and combed his surroundings for any type of stick he might use as a crutch. He had to make it back to save his oxen. Then he almost laughed out loud. What good would saving the oxen be if the Indians killed him? But he must try.

Hopping on one leg, half-dragging the other, he finally found a stout branch that had come down during the winter. Using it as a crutch, he hobbled painfully on. Still some distance from the cabin, Walking Fire Stick came to his side.

"You are injured, my friend."

Baptiste stopped and mopped his forehead. "I am."

"How did this happen?"

The coolness of his friend's voice did little to calm Baptiste's nerves. "I tripped on this." He thumped his hand against the snare on his shoulder. "A foolish thing to do."

Walking Fire Stick's expression didn't change. "What were you doing?"

"Trying to eat." The words came smoothly off his tongue without him thinking about them. And they may have saved his life.

His friend clouted him on the shoulder, nearly sending him sprawling again. "You caught a big"—he held one hand toward the ground and the other level with Baptiste's head—"rabbit this time. You will eat good for many days." His laughter startled a trio of birds from the branches overhead.

"Oui, of course, you are so clever." Baptiste grimaced at the other man. "Now perhaps you can help me to my cabin? You are easier to lean on than this stick." He let the makeshift crutch fall to the ground.

Walking Fire Stick moved to his bad side, and Baptiste grabbed him around the shoulders. Even with help, Baptiste was weary by the time they reached the cabin. But instead of going inside, he pointed to the barn.

"I must see to my oxen."

"You fuss over those beasts as a woman would a suckling babe." His friend couldn't—or chose not to—understand the importance of the animals. "You should eat them. Then you would not foul yourself in another snare." He laughed again but helped Baptiste behind the barn where the two beasts lounged in a bit of sunshine that had made its way through the branches to the corral below.

Their water trough was full, and there was enough grass to keep them happy for several days. With any luck, Baptiste would be back on both feet by then.

Once on the porch of his cabin, he leaned against the log wall and met Walking Fire Stick's eyes. They were dark and unreadable.

"Did the attack go as planned at the fort?"

His friend looked toward the river, then back at him. "It did not."

Baptiste rubbed the back of his neck. "I do not know what to say. For your sake, I am sorry. For mine, I am not."

"You wish the British to remain?"

"I have no love for Redcoats. But I have no love for war either." He spread his hands. "I am a simple farmer. I prefer to live in peace with my neighbors."

"And your friends?"

He nodded. "Especially my friends."

Walking Fire Stick grunted. They stood like that for several long moments, the only sound the birds in the trees and a soft wind sighing through the branches, carrying with it the delicate scents of flowering trees.

"There will be time for peace when the British are gone." He clouted Baptiste on the shoulder again. "Until then, stay away from rabbit snares." His dark brows pulled into a flat line. "And the fort."

Chapter 9

Baptiste had pounded the last peg into place on the repaired ladder when the *shlup* of oars reached him. He hung his head, hands grasping the ladder spread over a pair of benches outside his cabin. There must be many oars for the sound to reach this far. Another attempt at the fort? Probably.

The sun was almost directly overhead. It was no surprise attack then, but more trickery. Would they try the same approach just two days after it failed the first time? Would the soldiers be smart enough to see a second attempt for what it was?

He wasn't going chasing down the riverbank again to find out. He eased his full weight onto his lame leg and grimaced. He couldn't get there in time even if he wanted to.

And he didn't.

Walking Fire Stick's parting words had been a warning, pure and simple. He suspected Baptiste had been doing more than snaring rabbits. Being a fair-minded man, he wouldn't press the issue without proof, but he suspected.

Too much suspicion could get a man killed.

Baptiste wrestled the ladder off the benches and up against the house. One painful step at a time, using his arms as much as his legs, he climbed the rungs until he could see bits of the river through the trees. Many canoes all heading toward the fort.

He couldn't do anything, but his insides pinched at the thought of the petite mademoiselle with her almost-red hair and matching freckles. Why would she not leave his thoughts?

Walking Fire Stick had been pushing his sister at Baptiste for almost two years, ever since Henri and Dances Away left. If he wanted a woman in his cabin, it would be better to choose one who would solidify his standing with the Ottawas. Not an escaped Huron captive.

Better if he spent his time patching his roof than thinking about women.

He half-slid, half-hopped on his good leg down the ladder. After shoving the wooden pegs he'd whittled the evening before into the pouch at his belt with the awl he kept there, he grabbed a long sheet of cedar bark to secure to the roof. It was past time to stop the leak that dripped above his door.

Back at the top of the ladder, he worked the awl and watched the river. The sun had moved past its zenith—his stomach growled a reminder—but still he chipped away at the roof, laid new bark, and pounded in the pegs. And watched the river.

When the bad section of roof was replaced and he ran out of pegs, Baptiste stretched as far as he could to see through the treetops. Movement flicked between the trees downriver. He waited, unmoving, vision blocked by a section of denser trees. Minutes ticked past. A bee buzzed around his hat. Sweat broke out across the back of his neck.

Canoes. Tiny in the distance, but many of them.

Against his better judgment, he slipped down the ladder and grabbed the crutch he'd fashioned, then hobbled toward the river. He stayed back within the screen of willows near his hidden canoe. The warriors' canoes came into view from there. Each man working to best the strong current.

There were no captives among them. No signs of plunder. The faces he could see were stoic and grim.

Their plot had failed again.

Baptiste remained unmoving until the last canoe was out of sight. Although he had no love for the British, he felt an unaccountable satisfaction that Pontiac and his men had been thwarted again. Even though he knew this wasn't the end. The Pontiac he'd listened to four nights ago had pledged an all-out war against everyone British. He would lose standing and power within the villages if he quit now.

It was only the beginning.

Waiting her turn at the well, Maggie listened to the silly chatter of women around her. The British women prattled on about Major Gladwin outsmarting the heathens, about their brave husbands and fathers, about the inferiority of the savages across the river. As if some battle had been won. As if Pontiac would retreat to his village and never return.

The French women—wives and daughters of men who'd sworn allegiance to England's king in order to stay in the fort and protect their business ventures—said little, but their secretive smirks spoke volumes. At least they did to Maggie.

British and French alike gave her a wide berth. Word had spread about who she was and where she'd come from. No one had been outright hostile toward her, but neither were they welcoming. Most looked at her with worry and suspicion in their eyes.

As if she were an Indian.

Maggie said not a word, but when her turn came, she filled both buckets she'd brought and returned to the Robertses' house. She entered and pushed the door shut behind her, leaning against it.

Mrs. Roberts glanced up from the fireplace, her hand paused on the spoon she'd been stirring the pot's contents with. "Is something wrong?"

"The women at the well." Maggie went to the fireplace and set one of the buckets there, then set the other on the work table. "They speak as if a great battle were fought and won today."

"Perhaps one was avoided."

"Not avoided, only delayed."

The older woman straightened, a hand to her back. "You are sure they will return?"

Maggie nodded. As sure as night would follow day, and spring would follow winter. "Pontiac is a very..." She shrugged. "I do not know the word, but when he talks, people want to believe him."

"Charismatic, I believe, is the word you mean."

"Is it a good thing?"

"Not always."

"Then aye, he is this charismatic. The young men of the Hurons were ready to follow him"—she snapped her fingers—"at once. He held them as if in his hands. The older men and Chief Teata, they were more cautious."

Mrs. Roberts bent and stirred the pot again, the aromas of stewing meat and herbs filling the room. She took a sip from the spoon, then sprinkled in a pinch of salt. "I have been thinking that perhaps Mr. Roberts could secure passage for you on one of the ships when they sail for supplies."

A way out of the fort. Her heart gave a hopeful thump. But on the heels of that... "And go where?"

"'Tis the question I have asked myself." She laid the spoon across the top of the pot and faced Maggie. "I have a brother, several years younger. He lives with his family in Philadelphia. He has a daughter around your age. You could go there with a letter of recommendation from me. He is a good man, a barrister. I know he would help you find your family."

Maggie sank onto a chair and gazed out the window, the fort's high walls visible past the houses that lined the streets. "What if they are no more?" What if that was the reason Da had never come for her? Why nobody had?

"It may be best to send my brother a letter of enquiry first, asking him to find news of your family." Her kind eyes met Maggie's. "It could be months before we hear back."

"Months." While Pontiac camped just up the river, and Tree Sleeper lurked somewhere beyond the fort's walls.

Roof patched and the canoes gone, Baptiste worked on a new corral between his barn and the smokehouse. It would be safer to keep the oxen close rather than picket them in the meadows out of sight of the cabin. Safer, but not safe. If the warriors grew frustrated in their attempts to attack the British, they may very well turn their anger on something else. Something as docile and undeserving of it as Beau and Pierre.

His leg aching, he used the crutch while working, which slowed his progress. He should rest it, allow it to heal so that he could sow his corn soon. But the risk to the oxen was too great. Their wellbeing must come before his own, or his own would be in jeopardy.

Baptiste's stomach rumbled a sour note. He'd not eaten at midday. With a hand to shade his eyes, he glanced west at the sun. Above the trees, a thin ribbon of dense gray threaded into the sky.

Smoke.

Hog Island parted the river just north of Baptiste's farm. There were no British settlements or Indian villages on the west bank of the river in that direction. The fire must be on the island. A British man farmed it, tending the crops and cattle owned by the fort for half the value of what they produced. He knew the man, Fisher, an honest sort for a British ex-soldier. Hardworking and knowledgeable.

Neither of which would save him or his family from the wrath of Pontiac.

Hunger forgotten, Baptiste limped to the river once more. The thin ribbon billowed into an angry plume hovering over the island.

From where Fisher's cabin and barns had been.

Baptiste sagged against the crutch in relief that his farm and his oxen had been spared. Then he remembered that Fisher had a wife and several children. Why should he, a crippled man by himself, survive while they did not? Not that his death would have meant they lived. It wouldn't have. Fisher was British. That was his sin in the eyes of Pontiac.

Baptiste was French, and Pontiac wanted the French soldiers to return. He wanted to trade with them. He wanted their guns, powder, shot, and rum. The Ottawa women wanted their metal pots and woven cloth. If the British had been smarter, they would have kept supplying these wants as gifts. Instead, they expected the Indians to purchase—by trading—for what the French had freely given. The British expected the Indians to adapt to their rules of commerce. And the British had no intention of arming the tribes hostile to them, or supplying them with the demon rum. They were foolish in the ways of the frontier.

As long as he kept to his side of the river, avoided the fort, and disavowed any connection to the British, Pontiac and his warriors should leave him alone. Should.

There were no guarantees.

He returned to his cabin and made a meal of smoked fish and dried apples, having no more than sat at the table when Walking Fire Stick stepped into the doorway.

"You always arrive at mealtimes, my friend. Perhaps it is you who needs a woman to care for him."

White teeth flashed for a moment beneath the black paint on the Indian's broad face. "You are a good host."

"Sit." Baptiste stood and retrieved the last of the fish and two more dried apples from their barrel. He put them in front of the seated Ottawa, and they ate the meager meal in silence.

Walking Fire Stick licked his fingers and then slapped the table. "You will stay on this land. Do not go to the fort. Do not visit the other farms or the villages." He leaned over the table, his face drawn in deadly serious lines. "You understand, my friend?"

Baptiste did. Only too well. "If I do this, my oxen will be safe from the knives of the Ottawas?"

The other man grunted and glanced away.

"Without my oxen, I cannot grow the wheat Pontiac enjoys."

"We lived for a long time without wheat."

"Oui, but do you wish to live without it again? Do you also wish for chipped stone arrows instead of rifles? For cooking in a deer's bladder rather than an iron pot?"

Walking Fire Stick shot him an unreadable look, but one that had the small hairs on the back of Baptiste's neck standing at attention.

Baptiste spread his hands. "I mean the Ottawa no harm." He thumped his bad leg. "My death would bring no warrior honor. Who cannot kill a crippled man?"

Another grunt, a slight lessening of the tension across the other man's features. Slight.

"You are a good man, Baptiste Geroux of the French. You

stay here." He stood and strode away, stopped in the door frame to look over his shoulder. "Maybe I will send my sister to make sure you do."

He left, and Baptiste dropped his forehead onto his palms. Never had he felt so out of control of his own destiny.

Henri, where are you? Wherever it is, I hope you are safe.

"FIRE!" THE SHOUT BROKE OUT AND, WITHIN heartbeats, every porch held someone looking up and down the street, Maggie and Mrs. Roberts among them. Smoke was a part of life in the fort, each house's fireplace adding to the general condition. It'd been even worse in the Huron longhouses with their small roof openings and lack of windows.

But this was something worse. Gray and black billows towered from behind the fort, past the barns that held the fort's few horses, oxen, and cows.

"What is burning?" Maggie hadn't left the fort since setting foot inside and didn't know the surrounding countryside.

The other woman shook her head. "Mr. Roberts will know when he returns."

The day had been almost windless, but a slight ruffle of breeze from the west teased Maggie's hair. Would it blow hard enough to drive the flames to the fort?

Memories of the blockhouse at Fort McCord pressed on her. The top of the blockhouse, larger than its base, fully engulfed in flames. Tongues of orange lapping from the windows as the shutters had fallen away. The chest-burning stench, and finally, the sickening crash and sparks showering the area. The Lenni Lenape hauling her away, barely allowing her to keep up with his long stride lest she be dragged. Dragged away from Mama and Catherine and little Donald.

She sucked in a deep breath that brought her back to Fort Detroit—not Fort McCord.

"Come." Mrs. Roberts held the door open. "There is nothing we can do here. Let us start supper and await Mr. Roberts."

Maggie followed her into the house. A house made of wood. A death-trap to the tongues of fire. She suppressed a shiver. Best to keep her hands busy, as Mrs. Roberts had taught her.

"I can bake scones for supper, if you like."

"That would be very nice." The older woman's eyebrows rose. "What do you need?"

"Cornmeal, salt, suet, and water is how I have made them, but you have wheat flour, aye?"

Mrs. Roberts nodded.

"Then I will use some of that too, if it pleases you."

"It pleases me. I have a small crock of raisins as well." She showed Maggie where everything was stored, including a heavy iron griddle like Mama had used. The familiar motions of blending and patting and laying the flat rounds on the hot griddle eased some of the tension from her shoulders. Keeping her hands busy was a good thing. She must remember it.

The door opened, and the surgeon entered.

"Dinner is nearly done." Mrs. Roberts greeted her husband and pointed to the table already holding plates and mugs. "Sit. You can eat quickly if you must go out again."

He swept off his hat and hung it on a peg by the door. "There will be no need." Lines etched between his nose and the corners of his mouth.

"Tell us."

He dropped to the bench at the table and combed his fingers through his hair. "It was Mrs. Turnbull's place."

Mrs. Roberts gripped the ribbon tied at her throat. "And?"

"She and her two sons are dead." He glanced out the window. "Ask me nothing more."

Mrs. Roberts gasped.

Maggie didn't need to ask. She knew what had happened, or at least knew the types of things that could have happened. She was content to be spared the details, having seen and heard enough of such things. In their frustration and anger, nobody was safe from the warriors following Pontiac.

Maybe the French. The Ottawa chief had seemed to esteem them still.

Would that keep Monsieur Geroux safe in his cabin across the river? She hoped so.

Chapter 10

"The sloops are needed for the fort's protection. Their cannons are central to keeping the Natives away from our walls." Mr. Roberts tipped his cup and drained it before rising from the table. Abigail's hopes dashed, he grabbed his hat from its peg. "The major won't be sending them off until he's sure 'tis safe." He turned to Maggie, his brown eyes filled with something she hadn't seen in years until arriving at the fort.

Compassion.

Then he turned to his wife. "Write your letter. When the time comes, I'll see it gets aboard." And then he was gone.

Maggie went to the window and watched him stride away, the wind rippling the back of his coat.

"Yes, well." Mrs. Roberts rose behind Maggie. "He said to write the letter, and so I shall."

"I will fetch more water and then wash dishes." Maggie picked up the buckets, then paused. She glanced out the window again. "Maybe I will make two trips, and fill the pots and kettles too."

"Why, my dear?"

She couldn't say exactly, only that she had a bad feeling. It

95

had rained during the night, washing away the acrid tang of the fire that had burned for hours behind the fort. But even with everything freshly washed and warm sunshine bathing the street outside, she couldn't shake the sensation. It made no sense. Indians traditionally attacked at dawn. She'd awakened well before first light, expecting their war cries any moment. Nothing had happened. Again.

That made her more nervous.

What was Pontiac up to? Where was Tree Sleeper?

She took a firmer grip on the bucket ropes. "I am not sure."

"My mother once told me, when I was still a young girl, to listen to the small voice inside." Mrs. Roberts gave a hollow chuckle. "My father called it 'women's intuition,' but he trusted her many times when she felt that way. If you are convicted to do something, then you should do it."

Maggie nodded, grateful that Mrs. Roberts hadn't dismissed her notion as silly, and stepped out onto the porch. The wind buffeted her as she walked to the well. There were only two other women there, both French.

"My husband, he wants to leave the fort," the taller one said in French.

The other cast a glance toward Maggie, but answered in French, "Mine too, but where would we go to be safe?"

"To the farms across the river. They are all Frenchmen, non? They would not turn us away, would they?"

The shorter woman lowered her voice. "But what of our valuables here?"

The taller one huffed. "What of our lives?" She lifted her bucket and left.

Her bucket filled, the other followed, and Maggie stepped forward to lower her bucket. As it filled, Esther Boggs joined her, the young British woman she'd met several days before.

"'Tis Maggie, is it not?"

"Aye. And you are Esther."

"Fancy you remember." The woman smiled. "You must have met so many here in the fort since arriving."

"Not so many." Maggie hauled up the bucket and emptied it into her other bucket, before lowering it again. "Not many who wish to speak to me."

"Oh." Esther glanced around. "Some people just take a while to warm up."

"Some people fear I am tainted by the Indians."

Esther came a step closer. "I heard that you were a captive, and I cannot imagine how difficult that was."

Maggie tugged the well's rope, testing the fullness of her bucket, and then hauled it up. "I expected to be treated poorly by the Indians." She met Esther's eyes. "I did not expect the same here among my own people."

"Nor should you." Esther took the well's rope and sent her bucket down with a splash. "But people can be difficult."

"Aye." Perhaps people were people, no matter the color of their skin or the shape of their houses. Some of the Indian women had treated her kindly. Wind Over Waters had treated her as a sister. Others had tormented her when they had the chance. Long Pouch had never liked her, despite Stone Foot interceding on Maggie's behalf. Or maybe because of it. Still others had ignored her, as if to befriend her would be a mark against them.

"I pledge not to be one of the difficult ones." Esther tugged at a blond curl that had escaped the back of her cap.

"Befriending me may make others think poorly of you."

Esther tilted up her nose. "They can think what they wish. I say you are a courageous young woman to have survived and escaped the heathens."

Maggie swallowed the lump that pushed against the back of her throat. "Then I would cherish your friendship."

Esther stuck out her hand, and Maggie placed hers inside. She knew about hand-shaking, but she'd never done it herself, not that she remembered. The other woman's hand was callused and warm, a capable hand.

Maggie squeezed it.

"Here we are, two young women on the frontier." Esther looked around the fort. "Waiting for an Indian uprising."

The other woman's fingers trembled the slightest bit. So she felt it too?

The soil was begging to be worked after the night's rain, but Baptiste's leg would have none of it. He'd done too much the day before. The leg needed rest, but his smoke-house was almost empty. Sitting in the canoe would not tax his leg as hunting or farming would, and it might fill his belly. After breaking his fast with some boiled cornmeal, he baited his fish trap with a bit of half-rancid meat and hobbled to his canoe.

He paddled against the wind to reach the center of the river and then let the current draw him toward his lucky spot. With practiced ease, he flipped the trap over the side, feeding out the length of rope until it connected with the bottom. Then he maneuvered the canoe toward the shore, caught a low-hanging branch, and secured the rope to it.

His lucky spot was halfway between his cabin and the fort. Hanging onto the branch to keep the canoe still against the current and wind, he glanced at the high wooden walls. All was calm.

Too calm.

Walking Fire Stick's warning echoed in his ears. With a

shove, he released the branch and dug his paddle into the swirling water. Within a few strokes, he was heading home against the current.

Something moved on the opposite shore.

An Indian. Two. Then three.

They were trotting along a path that would lead to the back of the fort. In broad daylight. Not taking care to remain unseen. If they took no care to be unseen, then they were growing bolder.

Baptiste gritted his teeth and continued to his land. He beached the canoe, then dragged it into its shelter of willows. He rested his hands against his knees, head hanging, catching his breath.

He and Henri had survived the French and Indian War unscathed. They had been too young to fight at the start, and the French preferred their farmers to continue to farm and thus feed the soldiers as well as the Indians who fought for them. Farming and their connections to the Ottawa made them more valuable on the land they worked. Maman died at the beginning of the war from sickness. Père had worn himself out on this patch of land granted him by the Ottawa. If Père still lived, Henri would not have gone west. Baptiste being barely a year the elder, he'd had no authority to keep his brother from leaving.

Now, if only he would return.

But would Henri stay if he came back? Always the adventurer, his brother had only tolerated farming to please Père. He was truly happy when running the forest with Dances Away, when hunting and fishing and trapping. Always pushing himself to run faster, jump farther, climb higher, and fight harder. He reveled in the things that Baptiste could barely do with his bad leg. Henri was as much Ottawa as he was French. Not by birth, but by nature.

Baptiste limped to his cabin and slumped into the only chair. The place smelled like a cave. It looked like one. There was a broom somewhere, left over from when Maman had swept and kept the floor clean. If mice hadn't eaten the bristles. He didn't have the energy to look for it. In fact, he didn't have the energy for much. He coughed and rubbed his chest.

Maybe he should listen to Walking Fire Stick about his sister. Baptiste pressed the heel of his hands to his eyes. What was her name? He never went to the village anymore. Henri had. Often. But the warriors looked down their noses at him and his lameness. The women giggled and pointed, one of them probably the sister. For all her brother's prodding Baptiste, she'd never crossed his land.

Mademoiselle Kerr hadn't giggled. Hadn't pointed. Hadn't looked down her nose at his infirmity. Was that why she wouldn't leave his thoughts?

And then it hit him like a tree branch across the chest.

Baptiste was tired of being alone.

THE FORT'S TRADING POST WAS A SQUAT BUILDING, long and narrow with shelves everywhere. Maggie's eyes couldn't find a place to rest with all the things hanging on the walls, from the ceiling, and filling the endless shelves. Baskets, barrels, and boxes held things she'd never seen before. But Mrs. Roberts didn't pause until she came to the bolts of cloth standing like soldiers at attention.

"What do you think?" The older woman pulled several bolts out of their lineup. She ran her hand down a mossy green. "This would complement your hair nicely. I could see you dancing with a handsome ensign while wearing that."

Maggie touched it with one finger, worried she might soil its beauty. "'Tis lovely. It reminds me of the riverbank."

Mrs. Roberts nodded. "The blue is pretty too." She shuffled that bolt to the top. "Or the brown. A nice brown wears well." She leaned closer. "Doesn't show the dirt or stains as much."

It was the color of a tree trunk. The color of the forest. A color she could wear if she decided to escape the fort.

The thought had hounded her since listening to the French women at the well that morning. If they let the French leave the fort, could she ask to go with them? Would the French allow her, a British citizen, to join them? Probably not. But perhaps she could slip away while the gates were open, acting as if she were with them.

As much as she trusted the Robertses and appreciated their taking her in, the walls of the fort frightened her. Trapped her. They may keep the Indians out, but they wouldn't keep out the fire. She had to find a way to escape and take her chances in the forest.

Tree Sleeper would assume she'd stay in the fort. He wouldn't be looking for her anywhere else.

"So which do you think?"

Maggie pulled her thoughts back to the fabrics before them. "The brown."

"A sensible choice." Mrs. Roberts sighed. "If things were different, I'd insist on the green." She tucked the other bolts back into place. "But there'll be no parties or dancing or anything else until this situation with the Indians is resolved."

The man behind the counter cut the fabric as Mrs. Roberts directed, then bundled it and tied it with string. She paid him, and they were stepping into the street when a volley of shots erupted from behind the fort. Mrs. Roberts grabbed Maggie's arm and hustled her toward the house. Red-coated soldiers raced past them, muskets in hand. Someone yelled orders behind them. Doors banged shut, bars thumped into place, shutters were slammed.

And above it all, the Indians' battle cries.

Out of breath—for who could breathe properly wearing stays?—they arrived at the house and followed the same procedure as before. Once the doors and windows were shut and the heavy wooden beams in place to hold them fast, the two went upstairs to watch from the window in Maggie's room.

Mrs. Roberts sat on the bed, the long gun across her lap.

Maggie leaned against the window frame, uncaring who might see from below. There wasn't much to see anyway, but the almost constant retort of guns, both within the fort and without, weakened her knees.

She was trapped.

DISTANT POPPING BROKE THROUGH THE FOG OF Baptiste's mind. He jerked awake, hand pressed to his neck where it had stiffened from leaning against the high back of the chair. More popping. No, not popping. He slowed his breathing, which came with a slight rasp, and listened. Gunshots. A whole lot of gunshots.

The fort.

He stood, then careened toward the cabin's wall, catching his balance. The room tilted around him, dots dancing in front of his eyes. What was going on? He was thirsty, so thirsty. And damp. Sweat plastered his shirt to his back, his hair to his forehead.

Weaving his way to the table, he plunged the dipper into the bucket he kept there and drained it. Once, twice, three times. The dipper hit the bottom of the bucket. He'd have to walk to the river for more. It wasn't far. Not far at all, but he sagged onto the bench beside the table and let his head fall onto his crossed arms.

Baptiste couldn't remember the last time he'd been sick.

At some point later, for the sky was darkening, he brought his head up from his arms, eyes bleary, and scraped the bottom of the bucket for the last of his water. He needed to fetch more for himself and for Beau and Pierre.

He stood, his bad leg threatening to buckle until he grabbed the crutch he'd left by the door. He'd have to make two trips. He couldn't handle the crutch and both buckets, not even with the shoulder yoke that hung on the front of the cabin.

Two trips.

One staggering step at a time, he made it to the river. A series of gunshots came from the south. He rubbed his eyes with a finger and thumb. The fort was under attack. Nothing he could do, even if he'd wanted to. Walking Fire Stick's warning, the British... he had to work to hold onto his thoughts. He filled the bucket and made the journey back to the cabin, past it to the barn.

One black and one red face met him at the fence. Before he dumped water into the trough, he drank long and loudly, wetness dribbling down his front. He poured the rest out for the oxen. They lowered their muzzles and drank almost as noisily as he had.

The new corral had enough grass to keep them for several days. At least he needn't worry on that account.

The prospect of another trip to the river was too much. He'd have to do that later. He staggered to the cabin and paused in the doorway, the distant gunfire sporadically peppering the air.

The mademoiselle had traded one bad situation for another, it seemed. Although it was difficult to imagine that the tribes—even combined in numbers far greater than the British—could breach the high walls. A well-shot fire arrow could. Or if the commander made a fatal mistake, a blunder of judgment.

Baptiste swiped his sleeve across his forehead, then stumbled into the cabin to collapse onto his bed. The world swirled around him for a moment. He hadn't barred the door. The idea of rising again to do that floated before him into the blackness.

Chapter 12

"I cannot stay." Maggie had done her best to explain to Mrs. Roberts, but the older woman's stricken face was proof that her words missed their mark.

"My dear, did you not understand Mr. Roberts this morning? Captain Campbell and Mr. McDougall have been taken captive." She took Maggie's hands and squeezed. "Forgive me for saying so, but you know what that means more than I. Would you risk being taken back? After what you told me about this Tree Sleeper?"

"No." Maggie suppressed a shudder. Tree Sleeper's presence might be the only thing worse than being trapped in the fort awaiting the fires. But he couldn't know she'd leave the fort. He couldn't be searching the forests with the attack underway. "But I must go."

"How?"

"Even now, there are French asking permission to leave the fort. I could cover my hair, and smear my face with boot grease to darken my skin and hide my freckles. They will all leave with bundles. I will bundle my Huron clothing and change once I am safely away." It was a plan born of desperation, much like the plan that had brought her to Fort Detroit. There was no reason it, too, shouldn't work.

"Where?"

Therein was the problem. There was nothing on this side of the river other than the fort. She needed to cross it and hoped one of the French would allow her in a canoe. But then she faced the same problem as before. There was no way for her to cross the huge lake to the south. And even if she did get across, where would she go from there?

Her face must have reflected her thoughts.

"Your best hope is to secure passage on the sloop when it leaves. It will sail for Fort Niagara, and from there, you can gain passage back to civilization."

Civilization.

Did she want that? If the walls of the fort were too much for her, how would she take to living in a town? Had she ever lived in one? She stretched her memory back into the corner she had hung a blanket over years ago.

Running over the grass, childish laughter, adults calling. A large group of adults standing near a building with a steeply peaked roof. Wagons loaded in front, tarps roped over the bulging loads. Mama waving her to return. Someone's arms around her, a girl near her age, laughter turning to sadness. Da's shout. Running to the wagons and Da lifting her high, plopping her onto a seat next to Mama. So many buildings in view. So many people waving as they drove away. Baby Catherine on Mama's lap. Da and Reggie walking beside the oxen. Turning on the seat to watch the buildings disappear behind them. Sadness. Mama's hand on her leg. "'Twill be for the best. You will see."

Da had promised a new life on the frontier. Land of their own that he could farm. A legacy to leave to his children. Room to grow and live off the land. To leave the buildings and trappings of the town behind. True freedom such as his family in

Scotland had never known. Had the frontier he'd so admired been the death of him? Of Mama, Reggie, Catherine, and little Donald?

Would it be the death of her?

Or would the fort?

"I cannot stay." How to make this kind woman understand? "I fear being trapped behind these walls more than I fear the forest."

They fell silent for a long moment, then Mrs. Roberts rose from the table. "I'll help you pack your things and make sure you've enough food to last for at least a week." She turned to Maggie, her face scored with lines of worry. "I do not like this idea at all, but I cannot force you to stay."

Maggie followed her up the stairs, a weight on her chest. Part of the weight was the distress she was causing the other woman, part was the fear of staying in the fort, and part, if she were brutally honest with herself, was the fear of striking out on her own. Again. But Da's blood must live strongly within her.

She had to go.

Something firm lifted his head, but Baptiste couldn't pry his gritty eyes open.

"Drink." Walking Fire Stick's voice was harsh and low. "You are in a bad way."

Baptiste did as he was told, the cold water reviving him some. And then more splashed his face. He sputtered and wiped it off his eyes, finally getting them to open.

"What are you doing here?" Was that croak his voice?

"Bringing you back from the dead." The other man removed his hand, and Baptiste fell onto his bed with a groan. "You are sick, but you are strong. This will pass."

"My oxen."

The Ottawa answered with a snort.

"They need water." Baptiste coughed, pain lacing through his ribs.

"I will make you a trade, because you are my friend."

Baptiste had kept one eye open, enough to know his friend was deadly serious. "What trade?"

"You give me your powder and shot, and I will carry water to your beasts."

He let his eye close, relieved that he'd buried most of it days ago. How many days? How long had he been sick? How long since Beau and Pierre had been given any water? "That sounds fair to me."

Another grunt, then the door opened and shut.

He must have fallen asleep, because a hard finger to his ribs roused him again.

"You must have more." Walking Fire Stick held his powder horn and half-empty shot bag that he kept beside the door.

He nodded and pointed to the trunk at the foot of his bed. "In there." There wasn't much, of course, but if he'd had nothing, the Ottawa would have been suspicious.

"Have you no more?" Was that anger coloring the other man's voice? Or frustration? Did it matter?

"I had planned to go to the fort for more, but I wanted to get my seeds in the ground first." He rolled to his side and cracked open an eye. "That is why I was trying to snare rabbits. No shot to spare."

The Indian strode to the door.

"Would you leave me with nothing to protect myself? A crippled man?"

"The British will be gone soon." Walking Fire Stick stopped at the door and looked back. "You have no one to fear." And then he was gone.

Baptiste rolled onto his back, but he couldn't hold onto a thought before he succumbed to sleep again.

"MERCI," MAGGIE WHISPERED INTO THE DARKNESS TO the barrel-chested man who had taken her into his canoe to the opposite bank of the river.

"You should come with us. Our friends, they would keep you safe." But doubt colored his words.

He must know why her words sounded like the Indians' French, but he hadn't asked. And she hadn't offered. Better for him to be able to say he'd not seen an escaped captive. Better for his friends not to hide one. And better for her to go her own way.

He and the other four in the canoe should not be able to describe her much, for the grease had done its work on her skin, and her hair was bound in a dark linen cloth Mrs. Roberts had given her. They hadn't been able to disguise her diminutive stature, but they'd wrapped her middle with a spare dress and petticoat. Mrs. Roberts had hemmed the old dress of hers short enough for Maggie to wear if she needed. But mostly, it made her figure much rounder than she was. Her attempts at disguise and the darkness should keep any word of her from being connected with the escaped captive, Dappled Leaves.

She stepped away, waiting until they had moved out of sight and hearing before turning to the north. There was one place she knew to go. One person who had helped her before.

He'd be smart to turn her away this time.

In a hollow in the middle of a bramble patch, Maggie stripped off her clothing. The ungreased areas of her body showed eerily white in the darkness. She pulled her Huron dress and leggings from the bundle, and tugged them on over her moccasins. She stuffed the rest of her clothing into the piece of oiled tarp Mrs. Roberts had given her and retied it. Her heart squeezed at the thought of the dear woman's distress when Maggie had followed the French out of the fort.

They'd not mentioned anything to Mr. Roberts, who hadn't returned for supper. He and the fort's officers stayed close to Major Gladwin. Concerns ran deep for Captain Campbell and Mr. McDougall. Maggie wished the two men well, but doubted they'd ever be released unless the major agreed to vacate the fort.

Likely not even then.

In her more comfortable and familiar clothing, Maggie made her way north, pausing frequently, ears attuned to the normal night sounds. She stayed away from the river and picked her way past what looked like neglected fields in the thin moonlight, keeping to the trees that surrounded them. She passed two cabins with no sign of life. No lights. No chimney smoke.

Had Monsieur Geroux also left? What would she do if he had?

She pressed her back against a towering tree, searching the inky darkness with branches overhead blocking the stars and moon. A faint rustle. Wings. An owl on the hunt, probably. The clicking of insects. The distant murmur of the river. She pulled in a long breath, allowing her ribs to expand.

Away from the walls and the restriction of the stays, she relaxed. If Monsieur Geroux was gone, perhaps she would return to one of the empty cabins. Or perhaps she'd head northeast. Somewhere in that direction—a very long way—would be the great trading city of Montreal. She knew nothing about it other than what the Indians had said, but it was under control of the British now.

And beyond the territory of the Hurons.

She walked on until the moon gleamed down on an opening.

Fields rolled past a familiar cabin, the barn, and several smaller buildings behind. Monsieur Geroux's place.

No lights. No smoke. But something moved behind the barn.

Maggie squatted to the ground, still hidden among the trees that backed the cabin. A rhythmic sound she couldn't identify reached her, but it was followed by something like a belch, and then more rhythmic... chewing?

The oxen. Of course. She kept low to the ground and moved toward the noise. Two shapes, one dark as pitch and the other lighter, lay within the corral. Neither appeared aware of her. She kept to the dark edges of the barn and moved closer to the cabin.

Was Monsieur Geroux inside? Or had he left? Nay. He wouldn't have abandoned the oxen. Such animals were too few and too valuable on the frontier. He must be inside, or—the next thought brought an unexplainable sense of loss—taken captive or killed.

But what Indian would have left the oxen alive when there were stew pots to fill?

The ground from barn to cabin was open, clear of trees or brush. The cabin's shutters were closed against the night. The door would be barred as well. Was the cabin watched? She pressed against the barn, scanning the surroundings and then glancing at the moon. It was well past midnight. A cloud was drifting in the right direction. Maggie waited until it blocked the moon, then slipped away from the barn and onto the deep porch of the cabin.

She froze, listening and watching, hardly breathing. Nothing moved. No unusual sounds came from within or without. The latch string was outside the door. Perhaps he wasn't inside. Time passed, then a bit more time, before Maggie finally plucked the courage to pull the latch string. It clicked the latch, and the door swung open. She slipped inside and shut it behind her.

Someone breathed across the room. A wheezing sort of breath. The room stank of sweat and dirt and illness. With no light to guide her, she followed the sound to a bed. Heat rose from the form there, but he made no movement. She groped along the wall and found a braced set of shutters. With a shove, she got the brace loose and the shutters open. That bit of moonlight illuminated the cluttered cabin, including a bucket on a table. She pulled the linen from her hair and sopped up the last of the water before crossing to the bed again.

Monsieur Geroux had not moved. His breath wheezed in and out softly, his chest barely lifting. Maggie's years living with the tribe's medicine man had taught her much about dealing with illnesses. She pressed the wet linen to monsieur's brow, then rose and searched for a candle or oil lamp. Instead, she found flint and tinder and started a fire in the fireplace for its light.

Another bucket lay on its side near the door. She took it and the one from the table to the river, keeping in the shadows, ears alert for any sounds out of place. Back in the cabin, she found a bowl and a spoon. The linen had dried on Monsieur Geroux's heated skin, so she rewetted it from the bucket she had set near the bed—careful to keep it separate from the drinking bucket—and washed his face.

He mumbled something and feebly swatted at her. She pushed his hands down and finished her task. The beginnings of a beard roughened the lower half of his face across a firm jaw that tapered to his chin. His nose was straight, eyes deeply set, thick eyebrows with a slight peak to them. Black hair was long and lank, clinging damply to his skin. She smoothed it back with the cloth, exposing his ears.

He was beautiful, if a man could be thought so.

The difference between him and Tree Sleeper was the difference between a fox and a badger. The one was all clean lines and graceful movement, the other a bad attitude on four legs.

She glanced at Monsieur Geroux's legs, encased in breeches and long stockings, the one was normal but the other twisted, the foot set at a wrong angle. The fox comparison fell apart. Instead of graceful movement, his steps were awkward. Not that it had slowed him much. She'd had to trot beside him to keep up, the length of his legs more than making up for the lameness.

She rewetted the cloth and laid it once again across his brow, then spooned water from the bowl into his mouth. He sputtered at first but swallowed. After three spoonfuls, he roused enough that she put the bowl to his lips, steadying his head, and he drained the contents. She laid his head back on the mattress.

She'd found no herbs, no bark, no meat to make a broth. Fatigue pulled at her, but she rose and slipped outside again, taking a knife from the mantle with her. There were many willows along the river, and she collected several tender branches and stripped them of bark. A tea would bring down the fever, if it wasn't too far along.

The river glistened under the moon. Stillness filled the night as if all of nature waited. The Indians were out there, maybe closer than she knew. They would strike the fort again.

The peace that surrounded Maggie wasn't a lasting sort. It was a waiting sort.

But closer to hand, she had an ill man to tend, and busy hands kept worry at bay. If she'd learned nothing else at the fort, she'd learned that. And her busy hands might be the difference between Monsieur Geroux living or dying.

Maggie wanted him to live.

Chapter 12

B aptiste coughed. A burning pain filled his chest, while the scent of something herbal hung in the air. Something or someone moved in his cabin. Walking Fire Stick must have returned. He licked his lips, but his dry tongue brought them no relief.

"You are awake."

The voice was feminine. Had his mother returned from the dead to help him? *Non.* The words were wrong. French, but wrong. Too guttural, too—Indian. Had Walking Fire Stick brought his sister after all?

Baptiste groaned and rolled onto his side, bringing another spasm of coughing. Once it passed, he rubbed the grit from his eyes and opened them.

Mademoiselle Kerr's face swam into focus.

He was delirious. Sick in the mind. Perhaps it was the end of Baptiste Geroux. Henri would return to find his bones on the bed.

The womanly figure in the Indian dress he'd first seen her in knelt beside him, a bowl in her hands. "You must drink. Your body needs water." She slipped a hand beneath his head and raised it, bringing the rim of the bowl to his lips. He sipped the water, ignoring the bitterness in his need for liquid. When it was gone, she pulled the bowl away.

"More." His voice came out more whisper than word.

"In due time. Let your body accept that much first."

He blinked. It was the mademoiselle, not an Indian woman. He clenched and unclenched his fists, feeling his fingernails bite into his palms. He was still alive. But his thoughts were a tumble of confusion until they focused on one thing. "Beau and Pierre. Water."

Her brow creased as she leaned in, her blue-gray eyes close to his, her freckles muted by what smelled like boot grease across her face. "Who?"

"Oxen."

Understanding blossomed in her expression as she sat back on her heels. "I will see to them." She glanced at the door and back to him. "There are no Indians nearby, are there?"

He shook his head, then pressed one palm against his forehead. "Walking Fire Stick sometimes comes. Took my powder and shot."

Her brows lowered, lips flattened.

"My oxen."

She pushed against his shoulders when he tried to rise. "I will take them water."

He sank back into the mattress, its musty grass filling cradling his weakness. He'd have to trust her to see to Beau and Pierre. It was doubtful that he could gain his feet, much less make it to the river and back. He'd have to trust her.

The blackness closed in on him again.

ANOTHER POT OF WILLOW BARK TEA SIMMERING NEAR the fire, Maggie checked on her patient once more before gathering the buckets and stepping into the daylight. She'd much rather wait until the cover of darkness, but Monsieur Geroux was worried for the oxen, and a man didn't heal well or quickly who fretted over that which he could not do. That she knew from her years with Stone Foot. So despite her fears, she ventured to the river, keeping to the forest as much as possible.

Downstream from where the monsieur kept his canoe, she found a tangle of willows and brambles that spread to the riverbank. She crept to the water's edge.

Smoke rose from the direction of the fort.

Great billowing clouds rose from several areas, all close together.

Maggie choked back a gasp. For Mrs. Roberts, for Esther, for the major, for all those trapped inside the walls. The memories of Fort McCord rose within her again. She gritted her teeth and pushed them down. History repeated itself in front of her. All those people, trapped inside the wooden walls and wooden buildings.

She'd gotten away just in time.

Brushing wetness from her cheeks with the back of her hand, she lowered the first bucket into the river. There was nothing she could do for those in the fort, but she could tend to the oxen. She could keep her hands busy.

She could be strong.

Both buckets filled, she turned her back on the travesty downriver and made her way less stealthily to the corral behind the barn. The Indians were at the fort, not lurking in the forest. Still, she kept her eyes and ears open.

The reddish beast greeted her at the fence, his slobbery nose pushed over the top rail. Maggie set the buckets down and tentatively rubbed her fingers along the broad space between the animal's eyes. It leaned into her pressure, and soon she rubbed her palm against the rough hair. It half-closed its eyes in response. The black beast ambled up beside the other, and Maggie did the same, both her hands occupied for a few moments.

There was an empty trough on the ground. She upended both buckets into that. The grass in the corral was trampled, but they should have enough to eat for a while. A memory surfaced of Da with his oxen, driving them before the wagon, picketing them in the evenings where they could reach plenty of grass to feed on before the next morning when they would travel again. Maggie had perched on a brown one, Da had walked by her side, one hand on her leg to keep her steady.

The red ox lifted its face, water dripping from its muzzle. More boldly this time, she reached through the fence and gave it one last scratch. A long, slobbery tongue swiped out and slapped against her arm. She pulled away, not surprised. Had another ox at another time done the same? Maybe.

For the first time in a long time, she didn't stuff away the memories. Instead, she smiled.

Grabbing the bucket ropes, she started for the river again. Monsieur Geroux would need more water, both for drinking and for bathing. And she wouldn't mind ridding herself of the tacky grease on her face, neck, and arms.

But as she neared the river, the acrid tang of smoke stripped all thoughts of oxen or washing from her. What had been billowing before was massive now. The horizon blackened and roiling like an evil across the land.

An evil that would take her—again—if she wasn't careful.

———

ALTHOUGH HE VAGUELY REMEMBERED ROUSING ENOUGH IN the darkness to drink several times while hands steadied him, Baptiste was still surprised to awaken to the

117

sounds of someone moving around his cabin. He coughed, throat and chest sore but not on fire as they had been. Blinking against the light of the open windows, he found the source of the sounds that had awoken him.

The mademoiselle swept his floor, a great cloud of dust rising and swirling around her as she herded about four inches of dirt and debris out the door.

He coughed again, louder this time as the dust reached him.

"Monsieur, you are awake." She beat her hands down the front of her deerskin dress, ridding it of most of the clinging dust. Then she dipped liquid from his cooking pot into a bowl.

"My oxen? Beau and Pierre?"

"I took them water yesterday and again this morning. They are fine. But you need more water."

He struggled to sit up. "First I must go outdoors."

She set the bowl on the table and hurried to his side. "Let me help you."

"What I need to do does not require your help."

Her lips quirked to one side. "Perhaps not, but first you must make it to your feet, non?"

That he couldn't argue, so he allowed her to assist. Once the room stopped spinning, he looked for his crutch. Part of him rebelled against appearing weak in front of her, but the more practical part decided that landing on his face wouldn't make him appear strong anyway. As if she understood, she fetched the crutch from just inside the door. Next to his powder horn and shot bag.

Baptiste froze.

Hadn't Walking Fire Stick come and taken those? Or had that been a fever dream?

"What is it, monsieur?" She was very perceptive.

"Were those"—he pointed to the shot bag and powder horn —"here when you arrived?"

She looked toward them, then back at him, her brows drawn together. "I believe so."

Leaning heavily on his crutch, he hobbled to the end of the bed and dug through his trunk. The extra shot and powder were gone. Walking Fire Stick had been there again. How long ago? When had he returned the items hanging by the door?

And why?

Perhaps most importantly, had he seen the mademoiselle? While Baptiste considered the Ottawa his closest friend, with war brewing, even that relationship would be strained. He half-staggered outside and headed for the outhouse and then the barn to see Beau and Pierre.

He had opened the gate and turned the oxen into the other corral when the feeling that he wasn't alone prickled the hairs on the back of his neck. Scanning the surroundings, he'd almost convinced himself that he was too jumpy from being sick when Walking Fire Stick stepped from the forest.

The Ottawa joined him leaning against the top bar of the corral. "It is good to see you on your feet."

As long as he didn't see the mademoiselle. Baptiste resisted the urge to look at the cabin. "You brought back my powder horn. My shot bag."

"I did."

"Why?"

The other man shifted his feet. "It was not good to leave my friend with nothing." Then he turned and looked Baptiste in the eye. "But you will tell no one. And you will hide them well."

Baptiste nodded. "But of course. I am glad our friendship stands."

Walking Fire Stick's face drew into severe lines. "For now it does, but you must keep to your farm. Do not go near the fort."

"What has happened while I have been ill?"

The other man grunted, crossed his arms. "The British have burned their own buildings outside the fort. It was not Pontiac."

A smart move on the major's part. The land around the fort was clear cut for many rods. Without those buildings to hide behind, the Indians wouldn't be able to get close without being seen.

"The Hurons took possession of several barges of trade goods coming upriver." Walking Fire Stick raised one hand to stop the question on Baptiste's lips. "They did not harm the Frenchmen on the barges, just sent them on their way. The British were taken captive." He shrugged. "Some were killed. Perhaps the British will take notice and learn. Or we will wait and starve them from the fort."

"That would take a very long time." There were gardens within its walls, and a very reliable well for fresh water. Although there were cattle and pigs and chickens, they would eventually run short of meat, but it would take many months to starve them out. In that time, reinforcements from the east would surely arrive.

"Time is on our side." The Indian said. "We are not leaving this place. And Pontiac will not rest until the British are gone."

"Then for your sake, I hope they leave quickly."

Walking Fire Stick shot him a narrow glance.

Baptiste shrugged. "If this drags on all summer, who will tend and guard your gardens to feed your people in the coming winter?"

The clout to his shoulder almost sent Baptiste sprawling.

"That is why we are friends, Baptiste Geroux." A grating chuckle and a parting of teeth would have been loud guffaws and wide smiles on anyone else. "You will work the land that I"—he thumped his chest—"secure." With sharp nod, the Ottawa strode into the forest.

Pierre shook his shaggy red head and blew his nostrils clean.

More than ever, Baptiste's security rested on the two beasts before him. He glanced at the cabin, its door and windows open, but no sign of movement inside. She was smart, the mademoiselle. He didn't have to worry about her giving herself away.

But even the most careful person couldn't anticipate when Walking Fire Stick or another Indian might stop by.

MAGGIE CLUTCHED THE HATCHET, READY TO THROW it at the head of whoever came through the door. She'd never killed anyone, but if it meant the difference between being recaptured or not—

"Mademoiselle?"

A huff of relief escaped her, and she let her arms drop, still holding the hatchet.

"Monsieur?"

"I am alone, he has gone." After those words, the monsieur appeared in the doorway, his eyes drawn to the hatchet in her hands. "I see I was right to call out before entering."

"Oui." And she was glad he did. He gripped the doorway, still unsteady on his feet, his face flushed with the lingering fever. "Come in. You should lie down."

He nodded and made it across the room before sprawling on the bed as if he'd used up every ounce of energy to get there. And he probably had. She slid the hatchet back into its loop at her belt and dampened a cloth before pressing it against his forehead, the warmth there less than before, but still too hot.

"If I had meat, I could make you a broth." She fetched a bowl of willow bark tea. "I found corn and flour and dried peas, so I will make a porridge."

"Fish trap." His eyes closed. "Down river. Tied to a tree."

121

His head lolled to one side, but she slipped her hand beneath it and lifted it up. "You need sleep, but you must drink first."

His eyelids opened a crack, and he drank down the tea, grimacing at the flavor. It wasn't the tastiest thing to drink, but it was bringing the fever down, and that was what he needed. She eased his head back onto the mattress.

"Sleep now. I will find the fish trap."

She turned to go, but he latched onto her wrist, dark eyes boring into hers.

"Be careful."

"Oui." He released her. She rubbed her wrist. For one so sick, he had a strong grip. And eyes intense with a sense of concern—for her—before they drifted shut.

First Mr. and Mrs. Roberts, and now Monsieur Geroux. Three people who cared about what happened to Maggie Kerr. It was a notion that would take getting used to, but it wasn't unpleasant.

Not at all.

Swallowing her nervousness, she made her way into the forest and then to the river. If the fish trap was tied to a branch, then it was very near shore. With luck, she would be able to reach it. It took her a while, but finally she spied the rope tied to a sturdy branch that hung low over the moving water. Sturdy enough to hold her slight weight and leafed out enough to shield her from casual eyes.

She climbed the tree and scooted out onto the branch. It dipped a bit lower but held her as she inched down its length. She'd almost reached the rope when, through a parting of branches, the fort came into view, its walls shining in the mid-morning sunlight.

It hadn't burned down.

The buildings outside the fort still smoldered, but the palisade stood strong and tall. Mrs. Roberts would be safe inside. Another wave of relief washed through Maggie, as strong as the relief she'd felt at Monsieur's voice outside the cabin door. In a few short days, she'd grown very fond of the older woman. More fond of anyone since Wind Over Waters had died, leaving Redwing in her care. She missed the chubby boy.

But all that sentimentality wasn't going to feed her and Monsieur Geroux.

Maggie inched out a little farther, the branch dipping closer to the water as it became smaller, but her fingers reached the rope's end. She pulled, and the knot came away in her hand. How had she remembered that trick? And how fortunate that the monsieur had tied the same knot Da had used.

Working her way back off the branch, one hand tugging at the rope, Maggie reached the bank and hauled in the trap. Flipping, silvery bodies filled the bottom. They would eat well for several days. And then? She had no idea. It was enough to have food and shelter.

For now.

Chapter 13

For two days—or was it more?—the mademoiselle had tended to Baptiste. Each day he grew stronger and slept less. Would he have survived without her? That question niggled at him as he watched her stir a pot of something made with the fish she'd brought back. At great danger to herself.

To care for him.

She shouldn't have come. She should have stayed at the fort, well away from Pontiac's warriors. They hated everything British. Mademoiselle may dress and speak and act like the Hurons who raised her, but her red hair and freckles marked her as British to anyone with half an eye. She was...

Beautiful.

Her face was almost heart-shaped, ending with a chin that was more often lifted in determination than not. Eyes neither blue nor gray, they were a fascinating mingling of the two. Baptiste lost long moments studying them, which often ended with her freckles lessening as color invaded her skin. She blushed often and readily, something he was not used to. Perhaps it was a common thing to one with such fair skin and reddish freckles.

She turned from the fireplace and caught his stare, the flush rising to her cheeks as if his thoughts had prompted it. Which pleased him, although he couldn't have said why.

"Are you hungry?"

He was, but maybe not just for food. Having her here, in his cabin, which looked nothing like it had before she'd come, pleased him greatly.

Eased his loneliness.

"Oui." He sat up and flexed his neck and shoulders. The headache was gone at last. He pulled in a long breath and almost gagged. Days of sweat and illness clung to him like fog to a spider's web. "But first, I need to bathe."

She said nothing, but he caught the hint of a smile as she turned back to the fireplace. He rooted through his trunk for a spare shirt and breeches. He sniffed them. They weren't clean either, but better than what he wore. Grabbing a tattered piece of toweling, so old and worn he could almost see through it, he limped toward the door. He almost picked up the crutch from habit, but tried putting more weight on his leg. It held. In fact, it felt better than it had since the rabbit snare incident. At least something had benefited from the illness.

Baptiste stepped outside and squinted at the sun past its zenith. He'd determined not to fall asleep again until after eating at noon, but his body had demanded it. Again. Not tomorrow. Tomorrow he would get back into his fields. Beau and Pierre were growing fat and lazy in the corrals. He pressed his hand to his own belly. If not for the woman inside cooking, he would be the opposite of fat. As it was, he was still thinner than before.

The walk to the river helped to clear his head and fill his lungs with sweet spring air. The blueness of the sky and vivid greens of the land renewed him. He stripped at the river's edge and plunged into the frigid water. As much as he needed a long soak, he settled for a quick dunk and a vigorous rubbing, using handfuls of sand to scour his skin until it protested the abuse. Rising from the water, a man's voice reached him from a distance. He froze, panic working its way into his blood.

Mademoiselle Kerr was alone in the cabin.

But the voice came again, more voices, and he could pinpoint them from upstream. He reached the bank and wrapped himself in the toweling, easing behind the willows. The *shlup* of many paddles announced the canoes before they came into view. A lot of canoes, filled with Ottawa warriors.

Heading toward the fort.

Those without paddles held long guns in their hands. All were painted. Walking Fire Stick was among them. His head turned, and their eyes met. Baptiste dipped his chin in recognition, and his friend did the same. It was good he'd seen Baptiste here. It was good he knew that his friend was staying put, heeding the advice given. That he was over the illness. That and the coming battle should keep the Ottawa away for a while.

Should keep the mademoiselle safe.

IT HAD BEEN EASY TO FALL INTO THE PATTERN OF caring for the monsieur when Maggie had arrived. Nursing the sick was something she knew. Caring for a man who could barely stand on his own two feet involved little, if any, risk. But as she watched him through the open window, his stride uneven but not unsteady, she contemplated slipping away.

The walk to Montreal was long and would take the entire summer. However, it would not be too hard to find once she located the great river to the east of Teata's village and followed the shore of the second big lake. But the thought of being anywhere near the village again raised gooseflesh on her arms.

And brought back fears of Tree Sleeper.

She'd been able to block thoughts of him while she stayed busy cooking and cleaning. Remembering what it felt like to live in a cabin again. There had been much to clean. Much to keep her hands busy. But that would end soon. The building all but sparkled.

Mama would be proud of her.

Maggie shoved the unwelcome thought away. Ever since she'd escape Teata's village, thoughts of Da and Mama had plagued her at the oddest times. She'd spent years purposefully not thinking of them. Why would she?

They had abandoned her.

She'd been left to herself, to survive however she could, and nobody had come for her. She—Maggie Kerr—had learned to be strong. Had learned to survive. Had learned that the only person she could ever count on was herself. Caring for a sick man had not changed that.

It was time for her to leave.

She spread the oiled canvas sacking on the table and rolled up the clothing Mrs. Roberts had given her. Her Huron clothing was much more suited to travel the forests. She lifted the stays and considered throwing them in the fireplace, but maybe a woman would need them in a place like Montreal. She hoped not but rolled them and added them to the bundle anyway.

In the middle she put the hard bread, raisins, and dried apples that Mrs. Roberts had given her. It wasn't much, but she could forage soon. The woods were coming awake with fresh greens and mushrooms, and there would be birds' nests to rob of an egg or two. She never took more than that from a single nest, leaving something for the mother bird to brood over.

Monsieur Geroux appeared in the doorway as she tied the bundle with cording. He looked at the oiled canvas, then into her eyes.

His were very dark. She was used to people with dark eyes,

having been the only one without in the Huron village. But his were different, warmer, deeper. As if she were seeing into his very soul.

The shiver that tickled its way along her back wasn't unpleasant.

"You cannot leave."

She straightened. What right had he to say such a thing? She touched the hatchet hanging at her waist. "I am not your slave."

"Non." He shook his head, then tossed his dirty clothing into a corner. "The river is full of canoes. They sail toward the fort. It is not safe to return."

"I will not return."

He opened his mouth, shut it, and then rubbed the back of his neck. "Where else would you go?"

"Montreal."

This time his mouth dropped open and stayed that way for a moment.

"I know how to find it."

"Oui, it is difficult to miss, but you have no canoe."

"I will walk."

"Mademoiselle," he spread his hands, "it is too far."

She gathered her bundle, putting her arm through the long loop she'd left in the cording and sliding it onto her back. "I will leave now, while the warriors are occupied downriver." And as strange as it was, a lump formed in her throat as she strode past him.

Until he grabbed her arm.

HER MUSCLES TIGHTENED UNDER HIS FINGERS, giving Baptiste just enough warning to block her other hand, the one clenching the hatchet. They stood inches apart, her nose barely reaching the center of his chest. She was strong, he'd give her that, but not strong enough to overpower someone of his size.

And she knew it.

Her eyes filled with something he couldn't quite define, but it moved him. He lowered her arm holding the hatchet but didn't release it.

"It is too dangerous for you. The Ottawa are to the north of us. The Hurons to the south and east. The Potawatomi have been across the river, but I do not know if they stayed there. And the Chippewa from the far north will come. They are friends of the Ottawa."

"Let me go." Her voice was firm and low. Determined. Like her chin.

"We both know what will happen if they recapture you."

She glanced out the door, but the tension left her arms. "I will not let them take me alive."

"You will likely starve on the journey."

She snapped her face back to him, eyes blazing, all softness gone. "I can take care of myself."

He believed her. Against all logic, the little spitfire would probably make it, if not for the war brewing all around them. That changed everything. The Indians should be planting their own crops, fishing, and gathering as they did in the summer months. Instead, they were prowling the forests looking for British to kill.

Like the lovely British woman in front of him.

What was he to do?

"If not for the war, I believe you could."

Her lips thinned into a straight line. She stepped back, pulling free of him, and dropped the hatchet back to its loop. "I have always taken care of myself."

Somewhere in those words was a cry for help, but he suspected she didn't realize it.

"Stay here with me."

She glanced at the bed, then to him as she took another step back.

"Not like that." Although the thought held a lot of appeal, he knew his deformity was repugnant to others. He would not subject her to that. And somewhere in the back of his memory was his mother's teaching, her constant reminders not to linger with the Indian maidens. Not aimed at him, the lame son, but at Henri. It hadn't worked, of course. Not with Henri. But Baptiste had put all thoughts of a woman in his life out of his mind.

Until now.

He swallowed. "If you stay here, I will see you to Montreal myself after the harvest and before winter sets in." Whether or not Henri returned. "I will move into the barn. You can stay here." He swept his arm out, taking in the cleaned space.

"Non." She slipped the bundle from her shoulder and held it to her chest. "I will move into the barn."

"I—"

She shook her head, long braid dancing on her shoulder. "Your Ottawa friend, he would look for you here, non?"

He grunted, crossed his arms. She was right. Walking Fire Stick was apt to walk through the door at any time, at least, when he wasn't in a canoe heading for the fort.

"He has no interest in your oxen, and there is no food in the barn for him."

She made perfect sense, of course.

"But there is something you should know." Her voice was low and earnest, and her eyes met his with conviction. "And then you may change your mind."

"I doubt it."

She tipped her head a fraction and raised her eyebrows.

"There is a Huron warrior looking for me. His name is Tree Sleeper." Her words wobbled the tiniest bit on the name. "He is evil."

"You said you were not married."

"I am not." Her shoulders drooped, and she clung to the bundle as a drowning man clung to a piece of driftwood. "But Stone Foot—the medicine man who owned me—had promised me to Tree Sleeper when he raised the bride price."

"Ah." Instead of putting him off, the urge to protect her surged through him. "Then we must be careful. Very careful."

The popping of gunshots reached them from a distance. The fort was under attack. Again. How long would that go on? How long before this Tree Sleeper was free to come hunting his bride-to-be? How long would Baptiste have to...

To what?

Enjoy her company?

Fall in love?

———

SOMETHING SHIFTED IN THOSE DARK EYES, something that struck a chord deep inside Maggie. Baptiste Geroux was a good man. She'd sensed that from the beginning, when he'd limped toward her with the chains around his shoulder and a canoe paddle in his hand. When he'd taken her across the river simply because she'd asked. And when he'd asked for nothing in return.

But to stay with him? To live in his barn? What madness was that?

Tree Sleeper was across the river within earshot of the cabin. He was busy, but only for now. Once the Indians took the fort—and she didn't doubt that they could by sheer numbers alone—and he didn't find her inside, he would come looking for her.

He'd stop at nothing to take her back. Not to make her his wife, not anymore. To make her pay for dishonoring him. He was a proud man, and cruel. Her death would be one the village whispered of for years to come.

She shuddered.

"Are you all right?"

His voice startled her from her thoughts. "Perhaps I will sleep during the daylight hours, and rise in the evening. I can cook when I awaken and before I return to the barn at dawn."

"A good plan."

She'd see less of him that way. Be less tempted to—what? So many questions surrounded her hasty decision to stay. Questions without answers. Questions that only time would work out.

"I will make a place in the barn." She scanned the area from inside the cabin before stepping onto the porch.

"There is a ladder on the wall that leads to the loft. You will find some hay up there. It is not fresh"—he cleared his throat—"but it will make a decent bed."

"Do your oxen not have need of it?"

"Non. The grass grows well enough to feed them now."

She nodded toward his pile of dirty clothing. "After, I will wash for you."

"It is not safe—"

"Inside the cabin, and I will hang everything to dry inside as well."

He picked up the buckets. "Then I will fetch the water."

She watched him limp away before turning to the barn.

In the loft, she arranged a place to function as a bed, wishing she had a blanket, but the hay would have to do.

The monsieur's whistling reached her as he returned with the water. Monsieur Geroux was a handsome man, even with his infirmity. When he looked at her sometimes, a heat curled inside of her that she didn't fully understand. That it had to do with him and her being alone on the edge of the wilderness was plain. It was part of the reason she hadn't left for Montreal. She was willing to admit that to herself. She wasn't ignorant of the ways between a woman and man, but she'd never expected to be drawn to someone in that way. Never expected to need someone else—or to want someone else—to be with her.

Another long string of gunshots reached her. How long would the fort stand strong?

How long would she?

Chapter 14

On the third day of their new arrangement, Maggie was roused by a gruff voice. She froze, her breathing shallow, her ears straining to make out the words. They were French words, not spoken with the smooth lilt as Monsieur Geroux spoke them, but as she did.

There was no window in the barn's loft, but in several places, the chinking between the logs was missing. The monsieur had taken the oxen to the field with him that morning, so she crept to the wall facing the field and found a crack to peer through.

An Indian spoke with the monsieur, both men with their arms crossed, heads high. As their voices rose, she caught the words.

"I have barely enough for myself until the crops grow."

"Pontiac will take whatever you can send with me."

"I can send nothing."

"Then he will kill the animals." The Indian jerked his head toward the placid pair of oxen, yoked together and resting. He said more, but with his head turned, she couldn't understand him.

Monsieur Geroux's hand clenched at his side. His profile was all hard lines against the greening field behind him. "I cannot grow crops without them. If Pontiac kills them, he will get nothing from me again."

"Take care, my friend." The Indian's stance had shifted. "This is Ottawa land. You are here because we allow it. If you do not grow food, you must leave."

"Then maybe it is time for me to leave."

The Indian said something she could not hear.

Monsieur Geroux spun and stalked toward the smokehouse. She scooted to the other wall and found another crack as he flung open the door and pulled out the fish hanging inside. Fish he'd caught two days before. He thrust the fish, strung through loops of bent willow twigs, at the Indian who had followed him.

"This is all I have."

The Indian grunted but took the offering. There were five fish nearly as long as her arm. It was not a small offering. And it left them nothing for their own supper.

"Take it and go."

Without another word, the Indian left.

Maggie heaved a breath of relief, letting her lungs refill before she moved back to her pallet. The shadows on the ground said it was nearly noon. She would sleep again, and then in the darkness, she would bait the trap and take it to the river.

It was unfortunate the monsieur had only the oxen and not a milk cow. She could have done much with a cow's milk. She remembered how to strip the milk from a cow, and how Mama had skimmed it and set the cream to age for cheese. Her stomach rumbled at the thought, but she stretched out to sleep again.

Then she saw the hatchet still lying by her pallet.

She'd not taken it up when she'd heard the Indian. There had been no thought of escape, of running to the forest. Maggie Kerr had trusted Monsieur Geroux to keep her safe.

And he had.

Shots rang out from the direction of the fort, but Maggie rested her head, reassured of her safety.

At least for now.

───────

HIS DAYS HAD TAKEN ON A SURREAL QUALITY. Baptiste had worked in his fields and labored around the cabin, replacing chinking and shoring up the porch where it needed repair. Things he may not have considered if the inside had not been so clean. So cared for. He even repaired the broken chair that had been left in a corner since Henri's departure. The chair Baptiste had hurled against the wall when his brother had left.

During all this activity, in his barn slept a woman who never left his thoughts.

A gust of wind slammed into the heavy logs of the cabin, rattling the shutters and door. His corn was only starting to peek above the soil, so it should weather the wind and storm. The wheat as well. If they got too much rain, his peas would take the brunt of it. But such was the life of a farmer, and the reason he planted a variety of crops.

The door burst open with the next blast of wind, and Baptiste came to his feet, but it wasn't the wind. Mademoiselle Kerr blew into the room, turning to force the door closed. Baptiste added his shoulder to the shove, and for added measure, he dropped the bar into its brackets.

"Pardon me, monsieur, but the roof of the barn is leaking." She clutched her bundle to her chest, the blanket he had given her wrapped around her small frame.

He glanced at the roof above them, glad he had patched it. "Then we will hope this one holds."

She nodded, then put her items on the table. She shed the

blanket and hung it on a peg, revealing her womanly form in the soft deerskin dress that ended below her knees. Her legs were bare, the leggings she usually wore missing. When she bent over the empty pot hanging near the fireplace, the breath squeezed from his lungs.

"Did you fill the buckets?" She turned and caught him staring.

It wasn't *her* face that flushed. Heat surged from under his collar and across his cheeks. He hadn't shaved that morning, but by the lift of her brows, the stubble wasn't enough to hide behind.

He fetched both buckets from across the room. She took one, poured water into the pot, and swung it over the fire.

"I will wash this and then launder the clothing." She rubbed her hands down the front of her dress. "Mine at least needs cleaning."

It would be safe for her to be in the cabin today. No Indian would travel in such a storm. They would keep to their wigwams and longhouses. But she'd been up all night, prowling the forest, picking edibles that had greatly added to their diet, and then returning to cook their breakfast while he tended Beau and Pierre.

"You should sleep."

She cocked an eyebrow at him and glanced at his bed.

The heat nearly choked him. He raised both hands. "Mademoiselle—"

Something close to a giggle escaped her. She pressed the back of her hand to her mouth.

Was she laughing at him? Was the idea so absurd? Did she see him as a joke? Anger flared within him, quick and sure. "Mademoiselle—"

"Maggie." She slipped the name into the room. It quenched his anger like water over a fire.

"Maggie?"

She nodded, her eyes soft, more blue than gray in the flickering light of the fireplace. "We live together, if not *together*." The stress on the last word was not lost to him. "You should know my name."

He hadn't forgotten it. Hadn't forgotten anything about her. But to be given permission to use her name? A small flame of something kindled deep in his chest. Was it hope?

He bowed, as if they'd been introduced at a dance. "I am Baptiste."

Her chin dipped, but her eyes held his. "I remember, Baptiste."

Lightning cracked nearby, the flash of light around shutters and door almost lost in the following roar of thunder.

It was nothing compared to the storm brewing inside Baptiste.

THE STORM HAD RAGED FOR TWO DAYS, CHANGING the landscape with trees down and puddles the size of small ponds dotting the fields and meadows. The river rode high and noisy between its banks, but the sun had chased away the clouds at last.

Maggie kept busy in the cabin, stretching and working back to softness the deerskin dress she'd washed. Baptiste, although worried about his fields, was mending the barn roof.

For her.

She gave the deerskin a good stretch and peeked out the window.

His clean white shirt rippling in the breeze, Baptiste pounded a peg into the roof, securing a sheet of cedar bark he'd peeled off one of the trees that had come down in the storm. He climbed down, moved the ladder, and repeated the process.

Maggie leaned against the window frame. The same breeze that toyed with his shirt brought her the scent of freshly washed earth. The storm had been severe, but in its wake would come such bounty from the land.

What would it be like when the fields were tall and ripening?

Baptiste turned and stopped working, seeing her in the window. She lifted a hand. He returned the gesture. Maggie stepped back away from the window, the deerskin dress pressed to her chest.

What would it be like to belong here? To belong to Baptiste?

She shivered, but not from the breeze. To even be thinking such thoughts was unwise. Somewhere out there, Tree Sleeper lurked. And although she was not an Indian to be given away for a bride price, he saw her that way. Stone Foot had promised her to the Huron warrior. He viewed her already as his.

Maggie didn't. She wouldn't. No matter what.

A voice rose in greeting. Indian words she didn't understand. Maggie glanced around the cabin. There was a half loft above, tight under the roof, but no ladder to climb. Her belongings were few, but she gathered and slid them under the bed, squeezing in after them, pulling the full skirts of her British dress in last. Her hatchet she clenched in both hands.

"I am busy. I must repair the roof to keep my oxen dry and happy so they will work the land for me." Baptiste's voice was much louder than the other man's. He was letting her know that someone was out there beside him. Did he think her deaf?

If she'd been wearing her Huron dress, she'd have slipped out the back window, but in the light color and flimsy cloth of the dress Mrs. Roberts had given her, she would never be able to leave unseen. As Baptiste's shirt had done, the dress would catch the wind and draw the eye.

Another voice rose, still in a language she didn't understand, but not the same voice as the first. Baptiste was outnumbered.

"I have no bread today," Baptiste all but hollered. "You took my fish already. I have nothing to feed you." He sounded cross, as would be expected after the man had taken the fish away, leaving him with nothing. But Maggie knew there was more in his voice. He was warning her, and he was worried.

Fear crawled under the bed with her.

The door opened, a breath of air swirling across the floor and into her face. Maggie froze, keeping her breaths shallow and silent.

The Indian's voice rose, a mocking sound to the next string of words. His moccasins came into view as he stepped into the cabin, followed by another pair, and then a third.

Maggie kept her eyes open, even as her heart squeezed. Her hands trembled on the hatchet's handle.

"You would enter my home?" Baptiste's voice resonated with anger. And it should. Such rudeness was not tolerated by the Hurons either. A man's home was not entered without permission.

"You did not extend us a welcome, so we had no choice." One of the warriors answered in passable French, although with faulty logic. "Is this the same cabin?"

Of course. If they had been here before, they must wonder at the change. She'd arrived to a bear's den and turned it into a tidy home. She shut her eyes.

"I am fixing the place up." Baptiste's moccasins came into view. "I patched the roof here first, then cleaned, fixed my chair, and now I am working on the barn."

"You need a woman for this. I tell you, my sister would come."

"As you can see, I have done well for myself."

A grunt, a clang as someone checked out the pots around the

fire, and then one of the warriors sat on the bed, its ropes and ticking pressing against her shoulder. She didn't move. Barely breathed.

"I told you, no bread."

"Pontiac will want more food soon. You must give something." One of the warriors still spoke in French, perhaps because Baptiste was.

"I cannot hunt for meat." Baptiste made a disgruntled sound. "You have taken my shot and powder."

The weight lifted from Maggie as the men headed for the door. One turned before leaving. "We will return in two days. Have something, or we will take the animals." His voice lowered. "Pontiac has taken several from the other farmers. He has a taste for oxen."

They left the cabin.

Baptiste moved to the window, watching them leave, no doubt. Long minutes passed, and finally he sighed.

"Are you here?"

She scooted from under the bed, hatchet still in her hand. "I am."

"It is dangerous for you when they come like that. Better that you can return to the barn and sleep during the daylight again. They wouldn't look for food there."

"Who were they?"

"The one who speaks French is Walking Fire Stick. He is of Pontiac's village." He shrugged. "The others I do not know. There are many Indians here now that I do not know. Those wore the clothing of the Ojibwe, who normally stay to the north."

Another tribe joined with Pontiac, making four.

What if next time it was Hurons who showed up at the cabin? What if next time it was Tree Sleeper? If he found her, he would not give her up to Baptiste.

He would kill Baptiste.

***

How could Baptiste keep Maggie safe when the land was crawling with Indians? Fleeing to Montreal was perhaps their best option, but how to get there? The river would be watched on both sides. To walk over land when he had no idea where the tribes were was foolish.

And then there was Henri. If he returned and Baptiste was gone…

Baptiste dropped his head to his hands, elbows on the table. Darkness crept around the cabin. Maggie was foraging in the forest, a shadow in her Huron dress, as safe there as anywhere, he supposed. Although part of him wished he could lock her in the barn and keep her there. He snorted and pushed away from the table, moving to the door and stepping through swiftly so the light from the fire didn't outline him in the doorway.

In the barn wasn't where he wanted the woman.

He went to the river and stripped, plunging into the chilly water and scrubbing off the day's grime. With Maggie keeping the house so clean, it only seemed right that he keep himself clean as well. At least, that's what he tried to tell himself.

When he'd caught her look from the window, his heart had almost beat out of his chest. It wasn't the look of someone who found his deformity repulsive. It was a look that had seared him to his bones.

He waded from the water and shook the worst of it off. He'd forgotten anything to dry himself with. But no matter. He sat on a flat rock by the riverbank, one he'd used on other such occasions, and let the night air dry his skin. Between the water and the breeze, he was thoroughly chilled by the time he pulled on his clothing.

But he'd come to a decision. Tomorrow, he would ask Maggie to marry him. To stay and make a home here with him. They'd still have to keep her secreted away until after the war settled, or perhaps they'd have to flee for Montreal, but whatever they did—

They'd do it together.

Chapter 15

How did a man ask a woman to marry him? Baptiste wished for Maman's advice. Or even Père's. He was treading waters as turbulent as the river's. And he wasn't doing a very good job of it. Maggie had retired to the barn loft, his question still unasked.

A commotion outside drew his attention.

"Baptiste Geroux!"

Henri? Baptiste bolted to the door and flung it open. The line of men approaching jolted him with disappointment. They were French, but not Henri. He recognized many of them, neighboring farmers from both sides of the river.

"Bonjour, my friends." He raised his hand and his voice. Maggie would hear and stay put. These men would have no reason to go into the barn.

Several chorused out, "Bonjour." It was Claude Charles Moran who led the way. An important man in the area, he'd never set foot on Baptiste's farm before. This could not be good.

Moran stopped and crossed his arms. "We go to Pontiac to speak with him about the raiding of our farms, the killing of our livestock."

Baptiste nodded.

"We wish for you to join us."

"What can I add?" He was of little to no importance, a young man struggling to hold onto the northern most strip of farmland. Those before him were men with silver in their hair, the grooves of wisdom lining their faces.

"You are the closest to Pontiac's village. His warriors know you, non?"

"Some do."

"Your presence, it cannot hurt." Several of the men nodded agreement, one muttering that it wasn't likely anything would help. At least one understood what they were up against.

Moran waited, stance unmoving.

"I will come. Give me a moment." Baptiste returned to the cabin and added his tomahawk to his belt, checked that his knife was in its sheath, and then joined the men outside.

Moran slapped him on the back as he passed, following the rest to the river. They'd come in six canoes, so there was no need for Baptiste to haul his out. He joined the one he was pointed toward, taking the front seat and lifting the paddle waiting there.

His question for Maggie would have to wait. A part of him was relieved. The other part grumbled at the delay.

They paddled against the current until the well-worn landing of the Ottawa came into view, their longhouses perched on a small rise overlooking the landing. Warriors gathered at the sight of the canoes, men bristling with weapons.

It was not a welcome, they were guards watching out for Pontiac.

Baptiste's stomach tightened, the muscles across his shoulders bunching, his hands gripping the paddle hard enough to make his fingertips numb. So much depended on the first words spoken.

Then Pontiac himself appeared, dressed in a splendid display befitting his rank and honor among the tribe.

The Frenchmen jockeyed the canoes so that Moran landed first, stepping onto the shore and raising his hand. Baptiste couldn't hear what he said to the Ottawa chief, but they were waved ashore. They beached the canoes and walked past the line of warriors, including Walking Fire Stick.

Neither his stomach nor his shoulders relaxed until they were seated around a fire, each man arranged by importance, with Baptiste in the back. And even then, he didn't relax much.

Pontiac's demeanor was cordial, but he demanded to know the purpose of their visit, which went against the Ottawa's normal protocol of allowing the visitor to state that in their own time and fashion.

So many things about this war were contrary to the normal Indian protocols.

"We are here to discuss business." Moran said. "It would be good for the other chiefs to hear us as well."

Pontiac dispatched messengers to the Potawatomi and Huron villages. Since there were Ojibwe warriors already surrounding the Frenchmen, their chief must have been nearby.

Baptiste and the others were offered food and drink, and small talk was exchanged while they waited. The day was mild, but the sun beat down upon them. Baptiste removed his hat and wiped his forehead, then replaced it. More than one pair of unreadable eyes watched his movements. Maybe it wasn't only the heat that caused his sweat.

Once the chiefs arrived, were properly greeted and shown respect, Moran stood and approached Pontiac, also standing, and they faced the rest of those gathered.

"My brothers, you seem surprised to see us. We have come here only to renew the ancient alliance which our fathers made with your fathers, and which you are today destroying." Moran went on to describe the devastating consequences of the Indians killing oxen and other livestock that the Frenchmen needed—not only to feed their own families but also to supply the Indians.

When Moran continued, telling Pontiac that his warriors were threatening them, treating them like slaves instead of brothers, Baptiste could feel the waves of resentment coming from those warriors who still circled the group. But Pontiac only listened, his head high and arms crossed. It was impossible to read anything on the chief's face. But that didn't stop the itch that buried itself between Baptiste's shoulders.

Moran finished his speech by assuring Pontiac that the Great Father, the King of France, would not look with favor at the way his people had been treated when he came back to these shores.

Baptiste gritted his teeth, half expecting a tomahawk would take out his itch at the end of that speech.

Instead, Pontiac raised his hands and addressed the Frenchmen. "My brothers, we have never planned to do you any injury or harm, neither have we intended that any should be done to you." His voice was smooth, his manner polished. He was, in a word, charming. He blamed the incidences Moran had outlined on young men who were too impetuous, as he assumed young Frenchmen could be as well. He reminded the older men of the attack seventeen years before when he'd stood between the tribes from the north, the Ojibwe and Ottawa of Michilimackinac, and the very Frenchmen seated before him. How he had turned those tribes away, preventing the bloodshed of his French brothers. He accused some of those present of sympathizing with the British but graciously acknowledged that they were bound by their oaths and could not side with Pontiac. He asked only that they remain neutral.

The Frenchmen—to a man—agreed that they were willing to

remain neutral. Better that than to die where they sat around the fire.

In reply, Pontiac gave his word that none of his warriors, nor those of the other tribes, would harass the French farmers again. He asked only one thing in return. He asked that the Indian women be given free access to work the fields left abandoned when others had packed up and left.

Moran agreed, even offering that the farmers would plow the fields and make them ready for the Indian women.

Baptiste, who had uttered not a word, followed the rest to the canoes and paddled back home. The men did not talk amongst themselves. Thoughts were kept close. But there was no feeling of relief among them. No optimism. Very little hope that their words had changed anything. The undercurrent was that their livestock were not out of danger, for all Pontiac's pretty words. The entire afternoon, as far as Baptiste was concerned, had been a waste. He needed a plan to hide Beau and Pierre should the situation worsen.

Which it almost certainly would.

One thing was abundantly clear. No matter how lonely he was, nor how alluring Maggie was, nor even how much she needed his protection, it was not a time to be considering marriage.

SOMETHING HAD CHANGED BETWEEN BAPTISTE AND Maggie since the Indians had come into the cabin while she'd hid under his bed, but she couldn't figure out what. The past three days, a tension had stretched between them, like unspoken words that begged to be said.

Did he regret not sending her on her way to Montreal? She wouldn't blame him, what with the sporadic pop of gunfire from the fort, the Indians who prowled the land, both those who belonged to the area and those who didn't.

Including Tree Sleeper.

The previous evening, while foraging for the crinkly mushrooms Baptiste so enjoyed, a trio of warriors had passed far too close to her. Close enough for her to hear them and see their clothing even in the dark.

Huron warriors.

She hadn't recognized any of them. They were probably from Takay's tribe. But it wasn't too hard to imagine that Teata's warriors would be close by. They'd prefer to stay with the other tribe of Huron than mix with the Ottawa or Potawatomi. Or the fierce Ojibwe from the north.

No, she wouldn't blame Baptiste for wishing her miles away from his farm.

Her stomach rumbled. It would be dark soon, and she would be free to slip into the cabin and cook something for supper. Hurons or not, she'd found a large handful of the crinkly mushrooms. Baptiste had cleaned and hung another catch of fish in the smokehouse. The mushrooms boiled with some of the fish would make a fine supper. Her stomach growled in agreement.

She was ready to climb down the ladder when a footstep caught her ear. She flattened herself to the floor of the loft. The door creaked open, allowing in the last of the sun's fading light.

"Maggie?"

Relief washed over her. She reached the ladder and climbed down. "You have returned." She vaguely remembered hearing his whistle as he'd walked away around mid-morning.

"I have. And I wish to show you something." He held the door open. "Come."

Intrigued, she ignored her empty middle and followed. They moved into the forest, and she caught his sleeve. He stopped and turned to her, his dark features almost lost in the gloom under the trees.

"Last evening, there were three Hurons near here," she said.

He searched the darkness, then nodded, moving as quietly as his lame leg would allow. While it wasn't much of a problem for him in his fields behind the oxen, in the forest it was different. But he was still more silent than she could have been, if she'd been so hampered. Of course, he was used to his awkward gait.

They wove through a section of dense growth, then skirted a small meadow before reaching a patch of massive cedars. Several of the shaggy-barked monsters had uprooted in the storm, their woven mats of roots thrust into the air higher than Baptiste's head. He led her around to the side of them, where an opening allowed them through.

"A natural corral." He gestured around the enclosed space fenced with exposed roots and horizontal trunks. "The only opening is the one we used." He pulled a gate of sorts fashioned from limbs and vines from the side and planted it in the damp earth to cover the opening. "If need be, we can bring Beau and Pierre here."

"A perfect hiding place." Someone could walk past it, never knowing the oxen were inside.

"If there comes a time when I cannot get them here." He shrugged in that way Frenchmen did. "Perhaps you can."

"I would be happy to." Already she'd grown attached to the animals she shared the barn with. Beau with his quiet dignity and Pierre with his shaggy red hair not too different from her own.

"Good." He smiled then, the white gleam of his teeth cutting through the forest's darkness.

Before he could say more, her stomach groaned like a dog giving birth. She clamped her hands across her middle and suppressed a laugh.

"Perhaps we should return to the cabin, non?" He removed the gate but seemed reluctant to leave. As if the unspoken words between them were near his lips. Yet he put his hand against her back and ushered her from the enclosure, the words still unspoken.

He'd shown her the safe place for his oxen. Surely that meant he wasn't wishing her gone. Did it not? It seemed as if he was counting on her. As if she were a part of his life. The idea made her a little lightheaded.

Or maybe it was the hunger.

They'd walked a short distance when Maggie spied a turkey in a tree, already roosting for the night. She grabbed Baptiste's arm, and he froze. She pressed her finger to her lips while slipping the hatchet from her belt. With a well-practiced motion, she sent the hatchet spinning toward the turkey. Its squawk was cut short, and it tumbled from the branch it'd been roosting on.

"Good throw." He turned to her. "Can you do that every time?"

"Most of the time."

He picked up the turkey by its feet and removed the head with his knife, then they walked back in silence. He held the door to the cabin open for her, and she stepped inside.

A voice came from the darkness inside. "I never expected someone so pretty to come through that door."

BAPTISTE'S MOUTH FELL OPEN, THE BREATH KNOCKED from his lungs. He pushed past Maggie, dropped the turkey onto the table, and embraced his brother. The answering thumps to his back would likely raise bruises, but Baptiste didn't care. His brother had returned.

His brother was alive.

Henri pushed him back at arm's length, hands clamped on his shoulders as if he'd never let go. "You did not expect to see me again, non? But I am the proverbial prodigal son. Did our Père, God rest his soul, not say so many times?"

"Oui, he did." How Père would've rejoiced to see them together again.

"But what is this?" Henri stepped to the side, his focus on Maggie. "You have taken a wife while I was away." He cocked his head. "A white woman in a Huron dress, no less. Brother, you have much to tell me."

And he hardly knew where to begin. "Henri, this is Mademoiselle Kerr—"

"Mademoiselle?" A slight difference in his voice, a feral gleam in his eye, Henri stepped toward her. "So you are not my brother's wife?"

Maggie tipped her chin down, her knees bending in that graceful way a woman greeted someone. But when she lifted her eyes again, there was admiration in them.

For Henri.

His brother was the better-looking of the two of them, always had been. And even if he weren't, he was whole. His legs strong and sure.

"I am not. Your brother is keeping me safe here in his home." She half-turned and gestured out the door. "Or rather, in his barn."

"I cannot believe he would keep you in that nasty old barn when..." Henri swung around and twitched his brows at Baptiste.

As much as he'd longed for his brother's return, at that moment, Baptiste almost wished him gone. At least until he'd decided once and for all whether or not to ask his question. But that couldn't be changed, and Baptiste needed to make Henri understand the situation. To protect Maggie.

"She is an escaped captive."

Henri's face grew deadly serious, all humor and whatever else gone. "It is dangerous for her to be here, then. Old Takay's village was like an arrow-shot hornet's nest when I passed it."

As boys, they'd been stupid enough to do that once, shoot arrows into a hornet's nest. Only jumping into the river and swimming underwater for a long time had saved them from their foolishness. Henri's comparison was not off the mark.

"I was in Chief Teata's village." Maggie closed the door. "But there are those in Takay's village who would know me."

Henri eyed her up and down.

Baptiste curled his hands into fists, but this was his brother.

"I can see why you take such a risk, brother." He turned and grinned at Baptiste, in that moment a younger, more vital image of Père. With all his charm and wit.

Maggie's stomach growled again. "You two reacquaint your-selves, and I will make supper."

Henri slapped his flat stomach. "I could eat one of the oxen tonight."

"I have fought too hard to hold on to Beau and Pierre to lose them to you." By the look Henri shot him, there'd been too much bite in his words. Baptiste shook his head and motioned to the chairs. "Sit and tell me where you have been and what you have done. It is good to have you home again."

And it was—wasn't it?

Chapter 16

Baptiste was very aware of Maggie's movements preparing and cooking the turkey and some fried cornbread while Henri had regaled them with stories of his months away. Baptiste had done his best to listen about the widest rivers and tallest mountains, things that would normally have fascinated him, but the way his brother sometimes watched Maggie's moves grated on him. Like a hawk on a tree limb watching a mouse across the meadow.

From Maggie's sometimes nervous movements, she noticed it too. As soon as the meal was over, she piled the dishes in the washing kettle and bade them good-night before she slipped out the door. She normally stayed in the cabin after their meal and talked while he mended or cleaned or sharpened something. She would clean the cabin or prepare food for the morning. He'd even unearthed Maman's old sewing kit a few days prior, and she'd patched his clothing. It had all been so...

Companionable. Comfortable. In every way the opposite of lonely.

"Where is your mind, my brother." Henri jerked his chin toward the door. "As if I must ask."

"It has been a long day. I worked a field for the Ottawa

women to plant." He stretched, his back cracking with the pull of his tired muscles. "Pontiac asked us to do this in exchange for leaving our oxen alone."

Henri's dark brows drew together. "What do our friends"— he poked a thumb to the north—"think of Mademoiselle Kerr?"

"They do not know."

Henri leaned forward in his chair, the one Baptiste had recently repaired. "How long do you think you can keep her a secret?"

"As long as I must."

With a snort, Henri sat back. "No man can keep a beautiful woman a secret for long."

No doubt his brother was right, but what choice had he?

"I am only sorry that I came and interrupted you." He glanced at the neatly made bed that had been their parents'. "I see you are not sleeping in the loft."

"I haven't since you left."

"Non. This bed is much wider."

Baptiste pushed to his feet and crossed to the other side of the cabin, plunging a dipper in the water bucket and draining it. He hung the dipper up, then faced Henri and gripped the edge of the table.

"It is not like that between us."

"Non?"

"Non." Not yet. And now maybe not ever. "She stays in the barn loft during the day and prowls the forest at night."

"I have not prowled a forest in a while, perhaps I—"

"Non." Baptiste tightened his grip on the table, keeping it between them. Otherwise, he might give in to the temptation to knock that knowing look off his brother's face. "She is a good woman. She needed my help—not my bed."

"If I were you, I would have given her both."

Baptiste ground his teeth together.

"But I am not you." Henri shrugged. "And by the thunder-cloud on your face, I think we should speak of something else, non?"

"I am glad you are home." He was, if not happy about the timing. "Things are very tense here."

"So I gathered." He glanced in the direction of the barn and then shrugged. "We were stopped three times on our way up the river. Even Dances Away grew concerned after the second time. Potawatomi, Huron, Ottawa, all joined—"

"And the Ojibwe."

The air whistled through Henri's teeth. "That is not good for the fort."

"It is not good for you and me either. Not for any of the Frenchmen."

"They do not bother you, surely. The Ottawa and the French are brothers."

Baptiste snorted, released the table, and sank onto one of the benches. "We met with Pontiac two days ago, with Moran as our spokesman."

His brother let out another low whistle.

"The warriors come to the farmers and threaten them if food is not given, as well as powder and shot. And if it is not given quickly, they have killed and taken livestock."

Henri dropped his head against the back of the chair. "Perhaps I have returned just in time. I will go to the village tomorrow and see what I can learn from Dances Away."

"Then we should sleep while we can. You take the bed, I will sleep on the floor."

"I would not know what to do in a bed after all this time." Henri flashed him a grin. "And your little housemaid has kept the floor so clean, it will spoil me for sleeping on the ground again."

His little housemaid. Perhaps that was all she would ever be to him now.

WITH THE MOON STILL A SLIVER IN THE SKY, DARKNESS reigned beneath the tall trees, hindering Maggie's search for edibles. The darkness matched her thoughts. Baptiste's brother was nothing like him, but his arrival explained the second canoe paddle. While Baptiste was quiet and thoughtful, his brother was brash and boastful. That they were brothers, no one could doubt. The same dark eyes and hair, the same burnished skin. The same shape of their nose and chins. But looks were not everything.

There was something in the younger man that bothered her. Something in his eyes, his bearing, his... She paused, one hand on a tree trunk. Baptiste's brother was too like the warriors of Teata's tribe.

He was a hunter.

Baptiste was a farmer, a man of the soil. He grew things, tended things. He was a strong man in a completely different way. A way that made Maggie feel safe.

Made her feel at home. A sensation she hadn't experienced in seven years.

It was more than just the cabin, so like the one she'd lived in before the Indian threat had driven them to Fort McCord. It was more than the safety of the dark barn. It was... She pressed her back against a thick tree trunk.

It was Baptiste.

But the brother being there, it would change things. Perhaps not for the better.

And yet, she was happy for Baptiste, maybe even a little envious. If she could see Reggie once more, or little Donald—who would not be so little anymore. And Catherine. Maggie blinked back the mistiness. She would give much for a day with any of them.

She would not begrudge Baptiste his brother.

But neither would she turn her back to him.

———

WHEN HE HAD THE OXEN MOVED INTO THE CORRAL, Baptiste swiped the sweat from his brow and headed for the cabin. He'd finished working the second field for the Indian women. A dozen of them had been in the first field, planting and talking and watching him work. Several bursts of laughter had rubbed him wrong, always feeling as if they were laughing at him, at his stumbling walk.

He was glad to be home.

The cabin was empty. Maggie hadn't started supper yet. It was a little early. He grabbed a fresh set of clothing—an old set she'd unearthed from his trunk and mended for him—and went to the river to wash. The day was very warm for late May, and the cold water felt good. He scrubbed with sand, then did his best to untangle his hair. It needed cutting.

Perhaps Maggie would do that for him. He'd sharpen Maman's old scissors in the evening. If she didn't volunteer, he'd ask her. It wouldn't be hard, not like the other question he'd never gotten past his lips.

Aggravated—at himself—he dove beneath the water and came up with a shake, spraying droplets far and wide.

"So it is not just your cabin that you keep so clean these days."

Walking Fire Stick sat on Baptiste's rock.

"Non." He slapped his chest with wet hands. "It is good to keep me clean as well. You should try it, my friend."

"Do you say to me that I smell bad?"

Baptiste laughed. "How could I say what you have already said?"

The Ottawa stripped and walked into the river. He reached the drop-off and then disappeared, only to rise again and blow a mouthful of water into the air.

"It is good, oui?"

Walking Fire Stick grinned back. "It is a long time since we swam together."

"Too long." Baptiste sobered. "We must not let this war come between us. Not between you and me."

Walking Fire Stick grunted, looked away, and then shook his head, droplets flying from his hair. "This I would not like."

"Nor I."

"But Pontiac, he has big ideas." The other man met Baptiste's eyes, something akin to unease lurked in the depths of his.

Baptiste shrugged. "Not all big ideas are good, and not all are bad. Time will tell."

"Time." The Ottawa looked to the sky and spoke to the setting sun. "And more than time." He grinned at Baptiste. "Friendship." Then he smacked the water, sending spray everywhere. "And our brothers have returned."

"Oui. As we wished. But I do not know where my brother is now. As soon as I said I have a field to work, poof, he vanishes."

Walking Fire Stick laughed, smacking the water again. "That is Henri. But I know where he is."

"Oh?"

"He came to our village early. He and Dances Away have told their story many times already." His brows drew together. "Pontiac was impressed. He asked Henri if he would join our fight."

Join with the Indians against the fort? But of course, Henri had never given his oath to the British, and Pontiac would know that. That was the reason—or one of the reasons—he'd left with Dances Away.

Would Henri's return be a safeguard for Baptiste and the farm? Or would it plunge him into the middle of the war?

———————

SHADOWS WERE LENGTHENING AS BAPTISTE RETURNED to the cabin. He and Walking Fire Stick had swum for a long time and lingered on the riverbank even longer. They had not talked of the fort or the British or the raids on the French farms. It was as if both of them needed a break from the war that surrounded them. As if they needed to step back into a more secure time.

And that worried Baptiste.

Twice it had been on the tip of his tongue to ask questions, and twice he had swallowed them down. Not asking wouldn't make things better, but for this one evening, it was good to enjoy the company of his friend.

While they still could.

A curl of smoke lifted from the chimney, and he hastened his step, thankful that Walking Fire Stick had made no move to join him for supper. He pushed open the door, and the scent of roasting meat greeted him. Roasting meat and a lovely woman bent over his fire. A rabbit hung in the hearth, a drop of moisture dripping and spitting onto the coals below.

Maggie flashed him a smile, her hair curling away from her braid's attempt to hold it. She pushed the curls from her forehead with the back of her wrist.

"A rabbit?"

She straightened. "I set your snares last evening, but only one proved worthy."

"A welcome change from fish."

"I have always liked fish." She wrinkled her nose. "But not for days and days on end."

A sense of peace and wholeness settled on him. "I agree. But you did bring down that turkey."

"Which your brother ate his way through before it had time to cool."

Baptiste laughed.

She cocked her head. "You are different tonight. Is it because your brother returned at last?"

Was it? "Partly. And also because I had a long swim with Walking Fire Stick. A good swim. A good talk."

"Of the war?" She stiffened.

"Non. Of everything else." He shrugged. How to explain that to her? "Like old times."

She blinked. "Oui. Your brother's return had me thinking of my brothers and sister last night." Then her smile returned. "Of old times."

"Bonjour!" Henri's voice boomed from outside a few moments before he burst through the door. "I have returned."

"As we can see." Baptiste shook his head. Henri could be so dramatic. Then he paused. Was his brother giving warning of his arrival in case... Baptiste closed his eyes rather than glance at the bed.

Henri didn't believe him about Maggie.

Maybe that was a good thing. Maybe it would keep Henri away from the woman who had worked her way into his heart. He rubbed his chest.

"Something smells wonderful." With an exaggerated sniff, Henri pulled in a long breath and huffed it back out. "Rabbit. My favorite."

"How can you be hungry?"

Henri raised a brow.

"Were you not storytelling all day, sustained with what the Ottawa women shared to keep you talking?"

"Ah. You have heard." Henri grinned, that bad-boy grin that had always melted Maman's temper. "But there was no rabbit in the village."

"Sit." Maggie gestured to the table. "It is ready."

Baptiste sat, a little startled when Henri joined him on the bench, leaving the other for Maggie. Baptiste sniffed. "My brother, perhaps tomorrow you can find time for a swim in the river."

Henri tugged his shirt away from his body and sniffed, pulling a comical face. "Not a bad idea."

Maggie turned away, but not before Baptiste saw her lips twitch. She removed the rabbit from its hook, tore it into parts, then ladled boiled peas and some type of greens onto each plate along with a section of meat, and set them on the table before hesitantly taking her seat.

Her years of standing to the side while Stone Foot ate, and only then eating what was left, had been deeply ingrained in her. It had taken some coaxing for Baptiste to convince her to eat at the table with him, even though she'd admitted to doing so with the doctor and his wife who had taken her in at the fort. Perhaps because there she hadn't been the only woman.

He ripped off a bite of meat, the flavor occupying him for a moment. If nothing else, the Hurons had taught her how to cook. He swallowed before asking his brother, "What did you learn in the village?"

"That my brother is still respected among the Ottawa." Henri tipped his head, looking from Baptiste to Maggie and back again. "But only among the Ottawa."

He'd assumed as much. The other tribes didn't know him. Not much, anyway. He recognized some of the Hurons to his south, but they were a prickly bunch at best.

"The fort, she is in trouble." He rolled his eyes. "To hear the Ojibwe speak, they will march in and take it without a fight. Pompous bunch. But they are willing to take direction from Pontiac. For now."

"The fort has defenses, if not as many men." Baptiste rubbed his chin. "There are cannons, small, but large enough to kill many warriors with a single shot if they get too close. There are guns on the boats as well. They protect the fort from the river side."

"One of the boats has left, Pontiac assumes to go for help. But the Potawatomi now watch the river." Henri pressed a fist to his chest and belched. "It will not return without a fight."

"If it returns with soldiers and cannon, the fight might be over quickly."

"Let us hope so, for you were right. The warriors have already returned to the farms demanding food and taking livestock."

Baptiste bit back a curse. So much for talking to Pontiac. So much for the chief's smooth voice and charming words. They'd spent a useless day meeting with him.

"There is something else. Fort Sandusky is no more." Henri made a slashing motion with one hand. "The Hurons have burned it to the ground and killed the soldiers there. They returned today with many scalps."

Maggie set her spoon beside her plate, her face pale in the light of the fireplace.

"You might like to know"—Henri waved a rabbit bone toward Maggie—"that Chief Teata's Hurons have withdrawn. Pontiac is not pleased. Not pleased at all."

Maggie stiffened. "All of them?" Even her voice was tight.

Henri shrugged. "Some remain with Takay, the young warriors, the hotheads."

Maggie's eyes met Baptiste's and clouded. The man who

wanted her for a wife, the cruel one she feared—he would be one to stay. Would still be a threat.

Without thinking, Baptiste put his hand over hers on the table and squeezed. "He does not know you are here."

Henri sat back, eyes flicking from their joined hands to Maggie and then to Baptiste. "What have you not told me, brother?"

Baptiste gestured to Maggie. She looked at her almost untouched plate and spoke softly, telling Henri of Tree Sleeper.

Henri whistled between his teeth, then shoveled in a spoonful of peas. He chewed, looking from Maggie to Baptiste. After he swallowed, he pointed his spoon back and forth between them. "You two should marry."

The words hit Baptiste like a punch.

Chapter 17

"You two should marry."

Maggie hadn't been able to digest all the news Baptiste's brother had spewed before he said those words. Words that sent a tremble through her. It wasn't a bad sort of tremble, however. She'd grown fond of Baptiste. Perhaps more than fond. And the way they had been living had touched something deep inside her. Something she hadn't even known she'd been missing.

The sense of family.

"What are you saying?" Baptiste found his tongue before she found hers. "Did you not just tell us that war is happening all around us? That, in essence, we are not safe?"

"I did. But you would be safer together, I think." The other man thumbed his own chest. "This is how I see it. If she were your wife, there is little this Tree Sleeper could do to separate you, non?"

"He could kill me." Baptiste squeezed her hand, still under his warmth on the table. "He could kill Maggie."

"He will kill me, whether or not we are married." The words slipped out before she thought about them. It was true. Her days on earth would be short and brutal once Tree Sleeper discovered her. "And he will kill you too, if you marry me." She looked into the fire, away from those expressive dark eyes. "He may even kill you if you don't."

Henri slapped his hand on the table. "That settles it then. You have nothing to lose."

"This is no time for your humor," Baptiste snapped.

With raised hands, his brother said, "I mean my words not as humor, but as truth." He leaned forward, dropping his voice. "And you forget, my brother, that you have me nearby now. This Tree Sleeper, he has met his match in Henri Geroux."

Maggie shook her head. "You do not know him."

"I do not need to. Have I not survived the west? Do you think the Indians out there tame as hound dogs? They are not. I have earned the right to boast of my skills." His face hardened for a moment, then the grin returned. "I do not fear this Huron who hunts you. Perhaps I will hunt him."

When Henri Geroux met her eyes, there was in them something that disturbed her again. She did not trust this one, not like she trusted Baptiste. But maybe it was because he had the same ruthlessness as Tree Sleeper.

She shivered.

"You frighten her." Baptiste glowered at his brother.

"Good. Then she will see the wisdom of my words. You should marry soon."

"Père Potier," she said, drawing the attention of both men— Baptiste's startled expression and his brother's knowing smirk. "He is the Jesuit who lives in Teata's village and holds much honor. The leaders look to him for wisdom. He tried to keep the village out of Pontiac's war and would have succeeded had not Pontiac threatened to kill the warriors if they did not agree to join him." She looked at one and then the other. "He knows me."

The Jesuit has always been kind to Maggie. Had looked on

her with favor. Perhaps he'd even steer Tree Sleeper away from the farm. It was worth the chance.

"I could fetch him. Bring him here." The brother nodded, tapping the side of his nose. "Swear him to secrecy. If there is anyone I would trust with a secret, it is one of the Jesuits."

Baptiste's eyes burned with something she couldn't define, but it stirred an answering response inside her. It was not unpleasant, but it was not comfortable either. If she did this, she would belong to this man she knew little of. But what she knew, she trusted.

For the first time since Fort McCord, Maggie Kerr trusted someone other than herself.

FOR THE THIRD TIME IN HALF AN HOUR, BAPTISTE crossed to the window. Rain dripped off the roof, the deep overhang keeping it from the window opening, even when the wind lashed off the river and slapped the logs of the cabin. He glanced at the barn, part of him sorry that he'd mended the roof. Maggie slept there in the loft, high and dry.

Or did she sleep at all? Was her mind in half the turmoil his was?

"You will wear out the floor from walking, or the barn from staring. Go and talk to the woman." Henri sprawled in a chair, cleaning his fingernails with the point of his knife.

"It is not that simple."

"Of course it is. She is a beautiful woman. You are a handsome man. There is no reason for you not to marry. Go and tell her this."

Baptiste growled in the back of his throat. What did Henri know about marriage? For that matter, what did Baptiste?

Maggie would marry him for her safety, oui, but was there anything else between them? On her part?

On his, he had no doubt.

"Go. Speak with her." Henri grinned. "I will not disturb you, have no fear. Just bring her back in time to cook supper." He tapped his middle. "I have not eaten so well in years. For that alone, you should marry the woman."

"Maggie." Baptiste gazed out the window again. "Her name is Maggie."

"Oui, and when you make her my sister, I shall call her that. So make haste. I can fetch the Jesuit tomorrow. I would have brought him today, but it is Sunday."

"Is it?" How did Henri know what day of the week it was when Baptiste never did?

"Did you not hear the bell toll from the fort?"

Had he? Probably. But he didn't pay attention.

"I will talk to her."

"About time."

He passed his brother's chair and resisted the urge to slap the man on the back of the head. But as aggravating as Henri could be, he was often right. And even if he weren't this time, he was pushing Baptiste in the direction he wanted to go.

Jamming on his hat, he limped out into the storm.

The barn wasn't far from the cabin, but he was soaked through by the time he wrenched open the door and entered.

"Maggie?"

"Oui." She peeked from the loft above him. "What is wrong?"

"Nothing." He hoped. "We need to talk."

She pulled back from the edge, and then her feet appeared on the ladder. She climbed down wearing the deerskin dress, which left bare a whole lot of her legs. He remembered seeing her in the fort the day after he'd delivered her, in all the finery British women wore. The sight had stolen his breath. But here, in his barn, dressed as a Huron, she was no less breathtaking.

He cleared his throat and tore his eyes away from her sleep-warmed face and disheveled hair. "We should decide."

"Oui." She laced her fingers at her waist. "We should."

Now what? The silence stretched, not a comfortable silence. He needed to speak first, but what to say? Then, as if a lightning bolt split the room, he knew. Just ask the question that had rattled in his head for days.

"Will you marry me, Maggie Kerr?"

Her lips trembled, half-smiled, then firmed, her knuckles white at her waist. "Why?"

"Why?"

She wasn't supposed to ask that. She was supposed to say *oui* or *non*. Didn't she know how this worked either? But how could she, when she'd been so long with the Hurons? What a dolt he was. As little as he knew about marriage—a traditional French marriage—she probably knew less.

"That is a good question." He fumbled for time to come up with the right answer, the answer that would end with her agreeing to marry him. "For your safety. Of course."

Something flashed across her eyes. Doubt? Anger? Disappointment? Something not positive.

He swallowed but his mouth was too dry to accomplish much. "But also because I have come to like you here." He gestured around them. "Not here in my barn, but here"—he tapped his chest—"in my life."

The rosy hue that so fascinated him crept to her cheeks, lessening the darkness of her freckles. It brought a sense of relief. He must have said something right. But she remained mute. Should he say something more? Or wait? Or walk back to the cabin and give her time to consider?

Maggie moved, which startled him, as tense as he was at the

moment. She walked to the oxen's pen and ran her fingers down Pierre's face. The ox closed its eyes and leaned into her touch.

He envied the stupid beast.

* * *

How could Maggie's life have changed so much in the past month? Had it only been that long? It seemed a lifetime. Yet judging by last night's moon, that was how long since she'd fled Teata's village, fled from Stone Foot and his plans to marry her to Tree Sleeper. Ran rather than be given to a man not of her choosing. A man she loathed. A man she feared.

She didn't fear Baptiste.

He created other feelings, some pleasant, some disturbing, but none of them fearful. And she trusted him. Last evening, after she'd slipped away from the cabin and the brothers with their dark good looks and flashing tempers, she'd spent hours examining her feelings toward Baptiste. Marveling that, in such a short period of time, she'd learned to trust again.

On the heels of that, thoughts of her parents had followed her into the night. The parents who had never come for her. She'd done as she'd been told. She'd stayed strong—stayed alive even when other captives hadn't—but they'd not come.

No one had come.

Twisting her fingers in the longer hairs at the top of Pierre's head, she glanced over her shoulder.

Baptiste waited, tension lines around his eyes and mouth, legs braced and body stiff. Did he expect her to reject him?

Would she?

She turned and leaned against the gate to the oxen's pen. "Tree Sleeper will kill you if you take me for your wife."

He crossed his arms. "He may try."

"He will. If he learns that you have allowed me to stay here, he will kill you, whether you take me for your wife or not. He is evil." It hit her—hard—that she didn't want anything to happen to this quiet, handsome man. The man who had taken her across the river simply because she'd asked.

"Henri is here now. Although he boasts much, I would wish for none other beside me in a fight."

If it were a fair fight, perhaps. Tree Sleeper, however, would not attack until he knew he had the advantage. There was no way he'd returned to the village with Chief Teata. He was out there, she had no doubts about that, if not for the battle, then to find her.

"Perhaps it is best if I leave." Even as she said the words, she knew she didn't want to go.

In three steps, he was in front of her, strong hands encircling her upper arms. But not trapping her. Even without trying, she knew he would release her if she wished. Perhaps it was that knowledge that took away any such wish.

"I cannot let you. The danger is too great."

"I am used to taking care of myself."

He leaned over her, and yet she still didn't feel trapped. His forehead pressed against hers. His nose inches from her own. His breath warm across her face. "I do not wish you to leave."

She searched for the right words. He must understand. "Even if it could save your life?"

"Even then." His words were more breath than voice, tightening something deep within her. Something that responded to the words' intensity in a way she didn't understand and couldn't ignore.

"I could not be the cause of your death."

He snorted, a short puff of air that was half-laugh and half-dismissal. "Will any of us survive the war brewing around us?"

Maggie had seen too much in her years with the Hurons to dismiss his question. Life was sometimes very short. Sometimes it ended badly. Did she wish to have it end without knowing more about this man? Did she wish to die without...

It took almost nothing to bring her lips to his.

The explosion of feeling that followed, however, rocked her. Warmth and excitement and need filled her, blocking out everything else. His lips moved against hers, and hers parted, somewhat in surprise and somewhat by instinct.

He slid his hands behind her, pressing her closer. She splayed her fingers across his chest, moving them to his shoulders, and finally tangling them in the length of his hair. He groaned, a low sound she felt as much as heard.

Then she was smacked in the middle of her back, driven hard against Baptiste. He staggered, catching his balance and steadying her.

Maggie turned. Pierre shook his head, fuzzy red ears flapping, and then snorted. She giggled, pressing her fingers against her tingling lips.

Baptiste scowled at the ox and drew her around to his side, one arm securing her there. "And you, Monsieur LeBoeuf, must learn to behave. That is no way to treat the lady of the house."

The lady of the house. She liked the sound of that.

Then Baptiste looked at her again, his dark eyes smoldering with emotion. "The lady who will soon be my wife, non?"

"Oui."

Because she wanted to know more of this man before her. She wanted to live with him as his wife for whatever time they had left.

BAPTISTE TRIED FOR THE THIRD TIME TO TIE THE wrinkled cravat at his neck. It smelled of age and disuse, but he wanted to present himself as best he could for his wedding.

His wedding.

Henri had left before daylight to fetch the Jesuit, the holy man having stayed at Chief Takay's village when Chief Teata's people had withdrawn. Henri knew this from the gossip in the Ottawa village. Likely the Jesuit thought he could sway the other Huron chief away from war, as he'd swayed Teata. But the two chiefs were nothing alike, and it was doubtful he'd have any influence at all.

At the moment, Baptiste couldn't worry about that. At the moment, he simply wished to tie the blasted strip of cloth around his neck.

With a groan, he ripped it off again and flung it onto the bed.

The door opened.

Maggie stepped inside and closed it behind her.

His mouth dried.

She held out her arms and turned in a circle. "Will I do?" Wearing a British gown adorned with lace and gathered in folds that hugged her in all the right places and exposed others just enough to hint at the curves beneath, oui, she would do nicely.

He worked a little moisture back across his tongue. "You are beautiful."

Her freckles dimmed behind her blush.

Baptiste retrieved the cravat, even more determined to make it work after seeing his bride in all her loveliness.

His bride.

Could a man die from the sheer wonder of how his life had changed? He wasn't sure, but it didn't seem too far-fetched at the moment. He fumbled the cloth into the best knot he could manage with hands that were no longer steady.

He couldn't remember being this nervous before in his life. Ever. Perhaps it was a sign that he—they—were doing the wrong thing. But then she crossed the room, the dress swishing around her. She reached up and fussed with his cravat, brows pulled together in concentration, then stepped back and smiled.

He had no idea what it looked like, but if she was happy, that was all that mattered.

Taking her hands in his, he marveled at their delicacy and strength, that this dainty woman had survived everything she'd been through. That beneath the delicate appearance, she was a spitfire. That she would soon be his. "Henri will return soon."

She nodded.

He cleared his throat. "Are you sure?"

She nodded again. Was her throat as dry as his? Her tongue as thick? Her fingers trembled, and he squeezed them, oddly pleased that he wasn't the only one nervous. There was no fear in her eyes, which swelled his chest with a pride he probably hadn't earned. But it still felt good.

"As am I." He might not have been moments before, but with her in front of him, he couldn't imagine ever letting her go. He would die to protect her, if need be.

A very real possibility.

"Bonjour!" Henri's call reached them.

They turned together to face the door and there was a right-ness, an almost preordained certainty, that made Baptiste stand a little taller as his brother and the Jesuit entered the cabin.

To forever bond him to the woman at his side.

Chapter 18

T he memories of before her capture had been returning since she'd fled the Huron village, and Maggie could vaguely picture a wedding in a church before Da had moved them to the frontier. The pretty dress of the bride she remembered the most, which had prompted her to put on the nicer of the two Mrs. Roberts had sent her out of the fort with.

Baptiste's reaction had confirmed she'd done right.

The wedding itself, however, had been a mystery, both the one from her memory and their own that morning. Père Potier had spoken in a language she hadn't understood. He bade them to kneel and to stand and told them when to agree with his words about marriage. And then after what seemed like hours, the thing was done, Maggie being no wiser to most of what had been said or what it all meant.

Other than she now belonged to Baptiste.

Père Potier had recognized her from the start, she was sure, but he'd not balked at performing the ritual. She glanced over her shoulder from where she knelt by the hearth to prepare the midday meal. The Jesuit spoke in urgent tones to both brothers. They spoke in French, but quietly and rapidly, not something Maggie could follow from where she worked. She poked the venison haunch, happy that Henri had returned with both the Jesuit and the deer slung across his shoulders. Breathing deeply of the tantalizing scent, she closed her eyes for a moment and let her thoughts drift back to Baptiste.

Her husband.

"Are you cooking that venison, or teasing us with it?" Henri asked.

Henri, her brother-in-law. A man she didn't know and was still uneasy around, but the man who had brought the Jesuit to the cabin and had pledged to help Baptiste protect her. He was something of a riddle. And he was hungry.

"It is done." She fetched the large pewter platter she'd found under a pile of mismatched dishes on a high shelf while cleaning. In moments, the steaming venison was on the table with stewed greens she'd picked the night before and bread rounds she'd fried while the meat cooked. It was a feast.

A wedding feast.

Talk stopped as Père Potier mumbled a blessing over the food, then the men picked up their conversation, punctuated with pauses to swallow food and gulps of water. Maggie was content to listen, understanding more now that they were close. War talk, of course. None of it good.

Then the Jesuit turned to her. "Tree Sleeper stays in Chief Takay's village."

Even though she'd known he would, her stomach rebelled against what she'd swallowed, and she pushed her plate away.

"He will not learn from me that you are here, but I beseech you, my child, to return to the fort."

"Non." He couldn't understand the fear that her single word held. The fear of being trapped again. The fear of being stolen again or burned. Death itself did not hold as much fear for her as that.

"You would be safer there among your own people."

"Baptiste and Henri are my people." She met her husband's intent gaze. "We are family now."

"Family, oui, but it does not change you from being British, my child." There was a sad finality to the holy man's eyes that struck an uneasy chord inside her. "Sometimes family cannot protect you."

Nobody knew that better than Maggie.

PÈRE POTIER WAS PREPARING TO WALK BACK TO THE Huron village on the river, disclaiming any need for Henri to escort him, when the boom of a cannon silenced their good-byes.

Baptiste tensed. The four of them stood on the porch as distant screams carried on the wind. Then a second cannon blast. More screams.

He knew those screams.

War screams from the throats of Indians on the attack.

Not the start to their marriage that Baptiste would have chosen.

"Père Potier, it might be wise for you to stay a while longer." Henri moved as if to shepherd him and Maggie both back into the cabin. "Wait here while Baptiste and I scout out what is happening."

Maggie stepped forward. "I am going with you."

"Non." The word slipped out harsher than Baptiste had intended. He took her by the shoulders, her eyes large and troubled as she searched his face. "In that dress, you would be seen from a mile away."

Her lips gathered in an intriguing way—if not for the thundercloud brewing between her brows.

"My wife." He enjoyed the feel of the words as he spoke them. "Stay here while my brother and I see what is happening."

He more than half expected her to balk, but she finally nodded. "I will change while you are gone. In case..."

In case they needed to run.

But to where?

A glance at Henri showed that all traces of humor had been erased in the hard lines of his brother's face. Henri needed no paint to be what he was. A warrior. A Frenchman by birth, but as wild as any of their Ottawa neighbors. And as skilled.

As deadly.

Maggie and the Jesuit retreated inside the cabin, leaving the door open.

"Come." Baptiste stepped off the porch and made for the cover of the trees, the yells and screams not relenting. They stopped near where he dropped the fish trap, letting the overhang of limbs shield them from downriver. He sucked in a breath as Henri breathed out a curse.

Barges. Many of them.

One barge had made it over to the sloop tied at the front of the fort. The rest were in a line on the opposite bank, Indians jumping off and securing the vessels. Vessels that would be loaded with supplies meant for the fort. Powder. Shot. Food.

Now in Pontiac's hands.

The soldiers were bound and being dragged from the barges. Baptiste couldn't let himself dwell on them. They would not survive. At least, most of them would not.

Henri nudged his arm, motioning them to move back. They stopped when they were halfway back to the cabin.

"This is bad." Henri shook his head. "Very bad."

Baptiste pinched the bridge of his nose, closing his eyes. "This I know."

"I believe Père Potier is right. Maggie must go to the fort

now." He clamped a hand on Baptiste's shoulder. "And you must go with her."

Baptiste jerked his head up. "I cannot leave. My oxen—"

"Will most likely be killed whether you are here or not. But if you are in the fort, you have a better chance of surviving."

"I am a Frenchman—"

"In the past, that was enough." Henri shrugged. "Now, I do not think it will matter much." He lifted his chin in the direction of the river. "You and I both know what will be on those barges."

"Powder and shot. Food."

"Rum." The word hung between them in the damp forest air, a cloud of gnats buzzing through it.

Nothing made the warriors as crazy as rum. As unpredictable. Or as dangerous.

"How? When?"

"Go back to the cabin and secret yourself and your bride away. Tell the Jesuit to go back through the forest, not by the river. I will watch the Ottawas, and when they are good and drunk, I will return and take you across the river. Then I will bring your canoe back and leave it where you always do. It will look as if you have stayed on this side."

"What about you?"

Henri grinned, a feral look in the dappled light through the trees. "I will survive. I always do."

"You will be in danger."

Henri shrugged. "This I am used to, and besides, I am closer to our Ottawa neighbors than most. I do not think they will harm me. I will not support the British, nor will I tell them where you are." He turned to leave.

Baptiste grabbed his arm. "In the southeast corner of the wheat there is an oval stone the size of my fist. Buried underneath is my powder and shot. You may have need of it."

"Very wise of you. I should have known you were not taken by surprise." Henri, face even more grim than before, led the way back to the cabin.

Baptiste couldn't help but wonder if he and Maggie would ever come this way again. Two days ago, leaving his farm would have been out of the question. But two days ago...

Baptiste hadn't had a wife.

MAGGIE PUSHED THE GATE INTO PLACE, THEN STUCK several more branches into its rough structure. She stepped back and dusted off her hands. It would serve. It would have to. She leaned the yoke against the inside of the gate and hurried back to the cabin. The men might have returned by now, and Baptiste would be worried.

Furious, probably.

A sound reached her. The slightest scuff against the ground. Maggie pressed further into the concealing roots of the upturned cedar, then moved nothing but her eyes, wishing she'd taken the time to darken her hands and face with mud. Her best chance to remain unseen was to stay completely still. She hoped. Time stretched into more time, and still, she didn't move. Another sound. Closer. Maggie barely breathed.

An animal would make more sound, so it must be a man. But who would be here in the forest when a battle raged at the river? Who would avoid the fight?

Time passed without another sound, and Maggie was almost ready to move when a man stepped into the deer path not a stone's throw from her. She knew that profile. Only years of discipline kept the gasp from rising in her throat.

Tree Sleeper.

Of all the warriors to miss out on the fight, she'd not have expected him. Then a cold shiver worked its way across her skin, the hairs of her forearms lifting. Père Potier had come from Takay's village. Tree Sleeper had been there. The warrior wasn't looking for her, he was looking for the Jesuit. Why? What about the Jesuit had pulled Tree Sleeper away from the fight?

Something evil.

Tree Sleeper was coming from the north, away from the cabin. Had he been there?

Another shock of cold drenched her.

Had he found Baptiste and Henri there? Père Potier had left soon after them, not returning to Takay's village but heading north to Pontiac's. The holy man thought he might be of use. Might be a voice of reason.

As if there were any reason in war.

Shouts echoed through the trees, bouncing off branches and trunks with little clue to their origins. But Tree Sleeper snapped his head up, face turned toward the river. In a flash of movement without sound, he was gone.

Trusting he wouldn't return—hoping that he wouldn't—Maggie ran as soundlessly as possible for the cabin. Raised voices met her before she reached it, and she slowed and listened. No doubt now that they came from the river. And they were coming closer. She dashed the last few rods and slipped inside.

Across the threshold, Henri had a knife raised in his fist, but he lowered it with a grunt. "That was foolish."

"Where have you been?"

"Men are approaching." She and Baptiste spoke over each other.

"Where is Père Potier?" Henri asked.

"He is gone, headed to Pontiac's village shortly after you left. He thought he might be useful there."

Henri muttered something in rapid French and shook his head.

Baptiste crossed his arms. "Where have you been?" The authority in his voice gave her pause, as did the hardness of his face. Perhaps he and Henri were not so different after all.

"I moved Beau and Pierre to the cedar corral."

Henri turned to her. "The what?"

Baptiste waved his brother silent. "That was foolish. You might have been seen."

"I nearly was."

Baptiste's nostrils flared, an almost savage light entering his eyes. This man she had married, he was more warrior than she'd thought. Instead of repulsing her, it was strangely comforting.

"Tree Sleeper was in the forest. He was coming from the north—not from Takay's village."

"He'd been here?" Henri gripped the knife again.

"The noise from the river turned him away, he went to join them, I think. And they are not far away."

"We must leave." Baptiste said.

"I have packed." She handed him one of the two bundles on the table. "We can wait with Beau and Pierre until things calm down, carry them a supply of hay."

Pain wrinkled across Baptiste's forehead. "They will not survive on their own."

"Show me where they are," Henri said, "and I will look after them the best I can."

Burdened with the clothing and a few other necessities she'd packed, her hatchet in its loop at the waist of her Huron dress, at the last moment, Maggie grabbed the blankets from the bed and wadded them into another bundle. Who knew where or how long they'd be gone? Baptiste and Henri stashed knives and tomahawks at their waists, powder horns and shot bags around their necks. Each man thrust a canoe paddle through the straps across his back, and then took up his gun.

A small army, but not one easily taken down.

There was no time to carry hay to the oxen. The voices at the river were too close. Maggie led the way to the cedar corral, Baptiste a half step behind her, Henri bringing up the rear. Maggie took a slightly different path, not wanting to flatten a trail for some wandering Indian to stumble across.

The voices faded into the distance and only the sighing of the wind through the branches, the buzz of insects, and the occasional song of a bird filled their ears. Even Baptiste, with his lame leg, moved almost silently through the forest. They reached the cedar corral, Baptiste moving the gate aside and entering first.

Red and black faces turned toward them, Pierre ambling over, Beau keeping his distance.

"How did you find this place?" Henri whispered.

"There was a storm some weeks back." Baptiste gestured around them. "It made everything but the gate."

Henri knelt by a small trickling spring at one side. "It even provides water."

"But not much to eat." Maggie placed her bundles at her feet. "They will need hay brought in when you can."

Looking north, Henri mumbled, "When I can." Then he turned back to her and Baptiste. "Stay here. Stay quiet. I will come when the warriors are too full of drink to move." And then he glided away, melting into the forest.

Baptiste kept her hands in his, their warmth spreading through her, giving her courage. Then he pulled her against his chest, pressed her head to him and his chin to her hair.

"This is not what I wished for, but we must go to the fort."

"Oui."

He pushed her away, bending to peer directly into her face. "You agree?"

Was he so surprised? Did he think her completely unreasonable? "Tree Sleeper is near the cabin. It is not safe for me, and it is not safe for you either." Probably the only thing that could have forced her into the fort. She would not see Baptiste killed over her. For herself, she would have continued to take her chances in the forest. But for him…

His sigh moved the hairs around her face. "I was afraid I'd have to knock you in the head and carry you to the fort across my shoulders."

She suppressed a smile. In the midst of one of the most dangerous times of her life, this man could make her smile. The Maggie Kerr of just days ago might not have recognized Maggie Geroux.

Chapter 19

It wasn't the wedding night any man would wish for. Baptiste adjusted his shoulders against the windfall cedar root behind him. Through the roots above his head, he could just make out the stars, but not enough to gauge the time. It had to be well past midnight.

Maggie stirred against his chest, her braid loose, draping over his arm. She gave a sleepy sigh but didn't awaken. Her breathing returned to a deep, steady rhythm. If things had been different...

Beau jerked his head up. He stood like a dark silhouette over Pierre, as if on guard. Then his ears perked, and Baptiste tensed. Perhaps the ox *was* on guard.

Maggie moved, and Baptiste cupped his hand around her mouth. Her eyes met his, and he shook his head, then eased her away, picking up the gun by his side.

She slipped the hatchet from its loop.

They waited.

An owl hooted.

Baptiste put his hand over Maggie's on the hatchet's handle. He grinned at her, then answered the owl with chirp like a tree frog.

"You remembered." Henri's whisper came through the gate moments later.

As if he could forget their childhood signals. "Is it safe?" Baptiste opened the gate while Maggie gathered their belongings.

"As safe as it will ever be." Henri took the bundled blankets and shouldered them. "But we should make haste. Dawn is not far away. The warriors will awaken with fine headaches, but they will awaken."

Maggie touched Henri's sleeve. "Père Potier?"

"He was there. He appealed to Pontiac when the soldiers were…" Henri's words trailed off as his eyes met Baptiste's.

Maggie jerked on his sleeve. "I lived with them for seven years. I know what happened to the soldiers, or at least, I know enough."

"Oui. The Jesuit left hours ago, before the drunkenness took over." Henri's voice carried both sorrow and revulsion.

Oddly enough, Baptiste was gratified to hear it. Père had not drunk anything more intoxicating than wine and small beer. He'd taught his sons that strong drink made men into fools. Henri may be wild, but he hadn't completely turned his back on their upbringing. There was no scent of alcohol on him.

"Let us go." Baptiste led the way this time, straight to his canoe.

All was quiet, but to the east, a light gray misted above the trees. Not dawn. Not yet. But soon.

"Maggie." She turned to him, his wife. It didn't seem real yet, but in some ways, the wedding seemed a year ago instead of less than a day. "Change into your British dress."

"Are you sure?"

"He is sure you do not wish to be shot by a soldier," Henri said, taking the front of the canoe and lifting. "We will give you two minutes and no more."

Baptiste lifted the other end of the canoe, and followed his brother to the river. They'd have a few moments to talk without Maggie listening.

"It was bad, non?" Baptiste asked.

"More than bad."

"All of the soldiers are dead?"

"Non." Henri looked up and down the river, even though they were still screened in by tree limbs. "Most of them. Some were taken off the barges to be slaves. Maybe."

"Did Pontiac and the chiefs also get drunk?"

"Non." Henri kept scanning the river. "He tried to stop it. He broke many barrels and let it spill to the ground. The women helped him, but not soon enough."

Baptiste gripped his brother's arm. "I owe you."

"You are my brother. You owe me nothing."

Maggie appeared beside them, her Huron dress bundled in her hands. His beautiful wife, for whom he would leave his farm, give up everything he'd held dear, and go to live among the British. Largely due to Henri's help.

He owed his brother everything.

MAGGIE KNELT IN THE FRONT OF THE CANOE, paddling steadily.

Henri manned the other paddle in the back, Baptiste in the middle with his gun held at the ready. All three of them stayed silent, paddles dipped as quietly as possible, but the river's current did most of the work, and the distance wasn't far.

The walls of the fort came into view, as did the remaining sloop out front. Baptiste had already decided to approach the vessel, assuming the gates would be guarded outside by the warriors, and inside by the soldiers. Therefore, the easiest way to speak to someone would be to call out to the sloop.

"Lower your weapon and state your business," a soldier onboard demanded.

Maggie answered in English, "We seek refuge. I am British."

"State your name."

"Maggie... Kerr." She glanced at Baptiste with a shrug. After all, no one would know her by her new name. He gave her a brief nod without fully looking at her, his gun low against his thighs, eyes searching the surroundings.

"Who are the men with you?"

"French farmers who have given me safe passage, the brothers Geroux."

A rope ladder was lowered over the side. "Permission to board."

Maggie managed her skirts with one hand and the swaying ladder with the other. Her Huron dress would have made the climb much easier but the welcome less sure. Baptiste came halfway up the ladder, then took the bundles from Henri and tossed them onto the sloop's deck. He finished climbing aboard as Henri turned the canoe and slipped back across the river.

"Hey." One of the soldiers pointed a pistol toward Henri's back. "Where is he going?"

Baptiste stepped in front of the man and his weapon. "He returns to the farm to watch over things."

"Speak English, Frenchie, or I will shoot you."

"I will speak for him." Maggie would have stepped between them, but Baptiste held her at arm's length. "His brother returns to the farm to watch over it. He does not spy for the Indians. Would he have left us here if he did?"

The soldier lowered his weapon. "Not likely."

"Please tell Surgeon and Mrs. Roberts that I am here. They know me as Maggie Kerr."

"Do they now?"

Baptiste stiffened. His English wasn't very good, but he didn't need to know the words to hear the doubt and scorn in the soldier's voice.

"They know me very well. I was a guest of theirs weeks ago."

That made the soldier rub a gloved hand across his jaw. Then he barked at another soldier, hardly more than a boy, and sent him racing to the fort to alert them of Baptiste and Maggie's arrival. Since she'd been gone, the walkway between the sloop and the fort had been walled in, hiding movement from any Indians watching.

They waited in silence except for the river lapping at the belly of the vessel. Dawn crept up the tree line across the river, splashing the sky with vivid pink and orange. Maggie shivered, and Baptiste stepped closer to her, blocking the cool breeze coming off the water. Ignoring the handful of soldiers on the sloop, she leaned back against him, his quick intake of breath not lost in the stillness.

Before she could delve too deeply into what it meant, the young soldier returned, out of breath but still snapping into a smart salute.

"Captain says to bring 'em in."

The soldier who'd hovered nearby, obviously the man in charge aboard the vessel, grunted and pointed to the walkway. "Off with you then." He ordered the boy to accompany them, as if he were too busy and too important for such a task.

Maybe he was.

After all, it was men like him she would be counting on for her safety until the hostilities came to an end. Whenever that would be. Maggie picked up her bundles, Baptiste did the same, and they followed the boy. So different from the last time she'd approached. For one thing, she came with arms full of belongings.

And a husband.

How was she to explain that to Mrs. Roberts?

THE SPARSELY FURNISHED ROOM LOOKED THE SAME to Baptiste. The same maps on the walls. The same scarred desk behind which sat the same white-wigged officer, Major Henry Gladwin. But this time, instead of grilling Maggie with questions, the major's eyes bore holes through Baptiste, as if he could ferret out secrets even Baptiste himself didn't know.

Since he'd tossed in his lot with the British, it would serve Baptiste no good to withhold any information. He relayed what he knew about the tribes involved and their locations. He even went into detail about the Frenchmen meeting with Pontiac. Maggie interpreted when he ran out of English words. But it was apparent that he didn't know enough to be useful to the major. He had done what he'd promised the major in the beginning. He'd stayed out of the way, planted his crops, and minded his own business.

"And yet." The major slammed his palm on the desk, papers rippling under the force. "You return Mistress Kerr. How do you explain this?"

Maggie began to interpret, but Baptiste held up a hand. These words he understood. "I did not return Mademoiselle Kerr. I escorted Madam Geroux."

The major's eyebrows threatened to lift his wig. "Is that so?" The man turned to Maggie.

She stood straight, her chin high, and even with her diminutive height, managed to seem as though she was looking down her nose at him. Baptiste suppressed a smirk of pride in her spirit.

"'Tis, indeed." She slipped her fingers around his elbow again, as she'd done on the walk to the fort.

A gesture that did amazing things deep in his chest.

"We were married by Father Potier yesterday morning."

"The Jesuit missionary? He's still alive?"

"Very much so," she said. "And still respected by *some* of the chiefs, at least."

The major grunted, lacing his fingers together on the desktop. "Would that he could bring some sense to them. After yesterday's debacle..." The lines in the major's face deepened, highlighting the dark circles beneath his eyes.

Baptiste cleared his throat. "I am sorry for the loss of your men, sir."

"You are sure there are none to be rescued?" The hope in the major's voice was reedy, so thin one could almost have missed it.

"It is possible some were taken for slaves, but I do not know for certain, or where they would be." He shrugged. "My brother, he witnessed the deaths of those who reached Pontiac's camp."

Another slam of hand to desk. "What good do witnesses do? I need men who can stop this accursed siege. I need men who can return Captain Campbell and Lieutenant MacDougall."

"Do you have such men coming?" Baptiste asked.

The major's eyes narrowed to slits. "I think, Monsieur Geroux, until I know more about you, that it would be good for you to not ask such questions."

Maggie interpreted the words, even though Baptiste had understood enough. Enough to know that the commander of the fort didn't trust him.

Because he was French.

"Maggie!" Mrs. Roberts waited in the street, wrapped in a shawl, with a welcoming smile and open arms.

A lump rose in Maggie's throat as she stepped into the other woman's embrace.

"I cannot begin to tell you how worried I have been." She turned Maggie toward their house. "Come, we will get you settled back in your old room. Then you must tell me where you have been and—" She cut off the flow of words when Maggie pulled back.

"Mrs. Roberts." Maggie gestured to Baptiste, his gun hanging from its strap across his back, arms burdened with most of their worldly possessions. "Do you remember Monsieur Geroux?"

"Of course. You brought Maggie to us the first time. I am so relieved you have returned her. We will take good care not to lose her again."

"We"—Maggie motioned between herself and Baptiste— "need a place to stay."

The older woman paused, looking between the two of them.

"We were married yesterday, by Father Potier."

There was no mistaking the flash of relief behind the smile Mrs. Roberts beamed at them. Perhaps Maggie should have ordered things differently.

"'Tis a different kettle of fish, then. There are several empty houses, left by the French who moved out rather than withstand the siege." She patted Maggie's hand and tugged her in the direction of her house again. "In fact, there is one not far from ours. 'Twill be perfect for the two of you, at least until the owners return. If they return."

Maggie shot Baptiste an apologetic glance and allowed the woman to lead her away. He shrugged in that uniquely French way she was coming to expect and followed. He may be lame in one leg, but he was strong and capable of carrying their bundles.

Mrs. Roberts talked almost non-stop until they reached a single-story cabin made of logs, not unlike Baptiste's cabin on the farm. "I will have Mr. Roberts inform the major that you will be living here. 'Twill not be a problem." She pushed the door open and stepped inside, Maggie following and Baptiste behind.

It wasn't as dirty as Baptiste's cabin had been when she'd arrived, but it wasn't far from it.

"Oh, my. Perhaps we should look at another?" Mrs. Robert's face was a study of apology and chagrin.

Maggie turned to Baptiste. "This will do for us, non?"

"It is fine."

She searched his face and found nothing but honesty there. Of course, since he'd lived in worse, the mess before him may not have seemed unusual. Or perhaps he simply didn't care, as long as they were together. She wasn't sure where that thought came from, but it spread a web of tingling across her skin.

Baptiste hiked one eyebrow.

Maggie turned back to the cabin and reassured Mrs. Roberts that they would be very happy here, and happier still to be close to her and the surgeon.

"I will fetch cleaning supplies and return to help." She scurried away, leaving the door open, a fresh breeze coming in and stirring the dirt on the floor.

"She is coming back, non?" Baptiste asked.

"Oui. She will help me clean."

Baptiste looked around the room then, as if just noticing the dirt. "Then I will leave you to it." He dropped the bundles on a rickety table, that and two crates being the only furniture other than the roped bed frame in the corner. The ropes of which were too frayed for the previous occupants to worry about. "I will see if there is work to be had for a Frenchman."

Work. Of course. Baptiste would need something to do in exchange for food and necessities. She hadn't thought of that.

There would be no hunting here. They would have to rely on what they could barter for or purchase.

"You do that, husband, and I will make ready our home."

Baptiste pulled her close, leaning down until their breaths mingled, until she parted her lips in anticipation. All thoughts fled when their lips met until her heels touched the floorboards again. He steadied her, took a long breath, and pressed his lips to her forehead.

And then he was gone.

But he would return. He wouldn't abandon her. They might be boxed behind the fort walls, but they were together.

They were family.

And somehow, that made the difference.

Chapter 20

T he unaccustomed noise of the fort around the borrowed cabin might have awakened him, had Baptiste been asleep. As he should have been. But how was a man to sleep when such a perfect creature as Maggie lay curled against his side? Her head rested on the hollow of his shoulder as if she'd been made to fit there. Her breath rustled the hairs of his chest.

While he might have chafed at being in the British fort at any other time, at leaving unattended the farm Père had fashioned with his own two hands, at leaving the faithful Beau and Pierre to an uncertain fate, he would do it all again to keep the woman by his side safe.

He would do it all and more.

Just weeks ago, all he'd longed for was the return of Henri and fair weather for a good crop. And then this woman had stepped from the willows and asked for his assistance. He'd thought she'd reeked of trouble. Maybe she did, but it was trouble he was more than willing to join her in. Just to be close to her.

She sighed, her lashes lifting to reveal eyes that odd shade of not quite blue and not quite gray. She blinked, twice. Was she feeling the wonder as he? Did waking next to him mean as much to her as it did to him? He hoped so. Then she shifted, lifting herself to one elbow on the thin pallet she'd put together to cover the rough floor boards of the cabin. The bed she'd made for them.

"Good morning, husband." Her voice was whispery, like a feather across his skin.

"Good morning, wife."

She smiled, and even in the dim light filtering around ill-fitting shutters, her freckles faded behind the pink that washed across her cheeks. She ducked her head, allowing a thick tangle of hair to hide part of her face.

He pushed the hair away, the action bringing back vivid memories of the evening before. Memories echoed in the smoki-ness of her eyes.

"Are you hungry?" she asked. "Mrs. Roberts shared some supplies with us. I could—"

He pressed a finger against her lips, and her eyes rounded, then darkened. He slid his fingers into the hair at the base of her neck and drew her forward. Slowly. Tantalizingly. Enjoying the anticipation on her face and in his veins.

When her lips finally met his, he could not suppress the sound that rose from the depth of him. A sound echoed by Maggie. A sound more beautiful than any music he had ever heard.

Hungry? Oui. For his wife.

THERE WAS ONLY ONE OTHER WOMAN AT THE WELL BY the time Maggie got there. And no wonder, with half the morning gone. Maggie smothered a yawn behind the back of her hand as she approached with her bucket. Then she recognized the blond curls slipping from beneath the bonnet of the woman bent over the stone side of the well.

"Hello, Esther."

The other woman hauled the bucket up, set it on the well's stone side and turned. She broke into a smile. "Maggie! My goodness. Where have you been?"

"I left with the French, as you might know."

Esther nodded, eyes intent on Maggie but without malice or judgment.

"I took refuge in a farmer's barn." She passed the bucket's rope handle from one hand to the other. "And then we married."

Esther's mouth dropped open. "Well, 'tis not what I expected, I assure you. Who is he? How did you meet?" She stepped forward and pulled Maggie into a long hug. "Oh, you must tell me everything."

It was hard not to grin at the other woman's enthusiasm. Esther might be the only one who would have such a reaction. Mrs. Roberts had been tactful—but clear—that others would assume the worst when they learned of her hasty marriage. To a Frenchman, no less.

"His name is Baptiste Geroux."

Esther's smile slipped a bit. "A Frenchman?"

"Indeed. A farmer from across the river." She pointed in the general direction. "I met him first, before I came to the fort. It was he who brought me in his canoe."

"Ah." But the word held more bafflement than understanding. "And you were married?"

"By Father Potier, the Jesuit missionary to the Hurons." Maggie gathered the corner of her bottom lip between her teeth for a moment. How much should she admit to this young woman? They'd hardly been friends, not more than general acquaintances, really.

But something inside Maggie needed a friend. Mrs. Roberts was a dear woman, and one she'd always look up to and respect, but Maggie needed a friend, a confidant. Someone near her own age.

"Would you like to come to our cabin? 'Tis a story that will take some time telling, I'm afraid."

"I would love to."

Esther's lack of hesitation meant more than she could have known to Maggie.

Maggie filled her bucket. They stopped at Esther's house which was on the way and left her buckets there. Esther's house was similar to the Robertses', made of milled boards instead of solid logs. Maggie was a little chagrined when she ushered her new friend into the crude cabin they'd borrowed.

Esther looked around the single room with the loft above, her attention caught by the pallet of blankets on the floor, and then the bed frame with its frayed ropes.

"There are other abandoned French cabins and houses." She turned to Maggie, her smile as cheery and wide as before. "This afternoon, we shall visit them and see what has been left behind. Perhaps there will be some useful things to make you more comfortable here."

Maggie wasn't sure what to say about that. It had seemed presumptuous to move into this cabin at all, but to take from others?

On the other hand, none of them were certain to come out of this conflict alive. They could at least endure it with more comfort. Perhaps even a second bucket.

"Oui." Maggie shook her head. "I mean, indeed. That would be fine." She pointed to the crates set up near the hearth. "Please, have a seat. I have water hot and a few herbs for tea."

"Nothing for me, please. Nothing but your story, that is." Esther sat and folded her hands on her lap.

Where to start? If Esther was to be the friend she hoped for, she should start at the very beginning. At Fort McCord.

The telling took a long time, with Esther stopping her and asking questions throughout. As far as Maggie could tell, the other woman was shocked, but not repelled by what Maggie told her. But Maggie didn't tell the horrific parts. Some things were best left unsaid. Unremembered, if possible.

"My dear, what you have endured—and so young. I cannot imagine that I would have survived at all. I suppose you were fortunate, in a way, to end up with that Stone Foot. At least he treated you as family and not as... well"—Esther's cheeks reddened—"you know."

Maggie hadn't been ignorant of the workings between a man and a woman. Living in a Huron longhouse was far from private. She'd known that Stone Foot had given her a measure of protection. The tribe respected him, his knowledge of healing, his age and spiritual leadership. Because of him, she'd been selected as a bride for Tree Sleeper and not a slave. Although with Tree Sleeper, there wouldn't have been much—if any—difference.

Esther leaned forward and placed her hand on Maggie's knee. "You are a very special woman to have come through all that and then to this." She waved an arm, taking in their surroundings. "And with a husband, no less. I must meet your Monsieur Geroux."

As if summoned by her new friend's words, Baptiste entered the cabin. He stopped when he saw Esther, his face unreadable. Should she have asked him before inviting someone to their borrowed cabin?

"Baptiste." She rose and gestured toward her friend, "This is Mrs. Boggs. We met while I was in the fort before."

Esther stood and bent her knees in that graceful way of greeting that Maggie admired but hadn't quite mastered. "Monsieur Geroux, I am pleased to meet you."

Baptiste bowed. "Your servant, ma'am," he said in almost perfect English. When he straightened, a smile twitched his lips, his eyes seeking Maggie. She'd heard him speak English before, but she had a feeling that he'd done so this time to please her.

And it did.

That he would make the effort for her filled her with pride and something else she couldn't quite name.

"I believe I must be going now." Esther's voice contained a thread of amusement. "I am sure you have things to do. Shall we explore the other houses tomorrow in the forenoon?"

"Oui. That is, indeed." Maggie smiled to cover for her lapse into French. "Tomorrow in the forenoon."

Esther nodded to them both and left, closing the door quietly behind her.

Baptiste removed his hat and hung it on a peg by the door. "Did I interrupt your plans for the day?"

"Only a little." Tomorrow would be soon enough to go scavenging.

He came to her and pulled her into his arms, resting his chin on top of her head. She slid her arms around him, enjoying the sensations his closeness awakened.

"There is news, and it is not good."

She pulled back and looked into his face. "Tell me."

"Chief Wasson from the Saginaw Ojibwe has joined Pontiac."

The name didn't mean anything to Maggie, but the tightness in her husband's eyes did. She swallowed down the fear that threatened to rise again. The fear of being penned up in the fort. Trapped. "How do you know?"

"Three men who had been taken captive escaped. They made it to the fort today and shared the news. One of them is a French trader. The surgeon saw me and asked me to interpret."

"You know enough English to do that?"

He gave that classic French shrug. "Enough for what he say," he said in English, then grinned at her. "I have good news too."

"Oui?"

"The blacksmith needs help. Major Gladwin has charged him with turning every available piece of metal into a weapon. I have been hired to assist him."

"You are also a blacksmith?"

He laughed, the booming sound filling the room. A sound that filled her with imaginings of what their life could be like, if they were given the chance.

"Non, madam, I fear you have wed a simple farmer. He will put me to work doing what I can. And who knows? Maybe he will teach me a few things too." He thumped his palm against his chest. "Your husband, he is trainable."

A month ago, she'd fled from a man she didn't want. A man she'd feared. A man she'd loathed. Risking everything—her very life—to avoid marriage. Never could she have imagined that she'd be standing within the arms of a different man. A man she had first dismissed as a cripple. How foolish and shortsighted. Now, this was the man she wanted to be with.

Her husband.

⸻

"Hey, Frenchie. Come here," called a soldier from the doorway of the smithy.

Baptiste glanced at the blacksmith, who was called Smith. The big man jerked his head toward the door without looking up, the steady clang of his hammer never faltering. Baptiste released the handle of the bellows and approached the soldier. The sun beat down from directly overhead, adding to the heat of the forge and the sweat soaking through his hat.

"Oui?"

"Major Gladwin's orders, all Frenchies to gather at the flag-pole. Get a move on."

"But I have work—"

"When the major says all Frenchies gather"—the soldier jabbed his thumb down the street—"you gather. No questions asked."

The clanging stopped. Smith gave the bellows a few pumps. "You best go and do what he says."

It amazed Baptiste how much the blacksmith heard above the noise he made. For Baptiste, a man reared outdoors, a man used to the quiet of nature, to Baptiste, the constant noise of metal against metal drowned out all other sound.

He removed his hat and wiped away the worst of the sweat, then replaced it and started down the street. Should he go to the cabin first and wash some of the grime away? Should he bring Maggie with him? She was not French, of course, but as his wife, should she not be there? He turned in that direction. If nothing else, she could help translate any words he didn't understand.

The cabin was changed again when he entered. Maggie and her friend had spent the previous day scrounging castoffs from the other abandoned houses and cabins. They'd restrung the bed with strong rope and fashioned a ticking from a pair of blankets filled with what dried grass they'd found. It smelled slightly musty, but it was better than sleeping on the floor. A table sat between the crates they used for seats, and a cup graced the middle of it with three small blue flowers in it. Another table held a mismatched collection of dishes and utensils and a few things he didn't recognize. The cabin had everything—except his wife.

He poured water into a basin she'd found and scrubbed the worst of the sweat and dirt from his face and neck. He'd just finished drying off with an old shirt when Maggie rushed into the room.

"Oh." She stopped. Blinked. "I did not expect you to be here."

"The major has called all the French to the flagpole."

"All the French?" Her eyes narrowed in what he was beginning to recognize as her worried look. "Why?"

"This I will find out. You will come with me, non? You can understand much more." He shrugged.

"Of course."

He cocked his elbow. Her fingers gripped his arm, more tightly than necessary. Why did the major's order worry her? It hadn't worried him. Perhaps it should have. He quickened his pace until he noticed her almost trotting to keep up. It was one thing for her to do that in her Huron dress, but the cumbersome skirts of the British dress didn't allow for such ease of movement, so he slowed.

"I can keep up." Her chin lifted as if daring him to say she couldn't.

"I know." He grinned at her, and the tightness around her eyes lessened. "But I think to myself, why hurry to hear what he has to say? It cannot be that important, or he would be calling everyone, not just the French."

She nodded but shot him a sideways glance that told him she wasn't fooled. He'd married a smart woman. With each day, he learned more about her, and with everything he learned, he realized what a perfect wife she was for him. For a man who'd never considered marriage as an option—and certainly never marriage to a British citizen—it was a heady experience.

There were maybe thirty people milling around the flagpole. Most of the French had left the fort to take their chances outside its walls, trusting that the Indians would remember their friendship and treat them neutrally. As Baptiste had hoped.

Before Maggie.

He nodded to several he recognized but knew none of them well. There were half a dozen women in the group, but they rather pointedly turned their backs on him and Maggie. Baptiste must have stiffened, because Maggie patted his arm.

"Do not let it worry you," she whispered.

Not let it worry him? That his wife was snubbed in such a public way? He opened his mouth to reply but closed it again when Major Gladwin stepped onto the porch of his headquarters. He raised his hands for attention but needn't have. Everyone quieted to listen, most of them with arms crossed and scowls in place.

Gladwin raised a sheet of paper. "This letter was delivered in the wee hours of the morning. It comes from Fort Niagara. I have had it translated into French." He stepped aside, and a young man came forward with another piece of paper and started reading.

The war between France and England was officially over. France had ceded all the lands known as Canada, and all the lands of the Illinois territory, over to the British. It was done. No matter what Pontiac did now, the French would not return.

Baptiste held out no hope that the Ottawa chief would lay down the weapons of war and walk away. Even if the letter were read to him, he would convince the other chiefs that it was a lie, a trick by the British.

Pontiac's war would be fought for nothing. Men would die— Indian, French, and British—for nothing.

Across the sea, the rulers had made up their minds. The French would never return. It remained only for those on these shores to come to grips with it. To find a way to fit in with what remained.

Chapter 21

It'd been a fortnight since they'd arrived and taken up residence in the borrowed cabin. Maggie filled her days with visits to and from both Mrs. Roberts and Esther. She had cleaned the cabin until it shone, cooked what meager food they were able to purchase at the sutler's, and helped Mrs. Roberts with her small garden plot.

Every day it didn't rain, gunfire erupted mid-afternoon, generally sporadic and never anything that endangered the fort. In fact, the sound didn't even turn heads anymore. On a rare occasion, should the gunfire come with excessive war-whoops, the higher-ranking soldiers would climb the palisade to see what was happening.

The local Frenchmen who lived outside of the fort were allowed by the Indians to come and go as they pleased. Some days the fort had the feel of a market day from when she was a small child, except that food was getting scarcer. Even the French were suffering from the shortage, the Indians having raided their larders until they had nothing left to sell.

Baptiste worked from sunup to sundown, with a short break midday for a meal, and came home smelling of the forge and sweat. Tired, muscles in his arms and chest aching, but proud of his accomplishments. Proud of providing for her. And then, after supper, they would talk and touch and kiss until the worries of the day faded into the background. Until the only things that mattered were Baptiste and Maggie. They would fall asleep, her head on his shoulder, his leg across hers. And it all felt... perfect.

Until she woke again and the walls of the fort pressed against her.

She missed the fresh breeze off the water, the mumbled lowing of the oxen, the deceptive silence of the forest that melted into a symphony of chattering squirrels, clicking insects, chirping birds, and swaying branches.

Deep down, a part of her began to understand what drove Da to uproot their family, leave the town behind, and settle on the frontier. For years she'd resented him for doing that, resented him for putting them all in danger.

Blamed him for never coming after her.

If only the hostilities would end, she and Baptiste could return to his farm. She could relax and enjoy everything that went into being Madam Geroux. She could breathe easily. And together they would grow fine crops and, in time, fat babies.

Someone knocked on the door, jarring her out of her thoughts. She wiped her hands clean and set the cornmeal batter aside, then opened the door, a welcoming smile at the ready.

"Bonjour to the wife of my brother." Henri leaned against the door frame, his lanky length so like Baptiste, but without the twisted leg.

"Henri?" She opened the door wider to allow him in. "Is it safe for you to be here?"

He shrugged, an action so like Baptiste, and entered the cabin, looking around. "It looks like you and my brother found a good place."

"We are content." Mostly that was true. She was only discontent when she was alone and had time to brood.

"Where is he?"

"He works with the blacksmith, down the street and—"

"I know where it is." He waved his hand and winked at her. "Remember, I grew up here too."

"What news do you bring?" Surely he hadn't come just to check on them.

"I will save the telling for when my brother is here."

"It should not be long." She pointed toward her bowl in front of the hearth. "I was preparing to fry some bread when you knocked. Baptiste will be home soon."

He slipped his coat from where he'd held it draped over one shoulder, and from inside its folds, he pulled a string of smoked fish. "Allow me to contribute."

Maggie took the string, the aroma making her mouth water. Meat and fish were rare at their table, the fort being very low on both.

He sat on one of the crates and leaned his elbow on the table, his dark eyes following her as she returned to her work. Maggie cast about for something to say to fill the uncomfortable silence between them. At least, she was uncomfortable. She glanced at him studying her. What was he thinking behind those dark eyes?

"How are Beau and Pierre?" The oxen should be a safe topic.

"As well as when you left them."

"They have enough to eat?"

He cocked his head with an amused smile. "I am as much the son of a farmer as Baptiste. I know how to cut hay."

She couldn't picture Henri behind a plow, or sharpening a scythe, or anything as domestic as that. The man was too... dangerous for such mundane tasks.

Maggie tested the griddle and then shaped the cornmeal

batter into rounds and fried them. She was almost finished when Baptiste entered.

"Henri!" The two men embraced.

"Who is this muscled man?" Henri stepped back and examined Baptiste. "Your shirt is too tight. Is this from the blacksmith work or Maggie's cooking?"

"Both. You will eat with us, non?" He cast a questioning glance at Maggie.

She lifted the string of fish. "He brought the best part of the meal with him."

"Ah, you have managed to work the smokehouse, I see."

Henri chuckled. "I always knew how to use it, although I preferred not to."

"I am surprised they were not taken from you at the gate."

"Père did not raise any fools. I hid them in my coat."

Baptiste grinned. "And that fooled the soldiers."

Henri sobered. "Not just the soldiers. Pontiac does not mind the Frenchmen coming and going from the fort, but we are not to bring anything in. We are not to help. Instead, we are to report back to him what we see and hear."

Maggie set plates on the table, then filled three cups with water, and finally brought the food. Baptiste scooted to the edge of his crate and patted it. She sat beside him. The crate wasn't large enough for two, but it was all they had. And she didn't mind pressing so close to her husband.

As they ate, Henri told them what was happening outside the fort. Of more Indians joining the fight, including another village of Ojibwe. Of French traders arriving from Montreal and being set upon, their goods taken from them. Including barrels of liquor.

"They are taking from the French traders?" Baptiste shook his head. "The old alliances are crumbling."

"Pontiac does not seem to care. He acts as if..." Henri waved a hand in the air.

"He knows about the peace between France and England." Baptiste's words hung in the air for a moment.

Henri shot his brother a hard look. "So it is true?"

"Oui. Major Gladwin had the letter read to all the French in the fort."

Pushing his plate away, Henri rose and stalked to the hearth, leaning on the mantle and staring into the flames. "There is no hope of the French returning then."

"Non."

There was a finality to Baptiste's single word that turned the smoky fish to mush in Maggie's mouth. They hadn't talked much after hearing the letter read. It had bothered her husband, but he hadn't seemed to dwell on it. Maybe he had. Maybe she'd missed the signs. His country had abandoned them to the enemy. What must that feel like?

Like being promised that someone would come for you, and they never did.

"THE LIQUOR IN THE CAMPS, IT IS BAD, NON?" Baptiste asked as he walked back to the blacksmith shop with Henri by his side.

"Very bad."

"Even Dances Away and Walking Fire Stick?"

"Oui." Henri rubbed the back of his neck. "But only once that I know of. I have been staying close to the farm." He clouted Baptiste on the shoulder. "To care for your silly oxen."

"I appreciate that."

"You know, it is strange, but considering how much I wanted to leave the farm behind, I am finding it very..."

"Fulfilling?"

His brother shot him an unreadable look. "Maybe. Or maybe I was a little more homesick out west than even I knew. Or maybe I am staying away from the villages for now."

"*That* bad?"

Henri grunted, eyes casting around them, surveying the fort. "Taking supplies from the French traders is not good. You are correct that the old alliances are in trouble. And yet, Pontiac seems not to care."

"But you do."

"I do." He gave his head a shake, then glanced at Baptiste. "But you, things are well with you and your wife?"

Baptiste couldn't suppress the smile that any thought or mention of Maggie tended to produce. "Very well."

"Ah, my big brother, he is in love, non?"

Was he? He enjoyed Maggie in every way, not just in their bed. She was clever and resourceful, and he'd admired from the start her determination. His little spitfire. But love? What did a man like Baptiste Geroux know of love? Still... "Would that be such a bad thing?"

"Not bad at all, but risky." Henri shrugged. "Everything is more risky now."

"How so?"

"You and I, brother, have no country anymore. We live here only as long as the Indians allow"—he waved a hand toward the river even though they couldn't see it behind the palisade—"and I think they may not allow it much longer."

"Our friendships are dissolving." Had that swim with Walking Fire Stick been the last for them? The thought saddened him. Their fathers having done much business together, they'd known each other since they were small boys. He was the closest friend Baptiste had, French or Ottawa.

"There are more than four hundred and fifty warriors outside these walls. How many men inside do you think?"

Baptiste turned in the middle of the dusty street and faced Henri. "I do not know. I work with the blacksmith and keep my nose out of the fort's business as much as possible. And if I did know, I think it would be best if I did not tell you."

"Because if anyone asks, I can say I do not know."

"Oui."

"My brother, he is the smart one of the family." Henri grinned. "You always were."

"You have done well for yourself." Which was true. Not many men had ventured to the west as far as Henri and returned to tell the tales.

"Ah, but I do not have a pretty wife like my brother. Does Maggie have a sister?"

Baptiste started walking again. "She does, but she knows not where."

Henri slapped a palm on his back. "Perhaps I can find her."

They parted at the blacksmith's shop, Baptiste going back to work, Henri going who-knew-where. But the warning in his words stayed with Baptiste as he worked the bellows and tried his hand at a few of the simpler jobs that needed to be done. Had he found Maggie—and their contentment—only to die in a battle he didn't want?

Or worse, to lose her to it?

MAGGIE HELD THE DRESS UP IN FRONT OF HER, marveling at the softness of the material and its deep green hue. It reminded her of the forest at twilight. She pressed it to her front and looked at Mrs. Roberts.

"Oh, my dear. I knew that color would go beautifully with

211

your hair and skin." The older woman clasped her hands, fine wrinkles feathering the corners of her eyes.

"I know not what to say. 'Tis such a fine gift. Too fine—"

"Nonsense." Mrs. Roberts raised her hands to her waist, palms up. "After you left, I returned the serviceable brown fabric and asked to exchange it for the green." She shook her head. "I know not why, but something told me I would have need of it down the road. And I was right."

"Shall I try it on now?"

"Please do. Let me help you."

Within minutes, Maggie was wearing the stunning dress, the finest she'd ever known. The first new dress she could remember wearing. Made just for her. "'Tis so lovely." A lump pressed against the back of her throat.

"Shall we take a turn about the fort? We could stop by the blacksmith shop on the way back, just to let your husband catch a glimpse of you."

Maggie giggled. What would Baptiste say when he saw her? She treasured the memory of his reaction to her in the British dress on their wedding day, and that dress had been not half so fine. "Indeed."

The afternoon was warm with a stirring breeze, and there had been no gunshots. The Indians often waited until mid-afternoon to begin their futile shots from too far away to do any damage, but some days they did not shoot at the fort at all. On such days, a walk brought a welcome diversion from the monotony of life inside the walls.

Maggie pinned on the straw hat Esther had given her. It would keep the sun off her face, which the British women set great store by, disliking the sun to color their skin. Maggie simply enjoyed the shade over her eyes.

They talked of small matters as they turned one corner and then another, calling greetings to those they passed. Everyone seemed to know Mrs. Roberts. Indeed, as wife of the fort's only surgeon, French and British alike respected her. Most glanced past Maggie as if she weren't there.

When they turned at the corner near the commandant's office, Maggie stopped and drew in a quick breath. A circle of Huron warriors had gathered near the flagpole, and armed Redcoats in a wider circle kept watch.

"I am sure 'tis nothing to be alarmed about." Mrs. Roberts's voice lacked the conviction of her words. "But perhaps we should return."

Maggie had started to turn when a voice stopped her cold. The words didn't matter, didn't fully register, because the voice was Chief Teata's. She looked back at the Hurons, despite Mrs. Roberts's hand on her arm, urging her away.

The chief gestured as he spoke while Mr. La Butte, the Frenchman who interpreted for the major, translated. He was trying to assure Major Gladwin that he and his warriors wanted no part in the fight. He did not, however, mention his warriors who had joined with Chief Takay. Warriors like Tree Sleeper.

His name had no more than flicked through her mind when a warrior turned and looked straight at her. Even though his face never changed, she had no doubt that he recognized her. It felt as if someone had grabbed her by the throat and pinned her to the wall of the house beside them. Maggie could not move. Could barely breathe. Fear zipped along her skin, raising the hairs on her forearms until they itched like the bites of a hoard of mosquitoes. And still, she couldn't move.

His eyes were the same flat darkness, as if his soul no longer breathed within him. While she'd been wary of many of the Huron warriors through the years, avoiding them as much as she could, only Tree Sleeper had ever brought her to this level of panic.

"Come, Maggie." Mrs. Roberts tugged on her arm. "We must leave."

"'Tis him." The words barely slipped past Maggie's stiff lips.

Mrs. Roberts glanced at the Hurons and gasped, a sound that echoed in Maggie's heart. Then she stepped forward, putting her body between Maggie and Tree Sleeper, breaking the awful stare.

"Come." The older woman took her shoulders and turned Maggie around. "We are going home. He cannot follow you there. Not with the soldiers watching. They will make sure he leaves with the others and shut the gates behind them."

Maggie allowed herself to be ushered away, her feet moving almost of their own accord. The sun was hot overhead, but still she shivered. Tree Sleeper was inside the fort.

He knew she was here.

Chapter 22

Baptiste had not seen Maggie so agitated. She sat for only a moment, then was up again, finding some chore to keep her hands busy or gazing out the window. She'd told him about seeing the Huron—the one called Tree Sleeper—to whom she had been promised. She'd told him the warrior had recognized her.

His own reaction to her news had startled him. By nature, he wasn't a violent man. But the idea of a man who frightened his wife so much being anywhere near her had brought out a side of him he hadn't known existed. If the man had been within reach, Baptiste would have killed him. He'd spent their silent supper tamping down the urge to find and confront the man.

His attempts to assure Maggie of her safety had been met with stony silence and scowls. It bit into his pride that she didn't believe him. As if he were unable to keep her safe. As if he were just a cripple in her eyes.

And that was what bit the hardest.

He rose and went to the window, closing the shutters against the deepening twilight and dropping the bar in place to secure them. Then he closed the other window, the cabin having only two, and last he barred the door.

Maggie watched but said nothing.

He came to her, and she didn't move. He grasped her upper arms, and drew her to his chest. Where normally she'd melt against him, she stiffened. Anger and injured pride mixed badly with the supper they'd eaten.

"Do you still fear him, even when you are here with me?"

Her eyes, more gray than blue in the shadows of the cabin, flashed up to him. "I fear evil, and that man is evil."

"You do not think me capable of keeping you safe?"

She shook her head, and his stomach tightened.

"It is not that."

He breathed in twice before asking, "What is it, then?"

One of her shoulders lifted and fell.

He wanted to shake her. He wanted her to believe in him. Mostly, he wanted her to press against him and slip her arms around his back. He wanted things to be as they had been since they'd arrived at the fort.

Instead, he dropped his arms to his side and stepped back, turning away from her.

"Baptiste." She touched his arm.

He stopped but didn't look at her.

"You have not seen Tree Sleeper. If you had, you would understand, I think."

"Understand what?"

"Why I fear him. And why I..." She stepped closer, took a firmer hold on his arm. "Why I fear what he might do to you."

So the fear she was holding, it was for him? "You think me too weak to fight him?" His words lashed through the darkness.

"Non. Not that." She pulled him around to face her. "I think you too good. I think you would fight with honor. That one, he has no honor." Then she slipped her arms around his shoulders, pressing close, the scent of her hair filling him.

"I can take care of myself, Maggie." He bit off each word. "And I can take care of you."

She tugged his head down, her lips seeking his, her fingers tangling in the hair above his neck. His anger still simmered beneath the surface, but other forces—other emotions—took over for a time. Neither spoke again until much later, when sleep didn't come.

"Sleep, Maggie. I am here. The fort walls are sturdy. Men watch from the heights all night long." He smoothed the wayward hair from her face. "You are safe."

She snuggled closer to him, the ropes creaking beneath the ticking. "I know. I just wish…"

"Wish what?"

"That your brother was here."

A knife to his stomach couldn't have cut any deeper. He clenched his teeth when her hand cupped his face.

"You think him more capable than I." The words cost him, tearing something inside on their way out. "A better protector."

"Non. But he is something you are not."

A man with two strong legs. "Whole."

Her hand on his face tightened, forced him to look at her. "Ruthless."

Slapping the frayed cloth against the floorboards, Maggie took her frustration out on the dirt. Four days, and still Baptiste barely spoke to her. It was as if Tree Sleeper had come between them. Since that man had seen her, her husband had changed. He brooded. His dark good looks had become foreign to her.

Gone was the softness in his eyes when he returned from the blacksmith shop. Gone was the warmth in his words when he greeted her. At night, when he held her, she sensed he also held himself apart, so different from before.

Did he regret marrying her? Did he see her as more trouble than she was worth?

She slapped the cloth against the floor again, a spray of dirty water hitting her face. Mopping it with the back of her hand, she glanced at the beautiful green dress hanging from a peg near their bed.

After the encounter with Tree Sleeper, she'd returned to the cabin and stripped it off, donning one of her second-hand dresses instead. She hadn't wanted Baptiste to see her in it. Not then. She'd felt too…

She dumped the cloth back into the scrub bucket and finished her thought.

Too dirty. As if that evil man's eyes on her had marked her.

And maybe they had. Maybe that was why Baptiste kept his distance.

She glanced around the cabin, as clean as it could ever be. Since that encounter four days past, she'd been obsessed with cleaning. With keeping her hands busy so her mind wouldn't dwell on Tree Sleeper.

Unlike before, it hadn't worked.

She rose and took her straw hat from its peg. Perhaps a talk with Mrs. Roberts would help. Maggie had talked to Esther the day after everything happened, and the younger woman had listened with empathy, but Maggie needed something else. Mrs. Roberts, being older and wiser, might be able to help her figure out what.

The door banged behind her as a cannon roared. The soldiers had been shooting it off for several mornings. Esther had told her that the fort's small sloop was waiting on the great lake, and that the cannon was a signal for the men on board that it was safe to come up the river. But they had to wait until the wind was favorable.

That's what Maggie needed, for the wind to turn favorable in her marriage again.

It was a short walk to the Robertses' house, and she had barely knocked when the door opened.

"Maggie, I was thinking of you this morning." Mrs. Roberts stood back, opening the door wider. "Come in."

Tea was prepared, and they exchanged a bit of small talk, but once seated, Mrs. Roberts's face grew serious.

"Whatever is troubling you, my dear?"

The lady's bluntness shouldn't have caught Maggie unaware, for she'd always been forthright. But it did. She scrambled for the right words, the way to share what had happened without casting Baptiste in a bad light.

"Ever since Tree Sleeper—" She suppressed a shudder. "Ever since, there has been a change between me and my husband."

Mrs. Roberts set her cup of tea aside and leaned a bit closer. "How so?"

Maggie ran her finger around the rim of her cup. "In the little ways." She blinked back moisture that caught her by surprise.

"Go on." The urging was an encouragement, not a command.

Maggie blinked again, glancing at the ceiling and then at her friend. "As if I don't mean as much to him now."

Mrs. Roberts sat back in her chair, tapping her closed lips. Then she shifted to face Maggie more directly. "Do you think he fears Tree Sleeper?"

"No." Not like he should. "And because of that, I fear for him."

"For him?"

"Tree Sleeper will kill him if he learns Baptiste is my husband."

"Did you, perhaps, express this fear to him?"

"I did."

Brows drawn together, Mrs. Roberts shook her head. "'Tis likely the root of your trouble."

Maggie pressed her palm to her forehead, "Because I fear for him?"

"No, my dear, 'tis because you voiced your fear."

"He knew I feared Tree Sleeper. I told him before we were married." Maggie squashed the defensiveness that tried to worm into her. After all, she'd come for the purpose of hearing what Mrs. Roberts would say. Still, she added, "I kept no secrets from him."

The other woman looked out the window, finger tapping against her lips again. "'Tis not that you have fear of that man. Your husband would understand that, of course. 'Tis that your fear extends to him."

"I do not fear Baptiste."

"No, of course you do not, but you fear *for* him. And men, being the protectors of our households, sometimes see that as a lack of confidence in them." Mrs. Roberts gave a little shrug. "Men can be prickly that way."

"Prickly. Indeed, that is very much how he has been... Oh." Maggie stared into her tea as understanding blossomed.

"But all is not lost." Mrs. Roberts reached over and took Maggie's hand. "'Tis something to work out between you."

"I said something worse." Maggie raised her eyes to her friend. "I told him I wished his brother were here in the fort. Because he is ruthless."

"Oh my."

"How do I...?" Maggie searched the older woman's face for answers.

Mrs. Roberts winked. "I shall let you in on a little secret."

WITH A FINAL SMACK OF THE MAUL, BAPTISTE BROKE through the wall of the palisade. Arm and back muscles strengthened by weeks at the forge reverberated with the effort. The work did him good, giving him something to vent his pent-up frustration on. Sweat poured down his back as he straightened.

A red-coated sergeant bent and looked through the hole in the west wall of the fort. "This will keep those devils away." He motioned to a group of soldiers who surrounded the six-pound cannon. "Bring it up."

Baptiste backed away as the cannon was moved into position. The Indians had been using a well-worn road to the west, shooting harmlessly at the fort and jeering at the soldiers. On their next pass, they would be met with a round of grapeshot. It wasn't likely to kill at that range, but it would keep the Indians farther from the walls of the fort.

He could do something to help secure Maggie's safety, even if he weren't as ruthless as his brother.

"You, Frenchie," the sergeant barked. "Get back to work."

Baptiste finished his part of the job.

The sun was straight overhead when the cannon was secured, and he was hungry enough to eat a whole bear, though his stomach twisted at the thought of returning to the cabin for another silent meal. Back to the wife who wished for his brother.

But he needed to eat.

Halfway to the cabin, Henri joined him in the street. "You have worked hard." Henri's grin added to the sourness in Baptiste's middle. "I hardly recognize this muscled man in front of me as my own farmer brother."

"What are you doing here?" The words came out more surly

than he'd intended. Or maybe not. He wasn't sure how he felt about Henri at the moment.

"What has you sounding like a bull elk with its antlers caught in a tree?"

Baptiste grunted.

"You are missing the farm, no doubt." Henri glanced around the fort. "This is no way to live, behind walls. Fenced in like the oxen."

"How are Beau and Pierre?"

"Getting lazy. They eat, they sleep, and they grow fat."

"Are you staying at the cabin?" His cabin. It should be his and Maggie's, not the borrowed cabin in the fort, no matter how she'd cleaned and arranged it. It wasn't home.

"More or less."

Henri had never been able to stay in one place too long. He was always on the move. Perhaps Maggie was the same way. Perhaps that was why she'd left the fort the first time. In the past few days, he'd come to the conclusion that he'd married a woman he didn't know.

A thought that had brought him unexpected pain.

"If my brother were to invite me to eat with him, I may uncover something from my coat." Henri tapped the collar of the coat that was hanging over his shoulder.

"You have not been to the cabin yet?"

"Non. I saw you working on the wall when I entered, so I waited."

An uncomfortable tightness eased from Baptiste's chest. He didn't want his brother alone with Maggie. Not now. Not after what she'd admitted to him—that she believed Henri was better able to keep her safe than he was.

"We would be pleased to have you join us."

Henri shot him a puzzled look, but the two walked on in companionable silence. Baptiste pulled open the door to the cabin and motioned his brother through. The soft whistle from between Henri's teeth tightened his chest again. He stepped into the cabin.

In the green dress that had hung on the wall for days, Maggie raised questioning eyes to him before shooting a glance at Henri.

A glance he wished he could read.

OH, NO. MAGGIE'S WELCOMING SMILE SLIPPED AS Henri came through the door, his soft whistle filling the silent cabin. Baptiste followed, his face as tense as she'd ever seen it. Maggie stifled the groan that threatened.

Mrs. Roberts had been right.

Maggie could see it now. In the tightness of her husband's face. In the rigid set of his shoulders. And in the grim slash of his lips.

She smoothed her hands down the green fabric, as nervous as she'd ever been.

Henri whipped his coat from his shoulder with a flourish and held out a stringer of smoked fish. "For you, madam." He bowed as if she were someone important.

Maggie took the fish. "This is very welcome, as are you."

Baptiste's face darkened as he turned away from her.

What could she do? How could she salvage her plan? Something near panic pressed against the back of her throat as she waved them toward the table, already set for two. She gathered another plate, cup, and knife before joining them. She put the fish beside the bread and a jar of fruit compote that Mrs. Roberts had given her. She sat on the corner of Baptiste's crate, barely enough of her touching the wood to keep her from falling to the floor.

Henri looked back and forth between the two of them, his dark eyes unreadable. "I bring news, but I cannot tell you if it is good or bad. Yet."

"Then tell us." Baptiste broke off a piece of fish and a chunk of bread.

His brother did the same, then started his tale. Kinonchamek, the son of the great chief of the Ojibwe, had arrived and given Pontiac a very public dressing-down for his treatment of the French farmers and traders in the area. He'd chastised the Ottawa chief for not preparing for war as he should have, with provisions to feed his people without plundering the French. Even more, he had denounced Pontiac's tactics, most especially his barbaric treatment of captives. He told them that the French, when they returned, would not be pleased with Pontiac.

Baptiste had leaned forward, meal forgotten on his plate. "So Kinonchamek does not know of the peace between France and Britain? And he will not join with Pontiac?"

Henri shrugged. "Who knows? He may still, or he may not. But either way, Pontiac was shown in a bad light, and in front of all the chiefs." Henri tapped a finger on the table. "But I tell you this, Dances Away and Walking Fire Stick are also disillusioned with Pontiac."

"You are right to say this could be good or bad." Baptiste flicked a glance her way, then back to his brother. "Only time will tell."

Time, the one thing Maggie needed above all. Time to show Baptiste that she needed him. That she trusted him. Time to move them back onto the same footing they had begun on. Because she missed the man she'd married. The man she'd come to…

Love.

Chapter 23

With a full bucket in each hand, having purchased a second on Baptiste's account at the sutler's store, Maggie headed back to the cabin for another day of waiting. Waiting for the Indians to attack the fort. Waiting for the sloop to make it up the river from where it was anchored in sight but without enough wind to navigate the river. Waiting for Baptiste to respond to her overtures of mending their relationship.

It'd been more than half a month since Tree Sleeper had come to the fort. More than half a month since Baptiste had withdrawn from her. Some nights she thought they were getting back to where they had been, but then in the morning—

"Maggie!" Esther waved to her from her front door. "Can you spare a moment?"

Maggie hurried to the porch and left her buckets there, allowing Esther to pull her inside.

"'Tis such good news, I wanted to tell you straight away." The other woman's excitement was contagious, pulling Maggie out of her doldrums, at least for the moment.

"What has happened?"

Esther splayed her hands across her middle, puffing out her stomach. "I am with child."

With child? Thoughts of Redwing, which she'd pushed to the side for weeks, came crashing back. His sturdy little arms around her neck. His laughing face pressed nose to nose with her. A lump threatened to choke her, but she stepped into her friend's embrace.

Then she backed up. "When?"

"Surgeon Roberts says 'twill be winter time before the babe arrives, for which I am glad, since 'tis likely the uprising will be over by then."

"We will hope for that." She squeezed Esther's hands. What would it be like to know that Baptiste's child grew inside of her?

Then she paused. When had her courses run the last time? When she'd been in the barn. Before they had married. Before—

"Maggie?" Esther's voice reached her, pulling her back into the moment.

"I am just remembering." Maggie dropped her friend's hands and summoned a smile. "Did I tell you about Redwing?"

"The Indian boy you left behind?"

Maggie nodded. "I miss him still. 'Twill be good to hold a babe again."

And not just Esther's babe.

She'd speak with Mr. Roberts first, after she'd missed another course, but in her heart, she held onto the hope building there. The hope of a child growing inside of her.

Baptiste's child.

———

THE BOOM OF A CANNON—FROM OUTSIDE THE WALLS —threw the fort into a frenzy of activity. Shouts broke out, men and women both ran past the blacksmith shop. The pop of guns across the river. More shouting.

Smith stopped hammering at the forge. He jerked his head toward the open door. "Go and see what all the fuss is about." The gruff man rarely left his shop, preferring to send Baptiste on any necessary errands. He returned to banging on the iron in his tongs before Baptiste made it to the dusty street.

Outside the shop, the fort looked like the river at spawning time. People flooded the street, women calling questions to each other in two languages. Men grasping long guns. Soldiers racing past buildings or climbing ladders to the top of the palisade. But there was a general excitement that didn't bespeak panic.

Baptiste limped along with the crowd, catching phrases in both languages, enough to know that the sloop was in motion. A dark man hurried toward him, the slave of Major Gladwin.

"What is happening?" he asked the man in English, assuming he wouldn't know French.

"The sloop is coming in. That was her cannon, scaring off the Indians." He flashed Baptiste a wide grin. "She carries reinforcements."

And food, hopefully. The fort was getting very scarce of food-stuffs. Before the uprising, many of the Indians had stored their grain in the fort. Most of it was gone now, given to the fort's inhabitants by Major Gladwin's order. There were still a handful of cows that produced milk, their bounty given to the families with children, and the women's gardens were beginning to produce, but there would be no crops to harvest if the uprising continued. Or not much. Baptiste could only imagine what was left of his fields. The Indians would raid them, trampling as much as they'd reap. There was nothing he could do about it from the fort.

A glimpse of red hair pulled him to a halt.

Maggie came toward him, a basket over her arm, from the direction of the Robertses' house. Perhaps she'd been helping

Mrs. Roberts with the garden behind the building, as she often did. His stomach tightened at the sight, and it had nothing to do with the green pods visible in the basket.

It had everything to do with his wife.

He knew the moment she spied him, the quick breath that lifted the front of her gown. The old one, not the green that he'd not seen on her again since the day Henri had brought them the fish. How long ago? Ten days maybe. He wasn't sure. The days all ran together. He awoke, he worked, he came back to Maggie. And in between, he thought of little other than her.

She reached him, her lips curved into a welcome. She seemed happy to see him. She always did, but he couldn't let go of his doubts.

"There is quite the excitement, non?" she asked.

"Oui. And for good reason."

"The sloop brings more supplies."

"It brings more soldiers."

She gripped the basket in front of her and glanced down the street. "Do you think we will lose our place?"

Would they? The men would need to be housed somewhere, but there were several empty houses and a couple more cabins. "I hope not." She'd worked hard to turn what had been little more than a hovel into a home. As she'd done with his cabin on the farm.

And where else could they go?

For all his surliness over her insinuation that Henri could protect her better than he, in his heart, he knew she was right. His brother might have been able to keep her safe at the farm, but not Baptiste. Always he would be at a disadvantage. Always he would be hampered by a leg that didn't work as it should. And always he was aware of it.

What had burned him down deep was knowing that Maggie was aware of it too.

She'd said nothing about it since. In fact, she seemed to go out of her way to defer to him on everything. His little spitfire had tamed down.

He didn't know what to make of that.

"Surgeon Roberts said that Mr. MacDougall was in weakened health when he and the others arrived." Maggie placed their plates on the table while Baptiste hung his hat. "That they escaped at all was a mercy. It is not good that Captain Campbell remains a captive. Surgeon Roberts said the others did their best to persuade him to escape with them, but he did not. Perhaps he felt he could do more to end the uprising by remaining."

"Then he is a fool." Baptiste splashed water in the chipped basin and removed as much of the black forge grime from his skin as he could.

"You think they will kill him?"

"Oui. I do."

She remembered the man who had stood beside Major Gladwin that first day she'd arrived at the fort, and again when she'd gone to listen to the Ottawa warrior who had told of Pontiac's plans. He'd been a captive for close to two months. Her own situation had been different, being a child when she'd been taken. But she'd seen enough of other captives to know what his life was like.

And to pity him.

Maggie finished putting the meal on the table, including a crock of fresh milk.

Baptiste's eyebrows rose as he took his seat on the crate. "Milk?"

"Oui. A small herd of cattle arrived at the fort gates yesterday, including three milking cows."

Baptiste poured milk into his cup and drank, his eyes closed in appreciation. Then he thumped the cup back onto the table. "I cannot remember the last time I drank milk. Maman kept a cow, but it died a few years back." He looked at the cup, brows drawn. "Pierre was her last calf."

He missed his oxen. Her gruff husband had a soft spot for the gentle beasts. As did she. They'd kept her company in the barn those days and nights of hiding.

"Surgeon Roberts asked if I could help with the cattle, since I have no other duties during the day."

Baptiste glanced up.

"Da had cows. I remembered how to milk." She enjoyed the warm approval in his eyes. The repair to their relationship was a slow thing, but it was mending. And since her suspicions of two days past, that mending was all the more important to her. She'd do whatever it took to make up for her thoughtless words.

"Another French family has moved back into the fort." Baptiste waved a bite of the salt pork on his knife, some of the provisions brought in on the sloop. "That makes three. It would not surprise me if more came."

Her throat went dry. "Perhaps the owners of this cabin?"

"Perhaps." He bit into the salt pork and chewed. "I spoke to Smith about it today. He said if we lose the cabin, we can build a lean-to on the side of the blacksmith shop."

Living in a shed attached to the blacksmith shop held little appeal. The noise, the smell, the dirt. Especially the dirt. Maggie had grown used to living with floorboards beneath her feet again. But she would adjust as needed. She would be strong. And most importantly, she would be with Baptiste.

"Then we can rest easy." She summoned a smile, more than

gratified when it was returned. It seemed her husband had forgiven her for her hasty and poorly chosen words. That forgiveness—while never spoken outright—was restoring their relationship.

"Oui."

"Today there was not much gunfire from the Indians." She took a drink, watching his face. "They seemed to have left us alone. Do you think it is because Mr. MacDougall and the others escaped?"

"If it is, it does not bode well for us." He leaned back and stretched, his shirt protesting against the well-defined muscles. "Me, I prefer to see them outside the fort, wasting their shot and powder. When they are not in sight, they are probably plotting something new."

Something new. Each day, the gunfire reminded her that the fort was under siege, even though inside the walls things changed little. Most of the time, the soldiers didn't even return fire, knowing that the Indians were out of range and that their bullets fell well short of the walls. Always the red-coated soldiers stood watch, of course, but after so many days of sporadic gunfire that accomplished nothing, it seemed they'd grown to ignore it.

She and Baptiste finished their meal in a companionable silence. Maggie was putting the dishes in the wash tub when a pair of arms came around her from behind. A thrill shot through her at his touch, at his warm breath moving her hair, at the return to what had been normal before her thoughtless words.

She turned in his embrace. His dark eyes filled with the softness she loved. A softness that wasn't weak, a softness meant only for her, a softness filled with longing. Her fingers tangled in the long hair at his nape before she'd instructed them.

"Your hair is in bad need of a trim."

"So it is." His voice came in a low rumble that did delicious things to Maggie's middle.

"I packed the scissors from your cabin."

He tugged on the long plait of her hair. "You thought about my long hair even then?"

"One does not leave valuable tools behind."

"Then fetch the scissors and shear my mane, wife."

Maggie pushed him back toward the crate. "You must sit. You are too tall for me to reach."

He chuckled and sank onto the crate, but his eyes stayed on her, dark and filled with promise.

Her hands trembled slightly as she pulled the scissors from a leather pouch she'd stored them in. She took a deep breath and moved behind her husband, slipping off the leather tie that held his hair back. As rich as any sable pelt, the sleek locks cascaded over her hands. Maggie let them slide through her fingers until Baptiste shifted.

"Sit still." She pressed a hand to his shoulder.

"Get on with it." His voice was somewhere between a groan and a growl.

Maggie lifted the scissors and snipped the first lock of hair away, then another, and then another. She pressed closer, studying where to snip next, and allowing her clothing to brush against his.

"How long does it take to cut hair?" He asked, his voice tight.

How long, indeed? Maggie thrilled to the feel of his hair in her hands and the tension seeping from him in waves. "I would have you look respectable, husband, when you walk the streets of the fort."

He groaned then and gripped the crate until his knuckles whitened.

Maggie snipped a few more places around his shoulders and

back, evening the first cuts she'd made, then she bent in front of him to examine the evenness of the front.

The scissors hit the floor as his arms came around her. He lifted her onto his lap, his mouth seeking and finding hers, commanding her attention. Baptiste stood, Maggie secured to him with one arm. With the other, he closed and barred the shutters over both windows and barred the door. Then he blew out the single candle.

In the darkness, he lowered her to the bed.

Maggie ran her fingers down his shortened locks. "Perhaps I should trim your hair more often, non?"

The only answer before his lips reclaimed hers was a wolfish growl that matched the growing urgency within her.

"FRENCHIE, WHAT WEAPONS DO YOU HAVE IN YOUR possession?" The British soldier leaned against the open doorway of the blacksmith shop. "The major wants a count."

Baptiste wiped the sweat from his brow, glanced at Smith, and then approached the soldier. "I have a gun and a knife." He tapped the knife in its sheath at his waist.

"Nothing else? No tomahawk or axe?"

"My wife, she has a hatchet."

The soldier laughed. Baptiste kept his face stoic, let the man's laughter dissipate around them. The fool. Baptiste had seen Maggie throw the hatchet. He knew that, in her hands, it was a deadly weapon.

His laughter faded, the soldier pointed to the tools hanging on the walls of the shop. "Did you make any of these?"

"I am learning."

Smith banged his hammer against a piece of glowing metal, a shower of sparks lighting that side of the room. "He does well."

"Do not take any of them home, Frenchie. The major does not trust you Frenchmen. He thinks you would take up arms against us. That you would bite the hand that feeds you." The soldier spit outside into the dirt of the street. "Now make for the flagpole. The major has words for you, the whole lot of you."

He left, and Smith slammed the hammer down. "How do they expect me to get the work they require done when they keep taking my help away?" His voice roared through the shop, no doubt intended for the soldier, no doubt loud enough for him to have heard. But he didn't return.

"Go. Obey the major." Smith poked the tongs in his fist toward the door. "Come back when he allows."

Baptiste was halfway down the street when Maggie trotted to his side, one hand holding her straw hat in place against the wind. She took his arm, tension flowing from her fingers to his elbow. He patted her hand. "I am sure it is nothing."

"I wish I were."

"What has you so worried?"

She shot him a look he couldn't quite interpret, not while walking among the gathering crowd heading toward the flagpole. She leaned in closer, and he bent to catch her words.

"I fear the major might turn us out."

The thought had occurred to him as well, but Maggie was a British citizen. The major might not approve of her choice of a husband, but it was unlikely he would turn her out of the fort. It remained to be seen if he'd turn Baptiste out.

"I think not."

She pressed closer as they came to a halt on the outside of a growing circle of Frenchmen.

The major's spokesman came out onto the porch and raised his hands for silence. He read a letter from the major telling of a meeting between the French and Indian leaders from the different tribes. Pontiac was pressing the French outside the fort to side and take up arms with the Indians.

Henri. Would his brother rise to the call? For years he'd been as much Ottawa as French, as close a brother to Dances Away as to him. Now he would have to make a choice.

The Ottawa—or Baptiste.

Chapter 24

Baptiste had worked long into the evening, Smith having pushed both of them to their limits as per the major's orders. They would soon be out of metal to craft any more weapons, but the walls hung with every sort of knife, axe, sword, and pike Smith knew how to fashion.

Baptiste pulled in a long breath of the fresh evening air, glad to clear the black smoke from his lungs. He'd just turned onto the street where their cabin sat when a great shout came from the top of the palisade on the river side.

A shout of alarm.

Baptiste broke into his uneven trot, hurrying toward the shouting. Soldiers passed him, one of them shoving him out of the way. He tripped but managed to stay on his feet when another passing soldier steadied him. So it was with the British. There were those who would see him harmed, and others who would not. Perhaps humankind had always been that way. It was the same with the Indians. Some would befriend him, some would look down their noses at him and his twisted leg. Still others would see him dead. The French were more tolerant of his lame leg, but perhaps only because he was French.

The words flying around him were in English, but Baptiste

was becoming more fluent with that language each day. Barges had been sighted crossing the river, heading for the fort. A string of them, loaded with people and livestock.

French farmers. His neighbors. Fleeing their land. He braced his hand against the rough log of the fort's wall. All hope for Beau and Pierre was gone. Through a rifle slit, he could make out the shapes of the barges in the gathering dusk. A man on the front barge waved a white flag. Even in the gathering darkness and at a distance, he stood out.

Henri.

Behind him, fenced in with crates and trunks, were a red ox and a black ox.

A knot tightened in Baptiste's throat. He swallowed it down and made his way to the riverside gate. It took a while, since the men on the barges were questioned by those soldiers stationed on the sloop. Major Gladwin himself appeared and spoke to the apparent leader of the group. But at last, the people and animals were allowed entrance.

"Baptiste!" Henri tugged on the yoke connecting the oxen, forcing them to pick up their pace. "Look who I bring to you."

"I see. And I see that you are well, brother."

Henri scanned the crowd around them. "I am."

"Let us put Beau and Pierre away, and then we can talk. There are corrals not too far from the cabin."

They found a place for the oxen, then entered the cabin to the aroma of fried salt pork and something herbal.

"I had begun to worry..." Maggie's voice trailed off as she turned and caught sight of Henri.

He removed his hat and bowed. "It is good to see you, sister-in-law. I hope I am not unwelcome, even if I do arrive unexpectedly and empty-handed for supper."

Maggie's face flushed, and she took a moment to push her

hair back before answering. "You are always welcome in our home."

But there remained a bit of restraint that Baptiste could see in her eyes, that he hoped Henri didn't notice, and that he wondered about the origins of. He would need to think on that another time.

"Henri arrived on a barge filled with French farmers from across the river." Baptiste grinned at her, a weight lifting from him with his next words. "He brought Beau and Pierre with him."

"Oh!" She pressed her hands over her mouth. "Then I must cut for him the choicest section of the pork, non?"

They spoke of trivial things during dinner, and afterward, Baptiste barred the windows and door before asking Henri, "So what is the news?"

Henri leaned his elbows on the table, his hands knotted together. "One of the Frenchmen from the fort—I did not recognize him—came to Pontiac today and spoke eloquently of the need to not listen to the young Frenchmen, those with hot blood and few brains, who wish to fight alongside the Ottawa. He reminded Pontiac that the French, before they left, told him to leave his French brothers alone."

"And? Did he agree?" Baptiste asked.

"But of course." Henri half raised his hands, then let them drop back to the table. "He promised to not bother the French again, not to press them into the fight, but to only take volunteers."

Baptiste rubbed the center of his forehead. "Then why? Why the farmers on the barges?"

"Because the Potawatomi, the Huron, and the Ojibwe who remain would not listen. To them, the French are not brothers. The farmers fear for their livestock, their homes, their very lives."

"You said the Ojibwe who remain."

"Oui. The son of the great chief of that nation, after chastising Pontiac, went back home."

"Surely that is good news?" Maggie said.

Baptiste slid his arm behind his wife, pulling her closer on the crate, warming to the way she molded herself against him.

Henri shrugged. "It is not bad news, but the fort is still outnumbered at least two to one, probably more."

Even with the reinforcements from the return of the small sloop, it was probably more like three to one. Baptiste didn't know the exact numbers, but he could make an educated guess.

"What will you do, brother?"

Henri tapped his fingers on the table and turned to look into the fire. As much as Baptiste wished he weren't corralled at the fort, and wouldn't be if not for the woman beside him who had come to mean more to him than this own freedom, it must be more difficult for Henri. His brother was closer to the Ottawas and more at home in the forest than under any roof.

"I cannot join with the Ottawa while my brother lives in the fort." He turned back to Baptiste, his dark eyes unreadable in the dim light. Probably unreadable in broad daylight. His brother had always been like that. "And I cannot stay behind these walls."

"You are always welcome with us."

Maggie's voice was soft and earnest, but beneath his arm, Baptiste felt that lingering... something. Was it doubt? Did she not trust Henri? And yet, she'd wished him close not so very long ago. Baptiste would need to ponder it later.

"Of course you are," Baptiste said, returning his attention to Henri.

Henri raised an eyebrow and looked between the two of them. "You are newly wed, you do not need a brother living alongside you." Then he grinned. "Before you know it, the floor will be crawling with babes."

Maggie stiffened against him.

Henri spoke more about staying at the farm for the summer, then maybe heading west again to trap beaver. Dances Away already spoke of returning. Baptiste did his best to follow his brother's conversation while wondering why Maggie had reacted so strongly to the mention of babes. Did she not want a child? Was the idea of being a mother disagreeable to her? Had she not considered the natural outcome of their marriage?

Or did she worry that his deformity could be passed on to their children?

WITH BOTH BUCKETS FILLED WITH WASHED, WET clothing, Maggie returned to the cabin. She did their wash at the Robertses' house each week, since Mrs. Roberts had a proper wash kettle and a fire pit outside. With Henri's clothing added to their own, she was extra appreciative of the arrangement. Washing inside was nice during the winter months, but not during the hot and sticky days of July.

Henri had stayed with them for the night, even after his teasing words about babes, which had shocked her. Of course, he couldn't know. She wasn't even positive herself yet, but with each passing day she grew more confident. And she wondered how Baptiste would take the news. Would he be pleased? Or see the child as another mouth to feed in an uncertain time?

She plunked the buckets down near the rope Baptiste had strung behind the cabin. Frenzied gunfire erupted to the northeast. Gunfire was an almost daily occurrence, but this was different. A tendril of fear climbed her back and tightened around her collar. She left the buckets and ran to the street.

People gathered in knots around doorways, women called their young ones, dogs barked, and chickens scurried out of the way as soldiers yelled at people to get back as they raced toward the west wall of the fort.

Was this the attack they'd all been dreading?

Maggie stayed by their door, unsure what to do. Within moments, Baptiste joined her.

"Go inside, Maggie."

He followed her in, and Henri arrived out of breath. He leaned one hand against the door frame. The other held his rifle. "It is not good."

"So I gathered." Baptiste stepped in front of Maggie as if to shield her. The gunfire hadn't stopped, hadn't even let up.

"The major had ordered the American militia to go and dismantle some breastworks erected overnight, probably by the renegade French who have sided with Pontiac." Henri pointed his rifle toward the northeast. "They were ambushed."

Maggie peered around her husband. How did Henri know so much?

"They are asking for Frenchmen to volunteer." Henri glanced at her and then back to Baptiste. "To help the British put down the renegade French."

Baptiste took his gun from where it hung over the door. "I will go."

Everything within her wanted to pull him back, to tell him no. But Mrs. Roberts's words whispered in the back of her mind. A man was made to be the protector of his family. To show a lack of faith in him, especially in front of his brother, would be a blow to his pride. To their newly mended relationship.

He turned to her, his eyes guarded.

Maggie swallowed her worry and threw her arms around him. "Be safe." The words came out in a hoarse whisper, but it

241

was enough. The muscles beneath her hands relaxed. His small sigh blew across the top of her head. She stepped back, hands clasped at her waist, and nodded with her chin high.

What blazed in his eyes then was worth the fear she did her best to control.

Maggie had worked at being strong for so long. She'd taken care of herself. This learning to stand aside and let someone else take care of her was foreign. Uncomfortable. But it was the right thing to do. Even though her hands itched to grab her husband by the arm and pull him away from the door. Being strong also meant knowing when to take charge and when to step back. When to hold on, and when to let go.

Baptiste stepped past Henri and into the street.

Henri's eyes met hers for just a moment, and for the first time, she could read what was there. Approval. Admiration. And a promise. Henri would be at his brother's side. But would it be enough?

Would the father of her unborn child return?

Baptiste and Henri joined eight other Frenchmen, their faces grim and determined. They'd chosen their side. They would fight with the British. It wasn't a thing lightly done. For many years, the Ottawa especially had been their brothers. But the constant raiding of their farms and the threats had taken their toll. And among the Indians firing out there were the renegade Frenchmen, those who had volunteered to fight alongside Pontiac's warriors.

Other than Henri, the rest had family in the fort. Women and children to protect and livestock needed to continue with their way of life.

"You have no one here, Henri.," Baptiste said. "You could leave now, and no man would think less of you."

"How can you say that when you are here?"

"You know what I mean." Baptiste took the powder and shot given him by the officer in charge, then waited while Henri took his. "If you fight with us now, Pontiac will hear of it. You will not be welcome back in the village. Even Dances Away will turn his back on you."

"As Walking Fire Stick will to you."

Baptiste nodded. It hurt to think of the division between them now, but he couldn't change what was. If Pontiac had kept his word, things could have been different. He hoped that some day Walking Fire Stick would be able to see that.

"But blood is thicker." Henri cuffed him on the shoulder. "And I could not let you face this without me by your side now that I am here, could I?"

His brother's answer didn't surprise him. Even as children, they'd faced everything together, side by side. What had surprised him was Maggie's response. He'd been prepared for her to argue, to plead, or to demand that he not go. She hadn't —even though he knew she'd wanted to.

His little spitfire hadn't fooled him. But she'd made him proud. Sometimes it took as much strength to stand aside as it did to join the fight. He could never have stood aside and watched Henri go without him. Maggie, on the other hand, had found the strength to let Baptiste go.

Would he ever understand the woman he'd married?

Such thoughts were shoved aside as the officer in charge gave them their orders, then some forty British soldiers and the handful of Frenchmen marched out of the fort. Upon their arrival, the renegades—easily distinguished by their clothing— ran into the forest. The Indians, on the other hand, made a fight of it until the commander sent a number of men around to their flank. Then the Indians scattered, and the troops followed them for some way.

Baptiste, unable to run after the fleeing Indians, lent his strength to the soldiers who were pulling down and burning the breastworks. Henri stayed as well. They'd tossed the last of an old fence into the fire when the soldiers returned.

One man—an Englishman who had been a captive and escaped earlier that summer—swung a bloody scalp above his head and whooped.

"That will bring bigger trouble." Henri spit into the dirt.

Oui, it would. More than the skirmish, the taking of a scalp would fan the flames of hatred among the Indians. Flames that didn't need any help.

EVENING WAS THICKENING AROUND HER, THE shadows pressing close. No gunfire had rippled through the air for more than an hour. Maggie swatted a mosquito but refused to go inside the cabin. She leaned against the rough logs, one hand pressed to her middle, searching for a limping figure in the distance.

Where was Baptiste? Why hadn't he returned?

How had he come to mean so much to her? That was the pressing question. Since she'd accepted that nobody was going to rescue her from the Lenni Lenape, and then the Huron, Maggie had worked to be strong enough to survive on her own. She'd taken pride in not needing anyone. But in the past weeks, she'd come to realize that it had been a false pride.

Maggie swallowed down a load of emotions. What if he didn't return?

Could she survive being left on her own again?

It wouldn't be easy, not now, not when she realized how

dependent she was on those around her. Not when her heart would be broken—again—by someone she loved.

She closed her eyes for a moment and allowed herself to feel the emotions she'd stuffed away years ago. The longing for Mama. The anger at Da for not coming for her.

Another mosquito roused her from slipping deeper into that mire. She slapped her arm but didn't let it drop as a figure solidified in the gloom. A figure with a limp.

Maggie pushed away from the cabin, picked up her skirts and ran. She ignored Henri and the other men straggling back to their homes as she wrapped her arms around her husband and buried her face against his coat.

"Come, Maggie." His voice was low and kind, not embarrassed by her display on the street. He pulled her to his side, and they walked together to the cabin, his arm never leaving her shoulders. Henri melted away into the darkness, so they stepped into the cabin alone.

"You came back to me." The words slipped out before she could stop them.

"Of course I did." His brow wrinkled, out of puzzlement or the stirrings of anger, she wasn't sure.

"Not everyone does."

He sighed as he hung up the rifle and shrugged out of his coat. "I am not defenseless, Maggie. I can take care of myself." The words were sharp.

"So could my da, but he…"

Understanding softened his features. "I will always return to you."

He'd always try, Maggie knew that. It was the type of man he was. But outside the walls of the fort were hundreds of warriors would who try to stop him.

Chapter 25

The door was open against the midday heat, so the knock caught Maggie by surprise. She jerked around from the hearth, where she'd put a pot over the fire to boil.

"Surgeon Roberts." She stood and smoothed the front of her dress.

He tipped his chin in greeting but didn't enter. "Mrs. Geroux, the major requests you to come to the parade ground. He has admitted a group of Hurons who say they wish to make peace."

Tree Sleeper.

Maggie braced one hand against the mantel. "Why me?"

"You are fluid in their language. You might hear something said among the group that would be useful."

What if Tree Sleeper were among them? Although if they came to talk peace, it wasn't likely. It was very unlikely.

"Of course." She could hardly deny the major's request after he had allowed her into the fort not once, but twice. "I shall join you in a moment."

He stepped back out of the doorway while she secured her braid around her head, and then pinned her straw hat in place. She scanned the room for any other reason for delay, and finding none, drew in a steadying breath and stepped into the full glare of the sun.

Mr. Roberts walked beside her, his quiet presence a calming contrast to her stomach, which was starting to rebel against what she'd eaten less than an hour before.

"Are you feeling well?" The surgeon stopped and faced her.

"A bit nervous, perhaps." But it wasn't only that. She pressed fingertips to her lips. Her stomach had been uneasy for the past fortnight.

The surgeon tilted his head, eyes narrowed. "Perhaps you should visit me at my office someday soon."

"Perhaps I should, but please say nothing of it."

A smile tipped the corner of his mouth. "I never do."

Of course he wouldn't. But he knew.

And soon, she'd have to tell Baptiste. Things between them were smooth again, like when they'd first come to the fort. Maggie was more than content. For the first time in a very long time, she was happy. While she marveled at the miracle of growth within her, a part of her worried that revealing it would change things. She wasn't quite ready for that yet.

They turned the corner to a large crowd of warriors, and she gasped.

Mr. Roberts took hold of her elbow, steadying her. "There are more here than I was led to believe."

"'Tis fine." There were twice as many red-coated soldiers stationed around the Hurons.

"Do you recognize any of them?"

Indeed, she did. Several. She nodded.

"They can do nothing to you. You are safe here in the fort." His reassurance helped, a little, but—

"They might demand that I be returned to Stone Foot. He is much respected in the village."

Mr. Roberts squeezed her elbow. "You will never be returned

to them. You are a British citizen. They had no right to take you away from your family in the first place."

She swallowed and nodded, even while her knees trembled. "Where should I stand to listen?"

"Perhaps 'tis best if we stand behind the group."

His use of *we* helped to bolster her courage. "But 'twill make hearing more difficult."

"Indeed. But are you sure you are up to them watching you?" True concern filled his face. Such a compassionate man, so well-suited for his profession.

"As long as you are sure I will not be given back to them, I will be fine."

"Mrs. Geroux, I will personally stake my reputation on that promise."

She stepped forward again and didn't stop until they stood near the flagpole. There, she turned and scanned the faces before her. Most remained stoic, but several eyebrows twitched, a few frowned, and one grinned. Then another movement caught her eye.

Baptiste.

Why was he here and not at the blacksmith shop? She shot a glance at Mr. Roberts. He nodded, and when Baptiste reached them, the surgeon stepped away.

"Why are you here?" she asked.

"Mrs. Roberts came and told me what they had asked of you." He crossed his arms and scanned the Hurons before them. "I would not have you face this alone."

She smiled, glanced down, touched by his protectiveness, and then back at the crowd waiting for Major Gladwin.

Right into the flat stare of Tree Sleeper.

EVER SINCE CAPTAIN CAMPBELL'S BODY HAD BEEN fished out of the river, Baptiste had been waiting for the reaction. It was said that Captain Campbell had been murdered in retaliation for the killing of an Ojibwe at the skirmish four days before, the Indian whose scalp had been shown to all. The warrior had been some relative of one of the chiefs. Since then, things had been quiet—too quiet—around the fort. No gunfire, no shouts, no sign of the tribes at all.

And now this.

Baptiste stood next to his wife, admiring her courage to face the same people who had kept her captive for years. Then she stiffened, and her eyes locked on one of the warriors toward the back of the group. She shivered, and he slid his arm around her back, tucking her close to his side.

"You should not—" She tried to pull away, but he tightened his hold.

"Let him know that you are mine?" Baptiste raised his chin a notch. "I would have the whole world know this."

"But he is—"

"Tree Sleeper." He said the name to spare her needing to. "And he is nothing to you."

She looked at Baptiste, but he kept his attention on the other man. Having grown up with a foot in both cultures, French and Ottawa, he knew that the man was dangerous. Everything about him, his expression, his stance, even the way he wore his hair, said he was a man to be watched.

He wasn't in the fort to speak for peace.

He was there to find Maggie.

Well, he had. And now he knew she wasn't alone. She was no longer some captive woman forced to do the bidding of an old medicine man. Non. She was the wife of Baptiste Geroux. He was claiming her boldly for the whole tribe to see.

Let Tree Sleeper make of that what he would.

Across the parade ground, Henri leaned his forearms on the railing of a porch. At the slight jerk of his head in the direction of Tree Sleeper, Baptiste nodded, and Henri eased the long knife he kept at his belt from its sheath. There was no one more adept at throwing a knife than Henri. Tree Sleeper would be wise to keep still. Very still.

Muttering had broken out amid the Hurons before Major Gladwin appeared and silenced them. Through an interpreter, agreements were made to grant peace if the Hurons returned all the British captives they held and all the merchandise that they'd taken from the settlers and off the traders' barges, peace would be negotiated.

More muttering, much gesturing, and through it all, Tree Sleeper never moved. Never spoke. Rarely took his eyes off Maggie.

For her part, Maggie ignored him, cocking her head and listening intently. That she pressed a little closer to Baptiste was the extent that she let her nerves show.

Henri tossed his knife in the air and caught it by the handle, over and over again.

And then it was finished, the chiefs having agreed to the terms. The Hurons made their way toward the gate. All but one.

Tree Sleeper approached where Maggie and Baptiste stood, Henri moving behind him like a wraith.

The Huron stopped an arm's length from them and spoke in Huron.

Maggie lifted her chin and answered in French, "I am no longer the property of Stone Foot. Whatever you have given him is your business. It has nothing to do with me."

Another string of Huron words, none of which made sense to Baptiste.

But Maggie answered again in French, "Go with the others and make peace. There is nothing for you here."

The Huron's hand dropped, but before he could draw the tomahawk at his belt, the point of Henri's knife was pressing against the base of his skull.

"Monsieur, I do not think you wish to do that." Henri's voice was low and menacing.

The Huron man's eyes flashed black anger before they settled on Baptiste. "You are a dead man," he said in French, then twisted away from the knife and strode after the others leaving the gate under the watchful eyes of the red-coated soldiers.

"That one," said Henri, sliding his knife into its sheath, "he is not to be trusted with peace." Then he grinned at Maggie. "Or with my beautiful sister-in-law."

"I appreciate your help, brother."

"That one will need to die, I think." Henri shrugged. "Sooner or later."

Maggie shivered at Baptiste's side.

"Sooner," Baptiste said. "Let us hope for sooner."

"Death is a consequence of war." Henri's grin was close to feral.

A soldier cleared his throat. "The major would see you now, ma'am."

Baptiste escorted his wife into the major's office. The Hurons had said nothing that worried her, she assured him. They might have recognized her, but those she knew from Chief Teata's village were the more level-headed men. Those most likely to truly want peace again.

All except for Tree Sleeper. That one, Baptiste would keep an eye on.

It would have been easy to believe that the Indians were serious about peace. For three weeks they had been almost silent. The futile shots at the fort had ceased. Two attempts by the Ottawas to burn the sloop with fire barges had failed. The Potawatomi were in negotiations for peace, although the general feeling was that they were not as sincere as the Hurons had been.

The Hurons had not been seen since returning their captives and merchandise. Maggie breathed a little easier knowing she was free indeed, her captivity being negated by the agreement as well.

Still, Maggie was certain that Tree Sleeper remained behind with Pontiac.

But today, she had other things to think about. She hummed as she prepared the evening meal. Surgeon Roberts had confirmed her to be with child. The babe was due after the worst of the snows and before the green-up of spring. She took extra care with the meal, making Baptiste's favorites—as well as she could with the dwindling supplies. At least the gardens were producing. The salt pork was gone, but Henri and two other Frenchmen were allowed to come and go from the fort, hunting and bringing back whatever game they could find.

True to his word, Henri did not stay with them. Maggie didn't know where he slept, perhaps under the stars, but often he ate with them. She always cooked enough, just in case. If he didn't join them, the extra food helped defray her growing appetite.

She glanced out the window. This time of year, the sun set very late. Baptiste would be home well before dark. The blacksmith was not busy much anymore, the raw metal having been used up. But they were making repairs to some chains and fashioning grappling hooks in case another fire barge was aimed at the sloop.

She lifted the lid of the pot, the aroma of stewed cabbage filled the room. While it was one of Baptiste's favorites, and used to be hers as well, the odor disagreed with her increasingly unsteady stomach. She had hurried to the door to draw in gulps of fresh, humid air when the limping gait of her husband caught her attention.

How could she have ever thought him a cripple? Tall and strong, the limp slowed him very little. And so handsome it almost hurt to look upon him. But look she did, as often as she could. From a woman who fled an unwanted husband to a woman who eagerly awaited the return of the husband approaching her. How much she had changed. All due to the man who had spotted her in the doorway, and quickened his steps.

As if the sight of her affected him as much as the sight of him affected her.

No words of love had been spoken between them. Not even in the darkness when they came together. Was it because no words were needed? Or was it because such words, once said, would leave a permanent mark on the one who spoke them? A vulnerability. Why should it be hard to be vulnerable with the one you loved?

Baptiste reached the cabin before she could summon an answer.

"Hello, wife." He stepped into the room and removed his hat before kissing her cheek. Something he'd taken to doing when he arrived. Something she looked forward to. And something that turned her insides to mush in the most delightful way.

"Something smells good."

Did it? Then why did it make her stomach wobble? Maggie drew in another long breath from the doorway to keep her sustained as she dished up the stewed cabbage flavored with onions and the last bit of bacon she'd hoarded.

Baptiste sat at the table, and Maggie carried the bowls over, holding her breath. But she couldn't do that for the entire meal. She perched on the edge of her crate and leaned away from the steaming bowl in front of her.

"Is something wrong?" Baptiste's brows drew together.

"Nothing." But she'd drawn in too much air to say the word. Too much cabbage-smelling air. With a hand pressed over her mouth, she raced for the doorway and ran around the cabin to gag.

"Maggie?" Baptiste's uneven footsteps followed her. He slid his arm beneath her ribs, supporting her weight as she bent forward and retched again. "I will fetch the surgeon."

She held onto his arm. "It is not necessary."

"You are ill. Of course it is necessary." His voice was strained. Worried.

Maggie's stomach empty, she straightened. This was not how she'd wanted to tell him. Not with the contents of her stomach at their feet, and her breath smelling like a gut pile in the sun. Ugh. And not with people walking past on the street.

"Come inside." She took his hand and led the way. She dropped it once they were inside and went to the drinking water, took the dipper and rinsed her mouth, spitting into the fireplace. Once. Twice. After the third time, she felt almost human again.

But she stayed across the room from the cabbage on the table, sitting on their bed instead. Baptiste followed her, and she drew him down next to her.

He pressed his palm against her forehead, and she gave him the best smile she could muster under the circumstances.

"I am not ill."

Confusion and concern flattened his eyebrows into a dark line. She traced her finger along one of them, smiling in earnest at the darkening of his eyes, the slight hitch in his breath.

"I am with child."

She'd had weeks to imagine what his reaction would be, to worry over it even, but she hadn't come close. He gave a shout that filled the cabin, then whisked her off the bed and into his arms. He turned in a circle, her skirts flaring out around them.

She clung to his neck and willed her stomach to behave, even as she laughed.

"I will be a père." His white teeth flashed against the dark stubble on his cheeks.

"Oui. That is how it works."

"A strong son to follow in my footsteps. To work the fields beside me." He twirled her again.

When he brought them to a stop she said, "It could be a girl."

His grin only widened. "A little spitfire like her maman. This would be good too."

Shouts reached through their celebrating, urgent and insistent. Baptiste carried her to the door as Henri appeared in the opening. His brother's eyes widened.

"I am sorry to interrupt."

Baptiste smile never faltered. "Nothing you say can dampen this moment, my brother."

"Nothing *I* say, maybe, but there are war chants rising across the river."

And just like that... her happiness evaporated like the mist at midday.

Chapter 26

T hree days of war chants were followed by fog so thick it was hard to see the length of Baptiste's arm.

The major didn't like the fog any more than the rest of them. Didn't trust the Indians—who were silent at last—not to sneak up to the walls and shoot fire arrows over them. He'd placed Baptiste and the other Frenchmen who had taken up arms with the British along the palisade before dawn.

Just as the morning's light was starting to penetrate the fog, a shout went up from the south side of the palisade. Barges sighted. A lot of them. More attempts to set fire to the sloop? Or something more sinister? Before they got much closer, fighting against the current, a cannon fired from the southeast corner of the fort. It was followed in mere moments by an answering cannon from the first barge.

The shout that rose from the walls was one of jubilation. A British cannon telling the fort that help was on the way, that at last, their relief and supplies had arrived. Baptiste grinned at the man next to him, but neither left their post.

Gunshots rang out from across the river, Indians firing at the barges. The fort's cannons boomed again, this time no doubt aimed at the opposing riverbank.

From where Baptiste was stationed, the barges came into view as they made their way to the fort and tied up near the sloops. Barge after barge, with men disembarking in a continuous line. More men than the fort had room for, but men needed to put an end to the uprising. He and Maggie would likely be turned out of the cabin.

He and Maggie and the child that grew within her.

He was still getting used to the idea of being a père. Still healing from the bruise Henri had left on his shoulder, a little over-zealous in his congratulations upon learning he would be an uncle. But he'd also seen a hint of something else in Henri's face. Not jealousy. More like envy. It did his heart good to know that there was a part of Henri that wished for a life such as Baptiste had. Such as Père and Maman had given them. That the wildness inside of him had not completely taken over.

"'Tis the last barge, that," one of the British soldiers said. "Twenty-two, and over two hundred and fifty fighting men, unless I miss my guess. With cannons."

"And food!" another from down the wall yelled in response. That brought a cheer from around the palisade.

The days of war chants had left the fort exhausted, too few men filling too many roles with too little sleep. As much as the food was welcomed, the extra men were needed. Even if it meant he and Maggie would be sleeping on the blacksmith shop floor until he could erect some kind of lean-to against it.

The men represented the best chance of quelling the uprising quickly. Perhaps even allowing them to return to the farm and his cabin. His and Maggie's cabin.

More than anything, he wanted his son to be born there.

Maggie had all their belongings packed as best she could, using their chair crates and buckets and wrapping more into their blankets. Everything had fit but the ticking, which Baptiste could carry. She didn't want to leave the little cabin, but with so many soldiers spilling across the parade ground, there was no way they'd be allowed to keep it.

It was a small price to pay for the men who would put an end to the war.

Restless, she left the cabin and visited with Beau and Pierre. The oxen drowsed in the sun that had finally beat back the fog. Pierre came to her at the fence, and she scratched the itchy spot between his eyes. Then she glanced toward the parade ground, even though it was hidden by buildings from where the cattle pens were.

Would so many mouths to feed put the gentle oxen in danger again?

She hoped not. Many barrels and crates had been unloaded from the barges. And so many barges. Surely there was enough to feed those inside the fort for long enough to stop Pontiac's attempts to force the British out.

A group of soldiers approached dressed in the uniforms of the American militia, most of them looking barely old enough to shave.

One of them, looking older than the rest, stopped and stared at her.

"Come on, Reg. We must hurry if we hope to get a bunk," said one of the departing soldiers over his shoulder.

She looked again at the soldier who'd stopped. He ignored his fellow soldier, not letting his eyes drift from hers. Slowly, he reached up and dragged off his hat, exposing a shock of reddish-brown waves and a freckled face.

"Kerr, get a move on," another soldier hollered from down the street.

Reg... Kerr. Could it be?

She took a step closer, and so did he.

"Maggie?"

Her heart skipped a beat, maybe two, before she could work any moisture into her mouth.

"Reggie?"

"'Tis true. I knew it." He ran toward her then, sweeping her into his arms. "You are alive."

So was he, solid and strong and nothing like the stripling boy she remembered... except his freckles and hair and voice.

He stepped back and took her face between his hands. "I would have known you anywhere. You are the very image of Mama except for your hair."

"Mama." The word came out in a breath.

Sorrow clouded her brother's eyes. "She died three years back. I always thought from a broken heart after losing you."

Moisture gathered in her eyes and clogged her throat, making the next words even harder to say, "Da? Catherine? Donald?"

Reggie nodded. "All alive, and Cynthia too. She was born after..."

After Maggie had been taken away from them. Something hardened inside her, wicking away the tears. They'd replaced her with another daughter. "He never came for me."

Reggie shook his head. "He couldn't, Maggie. Da"—he looked away and then back—"he took an arrow in the attempt. He can't walk without a crutch. He had to sell the farm. We moved back to town, and he works as a store clerk now."

Da crippled? What of the others from Fort McCord? "No one came for me."

Reggie's hands slipped to her shoulders. "They tried. Da tried." He gave her a little shake, as if to assure himself that she was really there. "For months and months they tried. They got all the others back, eventually, but you were not with them. No one knew who had taken you." He dropped his hands and looked at the ground. "Everyone said you were dead." His eyes snapped back up to hers. "I never believed them."

Her brother. As a child, he'd been her defender, her protector. She leaned into him again, wrapping her arms around his ribs and squeezing. "I am so happy to see you again."

"And I you, little sister."

She'd turned her face, pressing her cheek against his chest, when into her range of vision stepped Baptiste, face like a thundercloud.

"GET YOURS HANDS OFF HER." BAPTISTE PULLED Maggie to his side, ignoring her gasp of outrage. Outrage? When he found her in the arms of another man?

She stepped sideways, away from him.

Anger flared inside Baptiste, stealing his breath for words.

The soldier in question tried to step between them. "Unhand her!"

"Baptiste!" Maggie wrapped both of her hands around the fist he had cocked to level the soldier. "Non!"

She might as well have punched him.

"Baptiste, listen to me."

Listen to her defend herself for being in another man's arms? What did she take him for? An ignorant French cripple who could not control his wife. He ground his teeth when she tugged on his arm.

"He is my brother."

The words barely made it past the rage roaring in his ears, but after she gave him another none-too-gentle tug on his arm, he heard them. The fight seeped from him like water through a sack.

"Your brother?"

The soldier crossed his arms and met Baptiste stare for stare. The reddish hair and freckles, the same direct blue-gray eyes. Even the same chin, tilted in that determined way his Maggie often did. Oui, this must be her brother.

"Baptiste, this is Reggie Kerr. My brother." Maggie turned to Reggie. "And this is Baptiste Geroux, my husband."

"Husband?" Reggie's brows rose in momentary shock before lowering into a scowl and focusing on her. "You married a Frenchman?"

"Indeed." Maggie moved to Baptiste's side, and he slipped his arm around her back, an action that came without thought. "He is a good man. Being French or English does not matter in that."

Reggie's expression said he didn't agree, but he didn't argue.

Another soldier, an officer, approached.

Reggie snapped to attention.

"Kerr, have you secured lodging for you and your men?"

"No, sir, Captain Dalyell."

"What are you waiting for?"

"Sir, I have just been reunited with my sister."

The officer looked Maggie up and down, reconstituting the anger Baptiste had let go of. "Do you have a house, ma'am?"

"We do. A cabin."

"Very good. I shall assign your brother and five others to be quartered with you there. Please show him the way."

"Yes, sir," said Maggie, a grin breaking out as soon as the officer strode away. Then she gripped Baptiste's hand. "We will not be turned out after all."

No, but they'd be crowded with six soldiers spread out over

the floor. One of them the brother who still eyed Baptiste as if he smelled bad. At least his wife could keep her bed. In her condition, that was preferable to sleeping on the floor of the blacksmith shop.

"Come, we will show you the way." Maggie grabbed her brother's arm and tugged him forward, keeping her other hand on Baptiste's arm. She walked between them, her step light and her chatter brisk.

Baptiste said nothing. On the one hand, he should be happy that she was reunited with her brother, as she had been happy for him when Henri returned. On the other hand, he would be sharing their cabin—and her—with someone else. Someone he didn't know.

A British soldier.

"It will be fine, sister." Reggie came behind Maggie as she stirred the kettle filled with stew. "Captain Dalyell is a capable man, and besides, we have Robert Rogers with us. The men respect him, trust him."

"Respect and trust are all well and good, but you will be facing Pontiac and his warriors, not some uniformed army across a field." Maggie gripped the spoon with almost enough force to snap it. How could she bear it if Reggie walked out to meet Pontiac's men and never returned?

He took her shoulders and turned her around. "I am not a raw recruit. I know what I am about. I will come back to you, Maggie. I promise."

She summoned a smile for his brave words, but they lay cold in her chest. He'd written down Da's address. She'd learned to read and write as a girl, but she'd need Mrs. Roberts's help to write a letter. And for sure, she didn't want that letter to include losing Reggie in battle.

The evening before, while the other soldiers had been out, she'd shared with Reggie everything that had happened to her. Baptiste had stayed by her side, his support a palpable presence in the small cabin. Reggie had seemed to sense it as well, and the hostility he'd displayed initially had melted away. It had been... surreal for Maggie. The brother she never thought to see again, the husband she'd never thought to have, before a warm fire after a filling meal.

She could have been completely happy if only Reggie weren't going outside the walls again so soon, taking such a risk. But she couldn't talk him out of it. He was duty-bound to do as ordered by the men who thought they knew best.

"Tell me more about Da and my sister—sisters—and Donald." She prepared a huge batch of biscuits from wheat flour that had arrived on the barges. As he talked, she let go of some of the hurt of her past, some of the anger. Da a cripple. Not like Baptiste, who could do almost anything, if perhaps in a different fashion. Da, according to Reggie, was in great pain daily and had turned into an old man almost overnight. And as Reggie talked, she pushed the worry for his safety to the back of her thoughts.

Her worries wouldn't change anything.

"IT IS FOOLISHNESS." HENRI LEANED CLOSER TO Baptiste, his voice a low growl. "That man, Dalyell, he thinks to surprise Pontiac."

"You do not think it possible?"

"Non." Henri glanced around the oxen pen where they leaned against the pole fence. "There are too many ears in the fort, too many eyes, and too many loose tongues."

Baptiste agreed. "Would he listen to you?"

Henri snorted. "Would a British soldier listen to any Frenchman?"

It might be worth a try. Major Gladwin seemed even-handed in his dealings with the French. Perhaps—

"Even if I tried, I could give him no proof of the spies, no names."

Neither could Baptiste, though he agreed with Henri that there were spies within the walls of the fort.

Henri cuffed his shoulder. "But this brother who came off the barge, that is good for Maggie, non?"

"Very good."

"What is this?" Henri squinted at the tone Baptiste hadn't meant to infuse into the words. "You are not jealous of a brother, are you?"

"Non." Not jealous. Not exactly. After all, Henri joined them for meals often. A brother at the table was a good thing.

A brother with five strange men sleeping on his floor was something else.

Henri laughed, a pleasant sound to mix with the tension that zinged inside the fort. "But you wish to have Maggie all to yourself."

Baptiste fought the heat rising above his collar.

"I do not blame you, brother. If I had my own Maggie, I would feel the same." His teasing dropped away as a group of soldiers approached, then passed without comment. "She will be deeply grieved if her brother goes out and does not come back."

That was weighing on Baptiste as well. "Oui."

Henri pushed off the fence. "Perhaps I will tag along with the soldiers."

"Non." Baptiste clamped his hand on Henri's shoulder, his grip tight. "It is not your fight or mine."

"If the brother does not return?"

Baptiste exhaled and closed his eyes for a moment. "Then, for my wife, I will seek revenge."

"Then, for my brother, I will be by his side."

Chapter 27

Baptiste kissed the top of Maggie's head, her face pressed to his chest, the scent of her hair filling his senses. "I will keep watch with the other Frenchmen."

"It is so dark. Why do they leave when they cannot see? They do not know the country around us."

"They took scouts with them."

Maggie snorted, and Baptiste agreed with the dismissive tone of it. The scouts were Frenchmen or half-French and half-Indian. They could as much be spy as scout. Captain Dalyell, however, had not listened. It was said that Major Gladwin did his best to discourage the attack. Captain Dalyell, being an assistant under the command of General Amherst himself, had overridden the major's objections and set his plan into motion.

A plan which had, at best, a fifty percent chance of working.

Baptiste kissed his wife again, then stepped out into the humid night air. There wasn't a breath of breeze inside the fort's walls. He climbed to the top of the palisade, the misty clouds doing little to block the light from the sliver of moon overhead. At least it wasn't a full moon that would have illuminated the soldiers.

Below him, a long line of Redcoats left the fort. They made

enough noise to wake the dead, at least to Baptiste's frontier-trained ears. So many of them.

"How many are going?" he asked the sentinel beside him.

"Almost everyone who came on the barges."

Leaving the fort with too few defenders yet again. Who thought that a good idea? Not Major Gladwin. He was too savvy to have made such a decision.

Baptiste squinted at the stars through the mist. It couldn't be much past two o'clock in the morning, but the air was hot and muggy. He slapped at a mosquito that buzzed around his ear and pitied the wool-coated soldiers below.

A pair of barges, each equipped with one of the smaller cannons mounted on a swivel, launched into the river and followed the line of men. That was smart. Indians tended to scatter when grapeshot was lobbed at them.

But would it be enough? There were, at most, two hundred and fifty soldiers. How many warriors were there combined from all the tribes? There were Ottawa, Ojibwe, Potawatomi, some of the Huron who'd stayed in the fight, plus both Lenni Lenape and Shawnee had been reported in the area. In all likelihood, the count was four hundred or more. Perhaps many more.

Maggie's brother was in the thick of it.

Setting aside his irrational reaction to the man's appearance —Baptiste was willing to admit to himself that it was irrational —it would devastate her to lose her brother.

Henri had been gone for more than two years. Until then, they'd never been separated for more than a few nights. And when he'd returned, Baptiste had been overjoyed. What must it be like for Maggie, having lost all of her family so many years ago, only to find one again in the fort? Against all odds.

They hadn't had a moment alone with time to speak of it, but her every movement conveyed her joy. The way she served

Reggie's meals, washed and mended his spare clothing, even cut his hair. All done with love in her eyes.

So much love.

Hence the irrational reaction on Baptiste's part. Seeing her love shared with someone else, even her brother, was... not to his liking.

Why?

He rotated his neck, easing the tight muscles.

Because Henri was right. Baptiste loved his wife. He may not know much about love in the broad sense, but in this sense he knew.

He loved Maggie.

But did she love him?

GOING BACK TO SLEEP WAS OUT OF THE QUESTION, SO Maggie tidied the cabin as much as she could, the floor being mostly covered with the soldiers' belongings. Daylight was still an hour away when she'd finished that task. To escape the heat and stuffiness of the cabin, she stepped into the street.

Houses and cabins alike glowed with candlelight. It seeped around every shutter, every door, and blazed out of those which were open. The whole fort was tense and waiting. Worrying.

A group of four soldiers, muskets in their hands and not at their shoulders, walked the street. They didn't march, they walked—more like stalked—peering into the shadows between buildings. The major was leaving nothing open to chance, like Indians infiltrating the fort while such a large force of men was away.

Despite the sticky air, Maggie hugged arms around her middle.

The soldiers reached her. One stepped forward, a veteran

with scars on his face and gray hair tied back above his collar. "'Tis best to stay inside, ma'am. And bolt your door."

"Perhaps so."

He touched his hat but didn't insist that she leave the street. The others ignored her, speaking to several others also in the street.

Waiting.

So much had changed for Maggie in the three months since her escape from Stone Foot and the Hurons. From Tree Sleeper. She hugged herself tighter. Was he out there? Was Reggie marching toward that evil man? Not that Tree Sleeper knew who Reggie was, but the thought sent a spurt of something close to panic through her.

Reggie.

Of all her family, it made sense that he'd been the one to cross her path. He'd played at being a soldier from her earliest memories, memories that had been unlocked during her flight, but not fully explored—not all of them—until Reggie's arms had come around her. It had been as if a log had struck a beaver dam and broken it open. Some of the memories were so fresh it almost hurt her to think on them. Many of them with Mama and Catherine, little Donald. Others pained in a different way. The memories of Da.

She'd all but worshiped him. He'd called her his little princess and told her fables about princesses of old. While she'd helped Mama in the cabin, it had been her chores in the barn with Da that she'd relished. Learning to milk the cow, gathering the hens' eggs, even walking the fields with Da and dribbling seeds into the dirt. Da had been patient and kind and everything a father should be.

Until he hadn't come for her.

She'd blamed him for that for years, had come close to hating him for it, and in the end, had done her best to erase him from her memory. In her mind, she'd wished him dead. Better dead than having refused to rescue her.

No longer. Reggie's news—very old news—of Da's lameness had begun the process of changing Maggie's heart. How odd that Da and her husband would share the same affliction.

Yet she couldn't imagine a situation where Baptiste would not come looking for her… would not find her. But Baptiste had no one else. In fairness, Da had Mama and the other children to support and care for. Reggie had said that others had looked for months.

Perhaps Da had done the best he could. Perhaps it had been above Da's ability to find her or hire others to find her. Perhaps —as she reflected on the man she now allowed herself to remember—Da had failed to rescue her because he simply hadn't been able.

Da was only a man, not someone to be worshiped.

She leaned against the rough logs of the cabin and blinked back moisture. The little-girl vision of Da and her new adult perspective would take time to reconcile, but already thoughts of him did not bring anger or resentment—at least not as much —only sorrow.

Distant gunfire erupted to the north. A lot of gunfire.

Fear clawed at her middle as Maggie raced to the north wall, passing others stumbling out of their homes. She had no idea where Baptiste was on the wall, but she ran toward the sounds. The boom of a cannon, followed closely by a second, brought a bit of hope.

"Maggie!"

She skidded to a stop and searched for the voice, Baptiste's voice.

"Here!" He waved his hat, the gentle light of the moon and stars falling on his dark hair.

She sprinted for the closest ladder and climbed to his side, not caring if the soldiers would rebuke her or not. Most of them were outside the walls anyway.

He grasped her upper arm and helped her step onto the walkway.

"Can you see anything?"

"Non. But there is too much gunfire. The Indians have not scattered away from the cannon."

Another cannon boomed, and she pressed against her husband, needing the arm that slipped behind her. Needing his support. Needing... him.

"This is not good for the soldiers." He peered into her face. "I am sorry, my love."

My love.

Heart breaking for her brother and fighting panic for whatever else was happening out there, she clung to those two words for a several heartbeats before pulling away.

"I will go to Surgeon Roberts and do whatever he says."

"That is a good idea. Wounded men will find their way back."

She touched the side of Baptiste's face, then pressed her lips to his almost fiercely before breaking away and descending the ladder.

Reggie was in grave danger, which terrified her. But Baptiste loved her. Her heart could barely hold the conflicting emotions of the past few moments. Keeping her hands busy was the best way she knew to deal with everything. And if Reggie came in with the wounded... she must be there.

She would not leave him alone.

THE SOLDIERS RETURNED IN STRAGGLING GROUPS OF ten to thirty. Baptiste and every other available man—French and British—manned the heights with muskets and rifles. But no Indians came close enough to fire upon.

Henri appeared beside him, long gun in his hands. "It is bad."

"Oui." Baptiste nodded toward another group straggling in, several having to be supported by their comrades.

"There is a group of soldiers still out there, trapped," Henri said. "The one called Rogers led that group."

Robert Rogers. That meant Maggie's brother could be one of them.

Henri squeezed his shoulder. "I am going out with a group of soldiers to try and free them."

"I will join you."

"Non." Henri glanced down into the fort and back at Baptiste. "You stay here, for Maggie."

Baptiste bristled. "I go for Maggie. He is her brother."

"But I can—"

"So can I." Baptiste slung his rifle across his back by its strap and stepped onto the ladder. "I must do this."

"Brother." Henri climbed down after him, grabbing his arm once his feet hit the ground. "If neither of you come back, where would that leave her? And your child?"

Baptiste sucked in a deep breath of the muggy air. "Maggie is strong. She will take care of the child."

"This I know, but should she suffer the loss of the husband she loves as well as the long-lost brother?"

The husband she loves? Did she love him, truly? As he loved her? If he survived the night, he had every intention of asking her.

"I am going." Baptiste headed for the gate, Henri catching up to him with long strides.

"You would not come west with me on a trapping journey,

but you will walk into a battle for a man you barely know." Henri clouted him on the shoulder. "You are crazy."

"I barely know him, but he is Maggie's brother." Baptiste shot a glance at Henri. "She would do whatever she could for you, because you are mine. I can do no less."

"I suppose not." Henri pointed to a group forming on the parade ground. "There are the men we will join."

There were about half Frenchmen in the gathering, which surprised Baptiste. But maybe it shouldn't. These men had already sided with the British by being in the fort. Ending the uprising as soon as possible would benefit them all. The farmers could go back to salvage what crops were left. The traders could send for more supplies. Until the war was squashed, they could do nothing but wait.

Waiting wore on a man like a yoke of brambles.

Their leader barked orders, and the soldiers and Frenchmen formed lines just before the gates opened. They stepped outside the high walls as the sun turned the eastern sky to gray with a band of brilliant orange flaring from the treetops. There would be no hiding. This was an open march to battle.

He and Henri walked shoulder to shoulder, every nerve alert, eyes scanning their surroundings. Before and behind them were men who also knew the land and the people who lived there. Men who would fight, not for a king on a distant shore, but for their homes. There was a measure of confidence in that.

They had gone less than half a mile when gunfire resumed ahead of them. Their leader waved them onward, into a trot. If the others had run, Baptiste could not have kept up, but even with his uneven gait, he could handle the pace.

Henri bumped his shoulder, then used sign language. Baptiste wasn't as adept at it as Henri, but he caught the basics. There was a swampy area near Parent's Creek that boasted an island of sorts. The gunfire sounded from that direction. If the soldiers were trapped on that island, it would be difficult to get them out. The island had some trees for cover, but they'd have to cross the open swamp to leave it, exposing them to the enemy.

They reached the scene of the battle as dawn broke fully over the trees. Red-coated bodies sprawled across the ground. Too many of them. As Henri had assumed, the gunfire came from the island.

The commander came down the line issuing orders to hit the flanks of the Indians on both sides, to drive them farther north.

They shouldn't have been able to sneak up on the Indians, but to Baptiste's amazement, they had. The battle that followed was intense. Muskets and rifles were fired, then slung out of the way as hand-to-hand fighting with knives and tomahawks took over. The only guns that continued to shoot were from the island, and Baptiste hoped they were all good shots.

An Indian came at him, face painted and mouth open, screaming as he ran. Baptiste dodged and slashed with his knife. The Indian also dodged. They circled each other, and the Indian grinned when Baptiste's twisted leg caught on a fallen branch. Not a large one, but enough to make him stop. Enough to make him an easy target.

The Indian was screaming again, tomahawk lifted when a knife whistled past Baptiste and planted into the other man's chest. His look of surprise barely registered before he fell. Henri shoved him over with his foot and retrieved his blade.

"That was close, brother."

"Too close." Baptiste turned his back, knowing Henri would do the same, and they moved forward, protecting each other as they had so many times growing up. Then, it had been war games with Dances Away, Walking Fire Stick, and others.

The thought of coming across his old friend brought a twinge of pain. This time, it was no game.

Before he could dwell on it, another line of Indians charged. Several were dropped by good shots from the island, and then it was close fighting again. The soldiers on the island took the opportunity to cross the swamp. With their added numbers, and reloaded weapons, the tide turned.

Baptiste spotted Reggie in the midst of the charge. He fought his way through to the young man, Henri staying by his side. As they drew near, an Indian burst through a line of soldiers, one falling to his tomahawk and another grabbing a slashed arm from his knife.

Henri stiffened next to Baptiste and uttered a curse.

Tree Sleeper.

Chapter 28

Henri's knife sliced through the air, turning a perfect spin. But Tree Sleeper's reflexes were quick. Baptiste would give him credit for that. Instead of the knife finding its mark mid-chest, it caught the Huron in the upper shoulder. The *thwack* of it striking bone cut through the cries and shouts of the men around them.

Tree Sleeper recovered from his duck and dodge, kept his feet, and retreated back into the forest around the marsh.

Henri growled beside Baptiste. "To have wasted such a knife on that one," he muttered in French.

"'Twas some throw," Reggie said, having taken up a defensive position on Baptiste's other side. Perhaps he didn't understand French. Maggie had learned in the Huron camp, evidenced by her Indian-accented words.

"He still got away," Henri said in English. "That one needs killing if any man does."

The leader of their forces was signaling them back into an organized retreat. The three men kept their position as others, many supporting the wounded, made their escape.

"Why is that one special?" Reggie asked.

Baptiste shot him a glare. He knew nothing of what had

happened here. Nothing of what his sister had gone through. Baptiste reined in his flash of anger. Reggie hadn't even known she was alive. "That one, Tree Sleeper, had been chosen by her captor to be your sister's husband."

Reggie's mouth opened, then snapped shut.

Good. At least he knew when to be silent.

"Be thankful that my brother married her and not that"— Henri pointed toward where the Huron had escaped into the forest—"evil one."

Maggie's brother remained silent as they brought up the end of the retreat, then he stepped away from Baptiste and Henri to assist one of the wounded. One of the men who had been sleeping on their floor.

Walking backwards was challenging with his twisted leg, but Baptiste knew better than to turn his back on the warriors behind. So did several of the other local men. Together with him and Henri, they formed the rear guard all the way to the fort.

They entered the gate, and Maggie rushed to his side.

His—not her brother's.

"You did not tell me you were leaving." Her words came at him in rapid French. Rapid and angry French. "If something had happened to you, I would not even have had the chance to say good-bye."

She was flustered, hair clinging to the sweat of her face, and fire burning a smoky haze in her eyes.

She was beautiful.

She was his.

He pulled her close. She stiffened for a moment and then melted against him in that way she had. The way that filled him with a strange combination of longing and contentment.

"There was no time," he whispered to her. "Your brother was in danger. My brother and I, we had to go. We are family, are we not?"

The fire in her eyes was quenched with a film of moisture. "Merci for that." Then she took a fistful of his shirt and gave him a shake. "But never leave without telling me again." Then she pushed away from him and ran to her brother, who had deposited his friend against the wall of the fort.

His little spitfire.

"Oh, my brother. To find a wife like that one." Henri breathed a quiet whistle between his teeth. "You are a lucky man. I would give much to find one such as her."

Baptiste wished the same for his brother, he truly did, but he had to squelch the urge to step in front of Henri and block his view of Maggie. In truth, his brother was looking at his wife with too much... not desire, but deep interest, in his face.

FOUR OF THE SIX SOLDIERS QUARTERED IN THEIR cabin had returned injured. None of them mortally. Maggie walked among them as they stretched out on the floor. She filled cups with water and checked bandages as Surgeon Roberts had shown her, examining and smelling for any hint of infection. While the wounds wouldn't kill them, an infection might.

In her heart, Maggie rejoiced that her husband, her brother, and her brother-in-law were not among them. Perhaps that was why she took such diligent care of the wounded men around her.

Baptiste was never far away. With no metals to work with, none having come on the supply barges, he had little to do at the blacksmith shop. But she thought there was more that kept him close to her. His watchfulness, his silent scrutiny of the wounded men, it all spoke of his need to protect her.

Not so long ago, she would have scoffed at needing a crippled man to protect her. She'd not seen Baptiste as a threat because he wouldn't be able to catch her if she ran. Even in the cabin, when she'd returned from the fort, she saw him as a peaceful man, one content to work the land, not pick up a musket.

How wrong she'd been.

While she'd been leery of Henri from the start, he and his feral glances, his ruthless manner, she now realized that Baptiste was every bit the warrior. Not in exactly the same way, that was true, but just as fierce. But with Baptiste, there was a loyalty she did not see in Henri. She gave herself a mental shake. Of course she would not see that loyalty in Henri. He was not her husband. But was it not his knife that had pierced Tree Sleeper?

For that, she owned her brother-in-law much.

As they'd laid on their bed the night before, Maggie had clung to Baptiste. Not in a sensual way—how could one feel sensual with snoring men not an arm's length away? But she'd needed to feel his solid form next to hers. She needed to know that he was safe, that he was with her.

That he loved her.

He'd called her *my love* on the palisade wall. She longed to hear the words again, spoken softly from the heart, and not in the heat of battle. There had been no words between them. He'd lain on his side and snugged her back against his chest, his hand splayed across her still-flat stomach. Within moments, his breath had steadied to the deep rhythm of sleep.

"Ma'am?"

The voice jerked her out of the memory and splashed heat across her cheeks.

The soldier held up an empty cup. "Could I have some more water?" His face was grimy, his hair full of dried mud, but his eyes were boyish, as was his grin.

She filled the cup and brought it back to him.

He took a drink, then shifted and grimaced. "I also need to..." He jerked a thumb toward the door.

Before she could say anything, Baptiste was there. He helped the man to his feet and supported him to the door. Doubtless to the latrine. Her husband didn't want another man touching her. Not even one recovering from injury.

The thought made her smile.

"What causes my brother's wife to stand in the cabin and smile?" Henri stepped through the doorway, a willow twig circled in his hand with seven long fish dangling from it, some still flipping their tails.

"My husband's brother bringing fresh fish for supper." She turned to those lying on the floor. "What do you think? Fresh fish instead of salt pork tonight?"

The chorus of agreement didn't surprise her. The army didn't vary the men's diet much. They'd been pathetically grateful for anything she fixed them with the supplies they'd brought. Fresh anything—meat or vegetable—was always welcome.

"You will join us, of course?"

Henri laid the fish on the table. "I will. Where is my brother?"

"He was helping—"

"I am here." Baptiste supported the soldier to his bedroll on the floor and helped him settle before coming to the table and poking one of the fish. "You have the trap out again?"

"Oui." Henri winked at Maggie, then looked back at his brother. "I can still be useful, even in the fort."

"In that case—"

"Join me for a walk." Henri's voice leveled into a more serious tone.

Baptiste touched her shoulder, his eyes promising to share whatever it was Henri wanted to tell him.

Away from the British soldiers' ears.

Maggie set about cleaning the fish, listening half-heartedly to the soldiers' talk and hoping that whatever Henri had to say to Baptiste was good news about the war ending. About them returning to the farm.

About going home.

"I SPOKE WITH DANCES AWAY THIS MORNING."

Baptiste glanced around them as they walked farther from the cabin. The street was its usual level of busy. Women sweeping, children running, dogs barking, all under the eyes of the soldiers at the top of the palisade.

"You took a risk."

Henri shrugged. "Perhaps, but he is my friend."

"Even now, while you are living in the fort? Even after you helped the soldiers?"

"Even then."

"Was he there yesterday?" Baptiste's stomach tightened, but he asked, "Was Walking Fire Stick?"

"Oui. They were both there. Both are fine."

Baptiste let out a long breath. "I worried that I would see my old friend down the barrel of my rifle." He shook his head. "Or even worse, at the point of my knife."

Henri grimaced. "It was the same with me."

"And yet, you went."

"As did you."

At first, Baptiste had vowed to ignore the war, to remain neutral. Then Maggie had returned to him and changed everything. Most things for the better. Like her in his arms as he went to sleep. Like the promise of a little Geroux to carry on the family line. He couldn't regret his decision to come to the fort, but he longed for his farm. He longed for the blasted war to be over. And he longed for a lasting peace overseen by men with cool heads and steady hearts.

"Dances Away said that there was great rejoicing for the victory at Parent's Creek."

Baptiste nodded. There would be. The Indians had driven the Redcoats back to the fort, had killed and wounded many. But they had taken losses too.

"It is a hollow victory." Baptiste waved an arm at their surroundings. "The fort is manned by more soldiers, many more, and supplied by the barges with food, powder, and lead. Pontiac did not gain much."

"Dances Away knows this. He also knows that stomachs will be empty in the winter months. Too little has been done to tend the crops or dry meat for the winter."

"The fields I plowed for the Ottawa women to plant?"

"Left to grow deep in weeds."

Baptiste swallowed down a wave of irritation. That his work, his gesture of good will, had amounted to so little. "What else did Dances Away say?"

Henri stopped and faced him. "He wishes to return to the west, to trap more furs, to see more new land. To leave behind this war he does not think they will win."

West again. Baptiste's chest tightened as he looked to his feet. Henri gone for another year or two, possibly longer.

"I wished him good health and good hunting."

That jerked Baptiste's head up. "You will not go with him?"

"Non." Henri grinned and poked him in the chest. "And it is your fault, brother."

"My fault?"

"Oui. You and your pretty wife." He shrugged again. "How can I leave for who knows how long when my niece or nephew will arrive in the spring?"

Baptiste grinned and breathed a sigh of relief. "True. You cannot."

Henri sobered. "But there is another reason." He started walking again.

It took Baptiste a few steps to catch up. "What is this other reason?"

They reached the oxen's enclosure before Henri stopped and dropped his forearms to the top rail. Beau raised his head and flicked his black ears in their direction. Pierre dozed in the sunlight. The area smelled of rich manure, heated earth, and dusty bovines as he waited for his brother to find his words. It wasn't Henri's way to be rushed. He would speak when he was ready.

"The farm next to ours—to yours because you have been the one to work it—has been abandoned." Henri rubbed his nose with the back of his hand. "I think I would like to take it up. To work the land. To build something permanent."

"You?" If Henri had told him he was going to sprout wings and fly, it couldn't have surprised him any more thoroughly. "A farmer?"

"I am sure I will need much help from my big brother, non?" Henri flashed him a grin. "And maybe some of my brother's luck will rub off on me, and I will find a good woman to share it with."

"Maybe." Baptiste wrapped his arm around Henri's neck as they leaned on the railing. "I hope so."

To have the war over, his farm back, his wife and babe at his side, and his brother as a neighbor...

Could anything be better than that?

Chapter 29

"'Tis the truth, as welcome as the soldiers are for our fort and our safety, I will not be sorry to see them out of our home." Mrs. Roberts pulled a uniform coat from the cooling kettle. "The men quartered here are all mannerly, but there is scarcely room to turn around in the evenings."

Maggie grabbed the bottom of the coat, and together they twisted most of the water out, letting it run back into the kettle as much as possible. Maggie added it to her growing pile of wet clothing.

"I am glad they are all out of our cabin during the day now." Maggie wiped a trickle of sweat from her neck with the back of her hand. "'Tis good that all the men with us recovered, due to Mr. Roberts's good care."

Mrs. Roberts smiled at her. "He says that same about *your* good care."

Maggie dunked the last coat into the soapy kettle, giving it a vigorous stir with an oak paddle. "Stone Foot taught me a few things. Not everything—the old man guarded his secrets—but enough to be useful."

"Enough to see that the men healed fully and quickly. 'Tis not a small thing."

A few gunshots popped to the west of the fort. Maggie looked that direction, but Mrs. Roberts hardly seemed to notice. Every day since the battle, shot had been lobbed at the fort. Several times, Major Gladwin had sent soldiers out to meet the Indians, but each time the Indians had fallen back and disappeared into the forest. For more than two weeks, this dance of fire, counter-fire, and retreat had taken place. Tempers were short among many behind the walls. Maggie imagined that they were also short in the Indian villages. Neither side was gaining. Neither side was losing. Every day it was the same.

If the fort fell, it may be due to monotony.

One welcome change was that the soldiers in their cabin had been moved from the floor to the loft. Baptiste and Reggie had reinforced the planking and built a ladder from scraps they'd scrounged around the fort. The cabin was still crowded, but at night, at least she and Baptiste had the illusion of privacy.

It was all worth it, however, to have Reggie nearby. He was busy during the days and many evenings, but when they had time, he would tell her of her family. He even had a couple of worn and wrinkled letters from Da that he'd read to her.

Da working as a clerk after discovering he was very good with numbers. Catherine, who had turned sixteen the past spring, was a beauty. Reggie said the young men had started sniffing around her—his words, not Da's—before she'd turned fourteen. Da had his hands full keeping them away. He needed her at home for a couple more years to help with the little one. Donald was ten going on eleven. The chubby toddler she'd tried to protect was to be apprenticed to a brewer in the village in a few years. And Cynthia, born after Maggie's abduction, was obviously Reggie's favorite. His eyes shone when he spoke of her. She was six years old and motherless for half her life. Maggie's heart softened at the thought of the sister she'd never met. At least she'd had Mama for eleven years.

Together, she and Reggie had written a letter to Da and the others. Reggie doing the actual writing, of course. Maggie had been able to read some of the words, but not most. She'd need to learn to read and write again to keep in touch with her family.

Her family.

Part of her wished to travel to Pennsylvania and see them, but the rest of her balked at the idea. Her home was here now, not inside Fort Detroit, but at the farm across the river. With Baptiste. And he would never wish to leave it.

The letter had left on the sloop sent to Fort Niagara for more supplies and reinforcements. How long would it take to reach Shippensburg, Pennsylvania? Months, probably.

Maggie and Mrs. Roberts finished the laundry, and Maggie was staggering back to the cabin under the weight of the buckets overflowing with wet wool uniforms when a cry went up from near the major's office.

A cry of celebration.

AFTER ALL THE FAILURES, AFTER THE FORTS OF Michilimackinac, Sandusky, Venango, Presque Isle, and Le Boeuf had fallen under the Indians' combined forces—and likely others they hadn't heard of yet—yesterday's news of Colonel Bouquet's rousing victory near Bushy Run in western Pennsylvania had brought a sense of relief. The first absolute victory against the tribes, and with fall fast approaching, it also promised the beginning of the end.

Fort Pitt was safe and fully manned. Fort Detroit, while harassed daily, was standing strong. Fort Niagara had, as far as anyone in Detroit knew, never been besieged or endangered. The three largest of the forts stood strong. Pontiac couldn't break the British without breeching the walls of at least one of these strongholds.

"He knows this is not good for his war," Henri said, speaking of Pontiac. Henri had slipped off to visit Dances Away early that morning. "And worse for him, the other tribal leaders know it too."

"His own people?"

Henri shrugged. "Dances Away plans to leave by the next full moon."

Less than two weeks away. Baptiste hoped, selfishly, that Henri would not change his mind and go with his longtime friend.

"He will leave even if the uprising continues?"

"He and Walking Fire Stick, they are both disillusioned with the fight. They know about the letter the major had ordered read to the Frenchmen here in the fort, and they do not believe the French will return." He shook his head. "And they are not the only ones within Pontiac's village."

If Pontiac lost the confidence of his own people, the war would end. Could it be that simple? Could the British out-wait the Indians and call it a victory? That would suit Baptiste just fine. He had no desire to fight or kill anyone. It was in him to live in peace with those around him. And lately, he'd allowed himself to hope that the same was true of Henri.

"But I have better news. Tree Sleeper has not been seen in the village by Dances Away since the fight in the swamp."

"Do you think you killed him after all?"

Henri shrugged. "He did not seem the type to give up, non? But infection…"

Baptiste grinned at his brother. "Then perhaps we could be back on the farm for the end of harvest time. We could salvage what is left in the field, and have time to hunt and dry meat for the months of snow and cold."

Henri dislodged a rock with the toe of his moccasin. "Perhaps."

There was a wealth of uncertainty in that one word. Baptiste was thoroughly tired of uncertainty. "But?"

"There is little left of your crops, brother. I walked through there this morning."

Anger flared, then fizzled. What else could the Indians do? They could no longer trade, they'd long since taken everything the French outside the fort could spare and plenty they couldn't, and the warriors were surrounding the fort instead of hunting and fishing. The women needed to feed their children and the elderly. The coming winter would be hard on them with limited food preserved. Very hard.

"There could be enough for one person, maybe two..." Henri let the sentence trail off.

Not enough food to include a woman and the coming child. The thought hit like biting into a bitter berry.

MORE SOLDIERS HAD ARRIVED, AND MANY MORE barges with supplies. Enough to see the fort through the winter. But the men were packed into the barracks like kernels on an ear of corn, and every house quartered at least four soldiers. Thank goodness they hadn't had to take in any more, but the fort was bursting at its seams.

Maggie wasn't, not yet, but it wouldn't be long before the child she carried would round her figure. For reasons she didn't quite understand, she didn't want their child born in the fort. Mrs. Roberts had been uneasy when Maggie had admitted as much, but as the wife of a surgeon, that was to be expected.

Raised in a longhouse of the Hurons, Maggie had witnessed many births, even assisted in a few. It had been her hands into which Redwing had slid, warm and sticky and utterly fascinating. She still missed the little boy, but he was better off with his own people. She splayed her hands over her flat middle, impatient for her own little one to appear. A boy, for Baptiste. She smiled and looked out the window at the dusty street. Then a girl, for her.

Baptiste strode into the cabin, his face flushed, eyes eager.

"What has happened?" she asked.

"A boat is leaving in the morning, a boat that will take us to Pennsylvania."

They'd discussed this at length, a trip to visit her family and await the birth of their child. The babe wouldn't be born in the fort, and Reggie assured her there were several midwives in Shippensburg.

Maggie was filled with mixed emotions, foremost the realization of what her husband was sacrificing for her. That he would leave his home, his brother, his very livelihood to take her to her family... It was a humbling realization. A testimony to his loyalty to her and their child.

The time had arrived.

"I will pack our belongings." She glanced around the room. "But what should we do with them?" They couldn't take everything, of course. Anything left in the cabin would be claimed by those who lived in it after them.

"Henri and I will take them across the river and store them in our cabin. He will watch over everything, including Beau and Pierre, while we are gone."

"And we will come back, non?"

His face relaxed, a smile tipping his mouth and crinkling the corners of his eyes. Then he pulled her against him. She went willingly, raising her face for his kiss. It was many long and satisfying minutes before he spoke again.

"We will return." His voice was husky. "This I promise you."

"I must get busy. I will pack and join you and Henri—"

"Non." The softness left his face and his voice. "You will stay in the fort."

She planted one fist on her hip and poked a finger into his chest. It was like poking a rock from his hours at the forge, but she didn't care. She poked again. "I will go with you, my husband, and see with my own eyes how our farm has survived in our neglect."

"Maggie—"

"Baptiste. I am a free woman again, and Henri admitted that Tree Sleeper is gone."

Uncertainty wavered in the creases of his forehead, and she knew she'd won. Careful to conceal any smugness, she got to work folding, packing, and bundling. Behind her, Baptiste sighed and left the cabin. She danced a little jig across the floor to collect their pots and kettle. They would have to eat from the larder tonight, but that was fine. Tomorrow they would sail.

Before then, she would see the farm again. Hear the babble of the river's edge. Feel the fertile earth beneath her feet. Smell the wind through the pines.

She would go home.

AGAINST HIS BETTER JUDGMENT, BAPTISTE HANDED Maggie into the canoe. The dark look Henri shot him mixed with his own misgivings, but the delight on her face... that he couldn't deny. In her own way, she was a creature of the wild, a part of nature. Living behind walls had taken a toll on her. She leaned out over the point of the canoe, face to the wind, and he could not deny her.

If he were honest with himself, deep down, he didn't wish

to. Seeing her at the farm again would give him good memories to hold to until they returned. Or if he returned alone.

Going to her family was the right thing to do, both because of the situation at the farm and because she should see them again. It would be difficult for him, living in the midst of the British for an entire winter, but for her, he would do so.

For her, he would do anything.

But would she be content to return with him after a season with the family she'd lost so long ago?

Henri shoved the canoe into the water. It was a large vessel they'd borrowed, holding the three of them and everything Maggie had packed to store in the cabin. Things Henri would need once he returned to live there. He'd promised to stay in the fort until it was safe, but it would be safe for Henri long before it would be safe for others, even with Dances Away's defection. He would talk his way back into the good graces of the village.

They beached the borrowed canoe at his usual spot. A quick glance showed no sign of his canoe.

"I hid it behind the barn," Henri said.

"A wise move." Baptiste's worries had all been for Maggie, not a canoe.

Henri hefted one of the crates and settled it on his shoulder. "We can check later to see if anyone has found it."

Maggie had her eyes closed, her nose in the air, arms flared at her sides.

Baptiste shouldered the other crate and stepped beside her.

Her eyes flew open and met his, a wide grin parting her lips. "Does it not smell wonderful?"

He knew what she meant. The fort smelled mostly of dust, old wood, and dirty bodies. He filled his lungs. The crispness brought on a pang of homesickness. But when he put his hand on his wife's back, and she leaned against him, the feeling of home that came over him had nothing to do with the cabin, the farm, or the towering pines behind it.

His home was wherever she was.

They made two trips back and forth between the cabin and canoe, then left Maggie to put things away in the cabin while Baptiste and Henri checked the fields. They had surveyed the damaged corn and peas and were heading to check on the canoe when…

"Baptiste!" Maggie's scream broke the stillness.

Never had Baptiste hated his twisted leg more than at that moment. Henri sprinted away, knife in his fist, leaving Baptiste to follow as best he could. In his rush, he tripped and fell, calling himself all kinds of a fool for allowing her to come. For having left her side. He scrambled to his feet and turned the corner around the barn, grabbing the weathered wood to stop his forward momentum.

Henri stood with his arms outstretched, knife pitched twenty feet in front of him, facing the man who held Maggie by the hair on the porch of the cabin, a knife to her chin.

Tree Sleeper.

The evil man's eyes flicked to Baptiste, then back to Henri. "She is mine. I paid for her a fair price." His words were in a barely recognizable French.

Maggie's eyes were huge. She didn't move. Even her chest was still, as if she didn't breathe.

It tore at something deep within Baptiste as he lumbered halfway to the cabin, the fall having twisted his lame leg. "She will never be yours. She has been mine for many months." And in her terror, she had called for him—not his brother.

A sneer cracked the warrior's painted face. "She is better off with me, a whole man, than a useless cripple."

Baptiste straightened. "Better a cripple than a coward who hides behind a woman."

"Baptiste." Henri started toward him, but Baptiste held him off with a raised hand.

"Come, Tree Sleeper. Let us see who is worthy of her." He tossed out the challenge, knowing the Huron man could not refuse. Knowing also that Henri would protect Maggie should he fail.

Tree Sleeper glanced between Baptiste and Henri.

Henri shook his head and backed away. "This is my brother's fight."

Maggie made not a sound, but her eyes filled. Were they tears of fear, sorrow, or something else?

Baptiste had no time to ponder them as Tree Sleeper shoved her away, drawing a tomahawk from his belt as he approached. Baptiste's tomahawk pressed into his palm, though he had no memory of drawing it.

They circled in the grass until Baptiste's back was to the cabin. Tree Sleeper needed his eyes on Henri and Maggie. That division of his attention was to Baptiste's advantage. When the Huron's dark eyes flashed toward Henri, Baptiste moved. Without raising his tomahawk, he swung low at the other man's legs.

Cat-like reflexes kept Tree Sleeper from the blow, but he stopped looking at Henri and concentrated on Baptiste. Something that might have been surprise brushed his flat features.

He hadn't expected Baptiste to take the initiative, so Baptiste moved quickly and struck again. The Huron blocked the blow and swung one of his own. While Baptiste's leg didn't allow him to move as quickly, his weeks at the forge had built a strength that even surprised him. He grabbed the Huron's arm and lifted him off the ground, throwing him free before the man's tomahawk could swing back and catch the side of Baptiste's head. But he landed and rolled to his feet in one fluid motion, charging Baptiste and swinging low... for Baptiste's lame leg.

Maggie screamed.

Baptiste twisted, avoiding the blow, but his leg gave out beneath him. With a tremendous effort, knowing it to be his last, he launched his tomahawk.

Tree Sleeper couldn't stop his forward movement. The tomahawk connected with the same shoulder that Henri had shot in the swap. The Huron's face twisted, a garbled string of words pouring from his mouth. Even so, it didn't stop him. He pulled back his good arm to throw his knife.

Henri scrambled to retrieve his knife from the dirt, and Baptiste rolled to the side, but he knew neither would be fast enough to beat the blade in the Huron's hand.

But Tree Sleeper arched his back, rose to his toes, and then collapsed, his knife hitting the ground beside him, a blossom of red on his bare chest.

Maggie rushed to Baptiste's side, and Henri stood over Tree Sleeper, his knife in his fist, but the other man didn't move, another blade visible thrust up from his chest.

Walking Fire Stick emerged from the forest.

Never had Baptiste been so happy to see his friend. The Ottawa man came to him then, arm outstretched. Baptiste grasped it and let the other man haul him to his feet.

Maggie tucked herself to his side.

Baptiste held Walking Fire Stick's strong arm. The arm that had thrown the knife that saved his life.

"I owe you, my friend."

"Henri has told me about this woman who put a spell on your good sense." He looked Maggie up and down. "And now I understand why." He chuckled. "My sister, she will have to settle for the other Geroux, non?"

"She will." Baptiste hugged Maggie closer. "She will."

Chapter 30

The wagon rumbled and bounced over the road leading into Shippensburg. Maggie held fast to the back of it, her legs dangling off the edge, the rough wood biting into her palms. Her queasiness didn't appreciate the bumping and jostling. It hadn't liked the pitching of the sloop either.

She and Baptiste had disembarked at the burned-out remains of Fort Presque Isle. Though the uprising was known to be over in that area, that didn't mean it was safe. Even this far east of Fort Pitt, they'd taken every precaution to travel unseen until they'd reached the major east-west road out of Fort Pitt. Reggie's directions and descriptions had proven accurate.

They'd no more than found the road when a line of freight wagons guarded by soldiers had pulled through. The driver of the first wagon, a man who'd introduced himself as Cully, offered them a ride. They'd gladly accepted. Maggie had crowded into the back with three other women and a total of nine children, refugees from Fort Pitt. From what they shared, they'd had a rougher time of the siege than Fort Detroit had. Maggie's heart pinched at the wan faces of the children, some too young to walk. They were worn down by hunger and fear.

Baptiste rode beside Cully on the narrow wagon seat. With

the wagons already full, the wagon driver's offer of a ride was generous indeed. She couldn't hear the men's voices, but considering the wagons had come from Fort Pitt, and she and Baptiste had come from Fort Detroit, it didn't take much guesswork to know they talked of the war.

"'Tis such a blessing to know that by nightfall we will be in a town," the woman who'd introduced herself as Annie said. "Once my feet hit the dirt of a real street, I will never leave that place again."

The other two women nodded and murmured in agreement.

Annie turned to Maggie. "Do you not agree? Are you not ready to live in a real town again? Where there is safety and sanity?"

Maggie glanced at the expectant faces. Thin faces of women who had survived much and didn't want to ever have to do it again. Was she wrong to wish for the forest and fields around her? To wish for the sturdy log cabin and a pair of soft-eyed oxen by the barn? To long for the babble of the river, the sighing of the pines?

"My husband and I will return in the spring."

Annie gasped. "How can you?"

Maggie glanced out the back of the wagon, at the one that followed, filled with more women fleeing what she so wished to return to. "Because it is my home." Her answer caused another round of murmurs, but how could they understand? They'd probably been raised in towns, taken west by husbands set on adventure. These women were going home.

Maggie was not.

She wished to see Da, needed to see him. Even after what Reggie had told her, there was still a spark of resentment—unforgiveness—for him leaving her with her captors. In her head, she understood that a lame man had limitations. In her heart, she still saw Da as the strapping man who could plow a whole field in a single day. The man who had carried her on his shoulders, so high off the ground that she'd squealed in fear even as she trusted him to never let go.

If the women were correct, she might see him tonight.

Had the letter reached him? Probably not. The sloop with the letter had sailed barely a fortnight before they'd caught a ride on the other sloop heading for more supplies. Would he know her, as Reggie had? Or would he have written her off for dead?

She twisted, looked at the straight, strong back of her husband. She wouldn't have to face Da alone, and for that, she was grateful. Baptiste would be with her, his arm around her back in that way that still made her toes grip the bottoms of her moccasins. She turned back around.

The moccasins had brought her some narrow-eyed looks when she'd climbed into the wagon, but the women had said nothing. Perhaps they thought she'd been unable to find better footwear and pitied her.

Da would know why she wore them. Would he look at her differently? Would he see the little girl of years ago? Or would he see a young woman raised to be an Indian?

Why hadn't she thought of that before?

———

THE TOWN'S LIGHTS CAME INTO VIEW AS THE SUN struck the treetops to the west. Baptiste drew in a quick breath. The place was easily four times the size of Fort Detroit. So many houses, smoke from the many chimneys sooty against the evening sky. Light poured from windows—probably through real glass—into the surroundings. He'd never been in a such a town before. It was... daunting.

"There's a welcome sight. The sooner I get these women

delivered, the sooner I can be about my business and return to Fort Pitt." Cully leaned closer to Baptiste. "There is a special woman left behind who waits for me."

Then it was a welcome sight for the freight wagon driver. But for Baptiste? What kind of welcome would he find from the father of his wife? The man had been crippled and lost his daughter during the French and Indian War. She was returning to him with a French husband at her side.

And ever at the back of his mind was the question that wouldn't be silenced. After she reunited with her family, would she still wish to return to the solitary cabin on the frontier?

With him.

Maggie's hands gripped his waist, and a welcoming warmth spread over him. She'd moved through the overcrowded wagon box and must have stood on her toes to look over his shoulder.

"That is Shippensburg, non?" Her breath brushed his ear, and her choice of the French words made him proud. There was no hiding his heavily accented English, but Maggie could slip between several languages and be understood in them all. His clever wife. His little spitfire.

"Oui. You will see your family soon. Your père."

The next breath that fanned his ear quivered a bit. She was nervous. He couldn't do much about that—what happened next would be out of his hands—but he wouldn't leave her side until and unless she requested it.

He fervently hoped she wouldn't make that request.

Cully leaned closer while keeping his face forward, his hands steady on the reins. "A word of caution. 'Twould be best if you spoke English around here." He flicked Baptiste a glance. "People have long memories."

Baptiste answered in English, "This I will remember."

They entered the town as twilight deepened the shadows between buildings.

"Whoa, Dusty. Whoa, Dan," Cully called to his team. They came to a halt outside of a tavern with an upper story filled with windows. Light and the laughter of men spilled from the door. Cully turned to the women in the back. "Jack runs a clean place. Colonel Bouquet said to charge the rooms to the army. Get a good night's sleep. The wagons will roll at daybreak."

Baptiste jumped down and helped the women from the wagon, then handed the smaller children to whoever held arms out to receive them. The older children, none standing higher than mid-chest on him, scrambled over the sides.

Maggie waited until last. He gripped her trim waist and swung her to the ground, not letting go.

"Reggie's directions so far have been good, but this." He nodded to the buildings around them. "It does not look like what he said."

"It probably does, but we could not picture all of this when he told us."

"I will go inside and ask for directions. Someone will know your father." He remembered to speak in English.

She glanced up and down the street, then hugged her arms around herself, the tips of her fingers twitching.

"I will not be long." He could almost smell her nerves, but she made no move to enter the building with him. She was as uneasy as he. They'd lived inside Fort Detroit for weeks, but it hadn't been like this. Even after the reinforcements had crowded into it, it hadn't been anything like this.

He looked back at her from the doorway before he entered. She stood like a statue against the side of the wagon, a small figure with her chin raised.

A DOOR BANGED ON THE BUILDING ACROSS THE street. A man hunched over in front of it for a moment, then straightened and slipped something into his pocket. He picked up a cane that had leaned against the building and stepped into the street.

He leaned heavily on the cane.

Maggie sucked in a breath. Could it be? Would it be so easy to find Da? He wore a hat, its brim and the fading light hiding his face. If only she could see his hair. Did it wave in russet disarray? Or his jaw. Was it square and firm with lips that tipped to one side when he smiled, covered with a bushy red beard?

He was angling away from the tavern, as if to continue down the street.

Maggie stepped into the street and followed him. His steps were slow, deliberate... painful. She tried to swallow the lump in her throat, but it wouldn't budge. She coughed, and he turned to her.

The lower half of his face was covered by bushy whiskers, but they were white.

"Ma'am?" The voice was low, the edges of the word tinged with a Scottish burr.

Her heartbeat skittered. "Reginald Kerr?"

He shifted the cane to his front, resting both hands on its knob. "Aye. Who be askin'?"

The lump almost prevented her from issuing the next words. "'Tis Maggie, Da."

His knees buckled.

Maggie rushed forward, supporting him before he tumbled, but his hat fell, revealing pure white hair. The shock of that dried her mouth.

"My girl?" The Scottish burr was much thicker in those words, the voice filled with wonder and something else. Something she couldn't quite grasp.

"Aye, Da." The once-familiar words slipped from her lips.

Steady again, he cupped her face with one hand and leaned close, peering at her. In the darkness, his eyes were dark and recessed, his face craggy.

Da was... an old man.

"Maggie?" Baptiste's voice cut through her scrutiny.

She called over her shoulder, eyes never leaving Da's. "I am here."

Her husband's arm came around her back. She still gripped Da by the elbows. His hand was on her face. None of them moved or spoke for a long moment, then tears leaked from Da's eyes and slid into the wrinkles of his cheeks.

"I canna believe this."

"'Tis true. I am here."

"How—?" He shook his head. "Nay. Not here. Come with me." He fumbled with the cane. "Come home with me. We will talk there."

"I will bring our things and catch up," Baptiste said.

Maggie linked her arm with Da's, his other gripping the cane. They made their way slowly down the street. A moment later, Baptiste appeared on her other side. Their bundles of belongings banging against his back with his uneven but long steps. So unlike the short, halting steps of her da.

They turned a corner, and Da opened the little gate in front of a two-story house. Light came from the windows—as with every house they'd passed. Da leaned on her as he climbed the two steps to the porch, then stopped with his hand on the doorknob.

"Your sisters, Donald, they will be..." He shook his head and let the words trail off as he opened the door.

Someone had baked bread that day, the yeasty aroma greeting them as they stepped over the threshold.

"Da? You are late tonight." The female voice came from the

back of the house, followed by quick footsteps. "I hope there was nothing... oh." A beautiful young woman stopped just inside the room drying her hands on a towel. Catherine. Her blond hair was gathered and knotted at the back of her neck, so like Mama had worn hers. Catherine was the only one who'd inherited those golden locks.

Unless Cynthia had as well.

Da hung his hat on a peg. "I hope there is enough supper to share."

A brilliant smile flashed across her sister's face. "Of course there is. Welcome."

There was no recognition in the blue eyes meeting Maggie's, but why would there be?

Maggie stepped forward.

"Catherine?"

"Yes?" Golden brows rose in confusion.

"'Tis Maggie."

The towel fluttered to the floor. "Maggie? My sister Maggie?" Disbelief colored her voice.

Maggie swallowed and squeezed out the word, "Yes."

Catherine looked to Da for his nod, and then came forward. She gripped Maggie's upper arms, peered into her face. "We thought you dead long ago." Wonder replaced the disbelief. "But you look so much like Mama." She tipped her head to the side, then back straight. "With Da's hair, of course." Then her arms came around Maggie.

Maggie hugged her little sister, her now taller and larger little sister. She wouldn't have known Catherine if she'd passed her on the street, so she couldn't fault her sister for not knowing her.

"Da?" A small voice came from the other side of Catherine, who let Maggie go.

"Cynthia, come and meet our sister."

The little girl was stamped with Da's unruly reddish hair. Her features, however, were like Mama's. Like Maggie's. Indeed, the child could have been Maggie years ago.

Maggie held out her hand, and the little girl grasped it.

"Are you really my sister?"

Maggie nodded and blinked back the dampness that had threatened ever since she'd left the wagon. "I am."

"Where have you been?"

Leave it to a child to ask the question. "I was taken away, a long time ago."

Cynthia pointed at Baptiste. "By him?"

"No." Maggie reached back and took Baptiste's hand. "He is my husband."

Da looked back and forth between her and Baptiste. He couldn't be surprised. Who else but a husband would have accompanied her? But still, there was something like relief in his face.

"Da, I would like you to meet Baptiste Geroux."

The old man drew himself up, his mouth a straight slash, all sense of relief vanishing. "A Frenchman?"

"No, Da. My husband." Maggie stepped back to Baptiste's side. She watched the emotions crisscrossing Da's face and waited.

Baptiste moved slightly, as if setting himself to speak, but she squeezed his hand. Best to wait and see what Da would say, to see whether they stayed, or moved on. Because one thing she knew without question.

She would choose her husband over the man who had left her in captivity for more than seven years. Even seeing him as he was, old and infirm, she couldn't fully shake the sense of abandonment that had been a part of her for so long.

Da limped forward, hand outstretched. "Welcome to our home, Monsieur Geroux, and welcome to our family."

Baptiste accepted the hand offered. "Call me Baptiste."

"And you may call me Reginald."

Maggie released a sigh, and Catherine caught her hand. "Now that that is over, let us put supper on the table... sister. Donald will be home soon. How surprised he will be. And we must write to Reggie, of course. Come along, Cynthia."

Maggie allowed herself to be dragged from the front room, but she cast one last look at Baptiste, and grinned at his wink.

Chapter 31

T he day had arrived, and Maggie was as ready as she could be. This morning they would set out for their farm along the river to join Henri and see how he had faired through the winter months. Baptiste had been like a caged wolf for the past fortnight, the farmer in him eager to be back in his fields, even though he knew the ground farther north would not be ready to be worked and planted for another month or more.

During that past fortnight, Baptiste and Da had been in long conversations, making plans and purchasing equipment, a wagon, and another team of oxen. Henri would need his own team if he were to stay and farm. If not, then Baptiste would have the pair to sell. Da had even bought a gift for Maggie, a gentle-eyed, fawn-colored cow who was due to deliver a calf in early summer.

It pleased Maggie to see her father and husband become friends. The two had so much in common, their love of farming, their love of the wilderness... and their love of Maggie. She knew now, beyond a doubt, that Da loved her.

It had taken weeks, months, before Maggie had been able to completely let go of the deeply rooted bitterness she'd held against her father for so long. But it was gone now. She had forgiven him. Or maybe more honestly, she'd realized that he didn't need to be forgiven, that he'd done the best he could do. And when it was all said and done, that was all anyone should expect.

Some of the maturity of her thoughts, she knew, had come after the bundle in her arms had been born. Little Josephine had arrived on the first of March, greeted by a proud grandfather, doting aunts, a fun-loving uncle, and a father who adored her. He'd named her after his mama. A beautiful name.

Maggie lowered her nose to the blanket-wrapped babe and breathed deeply. Would she ever grow used to the scent of her child? Ever grow tired of the weight in her arms? Or ever stop marveling that she and Baptiste had created something so perfect?

Cynthia called from the house, charging out the door waving something in her hand. "Maggie, you must take this for Josephine." She pressed a thread-worn doll into Maggie's hands.

Maggie knelt, keeping the sleeping babe tight to her chest. "But the dolly is yours. Why do you wish to send it away with us?"

"Because." Tears glistened in her little sister's blue-gray eyes, so like Maggie's. "Without it, she might forget about me."

Maggie didn't have the heart to tell her that Josephine was too young to remember her, doll or not. She pulled the little girl into a hug with her free arm. "'Tis perhaps best for you to keep the doll, and bring it with you when you visit." She hoped, someday, such a visit would happen. News had reached them of the peace agreement Pontiac had signed with Fort Detroit in late October, but nobody was fooled into believing that meant the uprisings were over. "Josephine can look forward to both you and the doll that way."

Cynthia pushed away to look at Maggie, her chin wobbling. "Do you really have to go?"

Indeed, they did. Maggie was as eager to reach their farm as Baptiste. Even so, a part of her heart would remain behind with the family she'd grown to know—grown to love—in the six months they'd been there.

"We must. I shall miss you, but we shall write letters. That I promise you." Maggie and Catherine had spent many nights at the table, the younger teaching the elder to read and write again.

"'Tis not the same," Cynthia wailed before she fell back against Maggie's side, ever mindful and careful of the babe. "I want you to stay."

Maggie laid her cheek against her sister's hair. She'd never dreamed the parting would be so difficult, so heart-wrenching.

HIS WIFE'S HAIR BLENDED PERFECTLY WITH HER little sister's. The sight added to Baptiste's unease. They were so alike it was uncanny, from the delicately pointed chins that lifted in determination when challenged, to the way they threw themselves into every project, no matter how large or small. And to the blue-gray eyes that now brimmed with unshed tears.

The oxen were yoked and hitched to the newly built, narrow wagon. Their belongings—so many new things purchased these past months—crated and packed into the wagon's bed. Barrels of supplies, including seeds for planting, lashed to its sides. Catherine emerged from the house with a sack, undoubtedly filled with loaves of bread and hard biscuits the women had baked the night before. Donald towed the reluctant cow from the stable behind the house. Reginald Kerr stood by the oxen, scratching the black-and-white spotted faces of the matched pair, his head bowed. It was time to leave, but could Maggie break away from the love she'd been surrounded by all these months? Could he ask it of her?

Would Baptiste and Josephine be enough for her after this?

For months he'd worried about little else. Pleased to see her enjoying her family, while living in dread that he'd lose her in the end. That her affection for them would be stronger than whatever affection she held for him.

He checked the straps on the canvas covering one last time. Working for a local blacksmith through the winter, he'd earned enough to purchase his own blacksmithing tools and enough iron to get a good start setting up his own shop. He'd still farm, of course, but he enjoyed shaping the metal, making and repairing what he needed with his own hands.

Maggie had packed her purchases to the front of the wagon —cloth for the babe's clothing needs, supplies for sewing and knitting and whatever else women needed. Catherine and Maggie had also made cheese, several types of which were under the tarp. The last thing to strap onto the back was a wooden crate with five hens and a rooster. Donald had built the crate and presented it to Maggie. Baptiste wasn't sure the chickens would survive the hawks, foxes, and coyotes, but he was pretty sure Maggie would never part with that crate.

The last strap tightened, Baptiste stepped back from the wagon. "Maggie, it is time."

Hugs and promises to write were passed around. Reginald thrust out a hand, but then pulled Baptiste into an awkward hug. "You keep my little girl safe," he said in a voice thick and rough. "My granddaughter as well."

"This I can promise you."

"You are a good man, Baptiste Geroux." Reginald released him and went to Maggie.

Maggie's eyes glistened as she faced her father, babe in her arms. The old man took the little one, and the babe awoke, arms flailing in the air. The gnarled hands supported her as Reginald gazed into his granddaughter's face.

Maybe for the last time.

Baptiste had learned that Reginald wasn't as old as he seemed, that the effects of the injuries he'd taken in the war, together with the grief of losing first Maggie and then his wife, had aged him beyond his years. But in the past few months, Reginald's steps appeared firmer, his hands steadier, his countenance lighter.

Guilt picked at Baptiste. Did he have the right to take away what the old man had already lost once?

Maggie hugged her father, gathered her daughter from his arms, and faced her family. "I will miss you all. These past months, they have meant much to me. To see you again. To get to know you." She tilted her face down, then back to meet her father's eyes. "To understand." Her voice wobbled on the last word, but true to form, her chin lifted. "I will not say farewell. I will say, until we meet again."

She approached the wagon, eyes glistening in the morning sun. Baptiste swung her and Josephine up onto the seat, then picked up his switch, and urged the oxen forward. "Come up, boys. Come up." He walked beside Maggie, her back as straight as the red pines behind their cabin.

"Are you sure?" he asked, keeping his voice low.

"Indeed." She wiped her cheek with the back of her hand. "I miss our home. I miss our river. I miss Beau and Pierre." Her lips trembled but pulled into a smile. "I even miss your brother."

"I miss him too."

"I love my family, Baptiste, but they are not my life." Her eyes were no longer clogged with tears. They were bright in a different way, a way that filled something inside of him. "You and Josephine, you are my life."

He reached up and grasped her hand. "As you are mine." He

brushed the switch across the oxen's backs again, more eager than ever to get back home.

Her fingers squeezed his, almost to the point of pain, and he glanced up.

"I love you, my husband." She spoke in French, her words more refined now. "I have not said as much, but I have known for a long time."

He stumbled on something but caught himself, not bothering to look at what had tripped him. It didn't matter. Nothing mattered.

His wife loved him.

His wife was going home… with him.

MAGGIE HADN'T BEEN COMPLETELY ALONE WITH HER husband in months. Da's house had been filled to the rafters, always busy, always noisy, and always someone wanting her attention. Baptiste had been very patient, although he'd often been the busiest among them, working at the blacksmith shop and making repairs on Da's house with Donald's help. Things Da couldn't do himself.

Josephine mewled and squirmed in her arms.

Maggie pulled back the blanket covering the little face. "Your père and I will not be truly alone for a long time to come." The babe blinked at her, then scrubbed her face with little fists, working up to a cry.

Maggie adjusted her bodice and settled the babe to nurse, ignoring the aches from the first day on the trail. She leaned against the wagon wheel, enjoying the lack of motion and the soft earth instead of the rigid wood seat. The ground was damp but not soggy, and smelled of the promise of new growth.

It'd been almost a year since she'd fled Stone Foot's longhouse. She'd never imagined what would happen once she'd gained her freedom. Hadn't dared think that far ahead. But this? She'd couldn't have imagined anything like this.

Baptiste had picketed the oxen and cow near the wagon. He turned in a circle, scanning their surroundings. She smiled at the way his eyes dipped to Josephine, the fascination he had for the babe. When his eyes met hers, something burned behind them that told her his fascination wasn't all for the babe.

"All is well?" he asked.

"Oui. I will find our supper when she is full."

"Non." He raised a hand as if to stop her from rising. "I will find it."

It was a cool evening, but they ate bread and cheese without a fire. Indians would be returning from their wintering villages soon, if they weren't already. Best to remain as hidden as possible.

Maggie pulled their extra tarps beneath the wagon, flattening one on the ground to keep the damp away, and rigging one overhead to keep the dew off. She and Josephine would sleep within the cocoon of canvas. Baptiste would sleep outside, his ears open to the sounds of the road nearby and the forest around them.

Protecting them.

A year before, could she have trusted anyone to protect her? No. A year before she had trusted no one but herself. Since then, she'd learned to trust Baptiste and Henri to protect her.

Fed and dry and soundly asleep, Maggie settled Josephine on a pad of blankets inside the tarps. The babe needed both her and Baptiste. Her for nourishment and care, Baptiste for protection and provisions.

"Maggie?" Baptiste called.

She backed out of the tarps.

Baptiste caught her at the waist, lifted her, and set her toe-to-toe with him. The rising moon glinted off his dark eyes. He inched his hands from her waist to her back, rubbing slow circles. She wore no stays to make feeding Josephine easier on the journey, so the heat of his hands seeped into her skin. He lowered his head until his forehead rested on hers, noses almost touching, and then he paused.

Her toes gripped the bottoms of her moccasins, her fingers digging into the loose fabric of his shirt, her breaths coming short and quick.

"Say it again." His voice was a deep rumble that filled her ears and melted her insides.

She couldn't think when he held her this way. Teased her with lips so close. "Say what?"

"What you said when we began our journey this morning." His fingers tangled in the back of her hair. "What you said that has made walking all day an agony of waiting."

Why had she chosen that moment to say something so important? It had surprised her as much as it'd obviously surprised him. The words had come on their own, without her directing them. She let loose of his shirt, tugged it from his waist, and ran her hands across his heated skin, the muscles of his stomach tightening beneath her fingers. "You wish me to say that I love you, is that right?"

"Oui." The word was barely breathed between them when he brought their lips together.

Under the stars and beneath the budding branches, they came together as husband and wife, joined as one body, bonded as one flesh. Nothing was kept from the other. Nothing was restrained. There was between them a new completeness.

Later, Maggie curled against her husband's length, her back pressed to his chest, her head pillowed on his arm, his other arm firm around her middle. "I should have said the words long ago," she whispered.

His sigh stirred the hairs on top of her head. "As should I, my love."

She squirmed around until they were nose to nose again. "You did. You called me 'my love' months ago."

"Did I?" His brows drew together.

She smoothed them with her finger. "You did, atop the palisade, and I never forgot." She pressed her lips to his, but his response was cut short when a thin cry reached them.

With a smile, she backed from his embrace and stood. Then she shrugged her best imitation of his classic French gesture. "I must see to your daughter."

"But of course." He also stood. "And I must keep watch."

As she crawled into the tarps to comfort and feed the babe, Maggie couldn't help but wonder, once again, at the change one single year could bring.

Chapter 32

They'd had a wait of many days at Presque Isle in the shadow of the burned-out fort there, but at last secured passage on a barge that was able to take on the wagon, oxen, and cow. It'd cost Baptiste almost all the coins he had, but it was worth it. Rumor had the Ottawa had settled along the west shore of Lake Erie. Because of that, it was better to wait for a raft to cross the water than to travel along the shoreline.

The wait had chafed Baptiste, who soon grew tired of the sideways looks and outright sneers by the British who had gathered in the natural port, most of them soldiers, some of them merchants who needed a place for their boats and barges to load and unload.

Now, the barge lifted and dropped beneath his feet. Clouds gathered along the horizon and the wind had risen over the past hour. The cow lowed her distress at the movement of the vessel. Baptiste paced, hands behind his back, until the captain approached.

"We need to seek shelter." The captain tipped his chin toward the clouds. "'Tis a warning to be heeded."

"Indeed." Baptiste had finally mastered using the British word for *oui*.

"There is an old French port along the shore." He pointed a gnarled finger to what looked like the solid forest of the lake's northern shore. "We could unload your wagon there and float it ashore."

Anger flashed through Baptiste. "You agreed to take us up the river."

"That I did." The older man rubbed his hand over the silver stubble on his chin. "But if that sky unleashes what I fear, 'twill likely wash your wagon off my barge."

Baptiste glanced at the sky again, its brooding clouds visibly darker and roiling. His anger deflated as he looked back to the captain. "Then your course of action is wise."

The old man stepped away, shouting orders to his crew of a dozen men.

Baptiste went to Maggie, who huddled out of the wind behind several barrels, their tarps stretched and weighted to provide the woman and child shelter.

"The captain, he is going to put us off before the storm."

"Put us off?" Her eyes darkened in that way they did when her temper rose. His little spitfire.

"The storm coming, he fears it will be too strong. He fears that we might lose the wagon."

"Oh." She struggled to her knees while keeping Josephine in her arms. "Where will we go?"

"We are nearing the northern shore. He says there is an old French port there where we can float the wagon to shore." He'd bought a wagon with a tightly fitted bottom, sealed with pitch, knowing they'd need to ford a few rivers. Never had he thought to float it, but there was no reason that it wouldn't work.

"The northern shore?"

"Oui."

Maggie's face paled, her freckles standing out in stark contrast.

"What is wrong?"

She pressed her fingers against her forehead, then lifted her eyes to his. "Teata's village is on the northern shore."

"Tree Sleeper is dead. You need not fear him."

"Oui, this I know, but—"

The barge tilted, and sailors shouted, several scrambled to lash down more of the cargo. Baptiste braced himself on the well-anchored barrels.

"I think we have no choice. If we stay on the barge, we risk losing everything." Another wave lifted the vessel. "Perhaps even our lives. We must do this."

Maggie clenched the babe tighter, bringing a whimper of protest. She resettled Josephine, then turned her face back to Baptiste. "Oui." Her lips were a flat line, whether to keep them from trembling or in determination, he wasn't sure.

They would have a long haul without a proper road. He'd have to rig the oxen to pull in single file instead of side by side. The wagon was narrow, built to work on the major Indian trails. On the others, he'd be wielding his axe and making a lot of noise. But it was possible.

Difficult—but possible.

MAGGIE TUCKED JOSEPHINE MORE SECURELY IN THE sling she'd fashioned to carry the babe. It was similar to those the Huron women wore but made of cloth instead of hide. She walked beside the lead ox, whom she had named Arthur. Oliver, the second ox, was directly behind, with Miss Brown, the cow, tied to the back of the wagon. Baptiste walked before them all, hacking at the growth to make room for the wagon.

It had been three days since the storm put them ashore. There'd been no way to get the wagon, or the animals, back onto the barge. The old port's dock had long since rotted away, unused since the fur traders had moved farther west a score of years ago or more.

With every step they took, Maggie breathed a little easier. Their progress was painfully slow, painfully loud, but it was progress. And they'd seen no Indian sign.

Yet.

"Whoa." Baptiste stopped and leaned against the handle of his axe. He swiped his sleeve across his forehead.

Maggie unhooked the gourd dipper they'd hung from the wagon's side and filled it from their water barrel, then hurried to his side. "Drink."

He drained the dipper and handed it back. "Merci." He straightened and scanned the area. "I had hoped we would find a main trail by now. Does anything look familiar?"

She shook her head, again. "As I have said, I traveled in darkness as much as I could. I am sorry I—"

"Non." He waved his hand at her. "Do not apologize." He huffed out a deep breath. "I only wish I knew this area, where to find a trail. There must be one."

"We could stop for a bit and make a fire. I could bake some cornbread."

"My Maggie." He tugged on the braid across her shoulder. "Always busy."

Something she'd learned from Mrs. Roberts, and it usually helped. But now... She was convinced they had landed well west of Teata's normal territory, but it was early spring and the hunters would be ranging far in search of meat. Every snap of a twig, every rustle in the brush, had her heart pounding in alarm.

The wagon, the chopping, the oxen... they were making so much noise, they couldn't be missed if anyone were within a mile.

After the break, with Josephine fed and dry, they started out again. How Baptiste managed, she didn't know. It was all she could do to walk beside Arthur, and even then, she held on to his yoke to steady herself. She'd grown soft in the fort and in the town.

Josephine squeaked and squirmed before drifting back to sleep. Motherhood might have something to do with the fatigue. Between Baptiste and Josephine, Maggie wasn't getting enough sleep.

Not that she minded.

She blushed, even though she was alone with her thoughts.

"Enfin!" Baptiste shouted. "At last!" He turned and waved her forward. "We have struck a path."

The Indian trail was wide and deep, one that had seen many years of use. But more importantly, it ran to the northwest, which was where they needed to go. Baptiste tossed his axe down and swooped her and the babe in his arms, turning on his good leg.

"We will make good time now." He planted a kiss on her forehead, then paused, eyes on her lips.

She pushed against him. "Set me down. If you start that, we will get no farther today, I think."

He chuckled and set her back on her feet. "Some things are worth the delay."

A shiver caught her unaware.

"Maggie?"

"I am all right, it is just..." She pointed around them. "We are so exposed now."

"Oui, but we will travel more quickly and more quietly." He hefted his axe again. "The path is smooth. Would you like to ride on the wagon?"

She nodded, relief and apprehension warring within her.

He helped her to the high seat, then pulled a rope from underneath the tarp and secured it to the ends of the seat and over her lap, not unlike how they'd anchored things to the barge.

"Grab the rope if you need to hold on." Then he took her place beside Arthur. "Come up, boys. Come up."

They'd traveled most of the afternoon when a flash of movement caught her eye on the trail ahead. Not the natural movement of branches in the breeze. Not the quick flash of a deer or the swoop of a bird.

"Baptiste?"

"I saw it." He didn't slow, but his knuckles whitened on the handle of his axe.

Maggie slipped her hatchet from its sheath with the hand not cradling Josephine.

But when the man stepped into the path, his hands were raised, and she recognized the long brown robe he wore.

"Père Potier," she whispered.

Baptiste turned his head to the side, so his low voice would reach her. "He may not be alone."

The shiver returned, and Josephine roused. Why now? She jiggled the babe in her sling. But Josephine was having none of it, between her next three breaths she worked herself up to an all-out squall.

The Jesuit folded his hands and waited as they approached.

"Bonjour," Baptiste said. "It is good to see you, Père Potier."

"Bonjour, my son." He lifted his eyes to Maggie. "Bonjour, my daughter."

Maggie nodded, doing her best to appease Josephine without feeding her and while watching the forest around them.

"It is good that you have returned," the Jesuit said.

"It is good to be back," Baptiste said, his voice wary.

"It is time for the Indians and the French to live in peace again, as brothers." The old man motioned someone else from the forest.

Maggie's breath caught when that man joined him in the path.

Stone Foot.

The man who had bought her from the Lenni Lenape. The man who had kept her captive for more than five years. He lifted his eyes to hers, and in their depths was something she hadn't expected.

Sadness.

He took a step forward, and Baptiste planted himself between him and Maggie.

"Non, Baptiste," the Jesuit said. "He means her no harm."

"With respect, Père, I do not know this. I do not know him."

"I give you my word. We come, just us two."

"I will tell you myself." Stone Foot spoke in guttural French and shuffled closer. "She is the daughter I never had. I would see her face up close, one more time."

Baptiste kept his stance for a long, tense moment, glanced at the Jesuit, then stepped aside.

Maggie suppressed a gasp. Would he not protect her now? Panic clawed at her throat.

"Dappled Leaves, it grieved me when you left." Stone Foot came no closer. "My home was empty without you."

A fiery anger shot through her. "You would have sold me to Tree Sleeper. You would have been alone even had I not run."

"Not sold, given to be a wife." He raised his hands to his waist, then let them fall to his sides again. "You would have remained close to me."

Josephine stiffened against her, cries becoming more stringent.

"And now, you have a child." The old man's eyes grew misty.

Nothing could have shocked Maggie more. After years of seeing Stone Foot only as her captor, there he stood, an old man, bent and emotional. His resemblance to Da caught her up. Words escaped her.

"My greatest wish was to see you settled with a good man who would give you children. Who would give me grandchildren."

Grandchildren? Maggie's thoughts swirled. Stone Foot nursing her when she'd fallen sick with a fever. Stone Foot threatening the village boys with a stick when they had teased her into tears. Stone Foot ordering Long Pouch to stop switching Maggie for disobedience when she'd been caught snitching food.

She'd always assumed he'd been protecting his property. Could it be that he'd done these things out of affection? Had she judged him as wrongly as she'd judged her own father?

"Help me down, Baptiste."

Her husband's jaw tightened in a way she'd come to recognize as his mulishness.

She raised her eyebrows, and he relented, untying the rope across her lap and lifting her as if she weighed nothing.

Maggie approached Stone Foot, who had not moved beyond the lead ox. He held her eyes for a moment, then shifted his attention to Josephine. She'd quieted, her eyes round. She blinked up at him. He held out his arms.

Baptiste growled low in his throat, but Maggie passed the babe over.

Stone Foot held the little girl to his chest and muttered a long string of Huron words. Even as close as she was, Maggie only caught enough of them to know he was giving the child a blessing. Then a tear seeped from between his closed lids before he opened his eyes again.

"What is her name?"

"Josephine."

"What does this name mean?"

Maggie turned to Baptiste, who shrugged. She looked back at Stone Foot. "It was the name of my husband's mother."

"It is the French way?"

She nodded.

"It is good then." He pulled in a breath and let it out as if cleansing himself of something. "Père Potier tells me that your husband is a good man. That is what I wanted for you, a good man."

Maggie couldn't stop the words that tore from her. "Tree Sleeper was not a good man!"

Stone Foot nodded. "This I know now, but I did not see it before. He is dead, Tree Sleeper. Killed by an Ottawa for assaulting a woman of their tribe. It was just."

Maggie forced herself not to look at Baptiste.

The old man straightened. "When word came that Dappled Leaves was cutting through the forest, I asked Père Potier to bring me to see. My eyes"—he swiped his hand over them—"they do not work well anymore. I wanted to see the one who is like my daughter before I can see no more."

He was going blind.

Sadness welled up in Maggie and lodged in her throat. This man had bought her from the Lenni Lenape who had captured her. He'd fed and clothed her, kept her safe. He'd thought of her as a daughter, and she'd never even realized it. She hadn't been as strong as she'd thought for so many years. She'd been closed off. She'd shut herself away.

Forgiving Da had opened her heart in many ways, but as she faced the old man holding her babe, tears clouded her vision. She opened her arms and hugged Stone Foot and Josephine together. The old man muttered another string of Huron words, this time a blessing for Maggie. They stayed in that embrace until the babe's mewling became shrill.

Maggie stepped back, taking Josephine with her. "I must feed her."

"And I must return to the village."

With no more words than that, the two men retreated into the forest.

Chapter 33

Maggie had been strangely quiet since her meeting with the old Huron and Père Potier three days past. Not brooding, not angry. He didn't detect anything unhappy about her, she was just... quiet.

Baptiste didn't know what to make of it.

She still hummed to Josephine, still spoke to the oxen and cow, calling them by name. And at night, she still slid into his arms and responded to him.

But she was different.

As he plodded along beside Arthur—whom Maggie insisted be pronounced as the English and not the more melodic French Artur—he should be excited about reaching the farm. Seeing his cabin. Reuniting with Henri. All things he was looking forward to, but behind him...

Was Maggie regretting their return to the wilderness? Was she missing her family?

He glanced back to the wagon. She lifted her head and smiled at him before turning her attention back to the nursing babe in her arms. That sight—repeated many times each day and a few more during the night—still created a stir in his chest.

His daughter in the arms of his wife. What could be more perfect?

Arthur swung his head at an annoying fly, knocking the cut end of the yoke into Baptiste's ribs.

"Stop that." He gave the blunted horn nearest him a push.

"Do you suppose he knows how close we are to home?"

"How could he?"

Maggie shrugged. "Animals sense things people miss. He may have picked up on our anticipation."

"It was a fly."

Her laughter carried like pollen on the wind, light and grace-ful. Then she gasped. "Look, Baptiste." She pointed. "Oh, non."

The brush along the trail blocked his sight for a few more steps, but then it came into view. A burned-out cabin backed by burned-out barns. Not his, but not far from his. There were seven farms along this bank across from the fort, which was not yet in view. His was the last, the furthest north. But if one was burned...

They passed the sad sight, then came upon another. Also burned. A short while later, a third.

At least they had arrived before planting season. He would have time to erect some sort of shelter. Maggie could stay at the fort, which was just coming into view. It stood tall and strong, never breached by Pontiac and his combined forces.

Baptiste stopped the oxen.

"Maggie—"

"Non." She shook her head, her chin up. "I will not stay in the fort while you rebuild."

How did she know what he was thinking? Maman had been able to read Père's mind like that. Maybe it was something all women could do.

"Think of Josephine—"

"I am. She needs her père nearby." Her chin dropped a bit. "As do I."

The huskiness in her voice and the smokiness in her eyes were his undoing. "Perhaps you are right."

Her smile showed she agreed. His wife. She could get her way with him too easily. But he couldn't find it in his heart to be upset by it. Maggie preferred being with him to living in comfort in the fort. What man's chest wouldn't swell with pride over that?

"We will rebuild," Maggie said.

"But of course." He urged the oxen on. They would rebuild, but he would miss the cabin his Père had built, the cabin he and Henri had grown up in.

The next farm came into view. It was still standing, a line of washing flapping in the breeze. Hope filled him, quickening his limping pace. The cow lowed behind the wagon, protesting.

The next farm appeared abandoned, but not burned. There was a strip of forest before the next farm. Before he could see it, a whiff of smoke reached him.

"Can you see anything?" he asked Maggie.

She shielded her eyes with one hand, squinting from her tall perch. "Not yet."

Baptiste gripped the wooden yoke, all but pulling Arthur along. They were so close. Any minute the farm before his would be in view. The farm Henri—

"I see!" Maggie shouted. "There is Beau and Pierre."

Baptiste whooped loud enough to startle the steady beast beside him.

"And Henri!" she shouted again.

They reached a break in the brush and willows.

Henri charged across the field, rifle in his hand, laughter reaching them before he did.

"My brother, my sister-in-law." Henri raised his eyebrows at the bundle Maggie held against her shoulder. "And who is this? Do I have a nephew or a niece?"

Baptiste lifted Maggie from the wagon. "Come and see."

He grabbed his brother's rifle as Maggie handed the bundle into Henri's arms. "Josephine, meet your Uncle Henri."

Henri froze, as if afraid of the babe, but when she cooed at him, he smiled as wide as the river. "She is a beauty." He glanced up. "She obviously takes after her uncle."

Baptiste laughed and slapped his brother on the back. Then he sobered. "The cabin?"

"Just as you left it." Henri winked at Maggie. "But maybe not so clean."

"When we saw the burned cabins south of here—"

"Bah." Henri grimaced. "The farmers left and burned their own buildings in protest rather than have someone take them over." He handed the babe back to Maggie. "Like me. I have moved in here and am ready to work the ground soon."

"We will be neighbors." The idea pleased Baptiste, very much.

It was good to be home with his wife and daughter. It was good to have a home to come back to. And it was good to have his brother nearby.

If only he understood the difference in his Maggie.

MAGGIE AWOKE TO JOSEPHINE'S SQUAWK. SHE RUBBED the sleep from her eyes, then smiled. For the first time since they'd married, she'd slept in their own cabin. Henri had been right about it needing a good cleaning, but she would soon rectify that.

Baptiste was gone, no doubt walking his fields or checking on the oxen or setting the fish trap. He teased her about being busy, but he rarely sat still for longer than it took to eat a meal.

Another squawk brought her out of their blankets. Once Josephine was dry and full, she happily snuggled against Maggie. The cleaning could wait for a while, the morning sunshine beckoned.

Maggie found Baptiste at the edge of his field, staring across the ragged remains of last year's carefully planted crops. She stopped beside him, and his arm came around behind her, drawing her close.

"Which oxen will you keep, and which will go to Henri?" she asked.

"Do you have a preference?"

"Non. I have Miss Brown. Milking her will be enough to keep me busy."

He grinned at her. "Then Henri can have the new pair with the funny names."

She elbowed his side.

"Look who has flown back for the summer like a pair of geese," came a voice from behind them.

Baptiste's arm tightened and then relaxed as he chuckled and turned. "And you, my friend? How did you winter here in the north?"

Walking Fire Stick came forward, arm outstretched. The two men clasped forearms, and there was genuine affection in the faces of both.

It brought a lump to Maggie's throat. She owed this Ottawa man much. "We met with Stone Foot on the trail—"

Walking Fire Stick's brows lowered.

"—you must have been the one to tell the Hurons about Tree Sleeper."

"I told them the truth." He released Baptiste's arm. "This

man is my brother. You are his wife. That man attacked the wife of my brother."

"We owe you much," Baptiste said.

The Ottawa grinned, showing an impressive display of teeth. "You have returned with a cow."

Which she would gladly give him and started to say so, but Baptiste crossed his arms.

"I seem to remember a young man who could not get enough of my maman's fresh buttermilk."

Maggie looked from one man to the other. "Then I will be sure to have buttermilk on the table when you visit. At least, once my cow gives birth."

Josephine roused, lifting her little head from Maggie's shoulder.

"And who is this?" Walking Fire Stick leaned close.

She turned the babe to face him. "Josephine, meet your Uncle Walking Fire Stick."

"Another uncle, oui." Baptiste nodded. "You are always welcome here. As family."

They returned to the cabin, Walking Fire Stick sharing the news that his village was done with fighting the British at Fort Detroit, but Pontiac and some warriors had left to join with other villages to the south in the Ohio territory. He had no wish to join them. Like Baptiste, he wanted to live in peace beside the river on the land he knew.

Maggie bustled around the cabin putting together their morning meal, her heart light, her hands busy, the husband she loved and their daughter nearby with her husband's best friend. So very much had changed in one year, but nothing had changed more than Maggie herself.

"COME HERE." BAPTISTE'S VOICE WAS HUSKY.

Maggie turned around, wiping her hands dry on her apron. "I am almost finished." The cabin was clean at last. She'd gotten their belongings put away and had washed their supper dishes as darkness descended around the cabin. She approached her husband's chair. "What do you need?"

He pulled her onto his lap, and she curled against him. His heart beat strong and steady under her ear.

"Are you happy?"

She sat up to look him in the face. "Of course I am." Had she given him reason to think otherwise? Or— "Are you?"

"Everything I love is here, under my roof. How could I not be happy?"

Maggie breathed a soft sigh. "I feel the same."

"Then…" He brushed his fingers up and down her arms, raising the fine hairs along with her expectations. "Why have you been so quiet since the meeting with Stone Foot and Père Potier?" His brow creased, and his dark eyes turned somber.

How to explain? She cast around for the words, trying to organize her feelings enough to express them. After so many years of denying emotions, she floundered at the task.

"Is it something I have done, or something I have not?" Worry crept into his low voice, tugging at her heart.

She took his face between her hands, loving the roughness of his evening whiskers against her palms. "You are perfect."

He snorted, his breath warm across her face. The urge to kiss him was strong, but if she did, the words she needed to find would not be said.

"Before you, I trusted no one. Before you, I stayed strong and took care of myself."

"My little spitfire." Love filled his voice, and her insides curled at the sound, but she couldn't let him distract her. It was time to talk.

There would be time for the other after.

"The past months have shown me that I was not strong." She pressed her fingers to his lips when he started to protest, then took them away when he started kissing them. "I had shut myself inside. Or maybe, I had shut everyone else out. I was angry at Da for abandoning me. I hated Stone Foot for purchasing me. Of course, I hated the Lenni Lenape for taking me, he whose name I will never say." She paused. How could he understand?

"But then?"

"But then you took me in. You offered me a place to stay without asking anything of me. Why did you do that?" Suddenly, his answer was of utmost importance to her.

"Because you were in need, and you were..." He shrugged. "Beautiful."

"You opened my heart again, Baptiste. Because of you, because you stood beside me, I had the courage to meet Da again. And I..." She sighed, a mixture of sadness and relief. "I was able to forgive him for abandoning me."

"Maggie, he could not have—"

"I know." She pressed her fingers against his lips again. "Maybe I always knew. He would have come had he been able. But it was easier to be angry at him."

Baptiste nibbled on her fingertips, and she frowned at him. He only grinned.

"Then Stone Foot came upon us, and he was just an old man going blind. Yet for me, it was as if I could see him for the first time. Even more, I could remember things he had done for me. Caring things. And when he said the blessing over Josephine... Oh, Baptiste. I knew I had hated him for no good reason. In my heart, I forgave him too."

"But he bought you and kept you a captive."

"He did, but before him, there was the Lenni Lenape." A

shutter rippled through her, and his arms tightened. "He was like Tree Sleeper. I fear that if I had stayed with him, he would have treated me far worse."

"But you did not. So for that, let us be thankful for Stone Foot, non?"

"Oui." He had seen so quickly what it had taken her months to figure out, her brave and smart husband.

"So, my love, why do all these thoughts make you quiet?"

Why, indeed? But with her willingness to forgive those two men, her heart had changed. A burden had been lifted.

"I think the anger and hatred I carried was not good for me. When I forgave both of them, something changed in my heart." She took his face in her hands again. "And I have you to thank for this, my husband. You are the one who taught me to trust again, who taught me to love again."

"I did nothing—"

"You saved my life."

"Non, it was Walking Fire Stick—"

"He killed Tree Sleeper, but you, my husband, taught me to love. Because of Walking Fire Stick, I survive. Because of you, I live." She let go of his face and wrapped her arms around his neck. "Without you, I would still be a slave to my anger and hatred, if not a slave to Stone Foot or Tree Sleeper. Because of you, I am calmer. I am…" She fought for the right word. When it hit, it was like a bright light in the dark cabin. "Free."

"Almost free." His voice was a playful growl.

"Almost?"

"Oui, wife, for you will always belong to me."

She would and was proud to. When he lowered his head, she wove her fingers into his hair and hastened his descent. She loved him with all of her truly free heart.

Please consider leaving a review on Amazon: My Book and/or Goodreads: https://www. goodreads.com/book/show/58484593-maggie-s-strength

Reviews help authors to find readers—and readers to find authors!

Join Pegg's Newsletter (writing updates, sneak peeks, fiber arts, updates, and personal content): https://www.subscribepage.com/PeggThomas

Author's Notes

True historical figures in this story include Major Gladwin, Captain Campbell, Lieutenant MacDougall, Robert Rogers, Mr. La Butte, Captain Dalyell, Father Potier, Claude Charles Moran, Pontiac, Takay, Teata, Wasson, Kinonchamek and Ninivois. Their parts are portrayed as historically accurate as possible from research done with two journals written by people—one English and one French—who lived through the events of the siege of Fort Detroit.

Pontiac organized the Huron and Potawatomi to rise up against the British with his Ottawa warriors. He forced Chief Teata to join with them under threat of attack. He arranged the first two attempts to gain the fort by trickery.

Mahiganne, one of Pontiac's Ottawa warriors, came to Fort Detroit to warn the British of the attack. He did so without asking for or receiving anything in return.

The attacks of May 9, 1763, against Mrs. Trumbull and the Fisher family are true events. The details were too gruesome to include in full in this story.

Pontiac swore that he would return Captain Campbell and Lieutenant McDougall after their meeting, but it was a lie. Claude Charles Moran was a French farmer and man of some importance to the area. Sensing Pontiac's deception, he tried to dissuade Campbell and McDougall from going, but they didn't listen. Pontiac took them both captive. Lieutenant McDougall was able to escape with several others, but Captain Campbell was eventually turned over to the Ojibwe and killed.

The meeting between the French farmers and Pontiac is a true event. They were given assurances by the charismatic leader that proved to be more lies.

Fort Sandusky fell to the Indians along with Forts Presque Isle, Le Boeuf, Venango, Ouiatenon, Miami, St. Joseph, and Michilimackinac. These lacked the size and manpower of Forts Pitt and Detroit which withstood the attacks.

Father Potier was a real Jesuit missionary who lived with Chief Teata and inspired many of his Hurons to believe in Jesus Christ. Chief Teata was reported to consult with Father Potier after Pontiac demanded the Hurons join him in the fight against the British. Father Potier was reported to be against it, but because Pontiac threatened the lives of the Huron if they did not comply, Chief Teata agreed. He pulled back out of the alliance as soon as he could, not partaking in much of the war at all.

The attack on the first supply barges was real. The resulting slaughter of the British soldiers was too gruesome to describe here in any detail. The following drunkenness was also real, although both the chiefs and the women poured out as much of the liquor as they could.

The letter that Pontiac had taken from a captive, and was brought to Fort Detroit by an escaped captive, told of the peace agreement between Britain and France. Pontiac had it read to him by an interpreter, but chose not to believe it. The letter was read to the French inside the fort as per Major Gladwin's orders.

Captain James Dalyell arrived with twenty-two barges and much needed food for the fort on July 29th. He led an assault against Pontiac in the early morning hours of July 31st—against Major Gladwin's advice—but was killed near Parent's Creek in the attempt at what was to be known as the Battle of Bloody Run. Reports of how many soldiers died are conflicting, and some were taken prisoner. Robert Rogers and his men were surrounded in a French house where they had taken refuge; the British army assisted in their safe exit. The marsh scene in this story with reinforcements from the fort is completely fictional.

Pontiac did reach a peace agreement with Major Gladwin at Fort Detroit on Oct. 31, 1763. He then moved his people south of the fort on the Maumee River near present-day Toledo, Ohio. But the war didn't end there. More battles were fought throughout the following summer, in and around present-day Ohio. Most of the tribes surrendered in September 1764. Pontiac's formal surrender to the British happened in July 1766.

No totals are known for the deaths of Natives or British during this time, but it is estimated as many as two thousand British citizens were killed in the uprising, up to five hundred of them civilians.

It is sometimes assumed that Pontiac's goal was to drive the "white man" from Native lands. That is demonstrably false according to several different journals from French and British sources. Pontiac's goal was to drive the British from Native lands *so that the French would return*. Pontiac wanted the French back to trade with and partner with. He didn't like the British because they didn't gift the Natives with presents the way the French had. The British—who were absolutely tone-deaf when it came to the Natives—expected the Natives to pay for or work for what they received. The French had gifted the Natives generously for the use of their land and for their friendship. It was the change from gifting to earning that Pontiac and others couldn't abide. It went against their culture. The French had come and learned how to work with the Native populations. The British came to dominate and thus triggered the resentment that sparked the war.

Pontiac was assassinated near St. Louis on April 20, 1769, by an unknown Peoria warrior. No reason is known, but speculation is that it dealt with quarrels Pontiac had with other tribes. He was a very charismatic leader, but not opposed to using coercion or force to accomplish his ends. Even so, he organized and led a rebellion that impacted the frontier of the American Colonies for more than two years.

About Author

Pegg Thomas lives on a hobby farm in Northern Michigan with Michael, her husband of *mumble* years. They raise sheep and chickens, plus keep a few barn cats and Murphy the spoiled rotten dog. Pegg is published in six Barbour historical romance collections, **won the 2019 Romance Writers of America FHL Reader's Choice Award,** was a **double-finalist for the 2019 American Christian Fiction Writers Carol Award** for novellas, a **finalist for the 2019 American Christian Fiction Writers Editor of the Year Award** and a **finalist for the 2021 Romance Writers of America FHL Reader's Choice Award.** When not writing, Pegg can be found in her barn, her garden, her kitchen, or sitting at one of her spinning wheels creating yarn to turn into her signature wool shawls.

www.PeggThomas.com

JOIN PEGG'S NEWSLETTER

writing updates | sneak peeks | fiber arts updates | personal content
www.subscribepage.com/PeggThomas

Made in the USA
Monee, IL
09 October 2023

44291338R00206